Call of the Raven

By

Julie Anne Gates

Copyright © Julie Anne Gates (2020)

The right of Julie Anne Gates to be identified as the author of this work has been asserted by her in accordance with section 77 and 78 of the Copyright, Design and Patents Act 1988.

All rights reserved. No part of this publication may be reproduced, stored in a retrieval system, or transmitted in any form or by any means, electronic, mechanical, photocopying, recording, or otherwise, without the prior permission of the Julie Anne Gates.

Any person who commits any unauthorised act in relation to this publication may be liable to criminal prosecution and civil claims for damages.

For my daughter, Natalie …

Prologue

Degannwy Castle, Wales, May 1201

It was the darkest hour of the night when Tangwystl awoke once more from the dream. Slowly she sat up. Then pulling the robe from the clothes pole next to her, she wrapped it tightly around her shoulders, before padding across to the adjoining room where her children slept. Without making a sound, she crossed the rush strewn floor to the bed where she stood gazing down at her son, Gruffydd, whose sleeping form lay spread-eagled on the counterpane with his sister, Gwenllian, curled up beside him. Behind a curtain on the other side of the room their nurse snored. She heard the creak of her cot as she shifted her ample bulk on the straw mattress before lapsing back into her rhythmic labouring once again.

Tangwystl stood for a long time taking in, perhaps for the last time, the shock of red brown hair and the smatter of freckles that peppered Gruffydd's nose, and the smooth curve of her daughter's face, before a cloud moved across the moon obliterating its light through the square mullioned window. She felt no sorrow for herself but she pitied the children, for she knew she would not live beyond the next few weeks. She could feel her life ebbing away, even as she stood with the coldness of the floor tiles seeping through the rushes and her hands clutching the roundness where the baby in her belly had not moved for days. The mid-wife had told her she was being fanciful, but Tangwystl knew these things. Just as her mother had known things before her. It was either a gift or a curse. And for Tangwystl it was a curse. She had no regrets, for she had loved Llywelyn, with all her heart. But it was not to be. Fate had determined that she would die young. And when she was gone her children would be taken to live with him at Aber Garth Celyn, his principle court. That would be her last request of the man she loved, that he take care of their children.

Tangwystl's eyes lingered on Gruffydd's small form for a moment. He had a great future ahead of him, the gods had decreed it ... *or had they?* a small voice asked. She shivered, remembering the dream again. It had come more and more often of late as her time drew closer, and she wondered if it were just the morbid fancy of a dying woman, or were the gods trying to warn her of something? Outside, beyond the castle walls, the distant rumble of thunder echoed across the valleys. The air was heavy and cloying in the chamber. Ominous. Behind her, a sudden gust of wind caught the window shutter and it crashed back against the wall making her jump, and thinking it might wake the children she held her breath. But neither stirred.

Going to the window, she caught the shutter before it could bang again, just as another rumble of thunder rolled over the valley. For a moment, she stood, mesmerised by the rhythmic patter of rain on the cobbles below. Welcoming the cool air. Then suddenly a great bolt of lightning lit the sky outside, flooding the courtyard, and briefly she saw it again. Instead of the buildings that crowded the sprawling inner ward, the imposing white tower from her dream reached towards the dark sky above, lit for a fraction of a second by the lightning. There were no stars visible above the tower, and she sensed that it was in a city that existed beneath a sky constantly hidden by a veil of smoke. A city far away from the hills and valleys of Wales.

A cold, heartless city ...

There was another flash of lightning and Tangwystl gripped the window sill, suddenly breathless with fear. People were running. Running fast to the foot of the tower, smoking torches streaming as they went. They were crowding around somebody lying there, but she couldn't see who it was, though now she could see the knotted sheets dangling from a window high above. With her heart pounding in her breast, Tangwystl leaned further out over the embrasure, desperate to get even a glimpse of what was causing the commotion. She heard a woman cry out piteously before a man pulled her away from the others and held her keening loudly in his arms.

Then the vision began to fade, and Tangwystl could feel the hot tears coursing down her face, mingling with the rain.

'Wait!' she called. 'Oh, please wait ... I must know ... who are you trying to warn me about? Is it my son? Please, I must know!'

But already the vision was indistinct. The veil between the two worlds was being drawn once again, and she could not reach past it to gain the knowledge she sought ...

'Mistress! Oh, Mistress! Wake up! I thought you were going to fall!'

Tangwystl blinked and rubbed her eyes, trying to remember where she was. One of the maids was frantically pulling her away from the window. The rain was sheeting into the room soaking them both. Beyond the window embrasure the tower had gone and the courtyard had re-ordered itself into the usual tangle of dark buildings. With a shudder she turned to the children, now wide awake and huddled together on the bed.

And she remembered the last thing that she had seen before the vision had faded. It was a flock of black ravens, swooping down in the grey misty dawn to settle on the tower's battlements.

Ravens, she knew, heralded death ...

Book One

Chapter 1

Aber Garth Celen, May 1201

No, it could not be true. The news was too devastating to take in. He could hear someone speaking, but the words were lost in a haze of confusion and disbelief. Llywelyn looked up. The messenger was addressing him again, stammering out the words as he was forced to repeat himself for a second time.

'I have a letter for you with her last request, taken on her death bed at Dolwyddelan, Sire. Please, will you not read it? It concerns her final wishes for her children. They're outside. She thought it best they come straight to you...' He faltered as the prince, feeling the colour drain from his face, stuck out his hand and groped for the table to steady himself.

'No.' Llywelyn shook his head fiercely in denial. 'No, I'll not believe she's dead. And in childbirth, never! Why, Tangwystyl birthed Gruffydd and Gwenllian as easily as popping peas out of a pod – there's no reason for it to be any different this time.'

'I'm afraid it's true,' the man repeated unhappily. 'It happened three days ago. I rode here as fast as I could, but with the children and their nurse accompanying me, well, the going was not as swift as I would have liked.' He paused as a squire hurried over with a goblet of red wine. Llywelyn reached for it blindly, spilling some onto the table where it slowly spread into the white napery. He closed his eyes, shuddering as he envisaged the sheets they would have had to have burned after Tangwystyl's final battle to force into the world the babe that killed her.

Around him, the hall had gone very quiet, save for the panting of the dogs at his feet and the distant sound of hammering coming from the bailey. He seemed to have aged ten years in the short space of time that it had taken for the news to be imparted. His initial anger had been replaced by numbness. The gut-wrenching pain would come later.

'I'll take that.' The voice belonged to Llywelyn's brother, Adda, who had appeared phantom like at his side. The messenger handed the letter over to him, Llywelyn let out a breath, grateful that he'd not had to touch it. For a moment his eyes alighted on his brother and in his present heightened sense of emotion, he noticed the imperfections he was usually blind too: the flattened nose, and twisted upper lip that marked Adda out as different to other men in the room. It was an affliction that he had inherited from their father, Iowerth Drwyndwn. One that, like their father before him, precluded Adda from inheriting the seat of Gwynedd, thus allowing Llywelyn to claim that right.

Oblivious to the sea of shocked faces that now surrounded them, Llywelyn hardly noticed Adda dismiss the messenger, or hear his roar as he bellowed for the rest of the household to leave. But soon the great hall was empty, leaving them alone with only the dogs, who silently retreated to a corner.

'Come,' Adda said, taking Llywelyn's arm and leading him towards the hearth. 'I'm truly sorry to hear the news about Tangwystyl's death. Childbirth is a dangerous time, but at least you have two healthy children who survive her. That must give you some comfort, does it not?'

Immediately a prickle of unease ran down Llywelyn's back, and he wished that Adda hadn't mentioned Gwenllian and Gruffydd who still waited outside in the bailey. Adda had never hidden the fact that he had disliked their mother; had believed that despite being both beautiful and captivating, there was also something of the fey about Tangwystl - something almost pagan that had interfered with his overtly Christian beliefs.

But if Adda had never hidden the fact that he had disliked their mother, neither had he hidden the fact that he disliked Llywelyn's children by her and, in particular, the fact that they were illegitimate. It was true the Welsh had a code of honour which did not distinguish between legitimate children, and those born on the wrong side of the blanket – a man could be a bastard-born child and a prince, and therefore could succeed in the same way as a legitimate one – but it was often the case with the arrival of the latter, that jealousy and rivalry would spread its ugly tentacles, causing nothing but dissention and trouble within a family. And that, Adda had made clear as he watched Llywelyn fight his own uncles and cousins in the bid for succession, was something he did not want for his own, or Llywelyn's sons in the future.

Suddenly Llywelyn was angry with his brother. Angry with the prejudices and pious opinions that so often got in the way of their sibling relationship. And he was angry, too, for his dead mistress who was not yet even cold in her grave, and before he knew it he found himself rounding on Adda - wanting to defend her honour, the love they shared.

'I know you didn't much like Tangwystyl, but she was my life and I should have married her when I could. She is ... *was* ...' he amended, his voice cracking, 'after all, the daughter of Lord Llywarch of Rhos. That should have been good enough for me. As a woman of high standing, she deserved better, she deserved to stand beside me as a princess of Wales, not just live a life as a concubine with nothing to show for it but the children who stand outside now ...' Llywelyn trailed off, confused and upset that in his grief he had revealed something of himself; a secret of the heart that he had vowed never to reveal to anyone, let alone Adda who himself had yet taken no woman for his own, but seemed to know a deal more about their make-up than he did.

Adda said nothing, but regarded him thoughtfully for a long while. Llywelyn knew that look well. It meant that his brother was about to say something that would not be welcome, but that he was going to say it anyway. And he was right.

'Some women are only ever meant to be mistresses, Llywelyn,' Adda began. 'That was Tangwystyl's lot in life, and with it, she was content. But now that she is gone, she has made way for another woman to come along. A woman more suited to be the wife of a great prince of Gwynedd. A woman who will bring with her the means by which you will unite principalities, and bear you more children, for the need for children is great when child mortality is such an unknown certainty, even for one such as you. You have one son, but so thought Henry of Anjou and his fourth now sits on the throne. That is your destiny, Llywelyn. It is God's will. Tangwystyl was not that woman. It is time you faced facts, brother. You cannot live on sentiment alone. And for the sake of your people you must marry well. And soon. And it must be a woman who can bring you the political advantages that Tangwystyl could not – border castles, alliances, *and*,' he said under his breath, *'a legitimate heir.'*

Even as Adda spoke, Llywelyn could feel the tension building in the room. Quickly, he glanced around, wondering that Adda did not feel it too. There was nothing. But there *was* something. He could the hairs on the nape of his neck prickle.

'I wish you to say no more on the subject, Adda,' he snapped feeling unsettled. We have had the conversation more than once before. I know that Gruffydd is illegitimate in the eyes of the Holy Church, and that you believe I must marry and beget more children. But under Welsh law he is still my heir. You cannot convince me otherwise, and now is not the time.

'Papa -'

Llywelyn froze, and turning, he looked over his shoulder. Slowly, Adda followed his gaze. Gruffydd stood in the shadow of the door frame, holding Gwenllian's hand. Their nurse was nowhere to be seen.

'Papa, Mama said that I was your best little prince, and Gwenny your little princess,' the little boy said, looking lost and confused as he regarded his father with serious eyes.

Llywelyn took a step towards him. 'Gruffydd, I don't know what you heard, but it's not what you think, I -'

'You said you loved Mama, Papa. You said you loved me, and Gwenny. I don't want a new Mama, and I don't want a new brother or sister! I want my old Mama back!' And with that he released his sister's hand, and turning on his heels, he ran back out of the door.

'Now look what you've done!' Llywelyn said, rounding on Adda. 'I know you cared not for Tangwystyl, but have a care how you speak in the presence of our children. In fact, you can deal with them now, I have business abroad.'

With that he turned and headed for the door, not caring that Adda might not have known that Gruffydd was there, or that he was too young to understand what he had heard, for he was already half-way across the hall. Moments later, he ran down the steps and into the bailey, completely ignoring the children who now stood huddled into their nurse's skirts, pausing only to fling himself onto his horse. They needed care but he could not care for himself, let alone two children who reminded him so starkly of the woman he had lost. He would return to them when his grief was assuaged; when he could look upon them without being reminded of the past, and see them instead as part of the future.

And then he was gone. Galloping over the drawbridge as if Satan was hot on his heels.

It wasn't until much later, when the children had been settled into their chambers, and he'd had time to sit down and reflect upon Llywelyn's abrupt departure, that Adda had time to examine once again the nature of his own feelings for Llywelyn's dead mistress. There was no denying that she had been an exceptionally beautiful and captivating woman, with her red brown hair and eyes the colour of honeyed mead. But as Llywelyn had surmised, there had always been something about her that he disliked; something distant and otherworldly that frightened and antagonised people and made them keep their distance from her. Only with the children and Llywelyn, the three people she truly loved, had she ever show any warmth or human emotion. And even in the short time that he had spent in children's presence today, he had the disturbing feeling that they had inherited those traits. Especially the girl, Gwenllian, who was clearly her mother's child, displaying the same unerring habit of being able to fix him with her strange eyes as if she could read his mind - see into his very soul and found it wanting.

Hastily he put the thought aside. Tangwystyl was dead. Any resemblance the children bore to her was purely down to their colouring, nothing more than that. He drummed his fingers on the arm of his chair as his thoughts went back to the matter of their illegitimacy. Caught up in his grief, Llywelyn clearly wasn't ready to discuss the possibility that this might cause problems in the future. But coming from a family in which rivalry had already cost them dear, Adda knew that he could not discount this from happening again. Gruffydd was already displaying signs of jealousy and resentment, railing against something which hadn't even happened yet. And that, mixed up with his grief, was a recipe for disaster. Sighing, Adda stood and went to stare out of the window, in the direction that Llywelyn had ridden away. His brother, he reflected, might be trying to run away from his pain, but one thing was for certain, he had plenty more to return home too.

Castle Caus, Shropshire, England, May 1201

Putting down the volume of Gerald of Barry's, *The Journey Through Wales, 1188*, that he'd been reading, Llewelyn looked around the comfy room within which he had taken refuge for the past few weeks, and sighed. That he had found himself in Shropshire following Tangwystyl's death came as no surprise, because it was here that he had spent much of his youth, following his mother Marared's marriage to the Marcher lord Sir Hugh Corbet when he was only ten. He smiled wryly. He knew that his mother had only married Hugh to protect him from his scheming uncles, Rhodri and Dafydd, whose treachery had deprived his father of his rightful inheritance after the death of his grandfather, Owain Fawr. But in the end, she had come to find some sort of peace, even a certain happiness, here, in the bosom of the Corbet family. And he had ridden to England wanting the same.

Crossing to the window he looked down over the bailey, remembering his step-father, a man for whom he'd come to have great respect, even though he was not of his blood. Not *Cymraig*, with the fierceness of a warrior running through his veins, and a deep, abiding passion for the mystic land in his heart. Despite this initial setback, however, Hugh had proved to be a kind and scholarly protector, who'd tried to instil in him some of the laws and values of the English way of life he'd suddenly found himself thrust into. And which, for his mother's sake, he had tried to adopt. As a well-respected English lord, Hugh had been able to provide him with the best schooling and religious education possible. From the start, he had been furnished with his own private tutor, whose job it was to teach him to speak the strange, Anglo-French tongue, native to those who lived in the kingdom in which he'd found himself. Another teacher had spent many hours instructing him how to ride a horse, and wield a sword the Norman way, before educating him in the art of manners and etiquette - so that he might eventually go into service as a squire to a neighbouring household, as was the custom in England. Weeks had been spent in the company of a priest, who had endeavoured to instil in him the Christian ways and values, that those dwelling along the borders thought the Welsh heathens beyond its fringes lacked. He had even been allowed to accompany Hugh as he travelled between his manors, collecting rents and tithes, so that he might learn something of estate management with which to run his own when the time came

In fact, Hugh had gone out of his way to accommodate him in every aspect of his education and welfare, so that he might come to enjoy his new life in England alongside his mother. Concerned that he was often alone, he had encouraged him to make friends amongst the local lads, the outcome of which had often been the requirement of a new tunic, or a stiff scolding from Marared after yet another fight. The acquisition of a new gelding, which he'd christened *Troy* - after the ancient city from which all Welshmen believed they were descended - had allowed him to venture further afield: to explore his surroundings and visit neighbouring towns and villages, in order to acquaint himself with the customs and ways of the people amongst whom he now lived. Hugh had even deemed it beneficial for him to have brief introduction to the opposite sex, turning a blind eye to his step-son's dalliance with a woman some years his senior, and far more experienced.

But, despite all Hugh's efforts, it had soon become apparent that his step-son could no more become an English man, a man of Shropshire, than he could suddenly grow wings and fly. Nothing had changed the fact that his earliest memories, formed through legend, myth and stories woven by his father and his forefathers before him, had instilled in him a longing for Gwynedd that could not be overcome by anything his step-father did. As he got older, he longed to return to the magical land; longed to see for himself the great mountains with their narrow deer tracks and forest trails, in the same way as he longed to see the wild gushing waterfalls that spilled down from their peaks, and fed the rivers that flowed through valleys beneath them. Nor did the smooth stone walls of the English castles and manors that he'd found himself living in, impress him. He had still woken every morning in Shropshire, yearning for the sprawling timber houses that had marked his childhood, and within which, he had learned the folklore and legends that surrounded his grandfather, the man he had aspired to be ever since he could remember. Inevitably, it had been this upbringing in an alien land, so different from the land of his birth, that had fuelled his desire for revenge upon his uncles, who, having dispatched with their rivals, had proceeded to divide Gwynedd between them. And so, instead of being the safe haven for her son that Marared had hoped it would be, Shropshire was the place, where, at the age of fourteen, he'd turned rebel, and together with his Welsh cousins, Maredudd and Gruffydd, had declared war on Daffydd and Rhodri in a fight to reclaim the land of his birth.

Sighing, Llywelyn pulled himself back to the present and picked up the letter that his friend and step-cousin Thomas had given him that morning. Thomas, careful of Llywelyn's privacy, had not said much, other to say that it was sent from Wales by urgent courier. And it was. It was from Adda who had hazarded a guess that England was the one place where he would be. Llywelyn smiled to himself. Adda might be of his blood, but he was wise enough to acknowledge that sometimes his brother needed the succour of their Corbet kin. To disappear to a place where he was loved, but not judged and found wanting. And most of all, he was not a prince with the weight of a realm resting on his shoulders. For a while he lingered over Adda's spiky writing, several pages of which outlined the arrangements that had been made for his children in his absence. He pushed those down into the neck of his tunic, not wanting to dwell on the fact that he'd deserted them. But still, an image of them huddled forlornly in the bailey at Aber rose before him, and not for the first time he wondered how much of his conversation with Adda, Gruffydd had actually heard.

It was the next part of the letter, however, that concerned him the most. Adda, not one to waste too many words, had put it plainly. In his absence a fresh outbreak of hostilities had erupted in Gwynedd. This time instigated by Maredudd - the very same Maredudd who'd helped him defeat his uncles all those years ago. Adda had not gone into much detail, only to say that upon his brother's death, Maredudd was now claiming his lands in the west of Conwy as his own. Lands, which according to an agreement between the brothers and himself at the time of his uncles' defeat, would pass to him when they were gone.

He frowned, and putting down the letter he went and poured himself a goblet of wine. Whether or not it had been his intention, Adda had made him feel ashamed. Running from Gwynedd had been a fatal error of judgement on his part, for he had not fought man and boy to become its prince only to lay the land open for plunder because of a single moment of weakness. Worse still, Adda was now alone with only a small garrison of men to protect him, because the rest had been dispatched to deal with Maredudd. Adda, the brother who because of his affliction had never learned the art of warfare and only knew how to defend himself with his wit, his guile and his tongue, which would be of little use in the face of invasion.

Llywelyn was about to go and find Thomas to say that it was time he departed, when a knock on the door signalled his arrival and, entering the room, he perched himself on the bed and began to flick through *The Journey Through Wales* that Llywelyn had been reading earlier.

Seeing Llywelyn regarding him, Thomas smiled. He was a likeable young man, not yet in his twenties, with a friendly disposition and shock of red hair to compliment his green eyes. 'I trust you found solace with us, as you hoped you might,' he said, accepting a goblet of wine from Llywelyn.

Llewelyn nodded. 'I did, thank you.' He paused for a moment, regarding his friend seriously. 'It has been too long between visits, and I must apologise that on this particular one I have not been much company. I confess that I have been sorely grieved over Tangwystl's death, and it has much occupied my mind over the past few weeks. Robert and Emma,' he said, referring to Thomas's parents, 'have offered me nothing but patience and understanding, and for that I am eternally grateful. I am very much aware that they are not obliged, what with Hugh and my mother being long since dead. Now though, I must return to my realm because -'

'Because,' Thomas interrupted, regarding him gravely from beneath his lashes, 'from what I hear, you have a new fight on your hands. With your cousin Maredudd this time, I believe?' For a moment, his eyes flicked down to the volume of *The Journey Through Wales* which still rested in his hands.

Llywelyn frowned as he followed Thomas's gaze, well aware of what he must be thinking, for in *The Journey Through Wales*, Archdeacon Gerald had given a brief, but flattering account of youthful exploits with his cousins in his quest to regain Gwynedd. 'Don't think that I have been reading that out of sympathy for Maredudd's plight,' he said stiffly. 'I'm reading it because Gerald has a wonderful way of reminding me exactly why we Welsh go to war with our own kin. Blood is no barrier to war when treachery flows through the veins of those closest to you. Even Gerald points out that foster brothers are often dearer to fathers than their own sons, and that brothers have been known to gouge out one another's eyes in the pursuit of their inheritance.'

'But Maredudd? He helped you secure Gwynedd. Can you not come to an agreement with him?'

'There was an agreement between us,' Llywelyn snapped. 'Upon each, or both of my cousins' deaths,

I was to receive their lands in Gwynedd above the Conwy, which coupled with mine below, would eventually give me rule over the whole of Gwynedd. The fact that Maredudd has made claim to his brother's lands does not change that agreement. Nor does the fact that he is my own flesh and blood. I have to stand firm on the matter, else I am seen to be weak in the eyes of the other princes of Wales. I cannot afford that if I am to become the ruler of the whole of Gwynedd.'

And you cannot afford it if you are to become ruler of the whole of Wales ... he whispered silently to himself.

For a moment, Thomas's eyes locked with Llywelyn's. 'And what if Gerald writes another volume of his *Journey Through Wales*, and paints you in a different light. What then?'

Llywelyn smiled grimly. 'That is his prerogative, of course,' he said, picking up his goblet and taking a deep draught of wine. 'But for myself, I mean to write other chapters in other volumes of history. And in those chapters I mean to be known as

Llywelyn the Great ... just as my grandfather was known as Owain the Great, before me.

And with that he finished his wine, and saluting Thomas he left to find his horse.

Aber, North Wales, June 1201

Bronwyn stood and surveyed her two charges thoughtfully. Gwenllian was very much like her mother had been, with her long red brown hair, slender frame, and eyes the colour of honeyed mead. Eyes which were fixed at that very moment on her brother, Gruffydd.

'Mama said that Papa would always look after us,' she said crossly. 'So why did he run away like he did?'

'Because he's a coward!' Gruffydd said angrily. 'It was his fault that Mama died, and he's not brave enough to face us and tell us so. And now she's dead, he's going to get married!'

'Hush, children!' Bronwyn said. 'You must stop this bickering, it's not becoming! You know very well that your father is seeking at this very moment to stop his cousin Maredudd from invading us. If he's not here now it's because he has responsibilities to his principality, and not because he is trying to hide from you. Or because he's planning to marry,' she added, looking sternly at Gruffydd.

'I hate it here,' Gruffydd said mutinously. 'I want to go back to Degannwy – why can't we go back, Bronwyn?' he asked, turning his tear smudged face imploringly towards her.

'Your mother wished you to be raised here, at Aber, Gruffydd. This is where your destiny lies. One day you will become the next prince of Gwynedd. Because of that, you must be schooled and nurtured in its principle court, under your father's wing.'

Bronwyn felt a sudden chill as she said this. Tangwystl's presence here wasn't as great as it was at Degannwy, but she still felt her will pressing down upon her. Forcing her to secure Gruffydd's inheritance; to ensure that he was the next prince of Gwynedd after his father, Llywelyn. She shivered. She must not fail Tangwystl. Tangwystl had gone to the grave tortured with doubts about Gruffydd's future, plagued by visions to which she could find no answer. And now it was her job to ensure that Gruffydd came into his own as the gods desired, no matter how she went about it. Bronwyn drew herself up. 'We'll go back to Degannwy for a visit soon,' she said, trying to reassure the boy.

Gwenllian still looked upset and angry, but she was now looking at Gruffydd with new respect. 'Is that true, Bronwyn?' she asked. 'Will Gruffydd be prince of Gwynedd after Papa?'

'Yes,' Bronwyn said firmly. 'It is.' Quickly, she crossed herself, knowing that if Gruffydd was right, and Llywelyn were to marry, he might beget a legitimate son, and Tangwystl's desires would not be met. 'Now, come children, let's clean up before supper,' she urged, ushering them out of the door towards their nursery. Behind her the shadows stirred restlessly and Bronwyn glanced back over her shoulder. 'Be patient, Tangwystl,' she muttered under her breath. 'Your will shall be done. There is plenty of time. There are still bridges to be crossed, for he is, as yet, still just a boy.'

From the door of the next chamber Adda watched them go with a frown upon his face. There was something that he didn't like about Bronwyn. Oh, she was attractive enough, with her dark brown hair braided neatly beneath her wimple, and her regular features set in the stern manner befitting one who had charges as young as Gruffydd and Gwenllian. But her clear grey eyes concealed something else about her: a wariness; a watchfulness that he did not trust. As she disappeared down the hall, Adda stepped into the chamber she and the children had just vacated. It was still and quiet.

Far too quiet for Adda's liking.

Chapter 2

Eifionydd, North West Wales, June 1201

Llywelyn sat atop his horse and looked out over Eifionydd. Just beyond the horizon smoke billowed from the stronghold within which Maredudd had taken shelter for the last few weeks of their standoff. It had been a testing time for him. At first, he'd sought to regain the territories that his cousin had so treacherously deprived him of by negotiation, and the magnanimous promise of a pardon if Maredudd accepted his diminished status and served him well in the future. It was a strategy that had worked well in the past with other rebellious family members. Upon his defeat, his Uncle Dafydd had accepted, not entirely willingly, exile at Ellesmere, his manor in England. Another cousin, Hywel, son of his Uncle Gruffydd, having seen the fate of others amongst his kin, had made the pragmatic decision to serve him rather than face the hardship of war, or the upheaval of his family to another land.

But Maredudd had broken the mould with his obstinacy. Greed and ambition had turned him into a pugnacious man, and he had flatly denied the existence of any agreement made between them previously regarding the disposal of lands upon either his, or Gruffydd's death. And so it was with great reluctance that Llywelyn had gathered his *teuleu* around him, and prepared to expel his cousin by force. However, expelling a Welshman from his own soil was not an easy task, as many would-be English conquerors had found out. Maredudd, true to his roots, knew the terrain like the back of his hand and had simply hidden himself in the high mountains with their jumble of narrow peaks and treacherous ridges that forbade even the nimblest band of foot soldiers access. But as quickly as May had turned to June, support and money for his cause had soon waned, for with no men to bring in the harvest below, came the threat of starvation, followed by the rumour of pardon and leniency if they defected to Llywelyn's side. Eventually, running out of food, and with his men deserting him, Maredudd had finally retreated to the small fort that, until now, had lain buried deep in a forest at the foot of the mountains.

Seeing his men making their way towards him, Llywelyn turned his horse's head, and, ducking low under some branches, he began to make his way down the track to meet them. Hywel was the first to round the corner at the bottom. Behind him came the posse of soldiers that he had personally chosen to flush Maredudd out of his lair. But Llywelyn could see no sign of the man himself. Or indeed, any other prisoners to show for the fact his fort now burned.

'Where's Maredudd? I told you I wanted him brought to me in person,' Llywelyn said with a frown, taking in Hywel's dirty smudged face and soot smeared hauberk as he came to a halt alongside him.

Hywel scowled, and reaching over to Llywelyn's pommel, he took a long draught from the wineskin that rested there.

'Well? Tell me what happened, man!' Llywelyn snapped, plucking the wineskin impatiently from his hands before he could drain it.

'It's not good news, I'm afraid,' Hywel said, wiping his mouth with the back of his hand and shrugging at him helplessly. 'The fort was burning as we arrived. There was no-one present, they had long since fled. But we found these,' he added, signalling forward a man carrying a sheaf of half burned letters.'

Llywelyn raised an eyebrow in question.

'They give us some idea of his movements,' Hywel explained, handing them over to him. 'It appears he's fled to Meirionydd for now. However, these were discovered still burning in the middle of the hall. Its correspondence with Gwynwynwyn of Powys. It appears, my lord, that he is intent upon forming an alliance with him. Against you.'

Llywelyn scowled. He had hoped that dealing with Mardudd would be a simple enough task. But looking at the stream of bedraggled men now lining the track behind Hywel, he realised how clever his cousin had been in outwitting them all. The burning of the fort had simply been a red-herring. One cleverly designed to draw his attention away from the fact that he had long since abandoned his safe-house, and was probably half way towards his self-imposed exile by now. Hywel and his men had wasted valuable time besieging the fort, which would have been torched by one or two faithful retainers once their lord was far enough away. In the ensuing chaos, it would have been easy enough for them to escape. Meanwhile, Maredudd was free to come to an agreement with Gwenwynwyn of Powys, and form an alliance against him in the future.

Letting lose a low growl of annoyance, Llywelyn pushed the sheaf of papers into his saddle bag. 'Well, for the time being we shall have to abandon our pursuit of Maredudd. But at least I can rest easy knowing that in his absence I can relieve him of Eifionydd and Llŷn, without the threat of bloodshed. Moreover, armed with these, we are kept abreast of his traitorous intentions. He would do better in future to make sure that he destroys all his evidence thoroughly before he leaves. Meantime, Hywel, I shall have to leave it to you to secure the remaining castles and forts, for I have to make haste for England. It appears that I have pressing business to attend to there.'

Worcester Castle, Worcestershire, England, July 1201

Llywelyn had never liked the tiny, half-timbered houses and narrow streets that defined the English towns and cities that he had visited in his youth, and he didn't like them any better now. But he had come to Worcester for a purpose. Turning away from the window he looked down at the piece of parchment that he held in his hands. It outlined the terms of a recent peace agreement he had made with King John of England, who was currently in France trying to save his Angevin lands from the plunder of the de Lusignans, and the French king, Phillip Augustus, after he had scandalously kidnapped his new bride, Isabella of Angoulême, from under the nose of her betrothed, Hugh de Lusignan. By all accounts Isabella was only twelve years of age, and incredibly beautiful, and it was said that John had become completely bewitched the moment he set eyes on her. For a moment Llywelyn wondered if the man was insane. To risk your lands for a child of but twelve summers, however beautiful, was an incredibly stupid thing to do in his opinion. Also, there was also the not inconsiderable problem of John's existing wife, Isabella of Gloucester. John had cast her aside, with the support of the Pope, on the grounds of consanguinity – declaring that he had never received the proper papal dispensation to marry a cousin in the first place. Ample enough excuse, so it seemed, for an annulment. If it was a king that was wanting one.

However, Llywelyn reasoned, the politics of the king of England's marriage affairs, was not of any concern to him. All that mattered was this treaty, for it was the first of its kind made between and English king and a Welsh prince, and in a private letter to Llywelyn, John had made it quite clear that he welcomed the accord between them, mentioning that it might prove beneficial to him in the future.

For a brief moment Llywelyn considered a rumour that he'd overheard at court, in which it was suggested that John meant to offer one of his illegitimate daughters to him. But the only one near marriageable age that he could think of, was Joanna, the daughter he kept at his side in France. And she was still only ten years old. Llywelyn pushed the thought away, sickened. He liked mature women, and, unlike John, would not be content to have a child in his bed. Anyway, it was far too soon even to think of marriage. He was still contemplating this, when a sudden gust of wind blew the shutter's closed with a resounding crash, making him drop the parchment onto the rushes. He looked around him. The room was bathed in semi-darkness, and he couldn't have said what it was, but it seemed to throb with anger. Shaking himself, Llywelyn bent and picked the parchment up off the floor before crossing to the window to open the shutters once again. Outside, it was still hot and humid. A haze hung over the bailey and a couple of grooms lethargically unharnessed a horse from a cart before leading it into the stable.

There was no breeze ...

Llywelyn shook his head, and turning he put the agreement down on the table and set off for the hall. He was becoming morose and tetchy. What he was in need of was some pleasant company, and a jug of good Rhenish wine. Tomorrow he would return to Aber. Now that he had relieved Maredudd of his lands in Eifionydd and Llŷn, and had fulfilled his business with the king's officials, he had no excuse not to return and reacquaint himself with his children.

Aber, North Wales, August, 1201

Adda read the agreement and sighed. 'So, you've signed the truce then, and you will pay homage to John as your overlord when he returns from France next?'

Llywelyn smiled grimly. 'In return, he recognises me as the ruler of Gwynedd above all others. An oath to the King of England is currency I am prepared to pay for that alone, if it spares us the price of Welsh blood. However, don't think that I will become a vassal of John's, for I will not. But there are advantages on both sides. On the one hand, John can rest easy in France knowing that with a truce in place we are discouraged from carrying out border raids on England in his absence. And on the other, with him as our overlord as well as theirs, Marcher barons such as de Braose and Will Marshall will think twice before they send their armies in to attack us.'

He paused, recalling the massacre of Abergavenny in 1175 in which William de Braose had invited Seisyll ap Dyfnwal, his son Geoffrey, and several other

Welsh princes, to a Yuletide feast under the pretence of a reconciliation and peace for his incursions into their territories. Once there, they had, as was the custom when attending a castle at a host's invitation, handed over their weapons for the duration of their stay. However, as soon as they were all assembled inside the great hall, de Braose had barred the doors and had them and all their attendants cut down in a bloody display of vengeance for the murder of his uncle Henry FitzMiles at Seisyll's castle several years before.

Llywelyn scowled to himself. He had not yet had the misfortune to meet "the ogre of Abergavenny," as de Braose was now known across the length and breadth of Wales, but he had promised himself that if he did, then the man would need to watch his back, for he had made an enemy of every prince in Wales and he was no exception. The Welsh might have a reputation for fighting amongst themselves, but they were also fiercely protective of their own heritage and people. This fact had been proven when, shortly after the murders, Hywel ap Iorwerth, Lord of Caerleon, had ordered the destruction of Dingestow Castle and had Abergavenny set afire.

Although the attacks carried out on de Braose were done by Seisyll's own kin in revenge of their relatives, they also served as a warning to any other Marcher lord who in the future might think to shift the balance of Welsh power into their own hands.

Seeing that Adda was looking at him quizzically, he plucked the piece of parchment impatiently from his fingers.

'As you can see, John has also agreed that not only do I own the lands in Wales that I've inherited in my own right, but I may also keep any lands that I might acquire in the future. Whether that be by stealth or force. That means that if I were to take the south from Gwynwynwyn as I propose, I would not have to answer to John for its acquisition. Therefore, I would become the prince of the whole of Wales, without any redress to England at all.'

Adda frowned, and Llywelyn knew that it was on the tip of his brother's tongue to remind him that Gwynwynwyn, too, had a similar agreement with the English Crown, and in the unlikely event that if it came to a fight and he won the battle for supremacy, then Llywelyn stood to lose everything.

However, he seemed to think better of it, saying instead. 'Don't be fool enough to think that John hasn't thought of that. Even if you did manage to overthrow Gwynwynwyn, John might well decide to curb your powers - lest you think to expand further out of Wales. And of course the problem of Maredudd has once again raised its ugly head, for I've been reliably informed that he is currently sheltering under Gwenwynwyn's protection.'

Llywelyn shrugged. 'I will deal with that when it comes. For the time being, keeping on King John's good side is imperative. As for Maredudd, I'm confident we will flush him out in the end.

It was well past the hour of Nones when Bronwyn ushered the children into the chamber. She had made sure that they had been scrubbed and were wearing their best clothing, but still she felt on edge about the coming interview.

A large desk sat at the centre of the room. Behind it sat Llywelyn, quill in hand, signing off orders for his reeve, Owain Morgan, who was investigating the theft of a cow in the township the day before. He was a small, sharp-eyed man with a propensity to look down his nose at those he disliked, which he was doing now as he regarded her, Bronwyn noticed irritably. Alongside her the children stood nervously waiting for their father to complete his business, which he did swiftly, dispatching Owain without delay much to Bronwyn's relief. Then he stood and crossed the room to where they waited and looked down at his offspring with a frown on his face.

'Your uncle Adda says that you are not content here at Aber. Are you not well enough provided for?' he asked more harshly than he had intended because they reminded him so much of Tangwystyl.

'I want Mama,' Gruffydd blurted out suddenly. 'You let my Mama die!'

'That is not true, Gruffydd, *bach*. You must believe me - I would have done everything in my power to save your mother. But these things, they happen; I would that they did not, but they do. And I miss your mother as much as you,' Llywelyn finished, realising that he was on the brink of tears.

'You went away, though!' Gruffydd said.

Llywelyn ran a hand through his hair. 'I had to go, lad,' he said. 'It was a matter of state. Your mother would have understood,' he finished, cursing himself for the lie, for it had been his own selfish needs that had led him to seek solace in Shropshire, with no thought for the needs of his children.

Bronwyn coughed. 'Might I suggest, my lord, that they have some time with you whilst you are here,' she said sternly. 'They are sorely in need of guidance. A proper tutor would not go amiss. And some companionship. Perhaps some children of their own age from the village?'

Llywelyn turned to Bronwyn, astounded that she had spoken so forthrightly regarding the management of his children. 'And who exactly are you?' he asked. 'You're certainly not the nurse that was in Tangwystl's employ when I last saw her.'

'I was Tangwystl's trusted companion and confidant. You didn't notice me because that is how my mistress wished it,' Bronwyn said. 'It was her last wish that I attend to the care and upbringing of her children. She felt that it was right that I have guidance of them ... that I make sure that they achieve everything that they should, as is befitting the children of a prince of Gwynedd.'

Llywelyn sighed. 'Very well, employ whosoever you see fit,' he said, feeling suddenly overwhelmed. 'I will see that they lack for nothing. But enough now. I would be alone for a while.'

And with that he turned and strode from the room without a backward glance.

Chapter 3

Criccieth Castle, North Wales, January 1202

'God's teeth, but its bloody awful weather out there. I shan't be travelling for a while, that's for sure, and neither will you!' Llywelyn said, staring intently out of the window at the thick flurries of snow that swirled down into the bailey, smothering the buildings and gatehouse in a crisp blanket of white powder so that they almost disappeared from sight.

Hywel frowned. 'Well at least it gives us time to plan. As I have said before, there is no time for complacency, Llywelyn. I might have succeeded in my quest to drive Maredudd out of Meirionydd on your behalf, but the downside of it is that I have just had word that he and Gwenwynwyn have now concluded their negotiations and formed a treaty of their own against you.'

'Much good may it do him!' Llywelyn said archly. 'I mean to deal with Gwenwynwyn myself. It is my intention to summon each and every prince of the realm together and have them swear allegiance to me. Then, with them behind me, I plan to invade Powys. It's only right that I should be acknowledged as the true overlord of Wales - though I don't envision Gwenwynwyn lying down and accepting me in that role readily. Not without a fight anyway.'

Hywel grunted in response. 'Well, you can count on me,' he said. 'My men will be behind you all the way. Gwenwynwyn is merely a stumbling block to be overcome in the future. What of King John, though? When he returns from Anjou you'll be obliged to swear your homage to him in person, will you not?'

'Yes,' Llywelyn said, glancing over to where Gwenllian and Gruffydd sat with chalk and slate, listening to what their tutor had to impart to them. 'John, however, has another agenda to address with me, I think. It is only the merest of hints at the moment. But reading between the lines, I'm certain he means to offer me his daughter, Joanna, as surety of my accord with him.'

Hywel put down the goblet he had been holding. 'Well,' he said carefully, 'do you intend to accept if that is the case?'

Llywelyn didn't miss the glance he threw at Gwenllian and Gruffydd, and taking his arm, he led him over to the hearth out of their hearing.

'Frankly, I don't know what to think, Hywel. Tangwystyl was my life. I still cannot believe that she is gone, that I will no longer find her waiting for me at Dolwyddelan or Aber, and I cannot contemplate entering another relationship – I feel that I will sully her name by doing so. Also, I have only these last few months won over my children. What would they think if I married a girl not that much older than themselves?'

'But think on it, Llywelyn! What advantages you would have if you married John's daughter!'

'She's illegitimate, Hywel,' Llywelyn cautioned. 'And, as I said, I can only guess John's intentions. But yes, there could be advantages to the match – I would not have to bed her until she is of a decent age, which will frankly be a relief,' he added, thinking again of his own children and shuddering.

'It will also give you good standing with the other princes of Wales. They will see the union as your link with a much greater power which you can wield at any time if necessary.'

'Hmm, we'll see about that,' Llywelyn said. 'Uncle Dafydd thought the same when he married John's father's half-sister, Emma of Anjou. And look what good that did him. Henry never once sought to help him in his strife. And neither did the Lord Rhys, when Rhodri took one of his daughters to wife. No, I am not naive enough to think that marriage into John's family will elicit a great change in John's attitude to Wales and its affairs. But still, it will give me good standing.'

'What will you do if John loses his lands in France?' Hywel asked suddenly.

'He's practically done that already.' Llywelyn said with a shrug. 'Arthur of Brittany and many of his French barons have joined the Lusignans and Phillip against him. I've no doubt that he will come crawling back to England sooner or later with his tail between his legs.' He frowned thinking of King John's nephew, Arthur, the son of his deceased brother Geoffrey, and Constance of Brittany. Although still only twelve years of age, Arthur was declaring himself as the rightful heir to the throne of England, having been named in King Richard's will before his untimely death at Châlus. However, the rashness of youth had not won him many followers in his cause, leading many in England to believe that John was truly the best candidate for kingship.

'Yes, but won't his failure in France reflect on you?'

'No, I don't think so. If anything, it will bind him even more to me. He would not wish to fail here as he has in France. And I have no doubt that we all, down to a man, will be invited to renew our vows of fealty to him as a mark of his favour whilst he re-groups his allies around him this side of the channel.'

Hywel shrugged. 'Well, you seem to have it all worked out then,' he said. 'I hope it comes to pass as you expect – you wear the mantle of state well, Llywelyn, and I for one shall always be at your side!'

'And I am happy to have you there, Hywel! We Welsh put little trust in our families - which is not surprising when brothers and cousins are wont to tear each other apart in order to secure a succession,' Llewelyn added wryly.

Hywel frowned. 'But Adda is always at your side? He would not forsake you?'

'No,' Llywelyn conceded with a fond smile. Adda has been my rock, especially after Tangwystyl died. But it is my duty to protect both him and my family now. That is why I strive so hard to build a principality fit for my sons.' Llywelyn didn't know why he had said "sons," instead of "son," but instantly the hairs on the back of his neck rose, as if someone was watching him. When he turned around however, the hall was now empty, save for himself and Hywel.

Degannwy Castle, North Wales, July 1202

'Do you see her, Gruffydd?' Gwenllian asked, tugging her brother's arm.

'Who, Gwen?' Gruffydd asked, peering in the direction she was indicating.

'Why, Mama of course!' Gwenllian said, looking at Gruffydd with interest. 'Are you saying that you can't see her?'

'Of course I can't see her, she's dead!' Gruffydd said. 'And you shouldn't go around saying that you see dead people, it's not nice!'

'But I *can* see her. Truly I can!' Gwenllian frowned, stung by Gruffydd's tone.

'Who can you see, *cariad?*' Bronwyn asked, hanging one of Gwenllian's bliauts on the clothes pole.

'I can see Mama, Bronwyn!'

Bronwyn froze in the act of reaching for another garment. Slowly, she turned. Gruffydd was watching her reaction with a look of scorn on his small face, and schooling her features she looked over to where Gwenllian was pointing. There was definitely something there. Something fuzzy, but with a distinctly human shape. Then after a moment it faded and disappeared, leaving an air of sadness in the room. Bronwyn shook herself, realising that the tiny hairs on the back of her neck had risen.

'Come on, Gruffydd, she's gone. We might as well go and find Cook and see if she has any cinnamon biscuits for us ... I do hope she has -'

Bronwyn could hear them chattering as they made their way down the newel stairs, and out towards the kitchens. Slowly she crossed the room to where the apparition had been. It was much colder in that part of the chamber, despite the heat of the day, and she reached out and moved the heavy curtain back from the window. There was nothing there.

'I promised you, Tangwystl, that I would see that your little prince follows his true path. And I will. You have no reason to doubt me! I promise you, as God is my witness!' Bronwyn whispered into the emptiness. She could feel the room throbbing around her, and, once again, there was a deep sense of unhappiness hanging in the air. Only this time it was tinged with anger, which somehow seemed to be directed at her.

Shaking her head Bronwyn made for the door, but at the top of the stairs she paused and looked back over her shoulder.

The shadowy figure stood where it had before, shimmering eerily in the shadows, and for the first time in her life, Bronwyn felt real fear ...

Chapter 4

Aber, North Wales, September 1202

'Gwynwynwyn is on the warpath,' Adda said grimly. 'His and Maredudd's troops have gathered together and united against us. They've not yet broached the border between Powys and Gwynedd, but word is they intend to do so!'

Abandoning the little pile of arrow heads that he had been inspecting before sending them to the fletcher, Llywelyn balled his fist and smacked it down hard on the table, heedless of the pain. 'What am I to do, Adda? I've summoned all the princes of Wales together to swear allegiance to me. And they all have. All but Elise ap Madog, Lord of Penllyn, who refuses to do as I command and take up arms! How then am I supposed to defeat Gwenwynwyn when I cannot command the one prince whose land stands between me and my prize, and who by refusing me, threatens the security of Gwynedd!'

Llywelyn was now pacing back and forward across the chamber, driving Adda to distraction. 'Perhaps it was too soon to try to assert your authority over Powys, and you should take a step back,' he suggested diplomatically. 'Rumours that you've raised a large army to invade his territories have obviously stung Gwynwynwyn into action.'

'Nonsense, Adda. Few, including Gwenwynwyn, can be unaware that I am the undisputed ruler of Gwynedd now, and in accordance with the laws of Rhodri the Great, and Hywel Ddato, it is my right to command the obedience of the lesser princes of Wales! This *ty hir,* this *llys,*' he continued, encompassing the hall in a sweep of his hand, 'is my principal palace, and I mean to have all the princes of Wales swear allegiance to me here. Even Gwenwynwyn, if it's the last thing I do!'

Adda sighed, seeing that it did no good to try to persuade Llywelyn away from this course of action whilst he was in the mood he was in. True, he had achieved a standing that was rare for any prince of Wales — he had power beyond his dreams, and wealth too. But Llywelyn's dreams were far too broad to be contained within the boundaries of north Wales. He lusted after the south as well.

Sometimes Adda feared for him, simply because he had no fear for himself. Which made him more likely to rush in where angels feared to tread.

'My lord,' Llywelyn's steward said, entering the room. 'Archdeacon Gerald is awaiting an audience with you. I have given him food and refreshment in your private chambers.'

Llywelyn's eyebrows shot up beneath his hairline. 'I'd not heard that Gerald was on his travels once more.'

'Yes, I wonder,' Adda said. 'To what do we owe a visit from the esteemed Archdeacon? Perhaps he's come to give you another volume of books. One in which you no longer feature as a terrier worrying at the heels of our uncles, but as a grown man in command of your own principality!'

'We'd better find out hadn't we!' Llywelyn said with a sudden infectious grin. 'I must say that I could do with a little diversion at the moment!'

Archdeacon Gerald unfolded his long, lean frame from the chair and stood to greet Llywelyn and Adda. He paused for a moment, noting that, whilst time had done nothing to soften the deformities that marked Adda apart from others, the boy he had briefly encountered on his journey through Wales with Archbishop Baldwin fourteen years ago to persuade men to join the third crusade, had changed indeed, for Llywelyn was now a tall, muscular man in his late twenties, though still with the same dark brown hair and lazy green eyes that he remembered.

If either Welshman noticed his scrutiny then they were too polite to say. Instead, seizing Gerald's hand Llywelyn shook it vigorously. 'It's a pleasure to see you, Archdeacon. Pray tell what brings you to Aber?' he asked, gesturing to the chair that Gerald had just vacated, leaving Adda to pull up a couple more whilst they talked.

'I am actually on my way to see the Bishop of Bangor, but as I was passing through Powys I was surprised to find large groups of Gwenwynwyn's men gathered near the border.'

'Yes,' Llywelyn said dryly. 'You know that I expelled my cousin Maredudd from his lands recently? Well, it appears that he has allied himself to Gwenwynwyn who objects to my growing power.'

'Is it true that you are planning to invade Powys, then?' Gerald asked, looking searchingly at Llywelyn's face.

'Yes, it is,' Llywelyn replied firmly. 'I intend to make haste for the border as soon as I have gathered my *teulu* to my side.'

Gerald sighed. 'That is why I am here. The Bishop is sending representatives from the church in the hope that you and Gwenwynwyn can avoid a war that is likely to be very costly in lives. You and Gwenwynwyn are the two mightiest princes in Wales, and he doesn't want to see the country torn asunder by conflict if it can be prevented. He also fears that now you have allied yourself with King John, he might send an army to help you in your efforts, and he wishes to seek to persuade you to avoid such a calamity. Many communities never recovered fully after the battle of Painscastle, when English troops joined de Braose to oppose

Gwenwynwyn. You must know that yourself, Llywelyn, for you lost many of your own men when you lent support to Gwenwynwyn, did you not?'

Llywelyn signalled his squire to pour him a goblet of wine whilst he considered Gerald's statement. 'I doubt King John will send troops to my aid,' he said eventually. 'He's much too caught-up with affairs in France, by all accounts. I had word today that he now has Arthur in his custody. The boy apparently besieged Mirabeau and held his own grandmother, Queen Eleanor, hostage. But that aside, I might be persuaded to discuss terms,' he said thoughtfully.

'What terms would those be?' Gerald asked as the squire bent over his goblet.

'Well, for one, I would require that Elise ap Madoc swear allegiance to me and forfeit Penllyn. I cannot risk a southern border prince such as Elise threatening the security of Gwynedd in the future. My presence in Powys will put Gwenwynwyn's nose out of joint, but it is a necessary condition for me to withdraw. Alongside this, I require all the princes of Wales to pay fealty to me as their liege lord. And then to King John, as mine. We are all John's vassals for our own protection. Even Gwenwynwyn, for he has sworn to John in the past and I must make that hold.'

Gerald nodded. 'I will travel on the morrow and speak to the Bishop. He can arrange for negotiations to begin on your behalf, and put your terms to Gwenwynwyn. We can take matters from there.'

'Will you deliver them yourself, Gerald?' Llywelyn asked.

'Nay, I have pressing business elsewhere. Other intermediaries will be found though, I promise you. But now that we are agreed on that subject we can enjoy your good wine perhaps,' Gerald finished, raising his goblet to Llywelyn, and then Adda, who'd sat in silence throughout the discussion.

'I'll drink to that!' Llywelyn said with a sudden grin, and with a signal to his squire to bring the pitcher, he downed his wine in one and held his goblet out for more.

Chapter 5

Chester, England, March 1205

Joanna picked up the tortoise shell comb that Rhoda, her ladies' maid, had used to brush out her thick dark hair and toyed with it nervously. She was the daughter of King John of England, and as such, she had to obey him in the matter of where she married. But she could not deny that she was scared. Mainly because of the stories that the acid tongued Isabella, her step-mother, had told her about the horrors of being bedded by a much older, and more experienced man. It was no secret that her own marriage to her father was still the cause of her father's on-going troubles over his dukedoms in France. That, and the disappearance of her cousin, Arthur. Arthur was the Countess of Chester's son, offspring of the union between her and her Uncle Geoffrey long before she had wed Ranulf de Blondeville, the Earl of Chester, following her uncle's accidental death on a tournament field several years before.

Joanna shivered. Sometimes she wondered what had really happened to Arthur. As far as she was aware, Arthur had last been seen with her father in Rouen. Was it true that her father had murdered him, as Isabella had so spitefully told her? Surely, he would not harm his own nephew? Joanna put down the comb. She was not so sure anymore. Her father had a reputation for being a cruel man. But it was also no secret that Isabella despised him, and therefore she might well have lied to her stepdaughter deliberately about Arthur's fate, knowing that she loved her father and looked up to him.

Still, she had been deeply hurt when Isabella had said that her father had Arthur blinded and thrown in the Seine. Even more so, when Isabella expressed delight that John's daughter would share her own fate, and marry a man much older than her. A man who was in his late twenties, and spoke a foreign tongue known as Welsh. 'See how you like having to spread your legs like a whore, or lie on your front, whilst a man the age of your father ruts you from behind like an animal!'

Frightened and appalled by Isabella's revelations, Joanna had run to her mother, Clemence. But any attempt to discuss her fears with the woman who had once been John's mistress, had brought about a serious thrashing and a round of admonishments regarding the behaviour, language, and topics that girls of her and Isabella's age should discuss.

Driven by fear Joanna had then approached her father, but no amount of pleading or crying would move him either. 'Yours is not a marriage for love,' John had told his tearful daughter. 'You are to marry this Welsh prince to secure a pact that I have with him. It is for the country you will do this thing, and I would advise you not to listen to Isabella's tales. I have warned her that I will not tolerate her acid tongue where matters of state are concerned. I assure you that he is a kind man. I have met his children and they are both polite and well looked after, as I have no doubt you will be, Joanna. Now, dry your tears, for I will have not one word more said on the subject!'

The fact remained, Joanna thought bitterly, that she was a chattel to be used anyway her father saw fit.

And in this case, it was to secure peace between England and some place called Wales, which she had been assured was full of heathens. But here she was. And in a few hours, she would be Llywelyn's wife. And a few hours after that, she would be tumbled in bed by him. Suddenly, she felt very sick.

'Come, Joanna,' the Countess of Chester said, popping her head round the door. 'Tis nearly time that you were at the cathedral! Ah, but you do look a picture, child!' she added, coming further into the room and eying Joanna's bliaut of fine blue silk, edged with gold thread at the sleeves and along the hem, where her elaborately embroidered red slippers peeked out. For a moment tears gathered in her eyes, and Joanna felt a surge of guilt, wondering how the Countess must feel having to oversee the marriage of the daughter of the man rumoured to have had a hand in her son's disappearance. But the Countess was made of sterner stuff than that and, coming further into the room, she picked up the gold circlet and veil which lay on the bed alongside her.

'Here, you are not quite complete,' she said, fixing the veil and circlet to Joanna's hair with pins from the dressing table. 'There, you look quite the blushing bride now,' she finished before turning and leaving the room in a flurry of skirts to see to her attendants.

Joanna felt nothing like a blushing bride. She felt like the child she was. A child who was shortly to be thrown to the lions. And the irony of that, when she saw her father's coat of arms emblazoned on her guard's surcoat, was to accompany her all the way to the cathedral.

The wedding meal was a tense affair for Joanna. The ceremony had gone well enough, and she'd not stumbled over her vows which was good. The Earl of Chester had given her away in the absence of her father who was still fighting a war in France, but Joanna was glad that he was not there, because she did not think she liked him much now that she found herself wed a man that she did not want.

The Earl sat now on her right, with the Countess. He had only just regained favour with her father, having been accused of conspiring with Gwenwynwyn of Powys against him while he was absent from England. But he was content enough it seemed to buy new favour by organising and paying for the wedding in John's absence. The Bishop of Chester sat on her left, beside Llywelyn, his bejewelled hand darting frequently to the laden trencher in front of him, whilst throwing her the occasional kindly smile.

There was food in abundance but Joanna scarcely ate it, so afraid was she of the coming bed ceremony. A dish of succulent roast venison lay between her and Llywelyn, which, according to tradition, they shared. Though Joanna noted that Llywelyn seemed to have no appetite either. She barely noticed the tiny succulent partridges, the chicken stuffed with quails' eggs, or the pike in galentine sauce which were paraded before her eyes, followed by pears in wine syrup, and the marchpane subtleties.

The only people she recognised other than the Chesters, were Matilda de Braose, minus her husband, William – who was abroad with her father – along with Amice and Richard de Clare, Hubert de Burgh's wife, and a handful of other marcher lords not attendant in France. She also recognised the boy who was squire to the Earl of Chester. William, she thought his name was. Will de Braose. Whom, if she remembered rightly, was the lady Matilda's grandson.

After the feast, there was dancing and tumbling minstrels for their entertainment. Llywelyn seemed less interested in this than carrying on a discussion with his friend, Thomas Corbet, who had arrived at the feast with him and had barely left his side since. They kept glancing her way every now and then and Joanna felt herself blush. She felt alone and small and she wondered if they were discussing her like they would meat from a butcher. Once again, she saw Isabella's spiteful little face swim in front of her eyes describing the horrors of the bed chamber, and she thought for a moment she was going to be sick.

It was getting late. Joanna had forced herself to dance a slow pavane with Llywelyn, and then a quadrille. But now she was tired. Partly from the strain of trying to appear pleased to be wedded to Llywelyn, and partly from the fact that she had been awake since the crack of dawn. After a moment, the Countess of Chester sat down beside her and touched her on the arm and Joanna wished that her mother was there instead, but her mother was in France, unable to attend her daughter's wedding due to ill health.

'It's been a long day, has it not?' the Countess of Chester said. 'But soon you must retire, I think.'

Joanna felt a slow flush spread up her neck to her face. 'I –'

'Hush, don't distress yourself. Prince Llywelyn is in accordance with me on the subject of bed ceremonies, and he wishes to spare you the ordeal. There is nothing worse than a crowd in the bedchamber, followed by a nasty display of blood on the sheet the following morning, in my opinion!'

Joanna looked around her at the still carolling guests. A few English, half in their cups, had already started fights with some of the Welsh guests, but these had been brought under control by the intervention of Chester's guards. Still, she felt a sudden rush of gratitude that she was not going to have to face all these people naked in her bed chamber. It would have been good sport to them, having consumed so much wine, but it would have been a personal humiliation to her, the daughter of the King of England.

'I have arranged somewhere more private within the castle for you and your husband to spend your first night together,' the Countess of Chester continued in a whisper. 'Thomas Corbet is swapping cloaks with him as we speak, and when the moment is right, I want you to slip behind this tapestry,' she said, indicating a large decoration depicting a hunting scene hanging on the wall behind her. 'There you will find a passageway that leads to one of the towers. When you are concealed, Thomas will make a dash for the door at the end of the hall. He and Llywelyn have the same height and breadth, and a hat will hide the brightness of his hair. He will also have at his side Llywelyn's dog, Gelert, who everybody knows accompanies his master everywhere. Hopefully, he will be mistaken for your husband and the wedding party will not know that they follow the wrong man!'

Almost sobbing with relief, Joanna sat back in her chair, and when the dancing resumed, she obediently slipped behind the tapestry where she found Will de Braose, the Earl's squire, waiting at the entrance to a dark passage. As soon as she appeared, he put his finger to his lips, and bid her follow him along a network of long, cold corridors towards a flight of newel stairs at the foot of a tower. At the top, he opened the door into a large well-furnished chamber, and ushering her in, he stepped back outside without a word, shutting the door firmly behind him.

Joanna looked around in delight. The room was a welcome haven from the noise and bawdiness below. Over in the corner, a small brazier burned, releasing a fragrant smell of herbs. Alongside it stood a table with a bowl of fruit, a pitcher of wine, and two goblets. Tapestries and hangings covered the length of the walls, where tapers burned brightly in their sconces. And everywhere, there were garlands of flowers. In the middle of it all stood a large wooden bed, heaped with soft furs and cushions of every colour imaginable. All at once Joanna's delight in the chamber disappeared as she remembered why she was there, and letting out a barely disguised shudder, she began to cry.

'Tsk!' Rhoda said, appearing from a small ante-chamber, bearing a pitcher of warm water and a bar of good soap. 'Surely you don't want the prince to find you sobbing like a baby!' Then, ignoring Joanna's distress, she began to prepare her for her wedding night, removing firstly her gown and then the gold circlet from her hair, before anointing her with oils and lotions from a bag she had brought with her from Joanna's own chambers in London.

They were nearly done when there was a gentle knock on the door and it opened, admitting Will's head. Seeing Joanna in a state of undress, he blushed furiously, before ducking back out to allow the prince entry, just as Rhoda finished slipping the soft embroidered night gown down over her legs. For a while no one moved, then gathering up her clothes, Rhoda gave a little bob and shuffled towards the door. Within moments she was gone, leaving Joanna standing alone, feeling very small and vulnerable in the presence of her new husband.

Llywelyn looked at the girl-child that was now his wife and wished that he had never broken off his negotiations with the pope for the Manx King's daughter who was far nearer his age.

'Sit down, Joanna,' Llywelyn said softly. He could see her shivering and he wasn't sure whether it was out of fear or cold, but it brought a pang to his breast, and he swore that he would not inflict marriage on his own children at such a tender age. There was no chair in the room, and Joanna reluctantly sidled over to the bed and climbed onto it, staring at him with eyes like a startled fawn.

Crossing to the table Llywelyn poured them both some restorative wine and, as he did so, he saw her draw herself back as far as possible, out of reach amongst the cushions.

Exasperated, he handed her the goblet. 'Drink some, it will do you good. Then you must get some sleep. You look exhausted, child.'

Joanna blinked but took the proffered cup from him. 'Are you not going to –'

'Going to what, Joanna? Defile a child ... goodness what do you take me for, a monster?'

Joanna flinched. 'But it is your right, Isabella said that when -'

'Isabella? What's she got to do with all this?' Llywelyn interrupted, wondering what sort of opinions Joanna's step-mother might have formed about a man she'd never even met.

'Isabella says that when you are a man's wife you must obey him in all things, even if you don't like what he does to you –'

'Enough about Isabella,' Llywelyn said brusquely. 'This is about you and me, Joanna. I married you today and legally you are my wife. And yes, you are correct - I could demand my rights here and now. But I shall not. You must learn to trust me first. We are tied together for life, and yet we have barely spent a day in each other's company. We must learn a bit about each other if we are going to make this work. But for now, we must both get some sleep as we have a long day ahead of us tomorrow,' he finished, giving her a reassuring smile.

He waited until Joanna had pulled back the covers and slid between the sheets before he undressed, blew out the candles, and slid in beside her. She lay stiffly beside him for several minutes, and he was convinced that she believed he wasn't going to keep his promise, but after a while she rolled onto her side. Moments later she was fast asleep, exhausted from the emotion of the day.

For Llywelyn though, sleep didn't come fast enough. And when it did, he dreamed of Tangwystl. She was floating across the river Dee towards him, ghostly and ethereal, her long, red brown hair, tangled and loose down her back.

You will secure my son in his inheritance as you promised ... won't you, Llywelyn? she called.

Llywelyn heard himself moan as she continued to float towards him. Her white chemise was bloodstained, and she carried the dead baby in her arms. Llywelyn could see the tiny face and small, perfect fingers of the daughter that he had never seen. *Never would see ...*

You promised me, Llywelyn ... do not fail me ... you must not fail me ...

Llywelyn woke with a start, to find Joanna shaking his arm.

'Llywelyn! Llywelyn! Wake up! What is it? You were crying out in your sleep!'

'Tis nothing,' he said brusquely. 'Go back to sleep, Joanna.'

Joanna let go of his arm and turned over. He could sense that she was hurt, but after a while she drifted into a deep slumber once again, blissfully unaware of the demons that haunted him as he lay alongside her.

Llywelyn rose. There would be no more sleep for him tonight, he knew. Tangwystl had seen to that, and for a moment he almost hated her. 'Go away and leave me in peace, Tangwystl,' he whispered into the cold night air. 'What will be, will be, and you haunting me will not change it.' He shivered. The room had turned to ice, despite the heat coming from the brazier, and for a moment he could feel her anger swirling around him. Then it was gone. And he was left alone with the flames and his memories.

The next morning Llywelyn watched as his young wife bent and petted Gelert, before turning to smile shyly at him, and he drew a ragged breath. It was going to be difficult to keep the promise he had made her the previous night - that he would not bed her until she was ready. She was not beautiful in the strict sense of the word, but there was something about her: her eyes were a stunning shade of blue, framed by thick brown lashes and finely chiselled eyebrows; a smattering of freckles dusted her nose, a bit like Gwenllian's, and her dark hair hung loose down her back in an abundance of thick curls. As a married woman, she should have covered her hair. But to assure her that he meant what he had said, Llywelyn had instructed that she be allowed to leave it lose - in consideration of her youth, and his intention not to rob her of her innocence, or feel pressured to fulfil the wifely duties she had doubtless been instructed to fulfil.

Drawing a deep breath Llywelyn made his way over to her. 'Joanna,' he said tentatively, 'we leave today for Wales, and you must say your goodbyes soon.'

Joanna bobbed a little curtsey, and Llywelyn had to control his irritation with her. If anything was going to keep him from her bed, it was the fact that she still acted like a child. Bobbing him curtseys where a simple nod would have done.

'I have told you already that you don't have to keep curtseying to me, I'm your husband now!' he said, more curtly than he intended.

Joanna's eyes immediately filled with tears.

'I'm sorry. Please don't cry, *cariad*,' Llywelyn said, suddenly contrite. 'I am just grumpy this morning at the thought of travelling. I did not wish to upset you. But please, don't keep curtseying to me. There really is no need.'

Joanna sniffed, and accepted the piece of embroidered linen her maid Rhoda handed her.

'Come now, child,' she said. 'Enough of that. You would not like your father to hear that you have been crying so soon after your marriage would you now? He would be most upset!'

Joanna obligingly blew her nose and dried her tears. 'I will have her prepared by mid-day, my lord,' Rhoda said, pulling Joanna's arm through hers and turning to leave.

'Oh, and make sure that you have good warm mantles to wear, and stout boots, for in some places we will have to lead the horses as the terrain is not good for riding. And when you are ready, Joanna, come to the stables to choose a horse for yourself. I have chosen two or three which might suit, but it is for you to decide,' Llywelyn called after them, with a sudden smile at his new young wife's retreating back.

Watching them go, he felt a sudden surge of longing for Crysten, his voluptuous mistress of a little over a year. Since Tangwystl's death he had not sought a new paramour from the women who had lined up to fill her place. At least not until Crysten, the widow of a rich merchant, had come along. He did not love

Crysten in the manner he had loved Tangwystl, but then he did not need to. She had understood his raw grief, and the need to assuage the pain of his loss without empty words of love or false promises of future commitment. For Crysten had loved her husband, too, and was not looking to replace him with another. Now, watching as Joanna rounded the corner, Llywelyn knew that when the time came for him to bed his new wife, he would have to give Crysten up. He also knew that Crysten would not be broken hearted. Only matter-of-fact. And for that, he would be grateful.

After a moment or two more revelling in his own solitude, Llywelyn turned on his heel and headed for the stables. Crysten was a day or two's ride away, and he needed to forget about her comforts - lest he turn into the sort of animal John had turned into, and found himself driven to mauling a child to whom he had made a solemn promise.

Joanna looked about the stables, seeking her husband. She found him standing by one of the stalls stroking the muzzle of a huge black war destrier; talking to it in the low, soothing, tones of a language that she now recognised as Welsh. Beside her, Rhoda watched with undisguised interest as behind them the door to the stables shut with a bang, blotting out the cheery tones of servants going about their work in the yard.

Llywelyn turned and spotted them. 'Ah, there you are!' he said. 'Come, you shall have your pick of horse. I have already chosen three that I think will be suitable, but it is you who will have the final choice, *cariad.*'

Joanna tilted her face up towards his. He was so large, this Welshman she had married, that suddenly she was scared. Quickly she lowered her lashes so that he should not see the tell-tale signs of fear in her eyes, and she took a step backwards as if she might dart back through the door.

Irritated, Rhoda pushed her forward so that she was near to the stall in which three docile looking mares stood, lazily nosing a bundle of hay in a trough along the back wall.

'What say you?' Llywelyn asked, coming to stand by her side. 'Which do you think is the prettiest? Just tell me. I will have her saddled up and you can try her out in the bailey.'

Joanna let out a deep breath as one of the mares ambled towards her. 'Why,' she exclaimed excitedly. 'She is exactly like a mare I had in France! My grandmother gave her to me for my tenth birthday. But she did not travel to England with Papa and me when we returned.'

The mare that Joanna referred to was pure white with a dark blaze on its forehead.

'Oh, she is lovely, my lady!' Rhoda said, coming to stand alongside her mistress.

'You shall have the other two for your attendants. It's a long ride to my court at Aber. I trust you do ride, Rhoda?' Llywelyn asked, raising his eyebrows in question.

'Oh yes, my lord,' Rhoda said with a vigorous nod of her head.

'Which do you like?' Joanna asked, interrupting them, and grabbing Rhoda's arm excitedly. 'I must have this one! But the roan over there, is she not pretty too?'

Rhoda looked aghast. 'But it is too much, I cannot take such a gift!'

'You must - for your mistress's sake. You cannot keep up with her if you ride an old nag. And Wales is a place of vast open spaces, which you will want to explore with her, I'm sure,' Llywelyn wheedled.

It was a clever ploy. Within minutes, the two horses were led from the stalls and being saddled by the grooms and, for the next half hour, Rhoda and Joanna rode happily around the bailey whilst the remaining horses were saddled ready for departure.

Later, the Lady of Chester entered the yard, Llywelyn could see her watching them with a frown on her face as Joanna laughed in delight at something Rhoda said.

'What is it?' he asked, crossing swiftly to her side.

She shrugged. 'I understand, my lord, that Joanna is very close in age to your children. I just hope it is an advantage, and they grow to like one and other.'

Llywelyn looked at her. 'Do you think they won't get on then?' he asked, voicing his own fears.

'I cannot say,' she said, glancing up at him with pity. 'But I hope that for your sakes they do.'

Chapter 6

Aber, North Wales, April 1205

The journey to her new home had been perilous in some places, mainly due to the process of negotiating very narrow tracks with the loaded wagons and horses. Llywelyn, however, was used to such journeys, and was familiar with the land, and so Joanna found herself trusting him more and more when he told her that a particular track was safe. Having crossed the river Conwy by ferry at a place known as Tal-y-Cafan, they passed through Rowen, where they crossed the pass of Penmaenmaw, a truly treacherous place with sheer drops down to where the surf crashed against the foot of the cliffs below. After several days had passed in comfortable silence, they began to drop into a valley that Llywelyn referred to as Aber. His palace, or *llys,* he said, was at a place called Abergwyngregyn, which meant: *"Estuary of the White Shells,"* in Welsh. Before it, he told her, was the Menai Straight, overlooking the Isle of Môn, or Anglesey, as some called it. Behind it, you could see the snow-capped mountains of *Eryri*, rising into the sky.

The sun was peeking through the clouds and as they made their way deeper into the valley and Joanna looked around, captivated by the sight of the wild sorrel and tiny daffodils that grew along the slopes. Lambing had just taken place, and the surrounding fields were populated with the fragile spindly legged creatures, little white spots against the jewel like greenness of the grass.

Then they rounded a corner, and Joanna had her first glimpse of the *llys* and the strange D shape of the royal tower peering over the curtain wall, nestled in the mouth of the estuary. Llywelyn had already sent a messenger ahead, and as they drew near, a drawbridge was lowered in welcome for the small party. Once inside the bailey, Joanna could see that the building was quite different to the Norman fortresses that she had spent much of her short life in. The tall D shaped tower she had seen on her approach, abutted a long stone manor house - the *ty hir* Llywelyn had called it - within which, was the private accommodation, and the majestically named

Princes Hall. Alongside the main building, there was the usual sprawl of outhouses: stables, brewery, bake house and kitchens from which the wonderful smell of freshly baking bread wafted. Finally, at Llywelyn's command, they came to a halt in front of the manor, where he dismounted and crossed to lift Joanna down from her horse.

'Welcome to your new home, *Siwan*,' he said softly.

'What does "*Shh … Shaaan*" mean?' Joanna asked, trying to purse her lips around this new, strange, Welsh word, but instead sounding like she was admonishing a naughty child.

'It's the Welsh for Joan, *cariad*. I thought it suited you. Now that you are my consort you must use it. Do you not like it?'

'Yes.' Joanna hesitated. 'No. I like my name in English, and I don't want to change it. Besides, I can't even pronounce it, it's silly.'

She saw Llywelyn frown, and open his mouth as if to say some more, but instead he indicated towards the huge wooden doors of the manor. 'Shall we go in?' he asked abruptly, leaving her in no doubt that she had somehow slighted him.

Nodding, Joanna followed him into a vaulted hall, and within moments servants were milling around them, taking their gloves and dirty travelling cloaks, and pushing them towards the fire that burned merrily in the hearth. For a while she stood alone and gazed about herself, watching as Llywelyn greeted friends and accepted the congratulations offered on their marriage in a foreign tongue. Nobody made the effort to speak her own and suddenly she felt very alone and trapped amongst these people with their strange lilting voices and sly glancing looks that told her she had no business marrying their prince. Or, for that matter, being in Wales. After a while a maid approached her with a ewer and a shy smile.

Gratefully, Joanna washed her hands before being shown to a seat on the dais alongside Llywelyn, just as great platters of food and goblets of wine appeared like magic from the kitchens and brewery beyond the hall.

Joanna had barely settled, when a man approached the dais slowly. The first thing she noticed was his disfigurement, for he had a strangely flat nose and twisted upper lip. Immediately, Llywelyn leapt to his feet and after much back slapping he introduced the fellow to her as his brother, Adda. Giving her a little bow, Adda took her hand and dropped a kiss on the back of it, before turning it palm up, and looking at the smooth white skin with an expression of barely concealed amusement. Snatching it away, Joanna tucked it down inside her skirts, aware that a slight had been made. Clearly, Adda did not view her as good wifely stock, and she wondered if she was expected to scrub floors and labour in the kitchens, in this ungodly place they called Wales.

Ignoring her discomfort, Adda took his own place alongside Llywelyn, who managed to eat with gusto whilst still enquiring as to the welfare of his children, who, it transpired, were visiting some neighbours and were unaware of the arrival home of their father and new step-mother. Joanna was conscious of the number of eyes that slid her way when Adda said that, and she began to wonder what they made of a child little older than Llywelyn's children becoming their new mother. It doesn't matter what they think of me, she said to herself. I'm the daughter of the King of England.

The meal seemed to last for hours before Llywelyn finally instructed a maid to show her to the rooms he had ordered made up so that she could rest after the ordeal of being scrutinised by the household. Following the girl, she was shown to two chambers adjacent to one another in the royal tower. One was furnished as a bedroom, with a pretty table and stools, a large wooden bed piled high with cushions, and a welcoming fire in the hearth. The other was a little dressing room, with a couple more comfortable stools, and another table - this time with her hairbrush and combs laid out neatly in a row, and a ewer of water with a bar of soap alongside. Behind a screen, she discovered the door to a privy chamber and the coffers containing her clothes waiting to be unpacked.

Re-entering the bedroom, she found Rhoda organising a pallet for herself in a corner, around which a screen was being erected for privacy, and, suddenly feeling very tired, Joanna plumped herself down on the bed. Within moments, she was fast asleep.

Gruffydd put the bowl of frogs that he had fished out of the freshwater carp-pool down on the table with a crash, slopping some of the water onto a list his father was writing, much to his annoyance.

'I don't want to meet her!' he said crossly.

'You don't have any choice,' Llywelyn said mildly. 'She's here now and she's my wife, and I expect you to have respect for her. Is that quite clear, Gruffydd?'

'I still don't have to meet her if I don't want too!' Gruffydd replied mutinously.

'You can't avoid her forever,' Llywelyn said patiently. 'After all, she's going to live here, under this roof with us – we might tour Gwynedd occasionally, but we will still have to return here often.'

'I want to meet her, Papa!' Gwenllian chipped in. 'What does she look like?' she ventured curiously, throwing a challenging glance at her brother.

'Well, you will find out soon enough,' Llywelyn said, smiling at his small daughter's earnest face. 'But I can tell you that she's very pretty, and I'm sure that she will think you're pretty too - and she told me that she's brought you both some small presents from France where she lived for a long time.'

'So, she's French?' Gruffydd said with a sneer. 'Which means she will speak only French, and have no Welsh!'

'She is French, yes - her father, King John of England, was brought up in the court of Old king Henry in France and inherited his Angevin empire, which is why he spends so much time there. Anyhow, she speaks mostly French and will have little English, but the main thing is she is willing to learn our language. So, you may have no fears there Gruffydd.'

Gruffydd scowled again, and Llywelyn felt the familiar exasperation that seemed to accompany any conversation with his son grip him once more.

Just then there was a knock on the door and Gwyn ab Ednywain, Llywelyn's seneschal entered. 'Look who I found wandering the corridors, Llywelyn,' he said with a grin. Beside him stood Joanna, smiling shyly.

'Come in, Joanna,' Llywelyn said with a nod to Gwyn. 'I was just telling Gruffydd and Gwenllian about you, so it is fortuitous that you arrived just as you did ...'

Joanna hadn't meant to intrude on Llywelyn's privacy for she knew that his children had returned to the *llys* and he would be spending time with them, but boredom had found her wandering the corridors in search of some entertainment. Now that she was here, though, she stepped further into the room and looked around; it was richly furnished and spacious, with arched windows that let in plenty of light. Behind Llywelyn another door stood open, and she saw a large bed similar to the one in her rooms, and she realised that these were Llywelyn's own private chambers. For a moment, she couldn't imagine anybody crossing the threshold without being invited, and she felt a little bit awkward that she had turned up so unexpectedly.

Llywelyn, however, merely held out his hand to her. 'Come, Joanna. It's time for you to meet my children, Gwenllian and Gruffydd - they have just returned from visiting friends.'

Joanna stepped forward hesitantly, and nodded to both in turn, taking in their shared appearance: red brown hair, and green eyes. The eyes were Llywelyn's. But the hair most certainly wasn't. Gwenllian threw her a beaming smile, but Joanna immediately sensed hostility emanating from Gruffydd.

Behind her Gwyn turned to go, but Llywelyn called him back. 'Stay, Gwyn. I will have a game of chess with you if you please.'

Ignoring the two men, Gwenllian took Joanna's arm excitedly and dragged her to a window seat. Gruffydd followed, dragging his feet, but one glance at his father warned him not to do anything rash.

'What was the wedding like?' Gwenllian asked in French. 'I hope you can understand my French,' she added as an afterthought. Both Mama and Papa secured us good tutors in the language.'

'Your French is lovely,' Joanna said, warming immediately to pretty girl sitting beside her.

A little dog suddenly jumped up from the fireside and shook itself before running across the room and leaping onto Gwenllian's lap, scattering ashes everywhere.

'Oh, you little rascal!' Gwenllian squealed. 'You've got dirty marks all over my gown!'

Joanna laughed. 'Isn't he lovely,'

'He's a she,' Gruffydd said, narrowing his eyes, 'And she belonged to our mother, so don't you ever forget that!' he finished.

Joanna realised immediately that this was some sort of warning. 'Oh, of course not!' she said earnestly. 'Your mother died, did she not? I'm so very sorry -' She broke off at the sheer look of fury that crossed Gruffydd's face, realising that she had made a very grave mistake.

Gruffydd struggled with his features for a moment, then suddenly he narrowed his eyes and leaned forward, so that his face was close to Joanna's. 'Gwenny sees her a lot. She haunts Aber, but not as much as she haunts Degannwy - that's where she died you see. At Degannwy castle. No doubt *you* will see her soon. Either here or there!'

Gwenllian was struggling not to burst into tears, when Gruffydd suddenly jumped to his feet and with a quick angry look at his father he stormed out of the room, leaving Joanna and Gwenllian gaping at his disappearing back in resentment.

Joanna turned a bewildered face to Llywelyn who had risen from the chess table, just as Gruffydd marched towards the door and slammed it angrily in his wake.

'I'm sorry for my son's bad manners, Joanna,' he said, coming to stand beside her. 'I shall have words with him. But meanwhile, why don't you and Gwenllian go and see the Flemish silks that arrived whilst I was away. Each of you shall have some new gowns made for you. I think you both deserve it.'

'Will he ever like me?' Joanna asked in a small choked voice, as they listened to Gruffydd's footsteps echoing down the corridor.

'Of course he will, *cariad*. It will just take time that's all,' Llywelyn said gently.

'I hope so,' Joanna whispered, staring into his eyes and seeing his words for the lies they were. Then turning, she took Gwen's hand, and without looking back they went to inspect the silk.

Llywelyn stood still for a long time after the girls had left the room, gripped by a sudden premonition: a feeling that Gruffydd would meet his end because of his stubborn unyielding nature and dogged assertion that life was being unfair to him. It was a feeling so strong, that he was forced to turn and grip the window embrasure to steady himself.

'Are you alright, Llywelyn?' Gwyn asked, coming to stand beside him.

'Yes … yes, I think so,' Llywelyn said, watching as Gruffydd's stiff little figure entered the bailey below and headed for the stables. 'I just hope that Gruffydd will be,' he finished as, once again, he felt the heavy threat of Tangwystl's anger hanging over him. Then throwing one last look at Gruffydd's retreating back, he plucked his cloak from his chair, and throwing it over his shoulder made his way down to the hall.

Whatever the demons were that his son was fighting within himself, until the day that he accepted his new step-mother, he was going to have to do it alone.

Chapter 7

Aber, North Wales, March 1206

Bronwyn gazed along the length of the hall to where Llywelyn sat, breaking his fast with his young wife. There was something about the little princess that Bronwyn didn't like, despite the months that she had been at Aber. She was a threat to Gruffydd. She could feel it in her bones.

And Tangwystl didn't like her either. She was growing stronger here at the *llys*. Bronwyn could feel her power. It came in waves. She could feel it now. Encircling her, drawing her in. Power like that only came from something invested with a dark magic, and she had come to the conclusion that one of the children, probably Gwen, had brought something of their mothers with them from Degannwy. Something personal. Something that had allowed her to follow them here to Aber. She frowned. She had searched Gwen's room, but the search had revealed nothing whatsoever. And when questioned, the child had denied it. She looked at her now seated on one of the high tables with some girls from the village. She was giggling over something that she had drawn on her slate, and her long red brown hair fell over her shoulders, deliberately shielding her face from her nurse's knowing gaze, as the ever-present shadows shifted restlessly around her.

After a while Bronwyn let her eyes wander back to Joanna. She was nearly a young woman now, and no longer the slender child she had been. It would not be long before Llywelyn noticed. Then he would take her to bed, and get her with child, for she had started her courses. For a moment Bronwyn toyed with her eating knife. She knew that Joanna was destined to have many healthy children, and that one of those would be a boy. For she had consulted the runes, and no matter what way she threw them, they foretold that *he* would succeed where Gruffydd could not, and inherit Llywelyn's title and lands.

Bronwyn placed her eating knife carefully alongside her trencher, no longer hungry. She could not let it happen. She must not allow Gruffydd to be robbed of his inheritance. But how to prevent it? There was no way of putting the necessary herbs in the girl's food to prevent her breeding. And even if there were, there was no certainty that it would work as the process took a lot of trial and error. No, that was simply not possible. And the consequences of doing such a thing if she were caught would mean her death.

But another plan was forming in Bronwyn's mind. She would just have to find a way to make the girl hate Llywelyn. She smiled. Already, she thought she had the perfect answer.

Later that night, as Gwen obediently rolled over onto her side and prepared for sleep in the bed she shared with Gruffydd, her hand curled around the trinket: the brightly enamelled little brooch that she had once belonged to her mother. It felt warm. She could feel its power vibrating softly. And with it, she could feel her mother's presence at Aber growing stronger. And so could Bronwyn. She was sure of it. She had been watching her knowingly of late, and she knew that she had been to her room and searched her belongings. Looking for something that might explain the strange atmosphere that hung over the *llys* recently.

Gwen shivered, and gripped the little trinket more fiercely. She knew she should not have brought the charm with her from Degannwy. That it was dangerous. But even though its power frightened her, she wasn't ready to give it up yet.

Gruffydd stared moodily out over the Menai Straight towards Llanfaes, the little village nestled on the eastern shore of the isle of Anglesey, now shrouded in mist. He had argued with Gwenny again about Joanna. Angry because Gwen showed no rancour whatsoever towards their step-mother, but rather had gone out of her way to befriend her over the last year and a half, and it was now he who was getting pushed out. He had even had to move rooms after he had deposited frogs in her bed the first night she had arrived, making her scream the palace down. His father had sent him to be horse-whipped for that, and he hadn't been able to sit down for a week. Sulkily, he picked up a pebble and threw it into the river. Flur, Tangwystl's dog, ran after it and plunged into the water, only to turn around and run out disappointed when it sank to the bottom beyond her reach.

Feeling thoroughly fed up, he turned for home, when suddenly he spotted Bronwyn making her way along the shore towards him. He scowled. He found his nurse's attention, and strange ways, cloying and claustrophobic. And anyway, he told himself, he was too old to need a nurse at ten! Undoubtedly though, she was here to scold him for missing supper, and irritated he picked up another pebble and threw it at a flock of seagulls, making them shriek and take flight with a noisy crash of wings.

Bronwyn met him half way along the path. 'What are you doing wandering out here alone? Your father would have you whipped if he knew, for it's not safe! Now come along. And don't dally, because he wishes to see you and Gwenllian in his rooms in an hour. Clean and tidy as a new pin if you please - no doubt you will have time for a bite to eat first!'

Gruffydd scowled. Private audiences with his father usually meant a scolding for some misdemeanour or other. But he couldn't think what, because his father had only returned from Criccieth with his escort that morning. And so, instead, he tried to think what he might have done in his absence to anger him.

'Come! Come!' Bronwyn said impatiently. 'Stop dragging your heels and get a move on, or you are sure to be late for your meeting with the prince!'

'Bronwyn.' Gruffydd came to a halt. 'Do you know why my father wishes to see me and Gwen? Have we displeased him in some way?'

Bronwyn turned and looked back at him. 'I'm sure he is not cross with you. He certainly didn't appear cross when I spoke to him. Quite the opposite in fact!' Bronwyn said, picking up her skirts and hurrying along the path once again.

Gruffydd sighed. There was nothing for it now, but to follow Bronwyn across the drawbridge and into the bailey. He was fairly sure that there was more to his father's summons than Bronwyn was telling him. She had the look on her face that, as young as he was, told him that she was concealing something from him, meddling in things that were not her business.

In his chamber, he found warm water in a ewer along with a cake of soap and a cloth. He washed quickly. Then Bronwyn entered the room, and set a platter containing some meat and cheese, and a small loaf of bread on the table alongside him. He hadn't realised how hungry he was, and forgetting the dreaded meeting with his father, he fell on it greedily.

He hardly noticed the sly smile that Bronwyn threw his way as she left, nor the air of confidence she exuded, for he didn't yet know of the plans that Bronwyn had for Llywelyn's little princess. Plans that would ensure that by the time the night was over, her world would be scattered in pieces around her.

Joanna picked up her tortoise shell comb, and passed it to Rhoda, so that she might tidy her hair. She'd been surprised when Bronwyn had handed her the note summoning her to Llywelyn's chambers that evening. It was true that she had never yet been summoned. Indeed, Llywelyn had treated her with the greatest respect - just as he had promised on the evening of their marriage. He was giving her time to grow. To mature and become a young woman. She had her own chambers and a great deal of privacy. He had even accommodated Gruffydd elsewhere so that he could not sneak into her room and fill her bed with frogs as he had done on her first night. But now he had summoned her. And Joanna could only imagine that because he had summoned her to his private bed chamber, and at night, he wished to make her his wife.

'Are you afraid, child?' Rhoda asked quietly, sensing her mistress's mood.

'Yes,' Joanna replied with a slight shake to her voice.

Rhoda smiled reassuringly. 'You have no need to be.'

Joanna let out a cross between a hiccup and a sob. 'Isabella told me what it is like for a woman in a man's bed,' she whispered. 'She told me that they act like animals. That they maul and paw you, with no thought to the harm they do to you in the process!'

Rhoda put down the comb down on the table with a sharp click. 'That girl is sick and jealous, Joanna. All the nasty things she told you were to frighten you.

Can you not see that because she is unhappy, she wants you to be too? Don't finally go to your marriage bed in fear, child. Go with happiness in your heart. You might find that you come away with wonder in it too, for love between a man and a woman can be a beautiful thing.'

Joanna turned to stare at Rhoda. For all her fussy ways, she had never thought that she might have a streak of romance inside her.

'You would have liked it at the court of Queen Eleanor, Rhoda. There, they talked of a thing called "courtly love." They encouraged the men to write poems, and sing songs to the ladies! Indeed, Queen Eleanor, my grandmother, received poems flattering her great beauty even at her age! Of course, I was too young ...' Joanna finished with a little smile.

'Come,' Rhoda said suddenly. 'I will accompany you to your husband's chambers. Mayhap, while you are happily occupied there, I may find a beau of my own!'

Gruffydd trailed to a halt in front of his father's chambers and knocked. Gwen was already there. Staring at the door blankly. 'I have already tried knocking,' she said.

Gruffydd shrugged, and getting no answer himself, he knocked again. Harder this time. Again, no answer. He frowned. He was certain they weren't late. And Bronwyn had definitely told him that they were expected in his father's chambers. She'd been most specific in that. Gruffydd continued to examine the door as if it could give him some answers. Then with a shake of his head he turned, and was about to walk away, when he thought he heard a shriek of laughter. Gwenllian looked at him. She'd heard it too. He was certain. Turning back, he put his ear to the door, but all was quite within. Had he imagined it, he wondered? No! There it was again. And it had definitely come from within the room! Gruffydd grabbed the door handle, and lifted the latch. The door wasn't locked, so he pushed it open and entered, with Gwenllian following reluctantly behind him. On the far side of the room, the door of Llywelyn's bed chamber was ajar. Now they could plainly hear voices. Their father's, and a woman's.

But he knew the voice wasn't Joanna's. It was too low and sensual.

Before Gruffydd could move towards the bed chamber, Gwenllian suddenly grabbed his arm. She was staring at something in the far corner of the room, and she seemed agitated.

'She's here!' she whispered.

'Who's here?' Gruffydd asked angrily, eyeing the door to the bed chamber from which the sounds emanated.

'Mama!' Gwenllian said hotly. 'And she's angry. Very angry!'

'Oh, for pity's sake!' Gruffydd said, shaking her hand roughly from his sleeve, so that she stumbled.

'Please, Gruffydd! Please listen to me!' Gwen cried, as a heavy sense of foreboding was suddenly unleashed on her senses. Ignoring her, Gruffydd grabbed a smoking tallow from the wall. Then striding towards the door, he threw it wide open and held it high.

Llywelyn lay sprawled on the bed, naked. Above him rose a voluptuous young woman, perhaps five years Joanna's senior. Both of them turned around in surprise as the door banged open.

Gruffydd stared at his father, hate written all over his face. 'So, you are servicing court whores now, are you?' he asked, his voice squeaking in disgust. 'Well, what of the whore you married? Do you finally agree that she is not worthy of you?'

But Llywelyn was not listening. He was staring at a point beyond Gruffydd's shoulder. Gwenllian was the first to turn around, just as a sudden flash of lightning came from nowhere, streaking down through a high window and lighting the doorway where Joanna was standing, staring at the scene in horror. Moments later she was gone in a flurry of skirts and loud distressing sobs, as outside the beginnings of a storm began to rage.

Back in her room, Gwen took out the little brooch and contemplated it sadly. She had only brought it here so that she could be closer to her mother. But now she was beginning to realise the folly of her ways, for Tangwystl was growing stronger. And now she was causing trouble. She was getting people into trouble, and that was not what she wanted. Quickly, she took out a piece of linen, and wrapping the brooch carefully, she thrust it into the little inlaid jewel box her mother had given her on a birthday long ago. Then, opening her coffer, she buried it as deeply as she could amongst her clothes.

Llywelyn eyed Joanna's stiff back. She had been like this for a week now, refusing to talk to him. And it was very trying. For a moment, his eyes alighted on Bronwyn who was sitting in the corner with Gwenllian, sewing. He was sure that she had something to do with Joanna discovering him with Crysten. He had sensed in the past that Bronwyn disliked Joanna immensely. If so, had Gruffydd and Gwenllian been placed there as witnesses in order to humiliate Joanna even further? But why was she trying to sour his relationship with Joanna anyway? Llywelyn wondered for the umpteenth time.

As if sensing his scrutiny Bronwyn raised her head, and her clear grey eyes met with his. He could read nothing. But still he felt uneasy. There was something not quite right about the woman, and he wondered for a moment if she was not a little touched.

'I would like to be alone with my wife for a while, please,' he said firmly.

Bronwyn threw Llywelyn a speculative look, but gathered her sewing up without a word, and nodding to Gwenllian she headed to the door.

'Please,' Llywelyn said to Joanna's back when they were finally alone. 'Can we not at least speak?'

'Rhoda says that Crysten is with child. Is it true?' Joanna asked, and he flinched at the hurt in her voice.

'It is true,' he said finally, sorry that Joanna had had to find out through castle gossip and not from him. 'But you must have realised that I would find solace with someone else – it was only to be until you were old enough to fulfil your wifely duties.'

'But she *is* with child.' Joanna said stubbornly.

'That cannot be helped,' Llywelyn said tiredly. 'She's going to go away to have the babe. It's best for you both if she is not here.'

'Do you love her?' Joanna asked, turning around to look at his face.

'It's not like that,' Llywelyn said gently. 'I just needed to fulfil my needs – the child was not planned, and I would not have hurt you for the world, Joanna. I would have you understand that.' Again, he thought of Bronwyn and the night Joanna had discovered him with Crysten. He was becoming more and more convinced that it was she who had set this messy business up; that had she deliberately arranged for him to be caught with his mistress. He was sure that she was not good for Gwenllian and Gruffydd, and now this. He would have to talk to her. The hold she had over his children must be broken, or else she must leave.

Stepping forward he took Joanna's chin gently in his hand, and looked down into her face. 'You have grown into a beautiful young woman,' he said, his eyes travelling down her body. Taking in all of her new curves.

Joanna flushed, suddenly shy under his scrutiny - he could see the emotion flitting across her face as she wondered if it mattered so much that he had laid with Crysten, and he bent down and planted a kiss on her lips. Then seeing that she was about to ask, he released her chin abruptly, and turning he picked up his quill and began to study the pile of parchments on the desk. As if he had forgotten she was there. He heard her gasp as if hurt at his sudden loss of interest in her, then, after a while, the sound of her slippers kicking at the rushes as she flounced across the room and threw open the door.

Llywelyn smiled, but kept his eyes down knowing that she would look back to see if he was still bending over the papers. If he was to have any sort of relationship with his wife, she would have to come to him of her own accord. Already, he could feel his erection hard against his chausses. It was going to be a pleasure de-flowering her. He only hoped that it would not be too long until she came to her senses.

'Who's that old woman?' Gwenllian asked Bronwyn, indicating a small figure with long flowing white hair, picking her way towards them along the wet sand.

Shielding her eyes, Bronwyn followed Gwen's gaze. Suddenly, her mouth felt dry, and her heart skipped a beat. 'It's only old Mab. She has a hut down in the valley. By the edge of the forest,' she said, grasping Gwenllian's hand firmly. 'She's harmless enough.'

'Oh, I remember Mama talking about her. She's a witch, isn't she? I wonder what she's doing here?' She turned bright eyes on Bronwyn who, despite looking nervous, stood her ground as the old woman continued on down the beach towards them.

'Well?' Gwenllian asked again, pulling her hand from Brownwyn's, which was damp and sticky, to stare curiously at Mab as she came to a halt a few feet from where they stood.

Mab must have been at least a hundred years old, and so frail and skinny that she could easily have been swept away by a stray sea breeze. Ignoring

Gwen's open curiosity, she turned her gaze on Bronwyn's now hostile face.

'You must cease your meddling!' she said without preamble, her voice ringing surprisingly clear and strong for one so old.

Gwen shivered. The sun was fading rapidly behind her. In the distance, she could hear the water crashing against the rocky shore, the only sound in the sudden silence that had descended upon them with the old woman's arrival.

'Tangwystl is wrong … the boy Gruffydd, her son, is not destined to sit on the throne of Gwynedd,' the old woman continued. 'There is one who comes after him. One who is more worthy. You cannot change that. You do not have the power, and you must stop meddling in things you know nothing about!'

'Is that why you are here? To tell me that, old woman?' Bronwyn cried, her voice brittle and challenging. She took a step back as a sudden wind rose from nowhere and swirled around them, flattening the old woman's work-worn gown to her skinny legs and blowing her hair wildly around her head.

Gwen shivered. The air was suddenly icy cold, and she felt the tiny hairs on the back of her neck rise as the two women faced each other, their eyes locked in some ancient battle of wills.

My son ...

She heard the words moaning in the wind.

Gruffydd ... my son ...

'Sweet Jesu!' she whispered. Her mother had followed down here! She had grown strong enough to leave the *llys,* despite the fact that the brooch was buried deep in the bottom of her coffer. And she was angry. Angry with the old woman. Suddenly she could feel it all around her: in the sand that was stinging her eyes, and in the wind that tore through the trees and whipped her hair into her face. Then behind Bronwyn, she saw something. A figure. Rising tall and ethereal. And full of hate. Not at all like the sad, beautiful mother that she remembered ...

Petrified, she caught Bronwyn's arm and shook her. Bronwyn gave a start, and unlocking her eyes from Mab's, she looked about her wildly: *she could see her too; feel her too ... and she was afraid!*

Giving a sudden sob, Gwen turned, and began to run up the beach. Back towards the safety of the *llys*. Behind her, she heard Bronwyn curse. Then the crunch of shingle beneath her feet as she turned to run up the path after her, followed by the distance sound of Mab's voice: 'The time will come when you will have need of me, Bronwyn. I will wait for then. But don't leave it too long, for the Lady Tangwystl grows strong ...'

The crone's voice faded away as Gwen turned the corner and streaked across the grass. Past the startled guards on duty at the gatehouse, and onwards. Towards her room, where she threw herself on her bed, and curled into a ball like a frightened kitten. Only then, did she begin to shiver with fear ...

Later that night, Brownwyn crept into Gwen's room, determined to discover whatever it was that the child possessed that was making Tangwystl stronger. It was only when the child turned over, and her fist uncurled, that Bronwyn saw it nestled in the palm of her hand. It was a little enamelled brooch. The one that Tangwystl had always worn. Pinned to her bodice, near to her heart. Picking it up with great reverence, Bronwyn stared at it. It looked so small and innocuous. But even as it lay there, she could feel the power radiating from it. For a moment, she looked at the child's sleeping form. Then, making a decision, she stood and tucked it down the front of her girdle. Power like that needed to be put to good use. And anyway, she had a feeling that Gwen would be glad to be rid of it.

Chapter 8

Trefriw, Gwynedd, North Wales, April 1206

Joanna looked about the hunting lodge with delight. Although not large, it was amply furnished and comfortable, with rushes strewn across the floor and sturdy benches laden with cushions. She watched as a maid built up a fire in the hearth then bustled off to prepare some food. She turned to Llywelyn. 'How long shall we stay?' she asked.

'A few days at the most,' Llywelyn said, smiling at her enthusiasm. 'I thought you would like to get away for a while. So that we can be on our own?' His voice sounded a little uncertain, and Joanna slanted a look at him from under her lashes, surprised.

'I know it is hard for you at Aber. Gruffydd has hardly been welcoming. And the incident involving Crysten, well -'

He broke off, as Joanna crossed the room and laid a hand on his sleeve. 'Pray do not speak of that here, my lord,' she said. 'It is my own fault ... I should have become a wife to you sooner ... I did not think -'

It was Llywelyn's turn to stop her mid-sentence. Pulling her to him, he lowered his mouth to hers. The kiss seemed to go on eternally, and was only broken off when the maid re-entered the room, bearing a tray of cold meats and cheeses and a pitcher of wine which she deposited on a heavy oak table in the centre of the floor. When she had left, Llywelyn shed his cloak and sword, and with Joanna's help, his hauberk. Then he gently drew her into his arms. 'I think that it is time to truly make you my wife,' he said. 'Although you are still young, you have matured much over this last year of our marriage – I should have noticed sooner.'

Joanna could feel her heart beating harder, and her breathing becoming thicker, as he gently cupped her breast. Immediately, the nipple sprung up beneath the fabric of her gown, and, with a moan, she suddenly pulled away.

'A goblet of wine, my lord?' she asked, pouring one with shaky hands.

Llywelyn took it from her, and replaced it on the table. Then he tilted her chin, so that she had to look into his eyes. 'Are you afraid, Joanna?' he asked gently.

'Yes,' she whispered.

'Come, you must not be afraid. I would not hurt you, and I will try and be as gentle as I can.' Llywelyn said, running his hands down her trembling arms.

Then, picking up the tray of meats and the pitcher of wine, he carried them over to a door. Behind it was a large, well furnished bedchamber. Joanna followed him, but remained hovering on the threshold like a timid bird. Now the time had come, she could not help remembering Isabella's bitter warnings of what she would have to endure in the marriage bed.

'Come,' Llywelyn said. 'Close the door. Lest you want the guards to walk in on our sport.'

Joanna did as he said, and perched herself nervously on the bed. Llywelyn picked up the goblet of wine she had poured for him, and came and sat next to her. The bed sagged slightly under his weight, and she was suddenly very aware of his size.

Taking a sip of the wine, he handed her the goblet. 'Here, drink,' he said gently. 'It will relax you.'

Again, Joanna did as he said, letting the aromatic wine linger in her mouth before swallowing. Outside, she could hear the sound of woodsmen chopping wood, and the warble of a chaffinch. Taking the goblet from her, Llywelyn drained it, and placed it on the floor beside the bed. Gently, he brushed a lock of dark hair from her brow, and cupped her cheek tenderly. Then, turning her face towards him, he kissed her again. Although still nervous, Joanna was suddenly conscious that her whole body was now alive, and tingling with anticipation.

Had Isabella not felt the same with her father?

No, a small voice said. Isabella had felt only repulsion –

Or had she? Joanna wondered, slightly confused as she remembered the sound Crysten's laughter coming from Llywelyn's chamber the night they had been discovered together. Perhaps it wasn't wrong to feel like this? Perhaps Isabella's comments crude comments about her father had simply been born out of spite, and rather than listening to her, she should learn something from Crysten's relationship with Llywelyn instead? Suddenly Joanna was no longer afraid, and almost unconsciously she leaned back as if offering herself to Llywelyn, letting herself sink back onto the bed as he slowly loosened the laces on her bliaut and slipped a hand down inside the neck of her chemise, releasing her breasts. He paused for a moment, and although she knew that they were full and rosy tipped, Joanna was suddenly assailed with the horrifying thought that they might not be to his liking: that he might reject her at the last minute because they were still too girlish, not womanly enough for a man of experience like him. As if reading her mind, Llywelyn lowered his head and took, first one swollen nipple in his mouth, and then the other. Then when she didn't resist, he slowly raised her skirts and began to run his hand up the inside of her thighs.

'My lovely Joanna …'

Joanna froze, then let out a gasp, as, encountering soft, tantalisingly wet flesh Llywelyn's hand came to a halt and he experimentally inserted a finger. At once, all thoughts of Isabella and her own inadequacies fled as she gave in to the new sensations that were taking over her body. She could feel the ripples of desire building inside her, along with an unbearable tension and the primal urge to have him fill her and use her. Until whatever it was that was happening raced to its final conclusion.

Withdrawing his finger, Llywelyn began to struggle with his close-fitting chausses and braies; to her surprise the loss of contact served only to heighten her desire, and she found herself moaning like an animal in pain. Finishing his undressing, Llywelyn begun to push her skirts impatiently up, and over her head, tugging at them until they lay in a crumpled heap on the bed beside him, and spreading her legs as wide as he could, he knelt before her. For a moment Joanna glimpsed his erection, large and powerful, and she was afraid again. Then all thoughts scattered as he entered her. There was a moment of pain only. Then an explosion, as he thrust once, then twice.

It was as if a molten river of fire had started between her thighs, and was now rippling up inside her. Suddenly, she cried out, clinging to Llywelyn's shoulders as he too found release, and let out a cry as old as the hills themselves.

Joanna lay still as the ripples subsided. She felt totally satiated. It was as if Llywelyn had released something deep within her. Opened a dam that she had never known was shut until now. And suddenly, she was utterly, and very thoroughly, content. And not a little bit pleased, that Isabella had not soured the occasion of her bedding with her wicked lies.

They stayed only two days more at the hunting lodge. They were days full of passion and pleasure. And, best of all for Joanna, peace away from the strains of running a household and maintaining a good relationship with Llywelyn's children. Particularly Gruffydd.

It was early evening on the last day of their stay, and Llywelyn sat by the hearth, toying with Gelert's ears as the dog dozed.

'Papa has asked that I visit him at Ellesmere,' Joanna said, waving the letter the messenger had delivered that morning. 'He will be passing that way soon, apparently to hold council with some of his barons in Shropshire.'

Llywelyn frowned. Following his Uncle Daffydd's death, John had passed Ellesmere on to him as part of Joanna's dowry, and as such, Llywelyn felt John had no right to demand that his daughter meet with him there.

'What is it?' Llywelyn asked, detecting the frown on Joanna's face. 'Are you not pleased to be summoned by your father? He has a deep affection for you, that much I know.'

'It's not that,' Joanna said quietly. 'Only, I don't seem to know Papa anymore - especially since he married Isabella ...'

'I know you don't like Isabella much,' Llywelyn ventured.

'She is cruel and vicious!' Joanna said vehemently. 'And she is bent upon making trouble. Why, she told me once that Papa murdered my cousin, Arthur of

Brittany, and had his body thrown in the river Seine because of his rival claim to the throne. I know that Arthur made a great deal of trouble besieging Grandmamma at Mirabeau, and siding with the king of France, but I cannot believe that Papa would murder my cousin. It would be a sin against God!'

Llywelyn regarded Joanna for a moment. Of course, he too had heard the rumours that John had blinded and gelded the boy, and had him thrown in the river Seine. And he believed them. It was whispered that William de Braose and Faulkes de Breauté, one of John's most trusted mercenaries, had assisted him in disposing of the body afterwards.

He sighed. He knew Joanna's father well enough to know that he was ruthless when it came to getting what he wanted. That he had a legendary temper, and if Arthur had crossed him – well, he suspected that John would easily have given in to a compulsion to murder him. What better way to rid yourself of the only other rival to the throne of England? If suspected, then he would only have to swear that he had never really meant to harm the boy. That he had simply done it in a fit of temper. But that didn't mean he would be forgiven. Not just because he was the King of England.

Llywelyn shivered. Thank goodness Joanna had a more balanced temperament than her father. 'I suggest that you don't dwell on it, *cariad,*' he said at last.

'But I do,' Joanna said sadly. 'But it's more than that, Llywelyn. Isabella wrote to tell me that his sister, my cousin Eleanor, is now imprisoned in Bristol Castle – indefinitely apparently. She tells me that Papa wants to hide her from the eyes of the world. To keep her silent, so that the truth can never be told.'

'I doubt she knows any better than we, the fate of her brother,' Llywelyn said with a sigh.

'Perhaps I could intervene on her behalf?' Joanna pondered.

'I should think it's best that you stay away from the subject of Arthur and Eleanor's fate,' Llywelyn said gently. 'We need to stay on the best terms possible with your father. His losses in France have borne him down, but when he returns to English soil it's important that we continue to foster his affection and trust. Yes, you must go to Ellesmere for a few days. To meet with him, and assure him of our loyalty and your continued love. But mention nothing of the rumours that surround Arthur. His troubles with the pope weigh heavily on him too, and you must assure him that I am keeping myself informed of his progress through the offices of the Bishop of Bangor, who is praying that there might be a quick and efficient solution to the affair. Now, come,' Llywelyn said. 'We must ensure that the marriage treaty kindly made by your father is pleasurable and fruitful. After all, what could the King of England wish for more than a grandson to secure our Anglo-Welsh union?' As soon as he uttered the words he regretted them, as immediately, the image of Gruffydd's angry face swam across his vision, and he found himself wondering once more about the fate of his first-born son.

Chapter 9

Ellesmere, Shropshire, England, May 1206

Joanna surveyed Isabella across the hall. She was very beautiful, in a brittle sort of way. Like coloured glass that might shatter if you touched it. At that moment, she was flirting with several of her father's barons. In particular, William de Braose, one of the men her father kept close to his side. Repulsed, Joanna tore her eyes away from her, for she offended every moral fibre in her body. She had just been hearing the most terrible tales of her infidelity from her old nurse, Cissy, and they had sickened her. The worst was of a young man found in Isabella's bed, whom, rumour had it, her father had ordered to be choked to death in front of his young wife as punishment for her sins.

Without wanting too, Joanna remembered another unfortunate young man - a former squire of her father's who had been found leaving the Queen's bed chamber. He had been locked in her father's dungeon and brutally beaten. The image once again brought to the fore thoughts of her cousin Arthur, and she shivered. It was becoming very clear to her that she hardly knew her father at all. Had she been so naive as a girl? She had worshiped the very ground that her father had walked on. When had that changed she wondered? When had he become so cruel? When had she begun to hate him ...?

When he married Isabella of Angoulême, a small voice whispered.

Joanna jumped as a hand fell on her arm. It was Richard de Chilham, one of her many illegitimate step-brothers by the sister of the Earl of Surrey.

'Hello, Sis,' he said, pecking her on the cheek. 'How are you finding marriage to your handsome Welshman?' he asked with an infections grin, his merry blue eyes missing nothing as he surveyed his sister frankly.

Joanna felt a telltale blush spread up her neck, infusing her cheeks with a rosy glow.

'Oh, like that is it!' Richard said, making her blush even more.

'Oh, do be quiet!' Joanna hissed, making him grin even wider.

A jig started up on the floor as the musicians livened up the tempo. Immediately Isabella dragged de Broase to the centre of the hall to join in, all the while laughing up at him and fluttering her lashes.

Richard frowned. 'She'd best be careful,' he said. 'Father misses nothing where she is concerned.'

Joanna eyed Isabella in disgust. 'She can't possibly like William de Braose – why, he's so … so … old!'

'So is Father. But the difference is she is married to him, and he gets mad when she flirts like that! Anyway, I suspect she's only doing it to annoy Lady de Braose,' Richard said, indicating to where the lady sat with a frown on her face. 'Isabella and Lady Matilda hate each other. But Isabella cannot rid herself of her presence at court because Sir William is so high in Father's favour. So, Instead, she does her best to rile Matilda by flirting with Sir William in her presence!'

Joanna looked at Richard in surprise. 'What on earth can she have done to incur Isabella's wrath? It must have been bad whatever it was!'

'Rumour has it that the lady has been, in the past, um ... intimate with Father, shall we say. Well, you must admit that for a woman of her age she is still very beautiful,' he said, seeing her surprise. 'And Father does have a thing for women with hair that colour.'

'Father has a thing for women with any colour hair!' Joanna snapped, as the realisation sank in even further that the man she had adored as a child had feet of clay.

'Hey, calm down!' Richard said, alarmed at her sudden outburst.

'I'm sorry, Richard,' Joanna said contritely. 'I didn't mean to snap. It's just that I have been hearing such dreadful things about Father these days, and I don't know what to believe.'

'Rumour is still rife, then? Even in the depths of Wales? Well, I've no doubt that some of it will be about cousin Arthur!' Richard said wryly. 'Nothing can be proved though, Sis, and it would be best if you didn't bring the subject up ... Father has an uncertain temper of late.'

'Bring what up?' King John suddenly loomed up beside Joanna and looked down at his daughter affectionately before stooping to kiss her.

'Joanna was just saying that she was sorry to have missed the last Christmas court, Father,' Richard said adroitly.

'Ah. Yes, you missed a treat, Joanna. But perhaps you will make the next one,' he said, catching sight of Isabella dancing with William de Braose, and frowning. Joanna flashed her step-brother a look of thanks for his quick diversion and made a mental note to be more discreet in future.

'What of your new husband?' her father asked. 'Are you pleased with him?'

Joanna blushed. 'Yes, Papa. Very! And thank you!'

'He has the oath of the other princes of Wales, I understand. Though not Gwenwynwyn of Powys?' her father said, scrutinising her face quickly before turning back to where Isabella was still flirting and dancing with William de Braose.

'Yes. He's a masterful politician and leader, Papa. I'm sure he will persuade the prince of Powys to swear his oath soon!' Joanna enthused, but her father was no longer listening.

'De Braose has been trying my patience recently.' he muttered.

Both Joanna and Richard looked at him in surprise, for de Braose was well known as their father's favourite.

'He's fishing for an earldom,' John continued. 'I hate greed in a man, and he for one is pushing for too much. Remember that, Joanna. I will be pushed only so far!' He turned and looked at her full in the face, before striding off to recover Isabella.

Joanna looked at her step-brother, her eyes wide. 'Was that some kind of warning?' she asked, suddenly dismayed. 'Does he think that Llywelyn will try to curry favour through me?'

Richard sighed. 'Father is mistrustful of everyone. But that's the first time I've heard him speak of de Braose like that. Although, I have wondered on occasions if de Broase has some sort of hold over Father that he is beginning to resent. Why, since their return from France, Father has done nothing but shower de Braose with lordships and knight's fees, but the man is constantly at his side pushing for more. You know what Father is like. He can be generous to a fault, but once crossed he will show no mercy. Anyway, don't worry your pretty little head about it, Sis. The likelihood of your husband jeopardising his position and overstepping the mark is very remote, is it not? Now, come and have a dance with me!'

But Joanna was no longer listening. She was staring at her father's retreating back, gripped by a sudden feeling of foreboding. A terrible certainty that one day she would have to stand between her father and the man she loved. And then she would have to choose between them.

John frowned as his fingers unconsciously struck a false staccato on the table. He'd had rather too much to drink and was feeling morose. Life was not treating him fairly at the moment. His argument with the pope and the looming threat of a papal interdict over the election of Stephen Langton as Archbishop of Canterbury was not going his way, with the Bishops still divided on the issue. Then there were the continuous rumours of unsettlement amongst his French barons, many of whom, outraged by rumours of the fate of his nephew, and the means by which he had acquired Isabella of Angoulême as his bride, had defected and joined forces with his duplicitous ally, Phillip Augustus, the sly, odious little man that was the King of France. Meanwhile, in England. He fixed de Braose with his coldly analytical stare. In England there was the growing power and arrogance of men who thought they could command a king. One of which was de Braose, who'd thought to increase his status by blackmailing him over the little problem of his nephew.

He looked up to see Joanna staring at him with a puzzled look on her face. Now there was another problem. By marrying his daughter to the ambitious prince of North Wales he had given him official status: had recognised him as ruler of a lesser, but not inconsiderable, power to his own within his kingdom. In return, Llywelyn had only to secure the oaths and exert his dominance over the minor chieftains in Wales who might infringe upon his own rule. The only flaw in the plan was the equally ambitious prince of Powys, who, having steadfastly refused to bow before Llywelyn, had started to expand his power in the south by launching regular raids on his Anglo-Norman neighbours. So far Llewelyn had failed to take up arms and subdue him, choosing instead to stick to the agreement made four years previously with the church - that he would not go to war with Powys.

He frowned. He found it very unsettling that Llywelyn had chosen to keep the peace with Gwenwynwyn for so long, as he was not unaware of his son-in-law's aspirations to take Powys for himself, thus becoming the undisputed ruler of the whole of Wales. Which, of course, if they remained on good terms, would be to his advantage. But then he had not pushed the issue through his daughter, because there was always the risk that if Llywelyn were to suppress Gwenwynwyn and reign supreme, he might well become a threat to him - become yet another thorn in his side to add to his already burgeoning troubles of trying to keep his own kingdom in check. For he had seen what power could do to a man. It corrupted them and made them greedy.

Picking up his goblet he took a large draught of wine. Mayhap he was worrying unnecessarily, but he had the feeling that the next few years were going to be the toughest of his reign.

As for Isabella, she had yet to produce him a son and heir. From now on, John resolved, he would keep her on a tight rein. Get a child on her. That would be an excellent way to curb her excesses elsewhere. It would also ensure that the child was his.

Slowly he rose, and taking Isabella by the elbow, he helped her to her feet. 'It's time to retire now, my dear. We shall have some sport before bed. And then, from this day forward, you will remain in my chamber or at my side at all times.'

As they made their way down the hall the other guests rose, and Isabella was forced to acknowledge the sea of smiling faces as they made way towards the doors. Even in the midst of his own problems, it did not miss John's attention that the only one she really noticed was Matilda de Broase's. Smiling smugly alongside her husband.

Aber, North Wales, May 1206

Llywelyn dozed fitfully again. Like he had since Joanna had gone to Ellesmere. The air in his room was heavy and cloying, despite the darkness and the time of year, and he shifted restlessly and opened his eyes. She was there. *Tangwystl*. Suspended above him. Her full round breasts dangled within reach, the dark nipples inviting him to take them into his mouth, explore them with his tongue. Llywelyn moaned as he felt his loins stir. A touch, feather light, as the sheet was pushed down round his hips to reveal his manhood. He moaned again, erect and hard now as she lowered herself down on him.

He came. Suddenly. Violently. And he heard himself cry out. When he opened his eyes again she was gone, and for a moment he wondered if he had dreamed it. But then he detected her scent lingering in the air. Frightened, he stumbled out of bed and over to the coffer, where, grasping a pitcher, he splashed water onto his face with shaking hands and dried it with a piece of cloth. Still breathing heavily, he looked round the room. It couldn't be true. He *must* have dreamt it. To think otherwise was madness! People didn't make love to ghosts!

It was only then that he saw the brooch lying on the coffer, alongside the pitcher. He stared at it in disbelief. It was the pretty little enamel brooch he had given Tangwystyl when they had first met. He hadn't seen it for years. For long moments Llywelyn stared at it, then he picked it up with unsteady hands. It felt warm. As if it had recently been worn, or concealed in someone's pocket.

Dropping it, Llywelyn stumbled to the privy. Where he was violently sick.

Chapter 10

Aber, North Wales, June 1206

Joanna awoke feeling sick again. With a groan, she swung her legs over the edge of the large bed and sprinted to the privy, where she spent the next half hour vomiting what little there was in her stomach. When she reappeared in her bed chamber, white faced and faint, Rhoda clicked her tongue loudly to register her disapproval.

'Have you not told him yet, then?' she asked, her face set in a mask of annoyance.

'Oh, do stop fussing, Rhoda,' Joanna said, climbing wearily back onto the bed and closing her eyes.

'Well, you have to tell him sometime. And I think you must be at least three months gone. In all likelihood, you conceived when he took you to Trefriw. You've been apart a lot since then, what with you visiting your father and him on tour in Gwynedd.'

'I know I should tell him, Rhoda. It's just that Crysten -'

'What of Crysten?' Rhoda interrupted sharply.

'Well, I don't know what to say to Llywelyn - after all, she is expecting a child too.'

'You are Llywelyn's wife. He will put all thoughts of you and his child first,' Rhoda said soothingly. 'Anyway, everyone can see how much he adores you. Crysten is no longer a threat, Joanna - she's not even here any longer,' she said as an afterthought.

I shall hope for a boy, Rhoda. And Llywelyn shall name him -' she broke off as a huge gust of unseasonal wind blew the window shutters closed with a crash, and the room went menacingly dark.

'What was that? What on earth is happening, Rhoda?' Joanna cried, sitting up sharply and looking around the room, which seemed to be vibrating with anger.

Rhoda hurried to the window shutters and threw them open again. Immediately, the feeling of anger dissipated as sunlight once more flooded the room. Then crossing herself, she turned back to Joanna.

'You must get a priest to sprinkle holy water on the bed before you give birth,' she said. 'For there is someone out there who has ill wished you, I fear!'

Then she hurried from the room. Leaving Joanna sitting on the bed, wide eyed in horror.

Aber, North Wales, November 1206

Llywelyn paused to watch Joanna organise the stowing of the newly carved cradle in the corner of the room. It was made of oak brought in from the forests of England at Joanna's command, and on each side there were three heart cut-outs of her own design. He smiled fondly as she rubbed her stomach where the child kicked restlessly in the womb.

After supper of late he had taken to joining her in her chambers where he would lie alongside her on the bed with his hand resting on the growing swell of her pregnancy, marvelling at the movements within. He would spend hours just holding her, feeling the baby move, and whispering endearments to her. On many occasions, he'd had to suppress the urge to make love to her, for the church prohibited lovemaking during a woman's courses, or if she was pregnant.

Joanna, well aware of his frustration, and anxious to prevent another incident such as the one involving Crysten, had invented new ways to keep him by her side. Subsequently, Llywelyn would often find himself leaving the chamber in the morning blurry eyed and tired from lack of sleep, whilst Joanna threw herself back down on the bed and ate plates of the sweetmeats she had developed a taste for during pregnancy.

Satisfied that the cradle was exactly how it should be, Joanna crossed to a coffer and started to arrange lovingly embroidered sheets and swaddling clothes neatly in its depths. Then she sent Rhoda to summon the chaplain to bless the bed and cradle with holy water.

Llywelyn watched her uneasily. He had never told Joanna about his dream – that was how he liked to think of it now - a dream. For to think of it as anything else was absurd. However, he sensed that Joanna knew something was wrong. That she, too, felt the tension that hung over them all; had the feeling that something or someone lingered there as a ghostly reminder of the past.

He shook himself. He was just being fanciful. Since that night in May, Tangwystl had not shown herself again. Or at least, he corrected, he had not dreamed of her again. He felt the small hairs prickle on the back of his neck as he remembered their ghostly lovemaking and, without wanting it to, his mind returned to her brooch, hidden out of sight in the depth of a draw somewhere. And not for the first time, he wondered if he should throw it away.

Aber, North Wales, December 1206

Llywelyn leapt to his feet as another rending scream accompanied by a series of muffled sobs echoed down from the tower where Joanna had been in labour for twelve long hours. Gwenllian crept forward and took his hand, her large, expressive eyes red from crying. Llywelyn had tried to send her away, but she had simply crept back to keep vigil with him until Joanna's ordeal was over. Gruffydd was nowhere to be seen, and even the servants had deserted the hall, remembering all too clearly that Llywelyn's first love, Tangwystl, had died in childbirth.

Outside, the snow-tipped caps of the *Eryri* Mountains rose majestically in the distance, and the winter sun bounced off the icicles clinging to the eaves of the scattered outbuildings in the bailey. But Llywelyn noticed nothing beyond his wife's pain, against which, he was helpless.

Joanna's head fell back once again onto the pillow. The sheets were soaking wet with her sweat, and the agonising labour pains were becoming more and more frequent, travelling between her back and her lower belly in waves that made her feel sick. Yet nothing was happening. She had still to expel the babe from her womb. The midwife muttered something to Rhoda, who mopped Joanna's brow with a cloth soaked in vinegar. Joanna's hair was loose so as not to bind the baby to the womb, and it spread across the pillows in wet tendrils. But still the baby did not come. The midwife exchanged frightened glances with Rhoda. Joanna could not last for much longer. And she, for one, didn't want the job of telling Llywelyn that his wife was dead.

Bronwyn entered the hall, hoping that she might persuade Gwenllian to come with her to her chamber, for it was not healthy for the child to listen to Joanna's screams. She shivered, she had never had children herself. She had never wanted them. In fact, she had never even been married. The day that her father had announced that he had arranged for her to marry the lecherous, red-faced innkeeper to whom he owed a large drinking debt, she had promptly put poison in her newly betrothed's food, fled to the farthest corner of the land, changed her name, and laid low. It was by chance that she met the Lady Tangwystl, who had soon learnt of her love of herbs and poultices, and, within days, she was installed with her new mistress at Degannwy, where she had contrived to stay out of Llywelyn's sight whenever he had visited.

As she crossed the hall, Llywelyn looked up. His eyes were red-rimmed and puffy, and he was unshaven and unkempt. The look of undisguised despair he turned on her as she crossed the room might have touched a chord in her heart … if she'd had one. Gwenllian was asleep, curled up on the bench alongside him, but before she could reach out and shake her awake, Llywelyn grabbed her arm in a vice-like grip. Startled, Bronwyn tried to pull it away, but Llywelyn held her fast.

'My lord,' she said, suddenly frightened, 'you're hurting me!'

'You have powers. Knowledge. I have heard it said! You can help her, Bronwyn ...' Llywelyn's voice was full of pain. 'Please, help her -' his voice cracked, and his hand fell away when he saw the look of contempt on her face.

'Why, my lord? You have never once welcomed me in your home ... in fact you merely tolerate my presence here and at the children's side. Can it be that you fear me?'

'Please -' Llywelyn whispered.

Bronwyn stared at him with interest. It had not occurred to her until now that it might be advantageous to her if she helped Llywelyn. Indeed, he might think long and hard if ever he decided to dismiss her in the future. Besides, the child that Joanna fought so hard for posed no threat. It would do no harm if it were to be born. For Bronwyn already knew it was a girl.

'There is someone who can help,' she said grudgingly, ignoring the anger that was pressing down on her. 'I will get my cloak.'

Inside the old log hut, the room was bare except for a stool and a battered old table. A fire burned in the hearth and with careful movements, Mab stooped and threw a handful of herbs into the flames. Immediately, smoke, acrid and thick, filled the room before disappearing through the badly repaired thatch, leaving long fingers of flame in which to see.

Mab looked hard. Searching for the Llywelyn's little princess in the flames. The child she carried was not the one that Tangwystl feared: the one that would displace her son in the succession and cause dissention and upheaval in the house of Llywelyn ap Iorworth. This child was a girl. A girl with eyes as black as sin, and a heart to match. For she had inherited the Satan streak. And the Satan streak was the curse of the Angevin's.

As she watched, the little princess writhed and screamed on the bed, twisting and turning as once more the labour pains gripped her from within like a vice and sapped her strength. But still, girl or no girl, if *Tangwystl* had her way the little princess would be dead soon.

Making a decision, Mab stood and reached for her rough spun cloak and bundles of herbs. Then leaving the hut, she made her way fast towards Prince Llywelyn's palace, knowing that she would meet the woman Bronwyn on route.

Joanna dreamed that she was being lifted from the bed and carried to the birthing stool. Bony hands supported her from behind, cupping the swell of her stomach. Images flashed: an old crone, tiny as a bird, shooing people out of the room; the midwife, disgruntled as she was sent on her way. The dream shifted slightly. She thought she heard Bronwyn's voice calling to her, encouraging her, bringing her back. The hands did their work. She could feel their power flowing into her womb, settling the baby. A strange smell, rich and pungent, floated around her. In the distance, she could see the sun, and she dreamed of the meadows of her childhood in France: her as a child, skipping through the green grass and red poppies. Careless ...

Then her way was barred by a woman standing in front of her. A beautiful woman, with long red brown hair, and eyes the colour of honeyed mead. The woman was angry. Darkness swirled all around her. Joanna was puzzled, but she smiled at her and skipped on the way she had been going. The woman called her back, but Joanna ignored her. She was heading for the sun. The light. Not the darkness.

'Goodbye!' she called. 'Goodbye!' She could hear the tinkle of her own laughter on the wind.

Yes, she was definitely heading for the light ...

Llywelyn stood and looked down at the child. His firstborn with Joanna, daughter of the King of England. He felt a moment of disappointment, followed by a rush of relief.

The child was a girl and not the boy that Tangwystyl feared. The one which would have replaced Gruffydd in the succession.

The knowledge came as a shock to Llywelyn. He should have known. How could he have been so stupid – even as he stood with the child in his arms he could feel Tangwystyl swirling around him, could feel the tentacles of her power reaching out. But she was placated for now: he could feel her fading away. Leaving only a trace of her previous anger hovering in the air.

Turning, he looked down at his young wife lying white and exhausted against the sheets, her dark hair spread around her in disarray. He knew now how close she had come to sharing Tangwystl's fate: to die in childbirth, her child with her, and suddenly he was full of anger.

'No, Tangwystl!' he whispered. 'No! Joanna was born to birth a son. A leader of princes. A proud and courageous protector of the realm. You shall not take her from me! My son will be born!'

Then, picking up his daughter, he pushed aside his fears for the future. 'She shall be called Glwadys,' he said, holding her to the light ...

Later that night, he took Tangwystl's brooch from the draw in which it was hidden, and he rode to the pool at the foot of the *Rhaeadr Fawr,* the water fall where the *Afon Goch* plunged over a sill of rock, into the foothills below. For a moment, he held it in his palm. He could feel it vibrating in anger, and, repulsed, he threw it as far as he could into its crystal depths.

He hoped he would never see it again ...

Chapter 11

Aber, North Wales, November 1207

Joanna was in her bower resting. News had come that morning of her new stepbrother, Prince Henry, born to Isabella in October. He was a healthy, happy boy it was reported. And her father was besotted with him. She glanced over at Gwladys, who was with her nurse, and laying her hand on her the soft swell of her belly where less than a year after Gwladys's birth, a new life lay, she suddenly had a yearning to have a boy herself, for she knew that it would please her father greatly if she did. She looked up as Llywelyn entered the room, and threw his wet cloak onto a clothes pole by the hearth and, without wanting it to, her hand travelled back to the pile of letters which still lay on the bed.

Along with the news of Henry, Richard had written to tell her of the sudden and meteoric fall of William de Braose from her father's grace, around which much speculation was being spun. She didn't know why, but she was beginning to become deeply troubled by the whole affair.

'My step-brother Richard thinks that Sir William had some sort of hold over Father, and that he may have been blackmailing him,' she ventured after a while, handing the letter over to him. 'Something to do with Father's involvement in the murder of my cousin Arthur, which he is using against him.'

Frowning, Llywelyn scanned the parchment. 'We don't know that Arthur was murdered, Joanna,' he said finally, though she could see that privately he thought it likely, and by her father's own hand.

'I know. But it says there that some fishermen dragged a body out of the river during the period that Father was at Rouen. They were pretty certain it was Arthur's. Father had previously had Arthur moved from his captivity in Falaise, to Rouen. It all fits you see,' Joanna said sadly.

'And if de Braose *were* blackmailing your father ...?'

'Well, I wouldn't like to think of the consequences,' Joanna whispered, remembering Isabella's viscous nature and her hate for the Lady Matilda, William's wife.

Later that afternoon, Joanna rode to Mab's hut. Bronwyn watched her go concealed within the great stone gates of the *llys*. The old woman would tell her what she was reasonably sure of herself - that Joanna was, like before, expecting another girl and not the boy she yearned for.

'You have no reason to fear,' she whispered, as behind her the shadows stirred restlessly. 'Gruffydd is safe for now. Your little prince is safe ...'

Chapter 12

Aber, North Wales, March 1208

Llywelyn waited for Gwyn to settle himself. 'Well?' he asked.

'The interdict is now official,' Gwyn said, handing him a pile of papers. 'John still won't accept Steven Langton as Archbishop of Canterbury, even though the monks themselves elected him, and Langton himself fears to set foot in England since his banishment. And now many other bishops are fleeing to join him in his exile.'

Llewelyn frowned. It was the worst news, for an interdict would bring hardship to the land, with no church services or burials permitted.

'And de Braose? ' he asked, glancing at Joanna who was sitting staring out of the window, her hand resting on the large swell of her belly whilst eating sweetmeats from a platter alongside her.

'The king has demanded the repayment of the five thousand marks loaned to him by the Crown to purchase the Irish honour of Limerick,' Gwyn said. 'But de Braose seems unable, or unwilling, to pay, and John is fast losing patience. He was also ordered to surrender the castles of Radnor, Hay, and Brecknock, which I am told he did with bad grace. As a last resort, his friends and family have prevailed upon the king to grant leniency, and give him more time to settle his debts. It's reported that John has agreed to a meeting at Hereford castle in April,' he added. 'Though I doubt he will change his mind.'

'Mmm,' Llewelyn mused. 'Do you think it's really the disappearance of Arthur that's behind de Braose's fall? Joanna,' he said, glancing in her direction, 'believes it is.'

Gwyn shrugged. 'It's no secret that de Braose was with John in Rouen when Arthur disappeared. And it's now widely believed that he has been using his knowledge about whatever happened to the boy to extort favours from John. The lordships of Gwent, the honour of Limerick, and others. Even an earldom, it's said. John won't stand for it; won't be blackmailed any longer, and he is now set upon bringing William down as an example to others. He has even turned on his son Giles, who was recently elected Bishop of Hereford, declaring it false.' Gwyn paused as Llewelyn's brother, Adda, joined them.

'Had it occurred to you, brother, that now, with the family having fled, and the king putting all his resources and energies into pursuing de Braose himself, his lordships along the Marches are vulnerable?' he asked, accepting the goblet of wine offered to him. 'Which, of course, means that Gwenwynwyn will almost certainly seize the opportunity to move in and take what he can from under the king's nose ... with the satisfaction of knowing that you are restrained from doing the same by your allegiance to John, and the fact that you are his son-in-law.'

Llywelyn snorted. 'Those are the very reasons that Gwenwynwyn will refrain,' he said shortly. 'He will expect me to make a move to protect my father-in-law's interests in his absence, which would mean war between us - something which we have avoided for years now.'

'No!' Gwyn interrupted, suddenly animated. 'No! Adda is right - Gwenwynwyn is greedy! He will not be able to resist! And whilst he is preoccupied with the acquisition of the de Braose lordships, that would leave Powys unprotected and ripe for the picking. None would blame you if you moved to secure Powys. Not whilst its lord is busy attacking lands recently reclaimed by the Crown in very public circumstances. You would be seen to be doing it as a favour to the king, whilst, in reality, you would be quietly and unobtrusively expanding your own kingdom!'

Llewelyn's eyes narrowed. 'John has a legendary temper. He would be furious,' he said, throwing a quick glance at Joanna, who was now absently stroking Gelert. 'But I'll not deny that recently Gwenwynwyn has grown bolder - harassing Marcher lords, and increasing his raids on my lands. Nor will I deny that I have considered taking up arms against him once more. However, out of respect for Joanna, and not wanting to pose a threat to her father, I have resisted. But now -' he paused, his eyes burning bright with sudden excitement, '- but now, if what you say is true, and Gwenwynwyn dares to attack the de Braose lordships right under John's nose, then he will be forced to retaliate. I'm sure of it! Now *that* would be the time to move into Powys - whilst the king is so busy defending himself against Gwenwynwyn and pursuing de Braose, that he is blind to my movements. The beauty of it is, I just have to be patient and wait!'

Chapter 13

Aber, North Wales, April 1208

Elen was born quietly and unobtrusively one balmy evening, just as the spring flowers began to carpet the footholds of the *Eryri* mountains and the snows began to melt, first to trickle, and then to flow down with the rivers from their peaks. Joanna gazed down at the little scrap who, if Mab was to be believed, was destined to have a glorious life marked by several marriages, two of which would be to earls, and one to a man who would try to break her.

She sighed as she handed the baby over to her to her new wet nurse. Mab had assured her that one day she would have the boy she desired. The one destined to rule Gwynedd in Llywelyn's wake. But, she had warned, it would not be before she birthed another girl as it was decreed. More than that she would not say, for Bronwyn stood glowering in the corner. Bronwyn, who Joanna did not understand, and could not control, because she did not know of the power that the woman had unleashed by making one fatal promise to a long dead woman.

A few weeks later, in the pool at the foot of the *Rhaeadr Fawr*, the little brooch, disturbed by the water flooding down from the mountains and several weeks of torrential rain, rose out of the deep and spiralled down with the great tide of water that had swelled the river, until it came to rest in a little pool by a rocky outcrop close to the *llys*, where it settled in the shingle to wait.

Aber, North Wales, June 1208

The lack of news had been the worst part of waiting. But when it finally came, filtered through from Madoc, it came as no surprise to Llywelyn to read that de Braose's audience with the king at Hereford in April had been a sham. William, hoping for a private interview, had in fact walked into a trap, and found to his horror that the king was not alone. Flanking him was his half-brother, William Longespée, the Earl of Salisbury, and William Marshall, the Earl of Pembroke. Alongside them, stood several other men William recognised from the close-knit entourage John gathered around him in times of trouble. Thus, he was prevented from speaking freely in the king's presence.

And if William had still harboured any hope of a reprieve, or of a thawing of John's ice-cold displeasure after the initial shock of his reception had worn off, then it was dashed immediately. For instead of showing any leniency to his former friend and ally, John had once again demanded the repayment of the five thousand marks owed for the honour of Limerick, along with another thousand incurred in pursuit of the debt. De Braose, wisely realising that any accusation in public pertaining to Arthur's disappearance would be tantamount to signing his own death warrant, had stammered out various promises and excuses, before finally capitulating under the king's accusing gaze and departing his presence a dishonoured and broken man.

Llywelyn frowned, and throwing down several pages that followed containing warnings on the matter concerning his own dealings with his father by marriage, he leafed through the rest until he came to the bit that both puzzled and excited him the most. It was simply headed with the words: *'Maude de Braose, June 1208,'* and it had been hastily scrawled - as if the letter had been torn open and a postscript penned at the last minute. Beneath the heading, Madoc had written:

Pray take heed, Llywelyn, the king's messenger called here today on his way back to England with news. John, angry at de Braoses continuous refusal to pay his debt, threw all caution to the wind, and last week he sent Faulkes de Bréauté and Peter de Athie to Bramber where the de Braoses are in residence, to discuss terms and secure some form of surety for repayment. However, the confrontation was a disaster. Maude de Braose, faced with the demand that she give up her eldest son and two of her grandchildren as hostages, has publically accused John of murder ...

Putting the letter down again, Llywelyn shivered. His father-in-law, well known for his cunning and devious mind, had played a clever trick when he had chosen to have witnesses present during William's humiliation at Hereford. But although the gamble had paid off, and he had successfully curbed the ambitious baron's tongue, he had been prevented from removing the man completely from his court or arranging for him a convenient end, knowing that if he did so the finger of suspicion would once more have been pointed at him.

But none of that mattered now, for even John could not have orchestrated the outcome that luck had dictated. For in the end it had been Maude's unbridled tongue that had finally sealed de Braose's fate. Once and for all ...

It was not long after Maude's outburst that de Braose and his sons made a desperate bid to try to regain possession of the castles they had surrendered to the king. Failing in the attempt, they had sacked and burned the nearby market town of Leominster to the ground, before fleeing England with Maude to take refuge in Ireland with their daughter Margaret, and their son-in-law, the Earl of Meath. Leaving, as Llywelyn had gambled, their lordships in Wales vulnerable and unprotected in their wake.

Chapter 14

Royal Court, Hereford, England, September 29th, 1208

'I hereby announce that on this date, 29th September, 1208, William de Braose - formally Sir William, Lord of Bramber, Gower, Abergavveny, Brecknock and Skenfrith - is declared traitor to the Crown. Furthermore, I declare that King John of England releases all his vassals from their allegiance to their lord ...'

The announcement went on interminably, outlining all of de Braose's crimes against the king. And although implicit, the message was clear: should anyone attempt to extort favour, blackmail John or threaten him in any way in the future, then they, too, could expect the same treatment.

Pausing in its deliverance, William Marshall took a deep breath before adding, 'the king also forbids any incursion in or around lands forfeited by de Braose, and from now on declared property of the royal demesne ...'

Stepping down from the dais, Marshall surveyed the sea of faces before him, many of them wealthy barons and one-time supporters of the king. Their expressions portrayed a variety of emotions - ranging from neutral to ill-concealed anger - that one of their own could be treated in such an appalling manner. Although not much liked, William de Braose's downfall had become the focus of attention for those concerned with the escalation of autonomy and power that John was hiding behind, in order that he could deflect attention away from his abuse of authority as king.

Many of the men in this room, Marshall thought uncomfortably as they parted to let him through, had willingly risked their lives in John's service. But judging by the wave of dissent rippling round the hall, that was a thing of the past.

Stepping out into the bailey Marshall paused to reflect on the future. Then, thrusting the roll of vellum he was still holding into the arms of a surprised guard, he pulled his shoulders back. As in the past, his loyalty was with the king ...

But, a small voice whispered, you did not turn the de Braoses away when they sought harbour with you recently ...

William scowled. John had not said as much, but he had taken note of this small deviation in loyalty when, unannounced, the de Braoses had fallen on his mercy on their flight through Ireland. And he would no doubt find ways to humiliate and subjugate him further in front of the court. Reading the proclamation against de Braose in front of his friends and compatriots was simply the first of many. With a last glance behind him, William Marshall kicked a small dog foolish enough to stray across his path and, signalling to a groom, he summoned his horse and rode away. Hoping to find solace in a tavern in the arms of a wench.

Aber, North Wales, October 1208

Llywelyn stood by the window, oblivious for once to sight of his beloved Gwynedd with the snow topped mountains rising majestically in the distance, as he reflected on recent events in England. It was almost three weeks since John's proclamation, and the reports of de Braose's exile had filtered through. The last he'd heard was that Giles de Braose had fled to France to join the other bishops taking refuge there. Then in the absence of any further news, his line of communication had fallen silent, leaving him pacing the length and breadth of his chamber in an effort to contain his anxiety in front of others.

But today his patience had paid off, and, at last, he had received the intelligence that he had hoped for. Amidst all the chaos in England, Gwenwynwyn, ignoring John's warning, was marching upon de Braose's lands. And he was attacking Norman manors and seizing livestock along the way.

Chapter 15

Aber, North Wales, November 1208

'The prince of Powys has been arrested and is being held at Shrewsbury Castle!'

What was left of the small party, gathered the day before to hear minor disagreements and matters of concern in the small township, parted in the hall to make way for a tall, dishevelled man who was pushing his way towards the dais.

Trying not to look too excited, Llywelyn rose from the table where he was, at that very moment, in conference with Gwyn on the matter of Gwenwynwyn's latest raids. Summoning his squire over with a jug of mead, he poured it into a goblet himself, before thrusting it into the hands of the exhausted man now standing before him.

'The prince of Powys is under royal arrest!' the man repeated, taking a swallow of the mead before launching into the full story.

John, it seemed, had responded with more force than Gwenwynwyn had expected to his unlawful incursion onto de Braose lands. Outmanoeuvred and outnumbered, the prince had finally capitulated before the might of the king's army, and been forced to agree to a meeting to discuss terms on the 29th October at Shrewsbury Castle. The man broke off, coughing. Then unable to continue, he thrust an oil skin into Llywelyn's hands containing several hastily scribed letters collaborating his story.

Waving the man away, Llywelyn broke the seal on the first letter with shaking fingers. Of course, the meeting had been yet another of John's cleverly orchestrated traps, and the moment Gwenwynwyn had set foot in Shrewsbury Castle John had placed him under royal arrest, thus denying him the opportunity of claiming any of his prizes or seeking terms upon which they might conclude a peace treaty.

It was no more or less than Llywelyn expected of his father-in-law, whose cunning and duplicity knew no bounds. John, Llywelyn was sure, had never had any intention of conducting peace negotiations with

Gwynwynwyn. No more than he would have bowed down to de Braose before him and offered terms. Llywelyn pushed this uncomfortable thought aside. More importantly for him, with its lord out of the way, Powys was left unprotected. And as he'd hoped, it was John who was providing the opportunity for attack. Sitting down Llywelyn picked up his quill, and began summoning his *teulu* - he meant to have Powys for himself.

Never mind, his conscience whispered, that you are taking it behind your father-in-law's back ...

Never mind that your wife, John's daughter, would be furious ...

Never mind that you might be drawn into one of John's devious traps ...

Behind him, in the shadows, something stirred, and a ripple of anger emanated around the room, causing Llywelyn to pause.

Take care of our son, Llywelyn. Remember your promise, and take care ...

Aber, North Wales, November 1208

Joanna turned to face Llywelyn, her hands clenched tightly at her side. The only sign of her fury at the events that had fast overtaken her world in the past few months. Events that had tested her loyalty to the limit, for she was torn between the two men that she loved the most in the world. Llywelyn. And her father, the King of England.

'You really don't know what you have done, do you?' she hissed. 'Papa is furious. Why, I had a letter from Isabella this very morning, demanding an explanation! Don't you understand how embarrassing it is to have a letter from that hussy, questioning my loyalty to my own father? And your loyalty *too* ...' she added in a whisper, her voice on the verge of breaking as she touched on the real reason for her distress.

She sniffed and rubbed a hand over her face in despair. This was not the first confrontation that she had had with Llywelyn over his sudden invasion of southern Powys. And, she reasoned, it would not be the last. Particularly as he was now preparing to cross into Ceredigion where Maelgwn ap Rhys, Gwenwynwyn's closest ally, had burned the castles of Ystrad Meurig, Dineirth and Aberystwyth in Upper Powys, to prevent them falling into his hands.

Llywelyn sighed, then laying his hands on her shoulders he shook her gently. 'Please, Joanna. Don't make the short time we have together more painful. You must understand that, with Gwenwynwyn under royal arrest in Shrewsbury, Powys was there for the taking. It was an opportunity that I could not miss. You know what I want for Wales? For us? I want to hold both Gwynedd and Powys. To forge them together as one principality. Under one banner - for our future! Can you really expect me to turn my back on such an opportunity, even for you?' he finished, wiping away a tear that had escaped and was now trickling down Joanna's face.

Joanna frowned unhappily. 'My father will never forgive you,' she said with more sadness than anger now, and pulling away she went and stood by the window, watching as Gruffydd streaked across the bailey with his sister in hot pursuit of a gaggle of angry geese. Then turning back, she gave a wan smile. 'There is always a price to pay where my father is concerned, Llywelyn. You of all people should know that by now.'

When Llywelyn gave no answer Joanna made to leave, pausing only to rest her hand over the soft swell of her belly where once again the beginnings of a new child lay. Another girl, Mab had said. One who, like Elen, could never do what a boy - a legitimate son with the King of England's blood in his veins - could do. And that was unite her husband and her father. And with that knowledge lying heavily in her breast, she scooped up her skirts and left the room without another word. Knowing in her heart of hearts that this was only the beginning of the breakup of relations between the two men she loved most. And that one day soon, she, Joanna, princess of Snowdon and daughter to the King of England, would have her own battle to face.

Chapter 16

Woodstock, England, October 1209

Joanna ruffled the fair tousled head of Henry, Isabella's son. The eldest now of her two half-siblings from the union between her father and the woman whom she considered the biggest jezebel in England. Henry was at the moment contemplating his baby brother Richard, as he lay in Isabella's arms, looking alarmed that such a small thing could eclipse his own importance in her eyes, even for a moment. At last, thoroughly disgruntled, he reached up a small fist, and pushing Joanna's hand impatiently away, he toddled over and proffered his most treasured of possessions, a soggy rag comforter to the baby, in the hope of attracting his mother's attention. When this did not happen, he promptly threw himself in the rushes and elicited a wail of such rage that his nurse, Ellen, hastened to remove his small, angry person from the room, scolding his conduct as she went.

Sighing, Isabella handed Richard over to his wet-nurse, who settled herself down to feed him some distance away so as to give the girls some privacy to talk. 'Are you not disappointed that so far you have given Llywelyn only girls, and not the son that he must so desire?' she purred suddenly, glancing after Henry pointedly, and then looking to where Gwladys and Elen played happily with a wooden doll in the corner, whilst their nurse looked on with Joanna's youngest, Marared, in her arms.

Joanna suppressed her anger at such an impertinent question. Marared, named after Llywelyn's mother, had arrived unobtrusively in the world two months' past. And being the quiet little girl Mab had already predicted, she'd hoped without notice. 'No, Isabella, I am not,' she said, standing abruptly and crossing to the window, where she could see Gruffydd indulging in some play fighting with Llywelyn's squire, their wooden swords clashing loudly and echoing round the bailey along with their shouts.

'But you know that must be what Llywelyn wants?' Isabella asked, raising one finely arched eyebrow, her hysop blue eyes glittering with malice. 'Llywelyn would not want a bastard Welsh boy to succeed him. Not now that his kingdom is, shall we say, secure under an Angevin overlord and protector like your father. No, my dear,' she said sweetly. 'You must produce an heir worthy of the title of prince of Wales. A legitimate son with Angevin blood flowing through his veins, and not the blood of a Welsh concubine,' she added spitefully. 'I know it's what your father wants. A grandson of Angevin blood to unite and bind the two lands together for the future.'

For a moment, Joanna was speechless. Then, turning, she faced Isabella squarely, determined not to succumb to the girl's spitefulness. 'It is a custom in Wales,' she said carefully, 'that any son, even an illegitimate one, can inherit the succession. The Welsh do not have the custom of primogeniture and, no matter what Father thinks, all Llywelyn's sons will share equally in his estates. Illegitimate or not.'

Even 'Tegwared?' Isabella asked sweetly, surprising Joanna by referring to Crysten's boy, knowledge of whom she was not even aware Isabella had.

With that she rose, and turning on her heel she headed towards the door, only pausing to give Joanna one last look. 'Llewelyn has got away lightly this time,' she said, referring suddenly to the reason that Joanna and Llewelyn were summoned to England. 'Llewelyn only has to renew his homage, and he will be forgiven for his impertinence in seizing Powys whilst your father was engaged in his war with Gwynwynwyn. In fact, I confess I am surprised that John's anger did not stretch further than it did - it is as well that Llewelyn had no designs on the de Braose lands himself. Pray that he keeps his oath this time Joanna, and that he does overstep his mark and ever seek to venture into England. Oh, and give him a legitimate son. 'Tis safer that way!'

With that, Isabella clicked her fingers at her lady in waiting and exited through the door in a flurry of skirts, leaving Joanna staring angrily after her.

Separated from the hunting party, Llywelyn pulled his horse up under a large oak tree and looked back at the imposing sprawl of Woodstock Palace. The place to which, nearly a year after the chaos in

England, and his invasion of Powys, he had suddenly been summoned to attend to renew his oath of fealty to his father-in-law, in order that he might be might remain safe in his conquests.

He scowled. Over the course of the last year he had managed to convince himself that the reason John had not punished him for his unauthorised incursion into Powys was not because he believed the reason he'd put forward - that Maelgwn and his brother Rhys Gryg would have done so themselves if he had not - but rather, that it was a sign that John was thawing towards his claims to the overlordship of Wales and had allowed him his prize, if not for his sake, then for his daughter's. Why John had ignored his other aggressive act - the seizure of Maelgwn's lands in Ceredigion - still remained a mystery to him, though, for despite the fact that he had handed the majority of it over to Maelgwn's nephews and kept only the Penweddig for himself, he'd still expanded his principalities without the John's permission. A fact that John would not have overlooked without a reason.

Llywelyn sighed, thinking of the months spent in an agony of uncertainty in the aftermath of his conquests until John had finally invited him later that year to join him in his campaign against the King of Scots, who was once again unwisely pressing his claims for Northumberland on him. At the time he'd thought that John had invited him to show that he forgiven him for his slight deviation in trust. But now he was he was beginning to realise that it had been done to show him that autonomy, even that of a son by marriage, was no defence against the King of England's wrath. In short, John had only invited him along to show him what would happen if there was a repeat of his rebellious activities and the might of his huge army was ever turned on him.

And today was John's *fait accompli;* for by demanding that he publicly renew his homage to him as the King of England, he was once again forcing him to abandon his dreams of independence and to accept him as his liege lord before the lesser princes of Wales, who would then only be obliged to pay fealty to him. Then, and only then, would Powys and the Penweddig truly be his.

He turned as Madoc rode up alongside him. 'You're thinking that because John asked you to join the campaign to Scotland last year, that he had forgiven you?' Madoc said mildly.

'Yes,' Llywelyn said shortly. 'But I was mistaken. I was under the illusion that John had at last seen me as his equal. That my acquisition of Powys, and the birth of legitimate grandchildren by his daughter, would put me on an even footing with him. But instead he insults me by bringing me here today to bestow upon me patrimony in my own land, rather than recognising me as its ruler. Other than marriage to his daughter, I'm no better off than Gwenwynwyn was as prince of Powys, or William as the King of Scots. We are none of us rid of John! By renewing my homage to him this afternoon, I am once more his puppet!'

'Well, at least, unlike Gwenwynwyn, you're still free,' Madoc remarked mildly, watching a hawk hovering above the hunting party who were now in hailing distance, prompting him to press his warning on Llywelyn.

Llywelyn opened his mouth to speak, but then closed again it as Madoc ignored him and carried on regardless. 'Gwenwynwyn has forfeited, not only his freedom, lands and patrimony, but he has had to hand over twenty hostages to John - most of them family. And although Maelgwn was not arrested, he too has been ordered to hand over several of his sons as a mark of John's displeasure. Just be careful, Llywelyn. Be grateful that you still have your son. That John has not taken him as hostage yet. Gruffydd is not Joanna's flesh and blood, and therefore he counts for naught in John's eyes. And don't forget that Joanna need not have care that her father might require the boy as a hostage in the future for your obedience, either. She is as much a pawn in her father's game as you are now. And if she gives birth to a son one day, then Gruffydd is even more at risk. Think long and hard on that before you act in haste again, cousin. Think long and hard!'

And with that Madoc turned his horse and rode away, leaving Llywelyn staring after him speechless.

Later that afternoon, as Llewelyn knelt before John in the great hall at Woodstock to renew his homage, he recalled Madoc's words and, glancing briefly to where Gruffydd stood along with his sister Gwen, he met the boy's eyes: *Tangwystl's eyes*. Feeling suddenly uneasy, Llywelyn turned back to John, who was now regarding him with a great deal of speculation, and he was only too aware that his father-in-law, the King of England, knew what he must be thinking; knew of the conflict that raged inside him every time he looked at his son, who was to John nothing but a living breathing bargaining tool – a symbol of the power he could wield if he chose to do so. It was then that Llywelyn truly knew that he hated John, and that had his sword been in his hand, the King of England would no longer be standing so smugly before him.

Chapter 17

Aber, North Wales, July 1210

William de Braose stood before Llywelyn, gazing down tiredly at the rushes strewn on the floor at his feet. Despite himself, Llywelyn was shocked to see the changes wrought in the over-bearing man who had once regarded himself as one of the greatest barons in England, and trusted friend to the king. Cowed now by the weight of the crisis that had befallen him, deep lines were engraved upon his face. A face once expectant with greed. And what was left of his coarse red hair was protruding in tufts around a balding pate giving him the air of a hunted boar. Pushing Gelert away, Llywelyn stood and signalled for all but Gwyn and Adda to leave him, then pouring the man a draught of wine he handed it to de Braose personally, knowing that although he could not find it in his heart to feel sorry for de Braose, neither could he turn him away. For now it was no longer just a matter of personal dislike. It was a matter of politics, and it needed to be faced. Even if that meant sheltering the man in defiance of his father-in-law's expedition to Ireland in pursuit of Maude and the rest of the family, who had, William informed him, almost certainly fled to Scotland by now.

'What is it that you think I can do?' Llywelyn asked de Braose. 'I'm not in John's favour at the moment. And even if I were, I should think twice about stirring a nest of hornets - John has laid waste to Ireland I hear, and I should not like the same to happen to Wales.'

'But it will happen to Wales,' de Braose said sharply. 'You surely did not think that your accompanying John on his expedition to deal with the Scots King, or your homage at Woodstock, was in anyway a truce, did you? John was merely biding his time and keeping you at his side where he could keep an eye on you. He's not forgotten that you invaded Powys behind his back, and although he keeps in mind that you are married to his daughter, it in no way precludes you from being on his list of men who have slighted him in the past and who must be dealt with in the future. Your time is near, Llywelyn. John has you in his sights - he has already confiscated Ellesmere as a mark of his displeasure, has he not?'

Llywelyn's face suffused a deep red at the mention of Ellesmere, for its confiscation had caused a great deal of argument between him and Joanna, who'd brought it to him as part of her marriage portion following death of his uncle Dafydd in exile there. Seeing this, Gwyn stepped forward hastily.

'As Prince Llywelyn has already said,' he said, 'I am not sure what it is that you think we can do. John is still in pursuit of your wife, and he will not take kindly to us harbouring you here in Wales! Furthermore -'

'No. No, de Braose is right!' Llywelyn said, recovering himself enough to interrupt Gwyn. 'John, despite outward appearances and false overtures of friendship, *is* displeased with me. And as a mark of his displeasure he confiscated Ellesmere. *But* he ceded me Powys and Ceredigion, and I perhaps have no wish to jeopardise that!'

'For pity's sake, please don't under estimate John, my lord!' De Braose said with feeling. 'He might have ceded Powys to you for now, but what if he releases Gwenwynwyn, lets him free to fight you for it? Think, my lord. If John does release him, it sets the Welsh princes against each other. Against you, even! Better to pre-empt him and side with the likes of Maelgwn and Rhys Gryg now - they have axes to grind - better to have them directed at John than at you if Gwenwynwyn is released and challenges your suzerainty.'

'I don't like to admit it, but I think de Braose may be right,' It was Adda's turn to speak. 'John is unstable and unreliable in his loyalties at the best of times ... if he does release Gwenwynwyn and turns against you, you should be ready. There are others who would join you, too. It is common knowledge that many English barons are alarmed at John's abuse of power; the treatment of their wives and daughters and ...' He trailed off, as if reluctant to mention Arthur's disappearance in front of a man who might well have been complicit in it.

But if William noticed then he made no sign, merely turning back to Llywelyn and picking up the theme enthusiastically. 'There's also my kin - de Clare, Lacy,

Mortimer and Derby. They are all outraged at John's cavalier treatment of, not just my wife and family, but also his abuse of power and his disrespect of the church. They would all heed the call if you were to lead a rebellion against John. And with him still in Ireland, now is the time to do it. Think, Llywelyn! With John shackled, your trophy could be Wales. You would no longer be subjugated to him. You would be a ruler in your own right!'

There was a long pause in which the four men appraised each other for signs of weakness. Then, satisfied that they were all together in their mutinous intentions, Llywelyn clicked his fingers at Gelert and strode from the room, knowing that he had yet to face the greatest confrontation his life - the one that would occur when Joanna when got to hear that, not only was he was harbouring her father's greatest enemy, but that he was also now planning a rebellion.

Later that afternoon, Joanna sank down on the rocks by the *Rhaeadr Fawr*. The stream that ran along the foot of the *Afon Goch*. The place she had fled to in order to escape the *llys* and de Braose, the unwelcomed visitor who'd come to burden them with his problems and place yet more radical ideas into her husband's head. Ideas that he had voiced to her privately in her solar later, having spent the morning huddled on the dais scheming with the enemy, and emerging set upon a course that, judging by the look on his face, he expected her to brook no argument too. She was so angry that she could have screamed. Instead, she thrust her hand down into the shallow waters of the icy pool beside which she sat, hoping to find a large stone that she could toss at the shrieking gulls whirling above her head. But in place of the large stone she had hoped for, Joanna's hand curled around something smaller. Something smooth and round, and with a bevelled edge ...

Aber, North Wales, August 1210

Nearly a month spent under his roof had not made Llywelyn warm to William de Braose any more than the day he had first stepped over his threshold. He was still an arrogant, boisterous and opinionated little man, and for all his bravado and promises, nothing yet had come of the endless plots and schemes he kept devising to usurp the King of England over copious amounts of Llywelyn's good food and wine. And despite the fact that Llywelyn had agreed to join him in orchestrating a rebellion, he was fast becoming accustomed to the idea that it was not going to happen. Not only because he had decided that it would bring too much trouble if he allied himself to Maelgwn and Rhys Gryg against John, but because the barons that William had said would rally to his cause had proved reluctant when it actually came to taking up the sword against their king.

Llywelyn looked up as Adda stepped onto the dais, interrupting him in his conversation with de Braose. For a moment Adda hesitated then, throwing a look of apology at Llywelyn, he turned to William and addressed him face to face.

'Your wife and several other members of your family have been arrested in Scotland,' he said abruptly. 'They were betrayed by Duncan of Carrick - a cousin of John's,' he added, by way of explanation.

William swayed, unsteady as a sapling in a storm as Adda's message sunk in.

'But there is worse,' Adda continued, still addressing William but with his eyes now on Llywelyn. 'John has landed in Fishguard and is marching on Bristol as we speak. And he has your wife and son with him ...'

'Does he know we harbour William?' Llywelyn demanded, his face darkening in anger as the seriousness of Adda's message sank in.

'Yes, he knows,' Adda said.

'What will you do?' Llywelyn asked, turning to de Braose. 'I fear it is no longer possible for you to stay here ... not with the king on the warpath and your wife and son as his prisoners.

'There is naught for it but to go to John ... petition him again,' William said fearfully.

Reluctantly Llywelyn's gaze strayed to where Joanna sat further down the dais, as far away from him and de Braose as she could manage without drawing attention to herself. They had argued heatedly these past weeks over the fact that he was sheltering an enemy of the Crown behind her father's back and, just for a moment, he wondered if she'd somehow managed to get word to him ... alerted him to the fact that de Braose was under his roof.

As if sensing his scrutiny, Joanna glanced in his direction. Her features were unfathomable, but he saw her hand go to the veil swathed under her chin where something glinted dully in the late afternoon light. It was the little brooch that he'd tossed into the *Afon Goch* all those months ago.

Feeling sickened, Llywelyn turned away, but not before he saw something stir deep in the shadows alongside Joanna ...

Aber, North Wales, December 1210

Joanna bit her lip hard, oblivious to the pain. But it was nothing compared to the pain of the betrayal and hurt that had been heaped upon her in the last few months since the conflict between Llywelyn and her father had begun.

William de Braose, having departed Aber soon after news that his wife was being held under royal arrest at Bristol Castle, was now reported to have abandoned all thoughts of rebellion and fled to France, leaving Llywelyn exposed to her father's displeasure. Richard had written to inform her that the demand for William's absolution was now forty thousand marks. Such a large sum led even Joanna to wonder if there was something more to their father's relentless persecution of de Braose, other than the accusations of blackmail and treachery he had levelled at him. Now she found that she could no longer ignore the many rumours that had circulated at court around the time of her marriage to Llywelyn. Particularly the one pertaining to the nature of Matilda de Braose's relationship with the king, which she had always believed was simply the product of the young Isabella's vicious tongue. Now, though, she was beginning to wonder if there was any credence to Isabella's allegations, as the sum of forty thousand marks demanded was so outrageous that even an earl would find it difficult to raise the amount at such short notice. There was, of course, she conceded, a certain irony in the price, for an earldom was in fact what William was alleged to have been pestering her father for. But still, now that her father had Maude locked up, it seemed that William was of no interest to him at all. He had simply allowed him to flee to France, presumably so that he could concentrate on punishing his wife for whatever indiscretions she might have committed along the way in his stead.

Joanna sighed. For a while she had truly thought that William's exile and Maude's arrest would mark an end to their troubles. But she had been wrong. With the de Braoses out of the way, her father was now concentrating on punishing Llywelyn for harbouring an outlaw and plotting against him by renewing his castle building policy on Welsh soil. In retaliation, Llywelyn had taken an army to the river

Conwy, where he had raised Degannwy to the ground in an attempt to keep it out of Norman control. This, however, had not prevented the Bishop of Winchester and the Earl of Chester from leading their own armies into Gwynedd, where Chester had re-built the castle right under Llywelyn's nose with her father's authority. Worst still, at the same time, her father had released Gwenwynwyn, who was now reported to be re-instated in Southern Powys.

For a moment, Joanna wondered if she too should not have fled to France. Taken refuge there in the land of her childhood, for she was no longer sure she was equipped to deal with the self-destruction Llywelyn was heaping upon himself by continuously opposing her father, or the cold indifference meted out to her by her father for merely being married to him.

'Are you well, *cariad*?' Rhoda asked, crossing to her mistress with a look of concern on her face. 'You've not eaten today,'

'How can I eat!' Joanna replied, more sharply than she intended. Then, seeing Rhoda's face, she was immediately contrite. 'I'm sorry, Rhoda, please forgive me for I'm sorely worried. You will have heard, of course, that now Gwenwynwyn is free he has allied himself with Maelgwn, who is seeking to re-gain his lands in Ceredigion from Llywelyn? My father has even provided money and men-at-arms so that he might do so,' she ventured, looking at Rhoda to gauge her reaction, for she no longer knew who to trust. Then seeing only sympathy in her old friend's eyes, she sat down heavily at her writing table and picked up the letter that had lain there since that morning.

'Oh, Rhoda, it's all so complicated - how can I even begin to explain?' she whispered, looking down at the unopened piece of parchment in her hand. 'You would only think me a silly girl with addled wits.'

'Try me, *cariad.*' Rhoda said, pulling up a stool and sitting down beside her.

Joanna sighed, and putting the letter down again, she pushed it towards Rhoda. 'Whereas once I had letters of love from Llywelyn when we were apart, now I have only letters of reproach. Reproach because he believes that I don't support him. And reproach for just simply being my father's daughter,' she said sadly. 'What am I to do? I fear to open this one for I know its content. Llywelyn is losing his war, Rhoda! For despite the fact that he assaults and burns Chester's Manors in Cheshire, then steals his livestock, Chester still remains firmly entrenched in Degannwy. Won't be budged. And now, with Gwenwynwyn back in power he has had to withdraw from Southern Powys, for he cannot hold out against the joint might of both Gwenwynwyn and Maelgwn. Llywelyn is fighting a war on two fronts. One that he cannot win. If only he had acted first, and allied himself with Maelgwn and Rhys as de Braose proposed!' she said, forgetting in her anguish, her anger at the plans Llywelyn had hatched under their roof with her father's enemy not so long ago.

Rhoda picked up the letter and frowned. 'But it's not just about this letter, or the fact that Llywelyn is losing his war against your father, is it, *cariad*?' I know you well enough to know that there must be something more to it than that ... you can tell me the truth, you know ...'

Joanna sighed. 'Ah, Rhoda, the truth … you want me to tell you the truth. Well, the truth is that I no longer know where I stand anymore. I only know that neither my father nor Llywelyn love me any longer – I know for certes that my father does not, for Richard writes to say he has another daughter now that he calls Joan … it was Isabella's idea, apparently. Done to replace me in my father's affections and make one of her own dearer to him than me …'

Joanna's voice trailed off, suddenly embarrassed that she revealed the real extent of her misery to someone other than herself. But even then, both she and Rhoda knew that her real misery lay in the fact that in naming another daughter Joan, John was not just replacing her in his affections. He was making the point that he had disowned the first.

Rhoda opened her mouth to speak, but she was too late, for Joanna was already on her feet and, with a sudden swish of her skirts and a loud sob, she grabbed the letter and turned and ran from the room …

That night Joanna slept restlessly. Her whole body ached for Llywelyn: to feel his hands caressing the contours of her body, for his weight to press her down on the soft feather mattress, for his fingers to invaded her most secret of places ...

'*Llywelyn*,' she whispered huskily, as her release came from deep within her body, rippling down in waves to explode between her legs in an agony of ecstasy ... and longing.

Joanna slept for a while after, her body limp and spent as the heat between her thighs cooled. Then, unbidden, she dreamed of Gruffydd. His angry face rose before her, full of hate and loathing for the step-mother he had never wanted. And in the background stood her father. His gaze lingered on the boy for a moment, before his cold blue eyes met hers, then slowly he turned his back on her and walked away.

Aber, North Wales, March 1211

Fed up with the girls constant bickering, Joanna picked up her skirts and marched towards the door of her chamber, wanting nothing more but for the soothing balm of the mountain air to engulf her, and to hear the steady pace of the water as it meandered over the rocks in the river *Afon Aber*. But as usual her wish was not to be granted as the clash of armoury being thrown down in the hall below drifted up the newel stairs, signalling the return of the scouting party.

With a sigh, Joanna pulled a wrap from the clothes pole, hoping that she could still escape by a postern gate undetected by Gruffydd. He would seek her out soon enough, for he liked nothing more than to impart news of Llywelyn's latest campaign to prevent Maelgwn from re-gaining his territories in Ceredigion, now that Gwenwynwyn was fully restored in Powys. Gruffydd had grown much in the past year and, in Llywelyn's absence, he felt duty bound to lord it around the castle, bombarding her with accounts of the border raids and skirmishes that kept him away from home in his conflict with her father. And, of course, to regale her for being John's daughter, and therefore the enemy in the camp.

Joanna turned now to the sound of footsteps mounting the stone stairs, ready with a retort should Gruffydd be in foul temper, and was confounded to find not her stepson but Llywelyn filling the doorway to the chamber.

'Llywelyn, I .... what ... what ... are you doing here?' Joanna stammered, taking in the look of rage that obscured his handsome features. 'I thought you were in -'

But she was cut short, as with two strides Llywelyn was standing before her, his hands balled at his side as if to prevent them from circling her neck. 'Your father's gathering a large army at Chester!' his roared, sending copious amounts of spittle spraying into her face.

Joanna stepped back, suddenly afraid.

'Not only has he summoned the prince of Powys, Maelgwn and Rhys Gryg, but he also has Madog ap

Gruffudd of northern Powys, and Hywel ap Gruffudd ap Cynan of Meirionydd,' he continued, listing two other major Welsh leaders, who until recently he had counted as allies in his cause against her father.

'Llywelyn, please! I know nothing of this -

But Llywelyn didn't hear. 'Is there no stopping his duplicity ... his conniving ... his ... his ... cunning!' he raged on, ignoring her, his voice echoed down the staircase, sending servants and animals alike running for shelter.

Shaking, Joanna groped for a chair and sat down, powerless against his anger as, running out of words, he crossed the room and poured himself a goblet of wine from a pitcher on the table before downing it in one gulp.

'Llywelyn, I -' Joanna began again, knowing that it was useless. Knowing that the final showdown between her husband and her father had begun ... with her stuck in between.

But Llywelyn was not listening. He was beyond listening. He was already on his third goblet of wine. And when he'd finished that, he turned his back on her and marched from the chamber. Leaving her shaking with fear. For she knew that the man she had married, the man she had dared to love, was not the one who had just left the room.

Within months, John, bound on the total subjugation of his son-in-law, marched his army into Gwynedd. Llywelyn, knowing his beloved land would offer no sustenance, no comfort, and little reprieve for such a large army, retreated ahead of the advance - into the uplands of Gwynedd and the shelter of his beloved *Eryri* mountains, where he sat, waited and brooded.

All the time Tangwystl was present. A shadow amongst the trees. A ghost in the wind. *Whispering. Haunting.* Reminding him of his promise to her; to his son ....

In his wake, his people followed like shadows. Burning their homesteads and bringing food, livestock and equipment with them, and taking refuge where they could - amidst the forests and trees, in caves and in the ancient mine shafts that still existed in the mountains, leaving little sign of life behind them. By the time John reached Degannwy, his army was exhausted, starving and demoralised. Their fear of the wildness, their hunger and the howling of wolves caused them to turn against each other. An egg was sold for a penny-halfpenny, horseflesh was found to be as good as the best dishes at court, and men began disappearing into the forests where vagabonds fell upon them and ended their misery. John was forced to turn his army around and retreat to Cheshire, his defeat and shame made plain with every staggering step of his once proud, now rag-tag army. This time Llywelyn had won. His scorched earth policy had brought the King of England to abandon his campaign and return to his own land shamed in front of his people.

But the wind whispered otherwise ...

Chapter 18

Chester Castle, England, July 1211

Ranulf de Blondeville, Earl of Chester, strode into the solar where his wife Clemence sat with her distaff hanging limply from her hands and a distracted look upon her face. Dismissing her ladies with a brief nod, he came to stand before her.

'He has calmed down somewhat and returned to his chambers,' he said, running a hand through his unruly brown hair in a gesture that was wholly familiar to her. 'It was one of his worst episodes since our retreat from Wales,'

'Is it true?' Clemence whispered. Referring, not to John's recent defeat at the hands of the Welsh, but to the rumours that had reached them that day of the cruel death of Matilda de Braose and her eldest son, Will. Rumours that John had incarcerated them in an oubliette deep within Windsor Castle, where they had starved to death back in the December of last year.

'I believe it to be true, yes,' Ranulf said tiredly, crouching down before her and gently removing the distaff from her hands.

'Then history is repeating itself,' Clemence whispered, her words full of such despair that Ranulf knew immediately that she was alluding to Arthur. 'He is the devil himself. Murder is of no consequence to him. His own kin, his barons, their wives are shown no mercy if they defy him! Tis murder, naught else,' she repeated, glancing fearfully around as if to be sure that they were really alone. 'And that child, Joanna. The daughter he had married here in this very castle, under this very roof. I remember you telling me that Constance placed the circlet on her hair and reassured her that all would be well in her new life as the wife of a Welsh prince. That Prince Llywelyn would treat her right. That her father and her new husband would be allies,' she finished, reminding Ranulf of the grief that his first wife had felt when she had placed the circlet on the head of the child whose father was rumoured to have been instrumental in the disappearance of her own. 'Ah, what is to become of us, Ranulf?'

Ranulf rose, and going to the table he poured himself a large goblet of wine. 'We grin and bear it,' he said eventually, having taken several gulps of the wine. 'We've been out of favour before, and then had to bear the humiliation of being restored to it in his eyes,' he went on, remembering with distaste a previous alliance unwisely made with the Welsh whilst John was absent in France. 'We grin and bear it. As does the Marshall and many others,' he repeated stoically, 'for I'll naught be out of favour again.'

Then with a heavy heart he turned away. 'His supplies are ready now, and his army. We march on the morrow!' With that he downed his wine and made his way to his hall, where John's justiciar, Peter des Roches, Geoffrey Fitzpeter, the Bishop of Winchester, William, the Earl of Salisbury, and several of his mercenaries, including de Breauté and d'Athée had gathered for a war council.

Dolwyddelan Castle, Gwynedd, North Wales, August 1211

'John has crossed the Conway and reached Bangor,' Gwyn said carefully, making his way to where Joanna stood, staring out at the distant glow that illumined the night sky from the top of Dolwyddelan's keep.

'He's burning it?' Joanna asked sadly. A tear escaped to run down her cheek as she remembered the beautiful cathedral that she knew her father, in his rage, would not spare. He would have desecrated it beyond repair. Destroyed it because it was a symbol of the institution, the church that had excommunicated him. The church that thought to bring the King of England to heel.

Gwyn nodded. 'Reports have come that the Bishop of Bangor was abducted from the cathedral, and ransomed for two hundred hawks.' He spat on the floor. 'A bishop, ransomed indeed! If he were not under interdict, he would not dare to do such a thing to a man of the church. A bishop, no less!' He paused. 'Robert,' he said, referring to the bishop by name, 'refuses to meet the king - refuses to meet an excommunicate! That was enough to enrage your father further and push him on. He has now penetrated deep into Gwynedd and, even as we speak, he is crossing into the *Eryri* mountains.' He paused. 'He has burned Aber, Joanna, *bach*. We cannot hold out anymore. It is time for you to go to your father. Speak with Llywelyn first. Convince him, *cariad*. Only you have that power.'

Joanna let the tears fall unashamedly down her face as, for the first time in her life, she had to choose: Llywelyn, or her father.

She chose Llywelyn ...

Joanna stood her ground as Llywelyn raged, his past ambitions now ashes in the wind. In his agony, he saw no spark left to re-ignite those ambitions again in the future. He was lost. He was dying. Dying as fast as his land died before him. Beside him stood Rhys Ieuane and Owain, the sons of the old Lord Rhys. The only ones to remain loyal to him. But they, too, had been hard pressed to hold on to their own lands in the south, and they were as impotent as Llywelyn was now.

Joanna barely noticed as the household gathered around them, their eyes darting uncomfortably between the two. She could not know that they had seldom seen their lord gripped by so much emotion, overpowered by so much rage, but then they had seldom seen him lose so much in so short a time, or seen him have to concede defeat and come to terms with the man he hated more than any other in the world. The King of England. His father by marriage. The very devil himself.

When finally Llywelyn's rage had subsided, Joanna said simply. 'I will go to him, Llywelyn.'

Bangor, North Wales, August 1211

Joanna faced her father across the chancery in the Bishop of Bangor's manor where he was camped with a large army led by the Earl of Chester, the Earl of Salisbury, his Justiciar, Peter des Roches, and the Bishop of Winchester. Behind them, the cathedral still burned. A chilling reminder of the sacrilege and devastation that her father's anger had heaped on Wales.

It was the first time that she had seen her father since she had visited Woodstock in the October of 1209, when Llywelyn had payed homage to him for the second time since their marriage. But those had been circumstances very different to the one she faced now, Joanna reflected sadly. Dismissing his squire, John crossed the narrow space between them to hug his daughter briefly, before bidding her to be seated at a window overlooking the west green, where a group of soldiers were taking shelter under a brightly coloured canopy from the mid-day sun.

Doing as she was told, Joanna smoothed down the fine wool of her gown, and adjusted the gauzy veil of her headdress under her chin, whilst she considered her position and the reasons that had brought her here today: to negotiate, nay beg, on her husband's behalf.

'Father I -' she began, but John held up his hand to stop her there.

'Your husband has overstepped the mark again,' he said without pre-amble. 'There is no discussion here, Joanna. He has turned rebel once too often.'

Joanna flinched as she heard the steel in her father's voice; saw his blue eyes turn to ice at the very thought of his enemy.

'But Father, there must be -' she halted as the door opened and Richard entered, along with a serving girl armed with goblets and a pitcher of wine. Another followed bearing a tray of sweetmeats, both of which were deposited on an ornate table nearby which, Joanna assumed, was not the property of the Bishop of Bangor who seemed to have led a seemingly monastic life, judging by the lack of any other adornment in the room.

'I thought you could do with some support,' Richard whispered, bending to kiss Joanna on the cheek before crossing to the table where he poured three goblets of wine.

John bore this sibling interaction with an inscrutable look on his face, accepting his wine with grace before continuing. 'There is no discussion here, Joanna,' he reaffirmed grimly. 'As I said, your husband is a rebel. No more. No less. He has showed no respect for his oaths to me as his sovereign, or as his father through marriage by you. Therefore, I have no choice but to deal with him as I have with those others in the past who have defied my authority.'

Joanna flinched, remembering Gwenwynwyn's fate, de Braose's, Arthur's, and others who had challenged her father's authority in the past. Llywelyn would never submit to such a fate - to be taken from his land, stripped of his patrimony, deprived of his liberty ... no, he would rather die than submit to such a life. Suddenly she leapt to her feet in a frenzy of anguish, spilling wine down her gown in her in her haste to say what she needed to say... to beg even ... for she feared for Llywelyn's life, and would do anything to save him. Even if it meant giving her own.

'Papa ...' she began, her head swimming. Then Richard was beside her, his hand on her arm and then round her waist as the nausea overcame her. After that she remembered nothing ...

When she came around, Joanna found herself lying on a settle in a small chamber adjacent to the one in which she had been seated with her father and Richard moments before. Several curious faces stared down at her. But she could only focus on one. One that contained a pair of deceptively guileless, hysop blue eyes.

'My God, you are pregnant!' Isabella giggled. 'Well! Well! Well! You must pray that it's a boy, for if it is, it may be the saving of you and your Welsh prince, my dear!' Then with a swish of her skirts and another giggle, she left the room ...

'Are you quite well now, Joanna?' her father asked her solicitously as they dined together privately that evening in his chambers.

'Yes, Father,' Joanna replied, pushing aside the plate of quail swimming in grease and selecting instead, a piece of bread, a hunk of hard cheese, and some fruit from the platter in front of her. 'Yes. Quite well, Father.'

'Hmm ...' John said, eyeing her speculatively. Then, after a moment. 'I have considered our - ' he paused. 'Dilemma. Is that the right word, Joanna?'

Joanna sat stock still. Unable to speak. Afraid to tip the balance. Outside she could hear the howl of a dog in the distance, and the shouts of servants going about their business.

'Do you love Llywelyn?' John asked, suddenly gentle. 'Do you really love him?'

'Yes ...' Joanna breathed. 'Oh yes, Papa, more than life itself.'

'Then he shall have safe passage and a choice of consort - as guarantee of his safe conduct. The choice shall be yours. But there will be terms. Terms that this time Llywelyn shall abide by, for he will have no other alternative. No other chance. Do we understand each other?'

Joanna nodded, afraid to speak. Knowing the terms would be harsh.

'Llywelyn will have to cede to me the four cantrefs of Perfeddwald that is Gwynedd Is Conwy, and several castles.' John continued after a pause. 'He will also have to be content with a realm of my choosing, and contain himself within it. He will rule still as a prince of Wales, but with a greatly diminished status. And he, and all the other princes of Wales, will answer to me, Joanna. Do you understand? Those are my terms. There is of course the question of a tribute, in compensation of my expenses – ten thousand head of cattle, forty war horses ....' he trailed of as Joanna stood and went to the window. 'Do you understand?' he repeated, as she gripped the window embrasure and took a deep breath of air.

Joanna nodded, almost imperceptivity. Then steeling herself she turned. 'May I go now Father, for I have lost my appetite?'

For several long moments, they held each other's gaze. Father and daughter. So alike, and yet so different now that there was an insurmountable gap between them; a void that would never again be filled.

'Yes,' John said. 'But there is one more condition ...'

Two days after his consort had arrived to escort him to the king, Llywelyn was in Bangor. Before him, he could just make out the stark outline of the burnt-out cathedral, with the army encampment in front, and the English standard flying over it in jubilation. This was the place where he was to finally subjugate himself, nay surrender. He who had been ruler of Gwynedd at his peak. He who had conquered Powys and nearly, very nearly, been the ruler of the whole of Wales ...

Behind him followed a small party, among which were his daughters, Gwladys, Elen and Marared.

Gruffydd and Gwenny were absent at Joanna's request.

'Do you want to make camp for a while?' William Longespée enquired of him, his weathered face inscrutable of feelings. Beside him Richard gave a small, imperceptible nod, and with a frustrated sigh Llywelyn settled himself down and waited whilst a small fire was made.

They sat, not in companionable silence, but at least one in which they could each take stock of their thoughts; make silent preparation for what was to come - Llywelyn for his coming humiliation and subjugation, and William and Richard for their duty to their king in what was to be the most difficult and unprecedented of circumstances.

Each in their own way thought of Joanna and her predicament: Llywelyn's heart raged between love, understanding and humiliation at the thought that he had sent his wife to beg on his behalf. He wondered if he would do the same for her one day, but he had no notion or care of the future.

William Longespée, half-brother to the king, had discovered on the short journey that in other circumstances he might have liked Llywelyn, whose stoic acceptance of his coming fate moved him more than his rages had done, and, in a way, he now understood how Joanna could love such a fierce and uncompromising man, despite his faults.

Richard, probably the closest to a true brother that Joanna had, cared only that Llywelyn accept his father's terms - for his wife's sake, if nothing else. Especially as he knew what those terms were. And that they were the only terms that could save Llywelyn ...

Llywelyn stood before John in the hall in the Bishop's manor at Bangor. Where, only a short while before, the manor had been a place for the Bishop and his prelates merely to sleep, or take sustenance between periods of prayer and worship in the cathedral and husbandry in the fields and vineyards beyond, it was now a place fit for a king. Along the middle of the hall, rows of trestle tables and benches had been brought in to seat the many courtiers who had dutifully followed John's progress into Wales. A further, more substantial table now stood at the farthest end of the room, with carved chairs lined along its length and a snowy white cloth to mark it as the king's own. And where once the walls had been bare, a number of brightly coloured tapestries now adorned them, between which sconces had been erected to throw an ambient light on the proceedings.

Sitting on an ornately carved chair amidst this makeshift court was the king himself, the sapphires and rubies glowing on his fingers as they hovered over the tray of sweetmeats being offered by a page in royal livery. On his head sat his crown. A mark of his status. A symbol of his authority. Around his neck hung several heavy gold chains of office. Symbols of the shackles that Llywelyn would in future be bound by - for shackles they would be, gold or otherwise ...

Llywelyn, stripped of his sword at the door, felt naked and impotent before him. Inside him burned a rage like no other before, fuelled by the anger that *this* man of all men should sit here before him and subjugate him - an excommunicated King, a devil no less having desecrated a beautiful cathedral and taken hostage a man of God in his own house.

'Ah, Llywelyn!' John said nonchalantly, interrupting the rising crescendo that mounted and threatened to erupt inside him. Then all of a sudden Joanna was at his side, grasping at his sleeve and imploring him with her eyes before turning and addressing her father.

'Might I have a private word with my husband, Sire? Before he has audience with you ... so that he might better prepare himself for your Grace.'

John's hands ceased hovering as he surveyed, first his daughter, and then Llywelyn, then: 'A chamber has been prepared for you. You may dress and present yourself to me before noon. No later!' he warned, before signalling to his squire to bring him more wine.

'He has demanded a hostage, Llywelyn. As part of his terms,' Joanna said, her eyes filling with tears.

'Who?' Llywelyn asked blankly.

'You must have guessed, Llywelyn ... you must have known ...?' Joanna said, coming to stand before him.

Llywelyn felt his head swim, realising now why Joanna had not asked that Gwen or Gruffydd to accompany him to John's court and, unbidden, Tangwystl's face floated before his.

You will take care of our son, Llywelyn ... you will take care ...

At noon, Llywelyn stood before John in his private chamber, fists clenched at his side as he listened to John's terms of surrender, his head still reeling from his conversation with Joanna. Much of it he could not take in, for it was even more harsh than even he had expected. Besides the surrender of Gwynedd Is Conwy, he was expected to forfeit and pay compensation to John for his expenses in the form of*: ten thousand head of cattle* ...' John's senchenel droned on, reading from the roll prepared ...'*forty war horses* ...'

Then Llywelyn's head snapped up. 'What did you say?' he asked, incredulous.

'You knew the terms when you married my daughter,' John said calmly. 'Had you had a son with Joanna, then he would have inherited your principality from you in its entirety. Now, should you have a son, he shall inherit only what remains of Gwynedd. That which *I* grant you, from you. If not, then it will revert to the royal demesne upon your death. Gruffydd and Tegward?' he queried, knowing full well the names of all of Llywelyn's children. 'Are Welsh bastards by mistresses unknown,' he continued, not entirely truthfully. 'They will not inherit; only blood mingled with blood from the true Angevin line shall succeed you. Do you understand?'

'But I have only girls by Joanna,' Llywelyn said blankly.

'You will stand before me before vespers,' John said, 'and publicly surrender. Those are my terms.' With that, John waved Llywelyn away derisively with one hand. Like a common serf.

Llywelyn stood before John in the hall for the third time that day. His audience was made up almost entirely of his enemies: John's barons and the Welsh princes who had deserted him to serve a foreign king - Gwenwynwyn, Maelgwn, Rhys Gryg and Hywel ap Gruffudd ap Cynan, among others. Only a few loyal friends stood by to witness his final humiliation - Rhys Ieuane and Owain, Gwyn, and the Corbets of Caus, who had risked so much to stay at his side. Joanna stood beside him. Unwavering now in her support, her mind made up. She, like her father, would not budge now of that she had made it plain where her loyalties lay, and Llywelyn was surprised at the sudden rush of gratitude and love that engulfed him as he sought his wife's eyes.

Then turning to John, Llywelyn steeled himself for what was to come as his sword was brought forward for him to surrender publicly, and subjugate himself yet again to the man he hated most in the world ...

Chapter 19

Aber, North Wales, August 1211

Bronwyn stood at the top of the tower looking down towards the gatehouse where a group of the king's soldiers, together with William Marshall, had gathered ready to escort Gruffydd into John's keeping at Chester, where the court had retired following Llywelyn's surrender. They had arrived that morning, but she had expected them sooner, for the gods had decreed it. With a shudder, she looked down at the little brooch she held in her hand. She knew it had returned for a purpose; Tangwystl would not let them forget. Not any of them. She had seen the shock on Llywelyn's face when he had seen Joanna wearing it in the hall the night of de Braose's departure and, although she had no liking for him, later that night when the castle was asleep she had made sure it had disappeared. Amidst the confusion of William de Braose's further troubles, nothing was ever said.

Suddenly angry, she turned and thrust it into the small coffer amongst the clothing she had packed for Gruffydd to take with him on his journey. 'Leave me be, Tangwystl,' she hissed. 'I can no longer serve you!' Then slowly she crossed to the door ready to make her way to the hall, knowing that she would have to send out a search party for Gruffydd who had fled at the sight of men-at-arms advancing upon Aber without his father at the helm.

Behind her the wooden lid of the coffer slammed shut, halting her briefly in her tracks, and crossing herself she turned and peered into the gloom. A shaft of light fell upon the bed where the coffer lay. Dust motes floated lazily above it, before falling to settle on the counterpane. Then, just for a moment, *she* was there. *Tangwystl*. Her eyes glittering in anger, her fury reverberating around the room at Bronwyn's rejection of her. Then the veil fell once more between the two worlds, and the chamber was silent. Empty once again. Save for a heavy throbbing in the air where she had stood.

For a while Bronwyn stared into the empty space. The tentacles of Tangwystl's power were reaching out and she was becoming more and more uncontrollable. It was then that the truth came to her in a flash: in making the promise she had made to her mistress on her death bed all those years ago, she had opened herself up to the forces of magic. Now, whether she liked it or not, she was Tangwystl's slave forever. No matter where the little brooch went ...

Chapter 20

Wakefield Manor, Yorkshire, England, February 1212

'Go away!' Gruffydd snapped impatiently, tired of Rhys's constant whining and demands for attention. Then, suddenly contrite, he rumpled the boy's red hair and cuffed him affectionately around the ear. 'Away with you now - go pester your brother Madoc!' he said, raising his hand to attract the attention of Madoc ap Maelgwn, the son of his father's enemy who, like himself, was part of John's swelling burden of Welsh hostages taken from all sides of the conflict as security against future rebellion. Although at first uncomfortable at being thrown together with the likes of Madoc, Gruffydd had soon found himself harbouring a grudging liking for the tall, red headed boy and his brother, despite their differing loyalties. Now he found himself hoping that in the future their fathers could put aside their squabbles, and come together to rid the country of the scourge of the English standard that hung over nearly every castle in Wales. Scowling again at the thought, Gruffydd pushed Rhys more forcibly towards his brother, before turning to see what the sudden noise was behind him.

John, as usual, was reclining in a chair on the dais, having consumed large amounts of the good burgundy he was so partial to along with his host, William, the Earl of Warenne, a cousin of his whom he had recently appointed as a warden of the Welsh marches. It was in this capacity that de Warenne now ordered the guards to bring forward an old man who was being restrained at the far end of the hall. The old man was little more than a beggar, and to Gruffyd's eyes could be no more of a nuisance than a few pieces of silver thrown his way could solve. And so, it was with interest that he watched as the witless fellow was pushed to his knees in front of the king, at once bringing a hush to the hall.

The silence seemed to go on forever as John examined the strange apparition before him, taking in the tufts of unkempt white hair and the long, straggly beard that now brushed the floor by his skinny knees as he knelt. But despite his complete lack of decent apparel and worldly goods, Gruffydd noticed that, far from being witless, he possessed a sense of purpose that belied the fact that he could have simply drifted in of the street and found himself thrust in front of the king by accident. Indeed, he seemed to regard his presence before the king as much his right as any other person in the room. A fact which he demonstrated by staggering clumsily to his feet so that he was standing somewhat haughtily before his sovereign.

Sighing deeply, John signalled for his men to take a step back. 'So, you are the hermit who has dogged my every step through Yorkshire and Wales, proclaiming that I am to lose my crown by Ascension Day - not this one I hear tell, but the next,' he said, addressing the hermit in a clear voice. 'You had quite a following in your wake,' he continued, 'particularly in Pontefract I understand, where you were heard to say, and I quote: "*A vision has revealed to me that the king shall not rule more than fourteen years, at the end of which time he will be replaced by someone more pleasing to God.*" Well, how say you, old man. Is this true? Shall I die on that day ... or how shall I be deprived of my throne? Well, answer me, old man,' John said, his upper lip curling in amusement, before downing the last of his wine.

The old man regarded John with pity in his rheumy eyes for several long moments, before replying. 'Rest assured that on that aforesaid day you will not be king, and if I am proved to have told a lie, do what you will with me.'

There was something so guileless, so compelling in this statement, that Gruffydd was suddenly glad that he was not in John's shoes, for he found himself believing every word that the old hermit had uttered. And he was not the only one. For all around the room he could see people murmuring to one another and making the sign of the cross before backing away, eager not to be in the sphere of influence that might taint them by such an omen.

Frowning, John stood, and taking a step down from the dais he went to stand before the emaciated figure. 'And who sayeth this? God, I suppose?' he asked sarcastically, peering curiously into the old man's face as if looking for some sign of insincerity; any clue that the man was a fraud.

'Yes, Sire. I am but an instrument of God. I seek to tell only that which has been disclosed to me by the Almighty in his wisdom,' the old man replied, his expression showing only the calm certainty of one who spoke the truth.

At this, John lost patience. 'Enough! Go back from whence you came, and cease your wagging tongue - I will hear no more of your confused babblings. They are but the invention of a witless old man - a beggar no less. You shall have a purse!' he said benevolently, signalling to his squire to bring forward a sum of money already contained in a canvas pouch designed for the purpose. 'Accept this, and we shall say no more on the matter.'

With eyes full of pity, the old man said. 'Sire, I cannot accept your money. And even if I did, it would not change that which I have seen, for I have the Sight. God has shown me this vision so that I could warn you; so that you could be prepared for another journey.'

For several moments more, John stared at the old man. Gruffydd could see the legendary anger building up in him and he wondered fleetingly if

John was foolish enough to strike down a prophet of God. Then as suddenly as it had come, John's anger dissipated, and with a wave of his hand he signalled the guards forward once again. 'So be it, old man,' he said. Then to the guards: 'Take him away. Have him confined in Corfe Castle until Ascension Day of next year when the truth shall be revealed!' Then reaching for his goblet once again, he turned his back on his audience and left the hall.

Gruffydd watched the king go with narrowed eyes and a cold, hard core of hate in his heart, in the knowledge that John had many months of worry ahead of him before Ascension Day 1213 came and went, and the truth behind the old man's prophecy was finally revealed. He also held on to the comforting thought that there would be good deal of ill-disguised amusement, and very little pity were it to be proved true.

Cambridge, England, March 1212

Gruffydd pushed his way through the throng gathering in the hall of the old castle at Cambridge, a buzzing university town in England where the court had adjourned for the Easter celebrations on the long march to Nottingham castle - the place in which John confined his swelling mass of Welsh hostages. His heart was pounding, and he was not sure that he truly believed the news that Madoc had imparted to him over breakfast: that his father was here, attending the celebrations as John's guest along with Joanna who, despite being in the last few months of her pregnancy, had made the long journey with him to visit her family.

Reaching the front, Gruffydd paused to watch as Llywelyn knelt before the king to kiss one of the bejewelled hands offered to him, before standing and presenting Joanna to her father. As if sensing his presence Llywelyn turned and, catching his eye, he held it for a moment. Then with a brief nod of his head, he turned back to John and begun to confer with him in low tones. Gruffydd held his breath, for although he could not hear the conversation, judging by the looks being thrown his way, Llywelyn was asking for time alone with his son. And, strangely enough, Joanna seemed to be in agreement, for her hand now rested on John's arm and she was giving him a beseeching look.

After a period of deliberation, John's eyes sought Gruffydd's and the warning was clear: he was to assure his father that for the last seven months' he had lived the life of a valued courtier, and been awarded the respect due to the son of a Welsh prince and stepson to the King of England's own daughter. And in truth he had, for he had found himself being treated better that most of the other hostages, having been given a great deal more freedom to roam within the confines of his captivity. However, Gruffydd could not fail to read the other message that John was conveying to him in that cold, steely blue gaze: that at no time must he forget that he was still a hostage, and therefore he must abide by the rules of his restraint. That meant that when he was alone with his father, he must at no time indulge in treasonous talk or make any plans for the future. Nor must he make any complaint pertaining to his treatment whilst in the king's keeping, for if word got back to the king that he had, John would no longer be responsible for his father's safety within the English court. For a moment, Gruffydd felt a resurgence of the hate that always seem to engulf him whenever he was in the vicinity of the King of England, for he resented the silken trap that he was caught up in, hated court life and all its privileges. And as young as he was, he hated King John. Even more so now that he had been given his first lesson in what it was like to hold the balance of someone else's life in his hands, and that that person was his father. And then it was gone as, with a magnanimous nod, John granted Llywelyn permission to go to his son.

'You are keeping well?' Llywelyn's voice was gruff with emotion as he searched his son's face for confirmation that John was not treating him badly.

'Yes, Father,' Gruffydd replied, and Llywelyn could see that he was trying not to succumb to the overwhelming mixture of emotions that were flitting across face – joy and fear, edged with just a hint of suspicion – at his unexpected appearance in England.

Sighing, Llywelyn gave him a moment to compose himself whist he took stock of the chamber which Gruffydd had led him to. Situated in the east tower, it was well away from the ever-growing mass of Easter visitors flocking to the castle. And, well away, too, from the prying eyes of the other hostages eager for news of their kin.

'And this is your room?' Llywelyn asked finally, looking around at the large oak bed and opulent, showy French furniture and hangings that adorned it, all somehow at odds with the simplicity of the rooms at Aber which they were used to.

'Yes, Father,' Gruffydd repeated, sounding like one of the brightly coloured parrots Isabella had sent for from the continent and then trained to repeat certain phrases for the amusement of her ladies. Then suddenly impatient, he grasped Llywelyn's arm. 'But what are you doing here - 'tis dangerous, is it not? Surely you are not here at the king's behest? You would not be so foolish to think that he has forgiven you ... it must be a trick ... and if it is, then Joanna must be party to it -'

'Hush now!' Llywelyn said, raising a hand to halt Gruffydd's babbling. 'As a matter of fact I am here at the king's request - he expressed a wish to see Joanna, spend Easter with her and play happy families for the sake of appearances, I imagine!' he finished with a mirthless laugh. 'But as you might suspect, things are not as simple as that. John has not once in his miserable life chosen to spend time with Joanna, lest it's to glean something to his own advantage. And, on this occasion, I suspect it is to ferret news out of me pertaining to politics of his own doing that are overwhelming Wales at the moment.' He hesitated. 'You know of course that I have kept my pledge with John in so far as that I have not resumed hostilities with him - for your sake?'

'Yes, Father,' Gruffydd replied. Then, breaking of all pretence, he blurted. 'But what is *really* happening? Tell me the truth! I am no longer a child, and I have ears! Madoc says that John has claimed Ceredigion for the Crown, and denied his father the very land that he fought against you for ... has even made Faulkes de Bréauté Sherriff of Glamorgan, and set him to building a new castle at Aberystwyth in the king's name!'

'I'm afraid it is more serious than that,' Llywelyn said, pulling out a chair and sitting on it heavily. 'John has indeed denied Maelgwn his land ...' He paused, as if trying to find a way of breaking it gently. There was none, and so he continued bluntly. 'In retaliation, Maelgwn and Rhys Gryg have rebelled against John's castle-building policy. Between them they besieged Aberystwyth and burned it to the ground, and they are now advancing on other English forts in the area and doing the same to them, too. They are at war. And Gwenwynwyn is on the brink, because John has sent Robert de Vieuxpont into lower Powys where he is raising the English standard on new castles as we speak. They are finally coming to realise that they made a fatal error in trusting John to reinstate their lands and allow them the right to rule their own principalities as before. John means to have all of Wales. For himself. At whatever cost.'

'Then Madoc and his brothers are in peril, along with Rhys's sons,' Gruffydd whispered, pulling out another chair and sitting down heavily alongside Llywelyn.

'Yes,' Llywelyn said, sighing deeply. 'Yes, they are. And so might you be, too, when you hear what I have to say.' He hesitated, and for a moment Gruffydd wondered if he had changed his mind about speaking. Then as if making a decision he leaned forward and took Gruffydd's hand. 'Look, Gruffydd … my son. I can no longer remain aloof from all of this and stand apart - not whilst John rapes Wales, beggars its people, and denies its princes their own birth right. In short, I can no longer tolerate his occupation of the Perfeddwlad in order to subjugate me, especially not whilst Maelgwn and Gwenwynwyn are facing such betrayal from John. And so, I mean to join the rebellion. And Joanna is in agreement. It's not just what's happening in Wales. Nor is it even about the fate of Maude de Braose and Arthur. It's bigger than that. Please believe me, I would not risk your life were it not otherwise. It's as the old hermit predicted - John's star is fading, and it's through his own folly, greed and debauchery. He steals from the church, makes profit from enforcing spurious forest laws, and commits terrible crimes against the Jewish moneylenders to fill his coffers. His goodwill only extends to Scotland in return for vast sums of money extracted from an ailing king. And in England and Ireland he taxes his barons to the hilt and deprives them of power, whilst at the same time, if I am to believe the rumours that abound, raping their wives and daughters!'

Llywelyn paused to look around the room in case it should sprout ears at such treasonous talk. Then satisfied that they were still alone, he continued in a low voice. 'The thing is that John is so heady with power that he now wants to cross the Channel and win back the lands he lost in Normandy. You must have heard by now that he is already mustering an army at Portsmouth which he intends to lead against Phillip Augustus later this summer - against the advice of his own council, I might add, who don't want the expense of a foreign war on their hands. In short, what I am trying to say is this, Gruffydd. Whilst John is preoccupied with calling men to arms and quelling dissention elsewhere in the land, I am in the perfect position to join the rebellion in Wales. In fact, I have already begun negotiations which I shall resume upon my return to Aber. I am on the verge of forming an alliance with Maelgwn and Rhys. With Gwenwynwyn, too, if all goes to plan. We will put aside past differences and become united in the cause for Wales once again. I am going to claim back my birthright! Claim back *your* birthright!'

There was a long silence in which Gruffydd took in the significance of his father's speech, unaware that even as the words left Llywelyn mouth he regretted them. For he knew that if Joanna was carrying a boy, then Gruffydd would forfeit that birthright. No matter what the outcome of his rebellion. Furthermore, he knew that his honey coating truth with promises that could not be met, was yet another betrayal of his promise to his dead mistress. The mother of the boy that sat before him, gazing at him with trust in his eyes.

Neither the boy or his father noticed the shadows deepening in the four corners of the room, and the sudden chill that descended as Llywelyn took leave of his son. Nor did they notice the raven that landed on the sill to stare balefully in, before letting out a loud caw and flying off into the slowly darkening evening ...

'You take your leave on the morrow?' John enquired of Llywelyn politely, before helping himself to another portion of the wild boar being offered to him by his squire.

'I do,' Llywelyn replied. ''Tis a long journey home, and Joanna is nearing her time.' Llywelyn sat back and contemplated the splendour of the hall, with its ornately carved furniture, sumptuous hangings, and flickering sconces. A perfect foil for the brightly dressed courtiers who had flocked to court at the king's behest to celebrate Easter. He did not feel hungry. In fact, he had hardly participated in the festivities that week, preferring instead, to eat alone in his chambers with his son where he could, for the debauchery and greediness of it all repulsed him. For a moment, he caught Eustance de Vesi's eye. De Vesi was a garrulous and outspoken Northern lord, whose loyalty and services had proved indispensable to John in his dealings with the Scots king. On the few occasions that Llywelyn had dined in the company of others he had found himself drawn to the man, and it had become apparent during these encounters that he was harbouring a grudge of epic proportions towards his liege lord. One that Llywelyn felt was not entirely due to the opposition that he could sense building amongst the English barons, concerning the aggressive methods that John employed to raise revenue for his continental expedition.

In the end, it was Eustance who broke their eye contact first, turning instead to fix his on John, who was leaning forward and whispering something in his squire's ear. After several minutes of close collaboration with the boy, John looked up and nodded towards de Vesi's wife, Margaret, who was sitting apart from her husband. Seeing the king looking her way, Margaret threw a startled look at her husband. It was a look which soon turned to resignation as she realised that she was being singled out for John's evening entertainment, confirming to Llywelyn the rumours he had been hearing concerning John's appetite for his baron's wives and daughters.

Feeling slightly repulsed, and not a little angered at John's blatant disregard for de Vesi, who'd had to suffer the humiliation of his wife being picked out from the other wives like a common strumpet, Llywelyn watched as de Vesi turned and grasped the arm of Robert FitzWalter, a powerful figure in the realm who held sway in Essex and London. His usual sallow complexion had now turned the colour of ripe tomatoes, and he looked fit to explode. The pair seemed to argue for a moment, and several oblique glances were exchanged with other barons around the room, many of whom Llywelyn recognised as being in John's private council - in particular, Geoffrey of Norwich, an exchequer official of standing. Then all the anger seemed to drain from de Vesi's face, and releasing his grip on Fitzwater's arm, he allowed himself to be led away from the centre of the room to where a small group of men were gathering near the door. In moments, they were joined by Geoffrey and several others Llywelyn vaguely recognised from the close-knit circle of men that John surrounded himself with, and after a brief, whispered discussion, one by one they began to slip away from the hall.

If John noticed this activity, then he said nothing, merely concluding his business with his squire and belching loudly before turning back to Llywelyn. 'Of course, your wife's welfare is of paramount importance,' he said picking up their earlier conversation as if it had never left off.

'As is yours,' Llywelyn replied, glancing pointedly to where Isabella sat surrounded by her ladies with several young courtiers vying for her attention, apparently oblivious to her husband's plans for the evening.

'She wants for nothing!' John said, his eyes narrowing in warning. 'As ought yours should Joanna have a boy this time around, for, like it or not, he will be the key to your future!' Standing to take his leave, he paused as if to consider something. Then he lowered his voice so that it was for Llywelyn's ears only. 'It has come to my attention that the pope is proposing to lift the interdict in Wales, and that you and the other Welsh princes will to be absolved of your allegiance to me should he do so.' For a moment, his eyes flashed cold blue in anger. 'Excommunicate or not, I'm both your king and your overlord. And you would do well to remember that! I *will* hang Steven Langton should he set foot in England. And I *will* hang the Welsh hostages, one by one, should you or the other princes forget it and oppose me!' With that, he turned and strode from the room, leaving Llywelyn alone on the dais. John, it seemed, had delivered his *fait accompli* on the eve of their parting. The gauntlet was thrown down. And it lay between them like an abyss.

Llywelyn pushed aside his platter still untouched, the meat cold and congealed. He felt sick at the thought of having to leave Gruffydd once again at the mercy of his father-in-law. He could only hope that within John's black heart there was a core of decency that would prevent him from lashing out at the boy. That if he had any respect for his daughter, he would not harm her husband's child for the sins of his father. For once he was back in Wales, Llywelyn meant to summon the Welsh princes to Aber once again. He meant to rebel. And he took little comfort from the fact he had done his best to warn and prepare Guffydd for the coming war. Glancing towards the door where the last of the group gathered with de Vesi and Fitzwalter had exited, Llywelyn at least took some heart from the fact that he was not the only one planning rebellion. The tide was turning for John. And it was not across the channel as he thought, but much closer to home. John's day of reckoning was coming fast. And Llywelyn could not wait.

Chapter 21

Castell Hen Blas, Flintshire, Wales, May 1212

Bronwyn stood at the top of the stairs leading to the solar and stared out of the narrow window, down towards the valley with its stream meandering like a snake between the hills. Behind her, in the room, a handful of women gathered around the bed where Princess Joanna lay, her frail body limp and exhausted from her efforts to expel the child that destiny had decreed would become the next prince of Aberffraw: the chosen heir to the throne of Gwynedd and ruler of the whole of Wales. The child that would deny a prince of the true blood the right of succession against all the laws of Hywel Dda and the old gods who still protected the land. This time there was no doubt that it was that child, for she had consulted the runes, and they had told her so. And the runes did not lie.

In the solar a serving girl banked up the fire, piling it high with kindling until the smoke rose, thick and acrid towards the hole in the roof where it escaped into the darkening sky beyond the *llys*. She paused, frozen, as Princess Joanna screamed a sharp scream, and stopping what she was doing she dropped to her knees and prayed to St Margaret, the patron saint of childbirth, to ease her lady's pains. Then, without a word to the others, she went in search of a priest.

From the shadow of the stairs Bronwyn watched her go. Waiting patiently as outside the night slowly closed in around the castle. In the distance she could see the moon hanging like a single pearl in the sky: round and perfect, its silvery light bathing the distant mountains in its glow. After a while she turned, and stepping into the solar she crossed to the hearth. The room was empty but for the woman, Rhoda, who stirred uneasily in her chair. For a moment she stood, staring into the fire. Then pulling a small packet out from within the folds of her cloak, she threw a handful of herbs onto the flames where they glowed for a moment like fireflies, before spilling a bitter cloud of acrid smoke out into the room. Bronwyn frowned. With the little brooch now in Gruffydd's keeping she was not sure that Tangwystyl would come. But if the gods were willing, and the power of her magic was enough, Joanna would die anyway. And with her would die the child that her mistress feared. Then, and only then, she, Bronwyn, would be free ...

It was midnight when the girl returned with the priest. He hesitated on the threshold of the chamber briefly. Inside it was hot and smoky, and there was a strange smell hanging in the air. Bronwyn watched as, without saying a word, he allowed the maid to lead him to the bed where, pulling out his rosary, he knelt and began to pray.

Outside it had begun to rain, and a sudden crash of thunder, followed by a flash of lightening woke Rhoda with a start. For a moment, she stared at the priest in confusion, and then at Bronwyn standing motionlessly by the fire. In the stillness, a candle in the corner of the chamber flickered wildly, before guttering and going out. Mesmerised, she turned towards it, watching as the smoke spiralled up towards the ceiling, before coalescing into a shadowy form.

Bronwyn smiled. *She* was here. *Tangwystl*. She was sure of it: she could feel her presence; could feel her anger radiating in the air around them. Satisfied that she had done what was needed, Bronwyn tucked the empty packet back into the folds of her cloak before throwing a final glance around the room. Briefly, her eyes came to rest on the rafters above the bed. As if she were searching for something. Then with a nod, she left to resume her vigil outside the door.

From her chair Rhoda watched her go. Then steepling her fingers in front of her face, she began to pray.

Joanna slept. She dreamt that she was floating beneath the rafters of her chambers at Castell Hen Blas. Curiously she looked down. Below her, her body lay inert on a bed, her white shift spread above her thighs but still covering the mound of her belly where the child squirmed inside her, desperately trying to get out. In the corner, a candle flickered and burned low before being extinguished by a sudden gust of wind.

Feeling strangely detached, Joanna floated nearer. Beside her body the shadowy figure of a priest prayed earnestly over his rosary, the beads clicking noisily in an otherwise eerie silence. Rhoda sat behind him in a chair, crumpled like a doll, praying to her own gods through twisted fingers. Only Bronwyn stood alone. Near the fire, which burned hot and acrid in its pit at the centre of the room. Crossly, Joanna called out. Wanting to tell them to stop what they were doing; that she could see and hear them, that it was not necessary to pray for her when she was right there, above them. Strangely, only Bronwyn seemed to know that she was there. Not in her body as she should be, but floating above it, and her strange grey eyes came to rest on her briefly, before, without a word to the others, she turned and disappeared quietly from the room.

Then suddenly the dream changed.

Joanna was floating above a meadow. A lovely green meadow, with bright red poppies and blue cornflowers scattered among the grasses. She was there with a woman. A beautiful woman, with long red brown hair, and eyes the colour of honeyed mead.

The woman seemed familiar somehow. Her eyes. She knew those eyes from before, somewhere ...

Casually, the woman reached out to her. Imploring her to leave her labours and cast away her pain. To come with her on a journey away from the effort of childbirth. She laughed a pretty laugh, and tossed her hair. Beckoning, coaxing Joanna to join her on the other side, to run free in the meadows, and amongst the flowers ... for all eternity ... *to give up the child that she laboured so hard for* -

Joanna floated for a while, tempted by the lure of the beautiful woman standing in the meadow before her. It was peaceful here, and she was weary. And her body seemed a long way away now as the pungent smell of flowers filled her senses ...

Then suddenly the dream began to lift, and she could hear a familiar voice calling her back. *Llywelyn's.* Her lips formed his name soundlessly. Slowly she looked around. Searching for him. He was down in the hall, his tall frame silhouetted by the light of the fire. He was calling her to him, his love enveloping her like a cloak, his promises dripping from his tongue like honey from a silver spoon. She tried to call him, but no sound came. Behind her the woman was desperate now. Holding out her arms, beseeching her. Joanna wavered. Llywelyn was getting smaller now, drawing away from her a look of infinite sadness on his face.

'Wait! Oh, please wait!' she cried. Then without another thought for her beautiful temptress, she turned and ran to him: to the safety of his arms; to the promise of a better future ...

Joanna woke suddenly. The woman was gone. The meadow was gone. She was back in her solar, and back in her body. An owl hooted in the distance, and mercifully the pain subsided as the child slipped the world.

Outside in the bailey, the rain had stopped suddenly and a loan cloud slid across the moon, throwing the castle into darkness. Bronwyn frowned, then, turning away from the window, she watched as

Llywelyn rushed up the stairs and pushed past her into the solar.

Moments later he was cradling Joanna's half-conscious body in his arms, she could hear him whispering words of love as he stroked the hair back from her damp face. Rhoda stood behind him, clinging to the tiny child that Joanna's frail body had finally spewed out onto the stained sheets.

Bronwyn stepped back into the shadows, confused. It seemed that the princess would live after all. And with her would live the child. The third and final son of Llywelyn Fawr. Grandson of John, King of England. And now, the legitimate heir to Wales.

Yet, the runes had foretold that both would die ...

'He shall be called Dafydd,' a voice said, startling her.

Bronwyn span round. Mab stood behind her. Older than the hills, and wiser by far. Her gnarled fingers wound round the knob of a willow staff. The only thing that supported her old bones now.

Bronwyn shivered. Words hung between them. Words uttered long ago: *'The boy, Gruffydd, is not destined to sit on the throne of Gwynedd. There is one who comes after him. One who is more worthy. You cannot change that, you do not have the power. You must stop meddling in things you know nothing about ...'*

'You knew all along, didn't you!' she hissed, and with a wild shriek she launched herself at Mab. The old woman stepped back, her eyes rolling in fear. The last thing she saw, was the thing she had failed to see in the fire she'd scried. The fire that had brought her here to witness the birth of the next prince of Gwynedd. And that was the knife that gleamed briefly in the light of the flames, before it sank deep into her bony old chest. Snuffing the life from her.

Mab, had failed to see her own destiny ...

Chapter 22

Aber, North Wales, May 1212

It was a gloomy day, late in May, when the Welsh princes finally came to Aber, well aware that the time had come to mend bridges. To forge a truce with Prince Llywelyn, the lord of Gwynedd. No longer could the King of England be trusted to restore them to their lands. Llywelyn was their only chance.

First to arrive was Maelgwn. He looked older than Llywelyn remembered: a short, stocky man, with receding red hair, cold blue eyes, and a permanent frown etched on a face now lined with worry on account of the number of his sons held hostage by John.

'I hear you have a boy now, by Joanna, the king's daughter,' he said, accepting the goblet being offered to him by a page no older than his son Rhys, the lad Gruffydd had taken under his wing at John's court in Easter.

'Yes,' Llywelyn said shortly. 'We called him Dafydd.' He picked up his goblet and peered at the contents, unsure about how to deal with the conflicting emotions that overwhelmed him each time mention was made of his new offspring, following the unsettling events of his birth at Castell Hen Blas.

'And yet, you have asked us here today to talk about forming an alliance against the English King? I find that mighty strange, given your new circumstances? After all, John is the boy's grandfather, and that cannot be ignored,' Maelgwn continued.

'It changes nothing,' Llywelyn said shortly. 'John is still our common enemy. It's time we all realised it, and fought together against him - rather than among ourselves.'

'And if we agree to a truce today, how can we trust you?'

'How can I trust *you*, more to the point!' Llywelyn snapped.

Maelgwn rounded on him, his blue eyes frosty with dislike.

'Do you really think that Gwenwynwyn and I have forgotten the years of bad blood, betrayal and downright mistrust that have passed between us? he hissed furiously. 'You made a grave mistake sneaking in and taking Powys behind Gwenwynwyn's back whilst he was being tricked by John. And you made an even graver mistake when you took Ceredigion from me! Even you cannot be unaware that your past history has not been good when it comes to forging alliances of confidence amongst your own chieftains!'

Llywelyn glared at Maelgwn, then looked away. Was he being foolish throwing his lot in with the Welsh princes and fuelling a rebellion against his father-in-law? Particularly when Joanna had at last produced the heir that John had promised would inherit the Perfeddwlad.

Cursing himself, he pushed the thought aside. No, he knew he would never be content with Dafydd inheriting Wales by dint of an agreement made under subjugation at Bangor. Especially one extracted in full view of those chieftains who'd fought on the King of England's side and taken relish in seeing him cowed at his feet. No, he wanted Wales for himself. But above all, he wanted, no, *needed,* to restore his pride in front of the princes. And the only way to achieve that was to put aside past differences and make a truce with these men who were now John's enemies. He could no longer dance to John's tune and sit back and do nothing like he had for the last ten months.

For a moment his mind focused on Gruffydd and the danger he was putting him in. Then, feeling slightly sick, he pushed the thought aside. The lure of his land was too great to consider the consequences of his actions for more than an instant. Gruffydd was now, and always would be, a casualty of war.

Just then the door to the hall was thrown open with a bang, and Gwyn entered with Maelgwn's brother, Rhys Gryg – or Rhys the Hoarse – a name given to him because of the tone of his gravelly voice, an affliction he had acquired following an illness when he was a boy. Following close behind him was the prince of Powys. A great bull of a man, with a mane of black hair tied back with a leather thong, and the thick neck and sinewy arms of a warrior well used to pulling the heavy Welsh bow so feared by the English.

Gwenwynwyn nodded at Llywelyn, his dark eyes fierce, his formidable countenance not dimmed by years of captivity, rebellion and counter rebellion.

Llywelyn relaxed suddenly. He realised that up till now he had been holding his breath. He'd been sure of Maelgwn and Rhys, Hywel and Madoc, and many of the other chieftains. But not of Gwenwynwyn, the fearsome ruler of Southern Powys. The man whom *he* had betrayed by stealing his lands behind his back. There was never any certainty where that man was concerned, for he bore grudges easily, and the loss of his lands to Llywelyn in the past could easily have led to his refusal to join him now in an alliance against the King of England. Llewelyn was painfully aware of how much he needed the man's support, for without him there would be no trust forged between the chieftains. And without that, the alliance would be weakened, and the rebellion lost before it was even won.

Outside in the bailey, a commotion marked the arrival of the remaining princes who were laying down their swords outside the door before being shown into the great hall. Llywelyn felt the stirrings of emotion, the first he had felt in months, for they were congregated at last. All in one place, and all to the same end: to free Wales once and for all of the scourge, the pariah, the leech that was the King of England.

When they were all assembled, Llywelyn gazed around himself for a few moments longer. Then he raised his hands for silence. 'As you all know, I met with the papal legate recently - just before Easter, here in this very court - and with him he brought news: the pope has formally released us from the interdict and freed us from our allegiance to the King of England.'

There were nods of approval all round.

'But there is more,' he said, pausing. 'I have despatched envoys to France in the hope of forging a treaty with King Phillip.'

A murmur went around the room.

'If we succeed,' he continued, 'the Holy Roman Empire will be behind us all, for the pope has plans to formally declare John a heretic and depose him as king. If that occurs, Phillip will have papal dispensation to invade England and place his son Louis on the throne in John's stead!'

'But what of the hostages? What of our sons? John will surely hang them if we proceed with this rebellion with you at its head,' Madoc interrupted, coming forward.

A rumble of agreement went up and down the hall.

'Nay, John will not murder innocent children!' Llywelyn replied confidently.

'How can you be sure?' one of the lesser princes asked. 'Old King Henry hanged Welsh hostages without a qualm. Why not John?'

Llywelyn paused. 'He will think of his own daughter in another land first,' he replied recklessly. 'A daughter who has a son now - his grandson, his flesh and blood - Dafydd! He will think on that first before he acts. He might have my son and yours, but I have his grandson and daughter right here in Wales.'

'His daughter is illegitimate,' Madoc said scornfully. 'What if he does not place much store by her?'

'He does ... he will,' Llewelyn replied, uncomfortably aware that he was not at all sure that was the truth.

'And where are your rebellious nephews, Gwenwynwyn? What of Owain and Rhys, where are they today? Do they not support us?' Another voice.

All eyes turned on the prince of Powys, who until that moment had remained silent.

'My nephews are weak,' Gwenwynwyn replied. 'They prefer to sit on the fence and lick their wounds. They think that by declining to join us they will be in a better position to serve the king if our rebellion fails and he calls upon them again.'

Llywelyn breathed a sigh of release. Gwenwynwyn had spoken, had used the term *'our rebellion.'* It was enough for Llywelyn.

'Are you with me, my lords?' He looked around the hall.

The nods at first were hesitant. But then Gwenwynwyn came forward and a murmur of approval went around the room as the two men faced each other and openly clasped hands for the first time in many years.

'That's settled then,' Llywelyn said, nodding at Gwenwynwyn. 'In the meantime, my spies inform me that John is headed north to aid the King of Scots. He leaves the bulk of his army mustering at Portsmouth ready to invade France upon his return. We must strike whilst he is occupied elsewhere. Whilst he does not yet know that we, the Welsh, are united against him and ready to rebel!'

Chapter 23

Castell Hen Blas, North Wales, July 1212

Joanna threw down the latest letter from Llywelyn. 'Christ's bones, Rhoda! I cannot stay here any longer. It has been more than two months since Dafydd's birth, and I feel like a prisoner!' she exclaimed, kicking the rushes angrily.

Rhoda shrugged. 'But you are safe here, *cariad*.'

And the woman Bronwyn is gone ... gone back to Aber in disgrace, but with no proof against her for the death of the old woman, Mab, or the witchcraft that occurred that night ...

The words hung in the air between them, and Joanna looked at Rhoda suspiciously. 'I don't want to be safe, Rhoda. I want to be with my children - what are you hiding from me? You are my servant. Speak woman!'

'Nothing! It's just that Llywelyn advises you that you would be better off staying here and getting some rest without the children. Anyway, he is often engaged on border raids now that he has forged an alliance with the other chieftains - you would be as lonely there as you are here. And you have no interest in war and politics,' she added.

'Ah, but that is where you are wrong,' Joanna said crossly. 'I would have much to say to Llewelyn - forging alliances behind my back, and going to war when we now have the child my father has promised will inherit Gwynedd. What is he thinking to achieve by going behind my back anyway, especially after I humiliated myself in front of my father at Bangor to win this fragile truce. Richard says he has had to write to father and advise him to return from Scotland and sort it out.'

She moved restlessly towards the window and stared out at the distant mountains. 'Anyhow, I won't be lonely. Not with the children around me, I won't! No, I won't have it! You will pack now, Rhoda. We make leave for Aber as soon as possible!'

Rhoda picked up Dafydd's shawl which Joanna had discarded on the floor, then crossing to the cradle she tucked it over the sleeping baby.

'I wouldn't advise it, madam,' she said, her back turned so Joanna couldn't see her face.

'Leave that!' Joanna exclaimed. 'It's too hot anyway. Just stop arguing, and go and pack as I ask!'

Rhoda sighed, and picking up her skirts she headed for the door, pausing only to look anxiously back at Joanna. 'Please,' she said, 'will you not reconsider? I have the most awful feeling that no good will become of you returning to Aber before you are summoned.'

But Joanna did not hear her, as heading for her desk she picked up pen and paper and happily began to plan ...

Chapter 24

Aber, North Wales, July 1212

'When is Mama coming home?' Elen asked, placing a hand on Llywelyn's knee and staring up at him with her huge blue eyes.

'Soon, *cariad*, soon. She is still recovering from the birth of your baby brother.'

'Harrumph!' Adda put down the letter he was reading and turned to look at Llywelyn, his eyebrows raised. 'Are you sure that's true, and you're not really keeping her there because you don't trust her with the knowledge that in her absence you have instigated yet another rebellion against her father, only this time with the full backing of the Welsh princes? Or that you're treating with Phillip of France to put his son on the throne of England in his place?'

Llywelyn scowled at his brother, then taking Elen's hand he led her to the door. 'Go and get Papa some of those marchpane sweets you helped cook make earlier,' he said, patting her on the bottom and making her squeal.

'Well?' Adda prompted, watching Elen go.

'Joanna has always known of my intention to form an alliance with the other chieftains, if and when the opportunity arose. She knows that I will not rest until Wales is mine. I have fought for it since I was a boy, Adda, and I am not about to give up now. You of all people should know that! As for Phillip, she will know about that soon enough!'

Adda frowned. He was not particularly fond of Joanna, he never had been. But for some reason, he felt slightly uneasy that Llywelyn had left her alone at Castell Hen Blas with the child that was, whether Llywelyn liked it or not, the blood child that John had sworn would inherit the Perfeddwlad should he be born. Nor was he convinced that keeping secrets from her was a good thing.

He sighed. 'There are other ways of settling your grievances with John without going to war - why not put a stop to this rebellion whilst you still can? Bring Joanna back to Aber, Llywelyn. Write to John, make much of Dafydd's birth.' He sighed. 'Is it not possible just to accept John's terms and go on ruling as you have done for the past eleven months. On the understanding that now you have a legitimate son, when he comes of age, he will inherit Gwynedd as John promised?'

'When Dafydd comes of age!' Llywelyn said scornfully. 'Why, that is not for another fourteen years under Welsh law! In the meantime, do you not think that John will find an excuse, any excuse, to invade Wales again - to strip me of all that I have left and subjugate me further? He has succeeded in making me a puppet prince already! I am not a chief, or even a ruler in my own land. He has made me *his* subject. *His* vassal. And even that is not enough, for he hates me with every bone in his body, and he will not rest until he has seen to my total destruction!'

'But -' Adda began.

'No buts, Adda. It's already too late to take that course even if I wanted to, for John has got wind of our rebellion and is on his way back from Scotland as we speak.' Reaching into his pocket Llywelyn withdrew a letter. 'You had best read this. It's from an informer of mine in John's court. He represents the barons. You should know that I'm arranging a secret council of war soon with those chieftains I know I can trust to discuss his proposition. I sincerely hope the fight has not gone out of you, brother, for I shall need all your determination and wisdom behind me if we are to proceed with the course of action proposed in this letter and win back Wales once and for all!'

Aber, North Wales, August 1212

A hazy shimmer hung over the distant peaks of the *Eryri* mountains, as Rhys and Maelgwn arrived at Aber for the second time since their alliance with Llywelyn in May. Dismounting, they left their horses to be fed and watered in the bailey, before picking their way curiously through the discarded pieces of scaffold that were now propping up parts of the *llys*.

'I have to admit I'm intrigued as to why Llywelyn wants us here so urgently,' Rhys commented, glancing at his brother.

'Well, it can't be the campaign for it's going to plan, so he can have no complaint. In fact, I've scarce time for this,' Maelgwn grumbled, 'my *teulu* is fighting without me!'

Handing their swords to a guard on duty, they followed a page up a flight of stairs and into a small chamber occupying the second floor of the tower, which proved a cool respite from the burning heat outside. Llywelyn was waiting for them inside the chamber, along with his brother Adda. Llewelyn's cousins, Hywel and Madoc, sat silently around a table at the far end of the room with the prince of Powys, the remains of a recent meal still before them.

'I trust that you have no concerns about the campaign?' Maelgwn asked, accepting the goblet of wine being offered.

'On the contrary,' Llywelyn said, smiling faintly. 'In June alone, we regained most of the Perfeddwlad. Only Degannwy and Rhuddlan castles proved impossible to penetrate, mostly due to bad weather and rough terrain. So far, John has responded with only one minor expedition to bring relief columns into Wales under Brian Delisle, which failed miserably.'

Rhys grinned. 'And between us, we have successfully taken most of the forts that John erected last summer,' he said, putting down his goblet. 'The English are scared. They can scarce take a piss on route between castles now, else they risk losing their heads to warriors who hide in the surrounding forests ready to ambush them. John's Lieutenant at Mathrafal burned the castle rather than let it fall into our hands, and his soldiers travel in large bands lest they be caught and slaughtered in the same way.'

Gwenwynwyn stood and came to stand alongside the brothers. He had a deeply suspicious nature which had now come to the fore. 'If this is indeed true, then why have you summoned us here so urgently, and secretly without the other princes?' he asked.

Llywelyn looked at him directly. 'I assume that you will have heard by now that John has learned of the spread of our rebellion. He's on his way back from the Scots border and headed for Nottingham as we speak. I've been reliably informed that he has put aside his plans to invade France, and is preparing instead to march on Wales. To that end, he has re-directed his army to muster at Chester on August 19th, and assembled more than six thousand labourers and two thousand carpenters ready with axes to re-instate his castles in his wake. He wants to end the war with us once and for all. And it seems he is very confident of winning.'

'We know all that,' Maelgwn said, interrupting his flow. 'You've already sent word. And, of course, we've been preparing,' he added hastily. 'But then you haven't brought us all this way just to tell us that, have you?' he asked, his eyes suddenly wary.

There was a loud scrape as Madoc pushed back his chair. 'Why don't you get to the point, cousin,' he cut in rudely.

Llywelyn glared at him. 'All in good time!'

Ignoring him, Madoc came to stand in front of the men. 'There have been developments,' he said bluntly. 'But it is for you to say if it's madness as I do.'

Maelgwn turned to Llywelyn and raised his eyebrows questioningly.

Throwing his cousin a look of reproach, Llywelyn put down his goblet of wine and, crossing to his desk, he extracted the letter that had given him so many sleepless nights since its arrival.

'As you know, we can now count among our allies Phillip Augustus and Pope Innocent. But crucially there is another development afoot. One which, up until now, I have not placed much store by. It concerns John's barons. I could not be certain of it before, but then, several weeks ago, I received this letter from an informer of mine at the English court.' He paused, and waved it at the expectant faces before him. Then, taking a deep breath, he continued.

'Among other things, my informer confirms certain rumours amongst a prominent group of magnates relating to the King's treatment of their wives and daughters, and the growing rate of dissatisfaction at court with his rule in general. *But,* and more importantly for us, he has confirmed the existence of a plot amongst the barons themselves. One in which they are planning to assassinate John. And if we agree, it will be carried out here in Wales with our help. And I have no reason to mistrust him,' Llywelyn said, handing the letter to Maelgwn, who scanned it quickly before passing it on to the others.

'I'm sorry I haven't spoken of it before. I did hear mention of such a plot when I was a court at Easter, but I needed to be sure that we weren't being fed a red herring and it was not really a plot to catch us in treasonous activities against the king. I also needed to be sure of all you first. It's a big step, and, as you know, the punishment for treason is certain death.'

Llywelyn watched the men's reactions carefully. After a moment he saw a look of dawning understanding spread across Rhys and Maelgwn's faces, followed by one of undisguised respect on Gwenwynwyn's as he handed the letter back to him with a grunt of approval. Only Madoc left. Picking up his tunic and marching out without a word.

Llywelyn watched him go thoughtfully. It had taken a while to convince Adda that his decision to join the barons was not a reckless one. But Madoc had not been swayed. Quickly he put aside his misgivings. It was too late now. Then glancing at the letter which was burning a hole in his hand, he crossed to the table and pushed it carefully under a map, before returning to the others and picking up his goblet of wine.

'If you are all in agreement, then there's someone here who wishes to speak with us,' he said, nodding to Hywel, who stood and opened the door to an adjacent room. 'He is here in secret, which is why I needed to be sure of you all first. For this man has risked his very life to be here at all ...'

Aber was deserted when Joanna arrived. She had hoped to be home sooner, but she had been taken ill with milk fever and been delayed by yet another month. She could see now that during her long absence the battlements and part of the tower had been propped up by scaffold. In the bailey geese scattered as she picked her way round a discarded hay cart, and headed for the main door of the hall, calling for Gwladys and Elen as she went. Behind her, the sentry frowned at Rhoda who stood with Dafydd in her arms, watching wearily as Joanna flounced about, her temper beginning to get the better of her after her long ride.

'Where is everyone?' Joanna demanded, returning to the sentry. 'Where's my husband? My children?'

'The children are down by the river with Bronwyn,' the sentry replied. 'Along with several guards for protection. There was a minor skirmish back in June when some English soldiers broke through, and they are no longer allowed out alone. My lord had already decided to make repairs to the *llys,* but they were brought forward after that happened,' he said, indicating the wooden scaffold. 'He wants to make Aber safer.'

Joanna spied some horses at the trough, and her attention was grabbed for a moment. 'Whose are they?' she asked, transferring her gaze to a very fine stallion being walked around the bailey by a fair-haired young man of about her own age. She couldn't be sure, but she thought she recognised him.

'Prince Llywelyn has visitors,' the sentry said firmly. 'He did not expect you home today.'

'Well, is there at least someone who can serve food?' Joanna enquired icily, losing interest in the horses.

'Most of the household been given the day off,' the sentry said mournfully. 'Though there is a cook and a handful of servants within. But they're not expecting you.'

Joanna sighed and, taking Dafydd from Rhoda, she began to make her way back through the rubble.

'Prince Llywelyn doesn't wish to be disturbed, Madame,' the sentry called after her. 'He's meeting with the chieftains in the tower.'

'He will see his wife!' Joanna muttered to herself crossly. 'And he will explain this mess!' she finished, kicking a bit of scaffold out of the way to make a path to the hall.

Inside the *llys,* Joanna headed up the newel stairs leading to her chambers at the top of the tower, hoping to find Llywelyn there. Halfway up she paused on a narrow landing, home to several chambers which Llywelyn often used for his private business. Suddenly a door opened and Llywelyn's cousin, Madoc, pushed past her and hurried down the stairs without a word, leaving it slightly ajar. Joanna paused. A shaft of light spilled out onto the landing, and the unmistakeable murmur of men's voices could be heard from within. Feeling like an intruder, Joanna hesitated. But then womanly curiosity got the better of her, and tucking Dafydd firmly under her arm, she moved closer and peered through the gap.

Llywelyn stood in the middle of the room. Immediately, she recognised the faces of several Welsh princes gathered around him. He was holding something in his hand. A letter? After a moment he disappeared, only to re-appear and pick up a goblet of wine before issuing an order to someone out of sight. The atmosphere in the room was tense. Expectant. Joanna felt a prickle of unease run down her back. She was about to knock and go in when she heard a door in the background open and close. There was a brief silence, then Hywel came into view. With him was another man: a tall man, powerfully built, well-groomed and, unmistakeably, of Norman birth. A man whom Joanna realised had no business being in Wales ...

It seemed an age before she finally crept numbly away. Even then it was only because a pair of blue eyes suddenly confronted hers through the gap, before, with a click, the door was shut decisively in her face.

Joanna spent the rest of the day in such a state of extreme agitation that when, surprised to learn of her unexpected arrival, Llywelyn came to find her in the hall that evening she quickly made her excuses and went to bed early.

Beside her, in the large oak bed, little Elen and Marared slept curled together like spoons, exhausted from the excitement of having their mother home with the new baby, but tearful that she would leave them again. Gwladys and Gwen had gone to their own beds, both having examined their new brother and judged him in their own particular way - Gwladys had been besotted with him immediately, exclaiming in delight as he curled a small hand around her thumb and fastened his pale blue eyes on her face. Gwen on the other hand had greeted Dafydd with a look of undisguised dislike, before turning sly eyes on her step-mother and asking grudgingly after her health.

Rolling over on her side, Joanna curled into a ball and stared into the dark, her mind returning unhappily to the afternoon's events. The man she had seen with the chieftains in the tower was unmistakably Eustance de Vesi, one of the more prominent barons from within her father's closest circle. She knew him well enough by sight to know she was not mistaken. She had needed no excuse to stay and eavesdrop after that, for there could be no good reason why a man so closely associated with her father's inner circle should be here in Wales. And so, without further qualm, she had stepped up to the gap and listened.

At first the men had talked only of the Welsh uprising, and the threat from the king's army which had been re-diverted from Portsmouth and was now heading for Chester - the place from which it would advance on Wales and subdue the rebellion once and for all. The voices had droned on, becoming more and more monotonous as they discussed the king's plans to re-build his castles in the wake of his assault and bring them back under the control of the royal demesne. Alarming as all this was, none of it was new to Joanna. Still puzzled by de Vesi's presence but no wiser, she had been about to leave when abruptly the conversation had turned to the existence of a treaty between the Welsh princes and

Phillip of France. One in which, she was astounded to hear, Llywelyn had denounced the treaty she had made with her father on his behalf the previous year.

Incarcerated in Castle Hen Blas after Dafydd's birth as she was, she had heard nothing of this, and she could only listen numbly after that as Llywelyn and de Vesi had gone on to discuss a plot by the English barons to assassinate her father on Welsh soil and put Phillip's son, Louis, on the throne in his place.

With Llywelyn now allied with the French king, all the barons needed to carry out the plot was for him to allow her father's troops to advance far enough into Wales so that he could be surrounded and either killed by his own army, or captured and held prisoner by the Welsh princes. That was why de Vesi was here, to make sure of Llywelyn's support. And that was why the *llys* was being fortified: to serve as a place of imprisonment, unfair trial and perhaps even murder … if her father was not already not dead on a Welsh battlefield.

But it is no less than your father did to Matilda de Braose, or Arthur of Brittany ... a small voice whispered ...

Pressing her fist into her mouth, Joanna let out a muffled sob of despair. What was she to do? Betray Llywelyn, or sacrifice her father? Making a decision Joanna swung her legs out of bed, and pulling a robe from the clothes pole she wrapped it around her shoulders. First, she needed to see proof. Llywelyn would not come to her tonight, she knew. Nor had she gone down to dinner. For even knowing that de Vesi would be kept out of sight, she preferred the company of the children to that of the men downstairs who plotted murder.

The fire had practically gone out in the hearth, but with a little effort and a few bits of kindling she was able to rouse a flame and light a candle. It took only minutes to creep down the newel stairs to the chamber the men had occupied earlier. Crossing to the table Joanna pulled out several draws, then finding nothing within she ran her hands over the surface. In no time at all she found a letter, carelessly hidden under a map. It took her only a matter of moments to read before, tucking it back in its place, she left the room.

It was with a heavy heart that she then put quill to paper. And it was gone midnight when she instructed her most trusted messenger, Owain, to deliver it. It was to be taken to England and handed over to no one but her father. To be put in his hands alone. Only when she had seen to Owain's safe despatch did she made her way to the chapel to pray.

The chapel was quiet when Joanna entered, save for a lone candle that guttered on the altar. She paused to let her eyes became accustomed to the darkness, before making her way down the nave to her usual seat. As she sat down she became aware that she was not alone - there was a young man sitting in the pew in front of her. She hesitated for a moment, wanting to be by herself, but at the same time afraid to ask him to leave in case he questioned her.

In the event, they both sat still for some while. Joanna tried to pray, but the events of the night lay heavily on her mind, blocking any thoughts of the scriptures. All she could think was that her father would probably laugh if he saw her praying, for he alone had cast aside the church and led Wales asunder. The only reason she could pray here now was because Llywelyn and the Welsh princes had come to terms with the pope, and once more the church doors were open in Wales.

After a while the candle guttered low, and the young man in front of Joanna stood to light another. As he returned to his pew, Joanna caught a glimpse of his face. 'Its Will de Braose, isn't it?' she whispered, leaning forward so as he could hear.

The young man turned a downy cheek to her. 'Yes, my lady,' he mouthed.

'I saw you this afternoon by the stables, did I not ... holding the reigns of a large stallion?'

'Yes, my lady, you did,' he confirmed, turning his head fully to her so that his large blue eyes focused on her face.

Joanna hesitated. She recalled him as being a passably good-looking boy when he'd served her at her wedding, many years ago. But now, well now he was probably the most handsome young man that she had ever seen.

'You're with him?' she asked suddenly, meaning de Vesi.

'Yes.' He hesitated. 'But your secret's safe with me.' Then, seeing that she didn't understand. 'You might have seen me in the bailey with de Vesi's stallion, but I saw you spying on your husband in the tower earlier - I was the one who shut the door,' he paused. 'I also saw you leaving the tower room just now, before dispatching your messenger. It didn't take much to put two and two together - but I shall not tell Prince Llywelyn,' he added hastily.

Joanna stood, suddenly very angry. 'How dare you spy on me!'

'I was not spying!' he said archly. 'Merely observing. As I said,' he repeated. 'I shall not tell Prince Llywelyn. But I shall warn the barons on my return to your father's court, of course ... to give them time to flee. After all, I owe it to my dead grandmother and my uncle Will not to let anyone else suffer as they did in your father's hands,' he said, echoing her own disturbing thoughts on the subject of Matilda's death earlier. 'We leave in an hour,' he continued, 'so we will not be far behind your messenger.' With that, Will stood, and taking her hand he bowed low over it. 'Let's just say that your beauty deprived me of all sense, Princess. So much so, that I saw nothing else.'

With that he melted down the nave, leaving Joanna shaking in his wake.

Chapter 25

Nottingham Castle, England, August 1212

'What the blazes!' John literally threw himself to his feet, knocking the table over with a crash, sending platters of meat and goblets of wine flying everywhere.

Richard glanced at Will Longespée, John's half-brother, in fright. Seldom had he seen his father in such a rage. 'What! What is it, Will?' he whispered. 'What can have happened?'

Silently, Will passed over the crumpled piece of parchment the fleeing messenger had thrust at him. He already knew its content, but he had been too afraid of John's temper to divulge the matter to John himself, so he had let others do it for him.

Richard scanned it for several long moments, then coming to the part that had undoubtedly enraged his father so much he raised his eyes to Will's, seeking acknowledgement of what he'd read there. Will merely nodded. He knew as Richard did the consequences of such information, for it stated quite clearly that Llywelyn had made a treaty of alliance with the French king. A treaty in which he and the princes of Wales agreed not to: *'truce, peace or even parley with the English.'* In short, Llywelyn had formally denounced the agreement his wife had secured from John the previous year, and taken up arms with Phillip of France.

'How did he come by this?' he asked his uncle quietly.

'He has spies everywhere,' Will said. 'Both here and abroad. John has suspected for a long time that Phillip's been planning to invade England with the intention of putting his son, Louis, on the throne. I doubt this was the news he was expecting, though, for if such a treaty exists, then Llywelyn is flagrantly throwing the terms of his surrender back in his face.'

'No wonder he's angry!' Richard murmured. 'He only came to the terms because of Joanna's intervention. If he'd done as he intended and had Llywelyn imprisoned, or even killed, he would have been less of a problem now.'

'Why now, though?' Will asked. 'Why would Llywelyn sign a treaty and take up arms against John when he now has Dafydd, the legitimate son that John promised will inherit Gwynedd should he die?'

'Because,' Richard said, throwing down the letter, 'he is stubborn, selfish and conceited. He doesn't want a legitimate son to throw a shadow over his own greatness. Like his grandfather before him he wants to add "great" to his name in the future, and he will let nothing stand in the way of that!'

Up on the dais, John was still venting his spleen by throwing goblets and plates at any hapless maid or page who had the misfortune to catch his eye. Richard met Will's eyes again, and realised they were of accord. Nodding, he turned and left the hall. He was going to despatch a courier for Wales as soon as possible. There was no time to be lost. For once in his life he was going to do the right thing by his sister. He was going to warn her of the consequences of their father's rage. Rage brought on by her husband's latest treachery in taking the field against him along with his enemy, Phillip of France.

Behind him he heard a clash of armoury as guards were ordered, and instructions given, to start building gallows out in the bailey.

As Richard suspected, John was about to use his Welsh hostages in retaliation. They were going to hang.

But even as he wrote, he knew that there was no hope whatsoever that his letter would reach Wales in time. And even if it did, he was sure Gruffydd would not be spared.

The King of England sat down to dinner that night oblivious to the sound of hammering floating in from the bailey, and the frightened cries of the Welsh hostages as they were ushered towards the dungeons to await execution. John's only instructions whilst he made his way through dishes of quail, sturgeon and boar, before rounding his meal off with figs in syrup, was to make sure that the hostages of the families closest to Llywelyn be the ones to be hanged first. 'Leave Llywelyn's bastard till last, though,' he added as an afterthought through mouthfuls of sturgeon.

Even Isabella didn't have an appetite that evening, picking at very little before making an excuse to take the children to a quieter part of the castle when John was sufficiently in his cups not to notice.

The next morning, John began drinking early. Richard immediately took it as a sign that his father might be showing some regret at his rash decision, but as the day went on it became apparent that this was not the case. Dismayed, he and Will approached the dais where John sat brooding, but nothing they said would move him from his course of action. The more that John drank, the angrier he became. Sometimes, he veered towards his original plan of invading France, but then in a flash his obsession and hate for Llywelyn and the Welsh princes would overcome him again. Together they pleaded, alongside the Marshall, that hanging the hostages would only result in a fresh outbreak of hostility; that instead of it simply being a war between countries, it would become personal with the families demanding *galanas* – compensation - for the murder of their loved ones. Richard argued that if John cared for his daughter then he would not hang her stepson. That he would not kill the lad because of the hate he harboured for his father. Would not cause a rift between his daughter and her husband out of spite towards the man, even in war. Then he argued that Gruffydd could prove useful to John in his dealings with his son-in-law in the future: a bargaining tool no less; an instrument to thrash Llywelyn with and alienate the other princes if their sons were hanged and his boy was not. Every argument was covered that morning, and at one point Richard thought that he might find the noose around his own neck. But John would not relent. The boy was to be hanged. And it was to be done at dawn the next morning, in full view of the court. After which, his body would to be cut down and sent to Llywelyn as a final and terrible reminder of John's displeasure.

When the hangings began at noon, Richard went to ensure that Gruffydd was kept in his rooms out of sight. John had ordered that he be left to last, but he clung to the hope that his father's anger would be assuaged long before that moment and Gruffydd would be reprieved. Then with his heart weighing heavily in his breast, he returned to the hall to see if, by some miracle, he could find a way to distract his father enough to delay the hangings – if not until his messenger had returned from Wales, then at least long enough to think of another plan to save Joanna's stepson.

The hangings were still going on when dinner was served. Isabella sat subdued at one end of the table as a mark of her disapproval, every now and then holding a scented pomander to her nose. Although not given to feelings, even Richard could see that Isabella was moved by the plight of the hostages, especially the younger ones, for she had given her ladies leave not to attend the meal.

As the sound of struggles and the cries for mercy drifted in from the bailey: a heart-breaking mixture of guttural Welsh and English, dishes of quail, perch and venison were being served by pages no older than some of those being hanged. Richard felt sick. He was not the only one. His uncle Will sat white faced beside his wife who could not prevent the occasional fat tear escaping down her cheek to plop on the table before her. William Marshall soon made his excuses of office and left, having touched nothing on his plate, leaving his down-in-the-mouth wife, Isabel, to play lady-in-waiting to the queen. And the Earl of Chester who had arrived earlier in the afternoon with William de Warenne, the Earl of Surrey, sat amidst the crisis looking appalled at events which, in his opinion, openly cast doubt on the king's sanity.

Only when the tables were cleared did John summon a travelling minstrel to play in order that he might no longer hear the sound of the executions still drifting in through the open windows. Then leaning back arrogantly in his chair, he watched as several pages entered the hall bearing something on their shoulders. It was a coffer packed full of the hostage's personal belongings – rings, brooches, goblets and silver plate, tokens of affection from their families left behind in Wales. They would be returned to Llywelyn on the morrow, along with the body of his son. Richard, still reeling with the horror of it all, was preparing to make an exit when the

Marshall suddenly re-entered the room looking both nervous and apologetic at the same time.

'A courier has arrived from Wales, Sire. I came across him outside. He carries a message that he will only entrust to you. He says it's from your daughter, Princess Joanna, and that it's of the upmost urgency.'

Making his way to the table, the courier fell to his knees before John. Richard recognised the man from a handful of Joanna's most trusted messengers. His name was Owain. For a moment he was confused. The messenger bearing his letter to Joanna had only left for Wales yesterday. Even if the man had changed horses and ridden all night, it was impossible for him to have made it there and for a reply to have been drafted and dispatched in such a short a time, for it was upwards of three days travel to Gwynedd and the same by return. Feeling light-headed, Richard sat down again. How then was Joanna's most trusted messenger here? And why now? Suddenly hope flared in his breast. Perhaps God had answered his prayers and he had not failed Joanna after all. He could only hope that the urgent nature of the communication now burning a hole in the courier's hand, albeit not related to the events outside, might just be the miracle needed to stay the horror of further executions.

Taking the letter from the courier, John dismissed him and prised the seal swiftly apart with his bone-handled eating knife. For several long moments he stared at it in disbelief. Then dropping it on the table, he stood abruptly and roared at the guards nearest to him to stop the hangings. Richard was still coming to terms with this sudden turn of events, when a commotion in the doorway signalled the arrival of another messenger, again bearing an urgent letter meant for the king alone. This time John fairly snatched it from the man's fingers before ripping the seal apart in his haste to read it. Then letting out a furious bellow, he threw it across the room where it was swiftly joined by the knife. After that pandemonium broke out with John shouting for everyone to leave the hall, save for Richard, the Earls of Pembroke and Chester, his cousin, de Warenne, and his half-brother, Longespée.

Time seemed to stand still for Richard as John paced back and forth on the cold stone flags, he had often witnessed his father in the grip of a rage, but seldom one as cold and calculating as this. It was Longespée who finally broke the silence. 'Sire, might you tell us what ails you?' he asked, glancing nervously out of the window where several of the hostages still hung from the gallows, swinging slowly back and forth in the soft breeze that accompanied the fading evening light.

John paused to wipe a hand across his brow which bore the sheen of several days heavy drinking. For several long moments, he considered their faces. Then apparently satisfied that they were all innocent of the crime he was about to disclose, he nodded.

'Take a look at this,' he said, waving the letter from Joanna in front of them. 'It was sent by urgent messenger as you witnessed, and it tells of a baron's plot ... a conspiracy ... against me!' He paused, and glared at each of them intently again, making beads of perspiration break out on Richard's brow, before throwing the letter down on a table by the window.

'Well, is it true? he demanded. 'Are they plotting to over throw their king?'

De Warenne took a step towards him and put a hand on his arm, but John brushed him aside and rescuing the other letter from the floor he thrust it at him. 'As you saw, I received this letter immediately after. It was also sent by urgent messenger. Only this time it was from the King of Scots warning me of the same thing. What are the chances of that, I wonder? Well, what have you to say?' he demanded, scanning their pale faces. 'Do the barons plan to murder me in the press of battle if I invade Wales? Or are they arranging for me to be captured by my enemies and murdered in secret? Is there treachery in my court, right here, right under my very nose? And if so, why!' he finished angrily.

Richard felt a flood of relief. Even though the letter was clearly not a response to the tragic events currently being played out in Nottingham, nevertheless it had contained news dire enough to have stayed John's hand - to have diverted him from continuing the bloody murder that he had embarked upon the day before – and for that he was grateful.

For a moment he wondered how Joanna had come across such information, for judging by the look on Will's face and those of the others in the room, none of them knew of any such plot in their midst. Then he realised that she could only have got the information from Llywelyn. And if that was the case, then Llywelyn must have been secretly plotting with the barons. Perhaps even without her knowledge. Maybe even whilst had been in the last throws of her pregnancy. And if Joanna had found out about it by accident ... if Llywelyn did not know that she had written ...

Suddenly, Richard was angry. Not with his father, but with his brother-in-law. Angry that, not only would Llywelyn risk Gruffydd's life by making a treaty with the King of France, but that he could also risk Joanna's by making her a traitor in the eyes of Maelgwn and the other chieftains, who would likely imprison, maim or even kill her if they knew what she had done.

It was Longespée who stepped forward first. 'Your Grace,' he said, addressing John delicately. 'I know nothing of a baron's plot. And even if there were one, they would not be so foolhardy as to carry it out, I'm certain.'

'There are always rumours though, Sire,' Richard interrupted, throwing a desperate glance at Longespée; willing him to understand, needing him to help keep John's mind occupied by something other than resuming the hangings of yesterday. For by whatever means Joanna had come by the information, he was not about to waste it if it could reprieve Gruffydd. He would worry about Joanna later. 'Grievances born out of jealousy, perhaps,' he continued, his mind racing. 'It is common knowledge that the barons resent your interest in their wives and daughters - though of course they should be honoured, Sire,' he added hastily, seeing John's face. 'Then there are the taxes,' he said slowly, his mind awakening to several whispered conversations inadvertently interrupted of late. 'It's well known that the northern barons resent paying scutage for a foreign war conducted from here, in the south. It is perfectly possible that they are aggrieved enough to plot, they are a troublesome lot the northern barons.' Richard held his breath, he could see John's mind working.

'Mmm, yes, De Vesi, Fitz Warren, they have always been rebels, malcontent's,' John acknowledged thoughtfully. 'And then there's Derby and de Clare, and the numerous other Irish lords who have held grudges since my Irish campaign. Even the Scots. And of course, there is Reginald de Braose and his brother Giles who are already in exile in France, and are crucially linked to Llywelyn by the French treaty. They are all capable of murder and treachery. He glanced at the Marshall, and Richard could see him weighing up the possibility that he was still not trustworthy because of his mistake in harbouring members of the de Braose family in the past.

'There must be others who bare grievances, Sire. Geoffrey of Norwich is ever discontent in his role as an exchequer,' Richard interrupted, desperate by now not to incriminate any baron in particular, but only to cause enough of a diversion so that John might forget all else; cease his hanging of the Welsh hostages, and concentrate instead on his own safety and the threat of immediate danger from within his private circle.

'Grievances! Plots!' John roared suddenly. 'Do I not clothe them, bring them to court, bestow them with gifts, gold, jewels, and feast them like they were royal personages themselves! They want for nothing, do you hear? Nothing!'

'Of course we might be wrong about this, we have no proof, only Joanna's letter and that of the King of Scots. The barons, they might -'

But Richard was cut off by John's almighty bellow.

'*They* know what the penalty for treason is. For regicide, no less! I would have every last one of them brought to court to answer for this, I shall drag the truth out of them myself!' he roared, flinging the chamber doors open with a crash so that the startled guards beyond sprang to attention. 'Go! Go!' he shouted, running down the corridor as if he had the hounds of hell on his heels, leaving a flustered William Marshall and Longespée to muster the guards and restore calm and order whilst Richard and de Warenne followed hastily in his wake.

Later that afternoon when John was calmer a council was called, and in light of both Joanna's and the King of Scot's revelations it was agreed to put off his invasion of Wales so that he could begin another campaign - one in which he would ferret out the ring leaders of the plot that the letters were alluding to, and bring the barons to heal. Isabella found herself suddenly plucked out of her sumptuous chambers along with Henry, her eldest son and, most importantly, John's heir, to be taken to a place of safe-keeping known only to the Marshall, Longespée, de Warenne, Richard and a few others. The rest of the children were to be shipped off to separate places of safety.

Alone now, and with only his most trusted of retainers, John planned his campaign to quash his baron's treacherous plans. Letters were drafted and sent demanding hostages from all those he suspected of plotting against him. Before the afternoon was out word came that Robert FitzWalter and Eustance de Vesi, both of whom John initially suspected of being the ring leaders, had somehow been warned that their impending betrayal had reached the king's ears and they had already fled court: FitzWalter to France, and Eustance de Vesi to Scotland, confirming his worst suspicions that there was indeed a nest of traitors lurking in his midst. John, upon hearing of their flight, immediately gave instructions to destroy two of FitzWalter's castles: Benington in Hertfordshire, and Castle Baynard in London. Geoffrey of Norwich was not so lucky. He fell into John's vengeful hands and was thrown into jail before he had a chance to flee the city, and Richard guessed no fair trial would be given. He would simply be left there to rot. Finally, John increased all security around him, becoming paranoid at the slightest thing, even sending for a food taster to sample all his food before consumption.

And John had not forgotten Gruffydd, or the few remaining Welsh hostages. He had left that to last, knowing that it might be an advantage to stay the executions in light of this new turn of events. Sitting back in his chair at the end of a long day, he laid down his quill and regarded Richard and Will with narrowed eyes. 'Were all Maelgwn's sons hanged?' he enquired searchingly.

'Only the youngest, Rhys. The others died earlier after being castrated on your orders, Sire,' Richard said, closing his eyes hoping to rid himself of the image of the small, pale, red haired boy pleading for his mother as he was dragged crying towards the gallows.

'And what of the others - how many?' he asked.

'Twenty-eight in total, Sire,' Richard replied. Will nodded affirmation.

'And Llywelyn's brat?' he enquired softly.

'He is safe under lock and key, Sire,' Longespée replied.

John nodded. 'I said to save him to last, not to spare him!'

Richard gulped, not wanting to look at John lest he betray himself. 'There was not time, Father. Not with night fall, and the letter -'

'Never mind,' John said, standing. 'He might yet be of use to us, not least for the fact that we've had to put the Welsh invasion on hold for the time being. It was fortunate for him that Joanna's letter arrived in the nick of time, and that my resources are needed elsewhere for now. Bring the boy here,' he said suddenly. 'And have the others confined to the dungeons until I decide what to do with them. They are lucky. Very lucky indeed.'

When dragged before the king, the cold, core of hate inside Gruffydd's belly hardened, and he raged silently. He was to be held separately from the few remaining hostages. Probably at another castle, for he was now the most single valuable asset in keeping the Welsh chieftains at bay and curbing any other plots they might conceive along with John's barons. However, he would not be kept in the comfort he had been accustomed to up until the day of the hangings. At the hands of King John, he would be made to suffer for his father's continuous treachery. Sometimes, he wished he had hanged along with the others.

That night, he slept for the first time as a prisoner in the Black Tower. Beside him, he felt the rushes upon which he lay stir, as if someone was there with him, and for a moment he thought he felt the whisper of a soft breath upon his cheek. Curling up in a ball, he clutched the tiny brooch he'd found amongst his belongings when he'd first been taken hostage. It was warm. And when he finally fell asleep, it with tears on his cheeks and dreams of his mother running with him through a meadow.

John said nothing further to Richard or Will Longespée about his decision to spare Gruffydd. But later that night Richard wrote another letter to Joanna, telling her how sick he was by what he had witnessed over the past few days. Gruffydd was safe for now and he was heading for Chester, he said. He needed to see his sister and forget the horror that he had witnessed. Perhaps she would come there. His plans were to make a new life for himself. To start again. He knew the letter would arrive long after the first, and that Joanna would have lived through hell with Llywelyn, but as he handed the message to the travelling minstrel to deliver as he wended his way through Wales, Richard could only hope she would forgive him.

Chapter 26

Aber, North Wales, August 1212.

'No, he would not have! He could not have!' Joanna whispered in horror, grasping the side of a table to steady herself, her mind trying to shut out the appalling news.

'But he has!' Llywelyn shouted, throwing down the letter from Richard that he had intercepted from the clutches of the breathless messenger, his face apoplectic with rage. 'He was building the gallows even as Richard penned this letter to you! He has hanged them! Every last one of them ... even the children, some as young as seven! Maelgwn's son, Rhys, was only that age, for God's sake!'

For a moment, Joanna swayed, remembering the freckled, red-headed boy with the engaging grin that she had met at Easter. The boy had been deeply attached to Gruffydd, she recalled. And for once, she had seen her stepson show some real affection for another human being other than his sister Gwenllian.

'Gruffydd!' she whispered, looking at Llywelyn's white face. 'Llywelyn, your son! Your son!' Frantically she clawed at Llywelyn's sleeve, ignoring the appalled faces of the servants in the room. With an almighty shove Llywelyn pushed her away, his face full of hate. Hate that she knew was directed at her for being her father's daughter. For a moment, she tottered on the brink of hysteria, not recognising the man who stood before her. He looked feral; ready to kill her.

'I will write! I will write! Now! To my father! Maybe he has not yet done it and he will reconsider if I beg him personally!' she cried in despair, spinning on her heels and running to the door, even knowing in her heart that it would be too late, for the letter was dated three days previously – days in which they would all have been hanged. Then suddenly remembering, she stopped short and turned to look at Llywelyn, slumped now against the table with his face buried in his hands. Tentatively, she took a step back towards him again. 'I have already written,

Llywelyn,' she said. Calmer now. More sure of herself. 'On another matter - to warn my father of the treachery within his court. Treachery aided and abetted by you and the chieftains. God help me, I thought I was doing wrong then – that my love for you should have blinded me to your cause. But now. Well now, that letter may have saved your son's life. One day you may thank me, for if it got there in time it may have stayed his hand.' But Joanna knew that Llywelyn barely heard her confession in his misery.

'What have I done? What have I done?' he whispered, his voice broken, not appearing to notice as the children's nurses made the sign of the evil eye and gathered them together one by one: Elen, Marared, Gwladys, Gwen, even little Dafydd, to be ushered, dragged or carried from the room, as if he had put a noose around their necks, too. And she knew that he did he did not notice that the hall had grown cold, or that the fire had gone out in the hearth before, finally, the servants slipped away to spread the gossip.

She only knew that in his despair, Llywelyn didn't notice anything at all ...

Llywelyn sat for a long while by the cold hearth, drinking himself into a stupor. It had occurred to him to take his *teulu* and ride to Nottingham, but what would that achieve? By the time he got there, they would all be long dead anyway. Signalling to a frightened maid to bring another pitcher of wine, he staggered to his feet, nearly tripping over Gelert. The hall was practically deserted. Had been since he'd ranted and raged at Joanna, venting his agony at the thought of Gruffydd's inert body dangling from the gallows: his face swollen and purple, his tongue protruding from his mouth. Swaying slightly, he stood and went to look out of window, but the sky was dark. Too dark to see. He ran a hand over his face, but the image of his son dangling from the gallows would not shift. Staggering a little, he crossed to a pallet and threw himself down, falling immediately into a deep, drunken sleep.

She was there. At first in full beauty: red brown hair cascading over her shoulders, her creamy white breasts suspended temptingly over his mouth, her hand down his chausses. He felt himself harden. His loins ached for her ...

Tangwystl ...

Suddenly, his eyes flew open. Above him loomed a spectre of the most terrible kind. Her hair was no longer red brown, falling in abundance over her shoulders. In its place, tufts of wiry grey sprouted from a chalk-white skull, sockets empty where once her eyes had sat. Eyes the colour of honeyed mead. And her skeletal body with its bony pelvis was astride him. Riding him like a harridan from hell ...

Our son, Llywelyn ... what have you done to our son ...

Llywelyn woke with a shout of horror to find Joanna staring down at him, a look of terror on her face.

For a moment, she stood transfixed. Then in a chocked voice, she said. 'I came to beg your forgiveness. To offer you hope that in writing a letter without your knowledge, I might yet have saved your son. But now, I think it is you who needs mine - forgiveness, I mean. May your son be safe, Llywelyn. And may you be safe from whatever haunts you ... for I fear you will never be free!' Then, crossing herself fearfully, Joanna fled from the room, leaving Llywelyn wondering if he would soon be haunted by his dead son, too.

The next few days were a nightmare for there was a gulf between them that neither Joanna nor Llywelyn could bridge. News had come that John had definitely hanged the Welsh hostages at Nottingham, and that it had been done whilst he was in the grip of a furious temper following the discovery that Llywelyn had indeed made a treaty with the French. But it had come in dribs and drabs. Travelling peddlers claimed to have information about the victims or survivors, at a price, of course. And bands of players re-enacted their gruesome last moments at the hands of the wicked King of England, for the titillation of any who would watch.

Llywelyn had not ventured from the *llys,* for fear that word might come in his absence concerning the fate of his son. Instead, he had written and despatched messengers to the other princes whose sons were being held hostage at Nottingham, offering neither condolences nor hope, but urging them not to listen to the spread of ugly rumour until it could be verified. Then he withdrew into himself. Not eating, drinking too much, and sleeping it off for several hours at a time, before waking to repeat the whole cycle again.

The children were really too young to understand what had happened. Only Gwenny understood, but strangely she didn't judge Joanna.

'Gruffydd's not dead,' she said simply, when Joanna sat down beside her on her bed, the day after the news of the hangings had arrived.

'How do you know, Gwen? You cannot know, surely?'

'But I do,' she said, tugging at a knot in her hair with an ivory comb, before placing it carefully on her bedside table. 'My mother told me.' For a moment, Gwenny looked at her stepmother with pity. 'You must know that she will never let Dafydd rob Gruffydd of his rightful inheritance?' she asked.

'I -' Joanna didn't know how to reply as the girl stared at her impassively with her strange eyes. Eyes the colour of honeyed mead. All at once Joanna remembered where she had seen those eyes before. They were the same eyes as the woman in her dream; the same eyes that had once belonged to the *creature*, the *thing* she'd witnessed astride Llywelyn in a sickening parody of lust and passion, the night they had thought Gruffydd dead. A shiver of fear ran down Joanna's back, and she opened her mouth to speak, but nothing came out. Instead she fainted. When she came around, she knew instinctively that she had get away. To run before she lost her sanity to this place. But then, knowing that it was futile to run away from her husband and lord, and that the other chieftains would be out there seeking revenge for the loss of their children, Joanna collapsed on her bed in despair instead.

It wasn't until the end of August when a minstrel arrived at Aber with a message. Joanna woke to be told that Richard was in residence in Chester Castle. She was to meet him there. He had news, the message said. But there was more. The mistral claimed that he had been summoned to play for John on the night of the hangings, and that he had witnessed them himself. Moreover, he had left the castle with Richard who was bound for Chester, and he knew conclusively that Gruffydd was still alive.

Llywelyn looked at the minstrel in disbelief. 'You were there?' he asked, as beside him Joanna clung to the arm of his chair for support.

'Yes, my lord,' the minstrel stammered.

'Playing?'

'Yes, my lord.'

'Good God!' Llywelyn exclaimed.

'I can assure you, your son was alive when we left.'

Llywelyn looked stunned. 'And the others?'

'Dead, mostly,' the mistral said, tugging at his moustache nervously, having clearly come to the conclusion that the fierce Welsh prince before whom he stood might execute him for being the bearer of bad news, rather than rewarding him for the knowledge that his own son was alive.

But Gruffydd *was* alive. And for that Joanna was grateful. However, her conversation with Gwen prior to the minstrels arrival had left her confused and all the more determined to leave; that and the fact that she'd had enough of Llywelyn leaving a room as soon as she entered it as if he could no longer bear the sight of her. At last, after much soul searching, Joanna decided she would travel to Chester. She would take the children; baby Dafydd could meet his uncle. She would be safe there, she reasoned, under the Lord and Lady of Chester's roof for a while. She would not venture further. Then, upon her return, she would travel to Llanfaes with the children, and she would stay there until she was sure about her future. Whilst she loved Llywelyn, she needed time to think and to make the right choices. With that decided, she went to inform Llywelyn.

'Why, *cariad*?'

Joanna flinched. Llywelyn had not used that term of endearment in a very long time.

'I must. I must think, Llywelyn. You have to allow me that at least. I need to see Richard first, though - to understand what has changed, for I no longer know my father,' she said sadly. 'That he could murder children -' her voice trailed off.

Llywelyn turned away tiredly. 'You may have a week, Joanna. A week with your brother, but no more. However, I cannot allow you to take the children.'

'But -'

'Especially Dafydd. He must stay in Wales. He particularly must not fall into your father's hands.'

'You would hold Dafydd as your hostage?' Joanna spat. 'Do you hate me that much, Llywelyn?'

'The decision is entirely yours as to whether you stay in England, or even return to France. I could stop you. You are my wife and I have every right too. But I will not. The children will be waiting for you at Criccieth in one week's time. If you do not return, you will no longer see them, for you will no longer be permitted into Wales.'

Llywelyn watched Joanna ride away that afternoon with sorrow in his heart. Once she crossed the border into Chester there was every possibility that she might not return. And could he blame her? He was as confused as she. Her letter had probably been the one thing that had saved Gruffydd, and for that he was grateful. But on the other hand, she had betrayed him. And for that alone, he knew a day of reckoning would come.

Turning from the window, Llywelyn summoned Gwyn and Adda. It was time to muster his *teulu* and resume the fight. Wales was still in peril. He'd had word that John was planning to send a flotilla to sail around the north Welsh coast and, wherever possible, land raiding parties to inflict as much damage as he could. He was running out of ways to contain him and his allies, that was clear. Worse than that, he was up to his old tricks of trying to set the chieftains against each other, and this time his elected supplicants were to be none other than his cousins, Owain ap Dafydd, and Gruffuddd ap Rhodri, both of whom were weak and easily lead. Llywelyn was reasonably sure that it would come to nothing. But it was always best to be prepared ...

Chapter 27

Chester, England, September 1212

Joanna's mood brightened a little as she rode into Chester to meet her brother. The road to the castle was bustling with peddlers and merchants making their way towards the outer bailey to ply their trade, selling ribbons, silks and pottery shipped from the continent to the busy port on the river Dee, from where it could be supplied to the household directly. It was a regular monthly occurrence which the Lady of Chester encouraged, for she enjoyed the atmosphere and pleasure it brought to her household: enjoyed watching as a serving lad purchased a ribbon for a giggling maid, or one of her ladies delighted over a length of peacock coloured silk said to be the latest colour favoured in the French court. Joanna watched for a while as a group of maids exchanged hard earned pennies for prettily embroidered linens and a cook bartered loudly over much needed utensils, finally leaving with nothing but a flea in his ear for his efforts. At last she made her way over the bridge, and into the inner bailey with Rhoda and her small group of guards, and leaving them at the stables she went to find her brother Richard.

Richard was alone in his chambers when she found him, the Lord and Lady of Chester having made their excuses and gone to visit neighbours, knowing that when she arrived the two would need time alone. He was gazing out of the window, looking down into the small courtyard below, and he looked tired and drawn, the horrors of the past few months having finally taken their toll on his health.

'Richard?' Joanna said softly.

'Joanna!' He turned around in delight at the sound of her voice. A few strides carried him to her side. 'You look well,' he said, kissing her on both cheeks.

Joanna sighed. 'I'm not sure that I am, Richard, after all that has happened. But at least Gruffydd is alive. Llywelyn was out of his mind with grief for a while, sure that he was dead.'

'It was your letter that saved him,' Richard said tiredly. 'Father flew into such a rage when he heard about the treaty between Llywelyn and the French king that he decided to hang the hostages on the spot. I've seen him in the grip of rages before, but never such a one as he was in that night. He was apoplectic; was practically eating the rushes off the floor.' He sighed. 'I never want to go through that again, Joanna. Maelgwn's son Rhys was only seven.' He shuddered. 'But when all is said and done, it was your letter warning Father of the baron's plot that saved Gruffydd. You alone can take the credit for that. If it had not arrived when it did, well -'

'Llywelyn doesn't see it that way,' Joanna said sadly. 'He sees it as the accidental outcome of my treachery against him. Albeit an outcome that saved his son's life. Oh, Richard, why is everything so complicated? Llywelyn now has to face the other princes who will blame him for his son living, whilst theirs are dead. They will also blame him for being married to the King of England's daughter; the woman who wrote the letter to warn her father that they were plotting against him. So you see, Richard, I am a traitor twice fold; by blood, and by my actions in trying to save father. But that's enough of me, what will you do?'

'I'm staying here for a while before heading to Dover. It's time I made proper acquaintance with Rohese, my betrothed,' he said, referring to the daughter of Faulbert de Dover, to whom which he had been betrothed since they were both children.

'Will you marry her soon?' Joanna asked, remembering the shy, dark-haired little girl she had met a handful of times at their father's court.

'Probably,' Richard said with a faint smile.

'And what of Father - will you still serve him in future?'

'Of course. I just need time to settle; to find a life of my own and have children. But what of you, Sis?' he asked, pulling her towards him and stroking her dark hair. 'What will you do now?'

'I have a week, then I will return to my husband and my children. Though I know Llywelyn calls me traitor ... and will probably do so for the rest of his life, and mine.'

'Do you love him though, enough to bear it, I mean?'

'Yes! Oh, yes, Richard. I love him!' She hesitated. 'But I fear there is another who loves him more. An old love. A mistress from beyond the grave. One who will not give him up because of a promise made long ago. And she is intent on destroying anyone in the way of her ambitions for him.'

Richard frowned. 'If you mean Crysten, then you -' he stopped suddenly. 'No, it's not Crysten. She's not dead, Joanna,' Richard said, floundering.

'I mean Tangwystl, Richard,' Joanna said calmly. 'I've seen her with my own eyes. She *is* dead. But she is not gone. And now I fear for Dafydd ...'

Richard and Joanna spent the week together. Not seeing anyone. Not even their hosts, save to attend the odd dinner out of politeness. During that time, they laughed over trivial childhood follies. But mostly they cried at the shame of their shared blood, and for the madness of their father who'd inherited the Angevin curse. They talked of their brother, John, a clerk now in London. And they talked of other brothers and sisters, scattered here and there in England and other lands where their father had left his mark. Finally, they talked of poor, bitter little Isabella, plucked from her betrothed to marry a tyrant king, and forced to live in a foreign land and bear him yet more children.

' Do you think she will stay here in England - if father dies first?' Richard asked one night as they lounged by the fire sipping good Rhenish wine.

'Oh no, never!' Joanna exclaimed. 'Never! She will abandon her children and flee back to France like a rabbit out of a bag. Once there she will marry her jilted betrothed, Hugh de Lusignan, if he's still free!' She giggled. 'I wonder where that insight came from, Richard!'

'Probably from the little minx herself!' Richard returned wryly.

Later they talked of Tangwystl. But Richard was inclined to think that Joanna's dreams and visions were the product of her overactive mind after the complicated birth of Dafydd. Only Joanna knew different. She knew that Gwen and Llywelyn both saw Tangwystl, as did Bronwyn. *Bronwyn*. A vision of

Bronwyn's cold grey eyes following her as she had floated beneath the rafters at Castell Hen Blas often haunted her at night. *Bronwyn*, whom she was now inclined to think she should have had punished and dismissed after Mab's terrible death there, but who had somehow avoided retribution for her part in it. Joanna shivered. Suddenly, she had an overwhelming urge to return to her children.

Chapter 28

Criccieth Castle, North Wales, September 1212

Joanna was kneeling in the rushes, playing with Marared and Elen, when there was a scuffle and Maelgwn came stumbling into the hall. He was followed closely by his brother Rhys Gryg, and the two guards who should have been on sentry at the gatehouse protesting loudly in their wake. For a moment, Maelgwn wavered on the threshold. Time enough for Joanna to notice his soiled tunic and bloodshot eyes, set in a face blurred and vacant from too much drink. He looked around himself, obviously uncertain as to why he was there, before taking another unsteady step forward into the room.

'Who's the mistress of this pile of -' He broke off, his eyes alighting on Joanna as she stood and carefully brushed the rushes from her skirts, before bidding the nurses to take the children back to the nursery.

'Well, what have we here?' he asked, belching loudly. Then taking a step towards her, he peered at her intently. 'Why, its Llywelyn's treacherous whore, is it not? What are you doing here? And where's your murderous husband, *my Lady of Snowdon*, hiding at Aber?' he asked insultingly.

'I am here with my children. And my *husband,* I expect, is out on border raids,' she said icily. 'As you would be. If you were sober, and had any sense,' she added, fishing for something to say to cover the fact that she'd not seen Llywelyn since her return from Chester. Silently, she crossed her fingers, hoping that he would not see past her bluff.

Maelgwn's upper lip curled in disgust. 'Shedding blood and rejoicing no doubt that his son was not murdered by your father like my sons were!' he said, his face contorting in a mixture of anger, pain and confusion. He wavered for a moment, clearly trying to form his next words, which, when they came, spilled out in a sudden rush of pent up fury. 'Well, *madam*! what do you have to say? Your husband clearly has no comprehension of what he's done - else he would have sent word before now. My wife had to find out through a travelling minstrel … she was inconsolable!' He clenched his fists as if he were about to strike her. 'Llywelyn's to blame for their deaths. And by God he shall answer for them, for he was the one who came to terms with your father. He alone agreed to offer up the sons of the chieftains alongside his own, whilst at the same time giving assurances as to their welfare on English soil! In my eyes, that makes *him* as much to blame for their murder as your snivelling, whoreson of a father, for he gave his consent to the hostage taking!'

'Please!' Joanna whispered, suddenly afraid. 'Please, Maelgwn! Just listen to me … it's not like that! Llywelyn sent word, I swear! He couldn't visit all the chieftains one by one, so instead he sent word. He's out there now intensifying his raids in reprisal for Nottingham. You must believe me, Maelgwyn! Llywelyn suffers as much as you and your wife!'

But Maelgwn was not listening. 'We trusted him when he said John would not murder children. That you as his daughter would offer a shield of protection against such a thing,' he continued furiously. 'But *he* was wrong! *We* were wrong!'

Joanna looked around frantically for help, and became aware that whilst they had been arguing a group of armed soldiers, swords drawn, had entered the hall unannounced and now surrounded Rhys and the guards who'd stood mutely behind Maelgwn during his outburst. For a moment she hesitated, confused by their sudden arrival, but unable to decide if they were friend or foe because Maelgwn had filled the space between them and was now looming over her like a big black crow.

'Look, Llywelyn knows he was wrong to trust my father, and he is sorry …' she said, desperately trying to sidle around him to see if she could find out who they were.

But Maelgwn, blind to anything but his own purpose in berating her for his troubles, grabbed her arm. 'It's too late now for remorse!' he spat, shaking her roughly.

Suddenly Joanna felt anger boil in her veins and, despite the threat, she forgot all about the new arrivals and rounded on him, totally unaware that for the first time in her life that she was about to display some of the characteristics of her father's legendary temper. 'You cannot blame my husband solely, my lord! You were sober enough when you gave up your sons. Sober enough when you agreed to sign a treaty with Phillip of France. And God knows you were sober enough when you plotted with Llywelyn to side with the barons against my father! I was there, remember! I heard you with my own ears!' She could feel herself shaking with rage as all the pent-up feelings of the past months poured out. Like a dam overflowing. Not directed at her husband as it should be, but at a man who was so overwhelmed by grief that he had fallen to the drink.

'I heard it was you who warned your father,' he said, unmoved by her outburst. 'I warned Llywelyn not to trust you. That your familial ties to the King of England would lead you to betray our cause!'

'I would that I had warned him sooner!' Joanna retorted. 'For then I might have saved your sons, too, and not just Llywelyn's! Do you think that I wanted their deaths to happen? Do you truly believe that I am so like my father that I would condone the death of innocent children for the sins of theirs? I am sorry, truly sorry that my letter was too late for your sons. But I cannot blame Llywelyn for being glad that his own son lives. And if you had half an ounce of decency in you, just half an ounce, then neither would you!'

At that moment, a second group of men entered the room, circling the first and disturbing the wretched scene.

Joanna unlocked her eyes from Maelgwn's with a gasp. Standing in front of the men was Llywelyn, looking hot and dirty from several days in the saddle. His face remained impassive as he regarded, first his wife, then Maelgwn.

'I think we should talk,' he said at last, turning to look directly at Maelgwn, before signalling for Rhys Gryg to be released. 'No, not you, *Swain*,' he said, seeing she was about to follow.

Joanna flinched. He only spoke her name in Welsh when he was displeased, for he knew she disliked it.

'We will talk later ...'

Joanna sat on their bed for so long that she thought that Llywelyn must have left the *llys*. If he had, she hoped he had left enough guards this time and ordered them not to trust anybody, even the other chieftains, for if Maelgwn's men could force their way through the main gate, then so might they. After a while she crept downstairs and, comforted by the sound of male voices coming through the chancery door, she inched closer, hoping make out the mood within.

'Its listening at doors that's got you into trouble in the first place,' Adda said, stepping out of the shadows.

Joanna jumped. 'What are you doing scaring me like that, Adda?' she exclaimed angrily.

Adda shrugged. 'I didn't mean to startle you,' he said mildly, 'I was only making an observation.'

'Well, you did - startle me, I mean,' Joanna said crossly. 'And why aren't you in there, anyway?'

'Because it's a matter between Llywelyn, Maelgwn and Rhys. What settles between them today will be the course they will follow in future. It's the course all the princes will follow, for it is not just Maelgwn who has lost sons. They need to find some common ground; regain the trust between themselves if they are to continue to fight John with Llywelyn as their liege lord, else they might as well throw down the gauntlet now and give up. But then that was your father's intention, I'm sure. With Gruffydd still alive, he is gambling that they will believe that he survived simply because of his status as your stepson. They will believe that, because it will make them feel better. They will have someone closer to home to turn on, and he is gambling that it will be Llywelyn. It's a game of chess really.'

'But they surely don't believe that Llywelyn had any real bearing on my father's decision to hang them, do they? It was that accursed treaty with Phillip which they all signed that tipped his balance. My father was pressed on all sides, Richard says he was in a mad rage, and vented that rage on the hostages in a fit of anger. And my father is not the first English king to hang Welsh hostages. Old King Henry did so before him. My father has Angevin blood,' she added lamely, realising instantly that it was a childish thing to say.

'It's not just the hostages,' Adda said. 'They don't trust *you*. But then you know that,' he finished, watching her closely.

'You mean Llywelyn doesn't trust me?'

Adda nodded, his face impassive.

'But I could not stand by and watch them plot to murder my father in cold blood!' She searched Adda's face desperately for some understanding, but it remained unchanged.

'If my letter had got there sooner, then all the hostages might have been saved. Not just Gruffydd. They would call me *saviour* then, would they not?' she whispered.

Just then the door opened and Llywelyn stepped out of the room, followed by Maelgwn. It didn't take long for Joanna to realise that she was once more in a compromising situation. Moments later Llywelyn raised his right hand and struck her fully across the face. Then he marched out of the *llys* and mounted his horse, leaving her lying crumpled on the floor.

Alone with Adda, and a triumphant Maelgwn staring down at her.

Chapter 29

Llanfaes, Anglesey, September 1212

Although Tindaethwy, the *llys* at Llanfaes, was his main palace on the island of Môn, and the place which he would normally bring his court, there was a smaller manor nearby which was quieter and better suited to Llywelyn's mood at the present time. And so, here he was. Restlessly pacing the lengths of its panelled hall, having ridden from Criccieth with the hounds of hell on his heels the day before after striking his young wife in front of Maelgwn. He was ashamed now. Mainly of the fact that he had lashed out at Joanna. It had been the shock, he told himself, for he had not expected to find her at Criccieth with the children. In fact he'd not expected her to return to Wales at all, but instead to have fled abroad: to France maybe, where she still had family. Anywhere that she could live out her life without the horror of the past few months repeating itself.

'You're going to wear yourself out,' Adda said, putting more kindling onto the fire and prodding it deftly with a fire iron.

'I don't know what to do,' Llywelyn confessed. He crossed to one of the windows and stared out towards the straights; looking for signs of a boat bobbing on the distant water, heading towards the port. Or a chestnut mare, perhaps, galloping along the track that lay between the sandy shore and the manor house. Any sign that Joanna might have followed him. That he might be forgiven. That they might at least talk. Seeing, not unsurprisingly, that she had not, he turned away and pulled up a chair by the hearth. Then beckoning a page over with a flagon of wine, he set his mind to unravelling the real reasons for his sudden anger with Joanna, which all seemed to stem from the fact that she was her father's daughter. The man he hated most in the world ...

That night, Llywelyn slept restlessly as images of Tangwystl invaded his dreams. He thought he felt her touch; her hot breath on his face as she slowly lowered herself down on him and he gave himself up to her. Then, as the bells rang out the midnight hour, he heard the sound of horses in the bailey and the low murmur of voices as a sentry hailed the visitors. Moments later Joanna's warm body was pressed up against his, and he could feel the hot tears on her face as she held him tightly.

'I thought I'd lost you,' he whispered, his voice cracking with emotion.

'Never!' She wiggled closer. 'Whatever happens, you will never lose me, for I love you more than anyone else in this world. Even more than my father, Llywelyn.'

Llywelyn turned, and rolling on top of her, he kissed her urgently. 'More than anyone?' he asked, still aroused by dreams of Tangwystl.

'More than anyone,' Joanna repeated brokenly, as a pair of impossibly blue eyes came unbidden to her mind.

In the corner, Tangwystl stirred. Angered at the intrusion, but slowly awakening to the boundless possibilities that hung in the room and mingled with the heavy scent of lust. Watching as Llywelyn pulled his young wife into his arms and made love to her. As if he would never let her go.

Chapter 30

Trefriw Hunting Lodge, Snowdonia, Wales, November 1212

Llywelyn reigned his horse in at the foot of the flinty mountain track from which he had just descended. Behind him lay the ancient woods, the trees twisted and knarred with age, where they had first spotted the stag in a grassy clearing. Shielding his eyes from the glare of the snow, Llywelyn searched for him. But he was gone. His tracks already disappearing in the new flurry of snow that had begun to fall from the heavy sky. Lowering his hand, he was surprised to find that he felt none of the usual frustration which generally accompanied the loss of a quarry. Instead he felt an overwhelming sense of relief that, like his son before him, the stag had escaped death at the last minute and was free to live another day.

The crunch of horse's hooves in the snow brought Llywelyn back to the present as Thomas Corbet pulled his mount up alongside him and reached for his wineskin, holding it to his lips before offering it to his friend.

'Have you heard from Gruffydd since Nottingham?' he asked, as if reading Llywelyn's thoughts.

'Not recently,' Llywelyn replied, taking the proffered skin. 'Joanna's still sends enquiries on my behalf, but her brother Richard doesn't move much in court circles now. I never thanked her, you know,' he said suddenly. 'For it was, without a doubt, her letter that saved Gruffydd's life. If she hadn't warned John of the baron's plot when she did, I fear he would be dead along with the others.

There was a pause while Llywelyn drank deeply before tucking the skin at the bow of his saddle. 'And the north, is it still on a civil war footing? Is John still taking hostages and punishing those he suspects of conspiring against him?' he asked casually.

'Yes,' Thomas replied. 'He's doing his best to stamp out the revolt, but disaffection amongst the barons isn't dead yet. Even now, it's being fuelled by FitzWalter in France who is declaring himself a martyr; telling all who will listen that he would rather live in exile than serve a heretic king and live under interdict. Ridding England of John is still the barons' primary objective. The only way for him to win back their loyalty is too give in to their demands and sign the charter they're proposing to reduce his power. That would require him, among other things, to re-instate their rights and stop stealing their wealth through unbridled taxation. Personally, I can't see him doing that at the moment, can you?'

'No. No, I can't. He would hang more hostages, incarcerate others illegally, and generally commit murder and mayhem before submitting to such a thing,' Llywelyn said softly, thinking of Maude de Braose and her son, Will.

'You'll have heard that the Marshall has persuaded John to make peace with the pope?' Thomas asked, throwing him a sideways glance.

Llywelyn nodded. 'Yes, I'd heard,' he said, wanting to hear more, but knowing that Thomas had already taken risks by coming to Wales to visit his friend, without divulging too much information about John's activities to his sworn enemy.'

Thomas, however, obviously had no such qualms, and after only the briefest of pauses to wipe away a drip that had formed beneath his nose, much to Llywelyn's relief he continued anyway. 'John's envoy is on his way to Rome as we speak - to meet with the pope's legate, Pandulf Verraccio. He hopes to agree terms along the lines of those offered last summer. The Marshall finally made him realise that the only way to prevent Innocent from declaring him an enemy of Christ and deposing him as King, is to accept the Church's absolution from excommunication. If he continues to refuse absolution, then Phillip will be offered both the realm and the Church's blessing in his stead.

'Harrumph! Llywelyn spluttered. 'Well, let's just hope that John doesn't get his appeal through in time then, eh? Phillip's already tottering on the verge of invasion. With the pope's support, it will be seen as righteously ridding the church of a heretic king. The way will be clear then for the barons to put Phillip's brat, Louis, on the throne.'

He retrieved the wineskin and took another mouthful before continuing cynically. 'Of course, we both know that Phillip has been preparing the way for months, portraying himself as the protector of Christianity and spiritual welfare across Europe, and John the heretic violator of the church's riches.' He thrust the wineskin at Thomas and grinned.

'We also know that, whatever happens, Phillip will invade anyway. With or without the popes blessing. And whilst John is occupied elsewhere, I shall be busy reclaiming my own lands!'

Thomas laid the wineskin on top of his saddle and frowned. 'Be careful, Llywelyn,' he warned. 'Phillip's not as secure in his plans to put Louis on the throne of England as he seems.' He looked around him, as if he expected a band of the king's men to spring out of the bushes and arrest him for treason, before continuing in a low voice. 'I shouldn't really be telling you this, but you'll probably have heard anyway.

Llywelyn raised his eyebrows and waited.

'Phillip has quarrelled with many of his own magnates. Primarily, Count Renaud of Boulogne, who's recently revived the coalition of princes in the low countries who once served King Richard. He's also at odds with Count Ferrers of Flanders, who is himself no longer certain of his position in France - on account of the fact that he's foreign and only acquired the county through marriage, which makes him unpopular among the people.

'And?' Llywelyn prompted.

'What I'm trying to say,' Thomas said, throwing a worried look at his friend, 'is that the odds have turned. Phillip now has enemies on his own soil. Friends to John who will support him in his claim for Normandy and Poitou, and who will support him in an invasion of France if he chooses to take that route. I know that at the moment John appears weak; that he lingers on the cusp of madness, wavering between his various enemies here and abroad wondering who to attack first. But in reality, he's still a force to be reckoned with. And if he goes to war with France and wins, what will become of you? You will have lost one ally completely, and the other will be weakened. John will then turn his attention back on Wales and his enemies at home, thinking he's invincible. For that's what madness does, my friend. It makes you believe you can do anything. It makes you its cruel and evil servant. If John comes back triumphant, he will come back a monster. And it will be a monster with nothing to lose! Think on that before you make more plans to win back your lands by supporting Phillip. And above all, remember that you're risking Gruffydd's life for a second time if John returns victorious and begins his subjugation of Wales again!'

Suddenly Llywelyn was angry. 'For Christ's sake, Thomas, I can do nothing more about Gruffydd - he is, and always has been since this whole sorry stand-off begun, a casualty of war!'

Contrite, Thomas leaned over and patted Llywelyn's shoulder. 'I'm sorry, I shouldn't have said that, perhaps I spoke out of turn. But might I suggest that you placate John by formally naming Dafydd ... Joanna's son ... as your heir before he leaves for France again? That way he is less likely to harm Gruffydd, or look to Wales for trouble when he returns.'

'The undertaking to ensure that only a son by Joanna may inherit from me was made in times of peace when I contracted to marry her,' Llywelyn snapped. 'When I was made to swear upon it again at Bangor, it was under far different circumstances. And now. Well, now I'm no longer sure that I want to stand by a promise made under duress, for it means that I am giving in all too readily to John's wishes.'

Thomas looked shocked. 'But if you defy him and refuse to formally name Dafydd as your successor, then John may yet murder Gruffydd out of spite!'

Our son, Llywelyn ... what have you done to our son ...

Without warning the sound of Tangwystyl's voice, followed by the vision of her ghostly form astride him the night that he had believed Gruffydd to be dead, entered Llywelyn's mind, and he jerked sharply on his horse's reigns causing it to whinny in protest. Spooked by his sudden actions, a robin abandoned its solitary search for grubs in the snow and flew instead to a nearby Rowan bush to fluff up its feathers in protest. Taking a deep breath Llywelyn peeked a glance at Thomas, wondering if he'd noticed. But his friend was gazing thoughtfully into the distance. At another bird, flying low over a marshy field.

It was a raven.

'Well, I for one am getting cold standing here arguing. This infernal Wales of yours will be the death of me, you'll see. Let's hasten back to the lodge before we freeze to death!' Thomas said, suddenly spotting the heavy snow clouds marching their way.

Letting his breath out slowly Llywelyn looked around. 'Honestly, you Englishmen, you have no stamina for the hunt when the elements are against you. Still, the stag can wait another day, and I could do with some good food and wine to warm my belly!' And shooting guttural orders to his men, he had them round the hounds up ready to make haste back to the hunting lodge. But even as they picked their way back along the familiar deer tracks, Llywelyn couldn't rid himself of the unsettling feeling that was beginning to hang over him like a dark, malignant cloud: the feeling that something, somewhere, was very wrong …

Later that night, in the hall of the hunting lodge at Trefriw, the men sat down to a meal of game caught the day before. Thomas, unashamed of his not inconsiderable appetite, plucked himself a large portion of the roast boar before passing it on to be devoured by the hungry huntsmen and faithful retainers of the hunting lodge.

'Where's Gelert … is he ill?' Thomas asked, frowning at the dogs milling about in front of the roaring fire, waiting to be fed. 'It's not like you to go hunting without him, Llywelyn,' he observed, waving his hand towards the pack.

Llywelyn snorted. 'No, but the silly old man got caught in some brambles this month past, so I've left him to keep watch over Dafydd and Joanna at Beddgelert,' he said, referring to the newly built palace that had recently been completed nearby – another place from which he could hunt or simply escape to with Joanna and Dafydd, perhaps even Gruffydd, if and when he eventually returned home.

Thomas's eyebrows rose. 'I thought Joanna didn't like the place – I seem to remember that it's a bit remote where it is in the footholds of the mountains, and out of the way of civilisation.'

Llywelyn shrugged, remembering Joanna's protests when he had told her that he would prefer her to wait for him in the palace whilst he went on to Trefwir to hunt with Thomas. 'Well, that's as maybe, but as Gelert's hunting days are over, I thought he might enjoy a new role as their guardian and protector. I do miss him, though,' Llywelyn added wistfully. 'He has a nose like no other, it's just a pity his legs can't keep up with it nowadays!'

'Thomas laughed, and standing he crossed to the hearth to warm his hands contentedly in front of the roaring flames, oblivious to the frown that crossed Llywelyn's face as he thought of his favourite hound curled up in front of another fire with his wife and son, patiently awaiting his return.

The solar was silent and chilly as Joanna rocked baby Dafydd in his cradle. She was exhausted and longed for her bed; just to feel the warmth of its heavy covers and the softness of its plump pillows beneath her cheek. But she was reluctant to retire for Llywelyn was away with Thomas, staying at his hunting lodge for the night, and without his presence here in this strange new palace at Beddgelert she felt vulnerable. Outside, the snow had begun to fall, deadening all sound save that of wolves baying in the distance. She wished again that Rhoda was beside her. But she had suddenly been taken ill, along with Dafydd's wet nurse and several other servants, who were now being cared for in the village away from her and the children. Now, apart from the guards on duty outside, the only other person not ill was Bronwyn. Bronwyn, who had simply slipped back to Aber and into her routine as Gwenny's companion as if nothing had happened at Castell Hen Blas on the eve of Dafydd's birth.

On the other side of the room, Bronwyn watched from the window seat as the shadows grew deeper and Joanna's eyelids fluttered, but bravely she resisted the urge to fall asleep. Even now, even knowing that she had failed at Dafydd's birth to fulfil Tangwystyl's dark wishes, she found herself trying to carry them out anyway, and she was surprised by how much she now hated the mistress she had once loved. The mistress to whom she had made such a rash promise on her death bed.

Reluctantly, her hand curled around the small vial of powder that she'd secured from a wise woman as a precaution as she made her way back to Aber all those months ago. She had not thought to use it until she was compelled to visit Beddgelert with Joanna, but as soon as they had arrived she had found herself lacing the servant's food with its contents to make them ill.

Beside her, the shadows stirred, reminding her that it was nearly the darkest part of the night and she would get no rest until it was done. In the corridor a sconce flickered, then went out. Only the soft snores of Gelert, asleep by the hearth, and the howling of the wolves outside penetrated the silence.

'It's time …' Bronwyn whispered into the dark, hoping that this time, if all went as planned, she would be free from Tangwystyl and the madness that was threatening to take over her mind forever. Then, taking a last look around, she hauled herself to her feet, and picking up the vial she crossed to where Joanna dozed keeping her vigil by the cradle.

Joanna woke with a start. Was it her, or was it excessively hot in the room? She glanced towards the fire where Gelert lay, his tail banging against the floor rushes as he dreamed of chasing rabbits across the valleys as he had in his youth. She yawned, and then realised that Bronwyn was standing silently by her side, a strange look on her face.

'Won't you retire now, my lady?' Bronwyn asked quietly. 'You are sorely tired I fear, and would want to be refreshed for the return of Lord Llywelyn on the morrow. I can watch over the child for a while, if you like? You can get some sleep, and I will bring him too you later.'

Joanna ran a weary hand across her face, before glancing warily at Bronwyn. It was unlike the woman to offer her services elsewhere in the household these days, other than to chaperone Gwen to whom she was fiercely devoted. Normally the woman kept out of the way, knowing instinctively that she was disliked and feared by the other servants since Mab's ghastly death at Castell Hen Blas. Anxiously, she looked around for Rhoda. But then she remembered that she and all the other servants had suddenly been taken ill and were not allowed near her in case they passed on their ailment.

'I can look after the little one for a while,' Bronwyn offered again. 'What harm can be done by getting some sleep? Else you too will be taken ill …'

Despite herself, Joanna hesitated. She was sorely tired and the thought of the deep bed covered in goose down quilts in the ante-chamber was tempting. 'You would summon me immediately, ere he should wake?' she ventured, still mistrustful, but willing to grab an opportunity to lie down on the soft covers while she had the chance.

'Of course, my lady. Go and lie down and I shall bring a hot posset to aid your sleep. The little one will be alright with me for a few hours,' she said, taking Joanna firmly by the elbow and leading her towards the bed chamber.

Llywelyn paced the length of the hall restlessly. All around him came the snores of his men who had bedded down where they could for the night. One man cried out, a wounded sound like a trapped animal, eliciting himself a swift jab in the ribs from his neighbour on the adjoining pallet, and muttered oaths from others trying to snatch a few hours between watches. Llywelyn stopped in his tracks. He couldn't dispel the thought that there was something wrong with his wife and son, and making a sudden decision he shook Thomas awake by the shoulder.

'What? What is it, Llywelyn? Thomas muttered grumpily. 'Can a man not rest after a day's hunting without being woken in the middle of the night for no reason?'

'Come,' Llywelyn said urgently ignoring his protests. 'We must make haste for Beddgelert. There is something afoot there, I feel it in my bones.'

Thomas sat up and pushed the hair out of his eyes. 'Can it not wait till the morrow, Llywelyn, I am sore tired, and it is half a day's ride in this weather.'

'No.' Llywelyn said decisively, 'I implore you as a friend, Thomas. Joanna and Dafydd, they are in danger. Don't ask me how I know, I just do. Now, come, we must make haste!'

Less than half an hour later, Llywelyn and Thomas rode silently out of the stable yard, accompanied only by a few men at arms. Behind them an owl hooted, and somewhere in the heart of England Gruffydd awoke to a strange strumming noise in his head, accompanied by the feeling that all was not well in Wales, but that it might yet be to his advantage.

It was nearing dawn, and the door was open when Llywelyn and Thomas strode into the hall of the palace. Llywelyn let out a frosty breath of air and looked around. Apart from a couple of guards slumped unconscious on the ground outside the doors, there was no one about. There was no welcoming fire in the hearth, and no servant ran to greet him with a sorely needed goblet of wine and a loaf of bread to break his fast. He stood still for a moment. The silence was oppressive, eerie even. Then with his heart in his mouth he beckoned to his squire.

'Go find the servants at once!' he barked. 'I would know what the devil is going on here! I would have an explanation!' Then flinging his gauntlets down on a chair, Llywelyn made his way across the hall and up the short flight of stairs towards Joanna's chambers. The door to the solar was ajar. With his heart thudding in his chest, Llywelyn pushed it open to find the room dark, but for the glowing embers of a dying fire in the hearth.

'Joanna?' Llywelyn whispered. The room was silent. 'Joanna?' he whispered again, noting the cot standing unattended in the corner. With a quick glance around him he started towards it, only to halt when Thomas entered the room with a lighted torch.

'It's uncommonly quiet here, Thomas,' Llywelyn said uncertainly, before taking the torch and holding it high. Just then Gelert crawled out from behind the cot and bounded forward, his old tail wagging furiously at the sight of his master.

'Gelert, old boy!' Llywelyn exclaimed with pleasure, crouching down to embrace his dog, only to stand again in horror when he saw that his hands had come away smeared with blood. Sick and afraid, Llywelyn pushed the dog aside, and with one quick movement he wrenched the cot curtain open to reveal an empty crib with only a faint impression where once his son had lain. There was a moment's silence in which Llywelyn's brain sought to comprehend the situation, then with a heart rending roar he swung round to face his hound.

Gelert's brown eyes never left Llywelyn's face as the master he adored plunged his sword deep into his side.

'Llywelyn ... Llywelyn, it's not your fault,' Joanna said carefully, before crouching down by his side. 'You were not to know.'

'Llywelyn -' Joanna tried again.

Llywelyn turned his head to focus bloodshot eyes on her. 'They have not buried Gelert with that wolf?' he asked listlessly.

'No,' Joanna said gently, 'they have not.'

'I did not know,' Llywelyn said in a flat voice.

'Gelert saved Dafydd, Llywelyn,' Joanna said, taking one of his large hands in her own.

Llywelyn felt warm tears run down his face. A search of the immediate area had revealed Dafydd alive and well abandoned behind the cot, one small hand still thrust in the small mouth where he had cried himself asleep. No more than a few feet away they'd found the body of the wolf, its throat ripped out and its teeth still barred for attack.

'I killed Gelert,' Llywelyn said blankly, then getting to his feet he crossed to the window embrasure. 'He only sought to please me, to show me what he had done to save my son, and I repaid him by killing him.'

'Where were you, Joanna?' Llywelyn asked suddenly, turning away from the snowy scene out in the bailey below.

Joanna flinched, she knew this was coming, 'I told you, my lord, Bronwyn was looking after Dafydd for me whilst I slept in the ante-chamber. All the other servants had been taken ill. I was so tired. And then I began to feel ill -'

'And where is Bronwyn now?' Llywelyn asked, turning back to the snowy scene outside. 'No, don't tell me. She has left the palace, I'll warrant. Disappeared as she did before in the face of trouble.'

'I sent her for the wise woman in the valley - to help find a cure for the servant's ailments. I knew she would be blamed, but as much as I dislike the woman and would like to say she did wrong, in truth I can't. She swears she only left Dafydd alone to go downstairs and get more logs for the fire – when she saw there were none in the hall, she went outside. She said that she must have accidently left the door open and allowed the wolf entry. Again, we cannot prove that this was a deliberate act and we must act within the law, have her questioned properly. But Dafydd is safe, Llywelyn - Gelert saved him from harm, remember that in you sorrow, I beg you, please,' she urged, privately swearing that if Bronwyn ever returned, and she was pretty certain she would not, this time the woman would be banished from their lives forever. For now, Joanna was quite certain the woman was mad.

Llywelyn drew her too him and kissed the top of her head. Surprised, Joanna tilted her chin and looked up at him.

'Do you believe in premonitions,' he asked.

'Yes … yes, I think I do,' Joanna whispered, recalling some of the strange things she'd witnessed since her marriage to Llywelyn had brought her to Wales.

'Well, I had one yesterday,' Llywelyn continued. 'Nothing specific, but enough to make me come back last night because I knew you were in danger. Perhaps Gelert's death was a warning to me, I don't know. But I do know that I've not been a good husband to you, or a good father to Dafydd since he was born. But I mean to change all that now. I have lived trapped in a web of my own uncertainty; have let my hatred of your father govern my decisions for too long. From now on I must go forward with more conviction, and be ruled by my head and not my heart. In truth, I realise now that you and Dafydd together are my future. Are *Wales's* future.'

Chapter 31

Aber, North Wales, March 1213

Llywelyn's step was positive as he strode into the hall following his latest meeting with the council of princes. It had taken months of bridge-building to reunite them all after the Nottingham hangings, to placate Maelgwn in particular after the loss of his sons. But if John had thought that by saving Gruffydd from the noose he could drive a wedge between them, then he had been gravely mistaken.

An attempt to send an English fleet to sail around the north Welsh coast to inflict as much damage as possible had been seen off with as much gusto by the Welsh princes as before the atrocities, leaving Llywelyn certain that John could no longer be left any doubt that the Welsh were rallying together very nicely, despite the cold-blooded murder of their sons. However, Llywelyn thought bitterly, that alone had not been enough to deter John from seeking to revive the old expedient of divide and conquer by encouraging the hapless sons of his late uncles, Owain ap Dafydd, and Gruffudd ap Rhodri, to turn on him and challenge his leadership of Gwynedd. Llywelyn scowled. Had it not have been for the fact that John, faced with his own problems abroad, and his barons at home, had offered them very little aid in their quest, then he had an inkling that they might have fared better. But, as Adda had reported only that morning, his would-be rivals, presented with a newly strengthened coalition of princes, had failed before they had even begun. A matter that had left him breathing a very large sigh of relief.

But it was to Joanna that Llywelyn turned his thoughts as he pulled up a chair and sat down. John's efforts to drive a wedge between the princes of Wales might have failed, but the unexpected outcome of the whole sorry debacle was that Joanna herself was now the cause of arguments between the chieftains. In fact, Llywelyn was not unaware that most of the chieftains were still of the opinion that in warning her father of the baron's plot, Joanna had acted treacherously. However, for the sake of the alliance they were willing to overlook her actions when he had reminded them that in the past she had proved herself to be a valuable mediator in affairs between them and her father. Maelgwn and a handful of others, however, could not forgive her for her actions. Maelgwn couldn't actually blame Joanna for killing his sons, but he could blame her for being the daughter of the man who had, and so he wanted her banished back to England where she could no-longer interfere in Welsh matters. Without wanting to, Llywelyn remembered Maelgwn's face when she had been caught once again with her ear to the door at Criccieth. It had been a mixture of triumph mingled with hate; the sort of look he usually reserved for those who had failed to pay the *galanas* for some mortal sin against him and his family, and for whom nothing short of death was now good enough to appease his thirst for vengeance. Llywelyn sighed. He knew Maelgwn would not dare to put a price on Joanna's head. But on top of everything else he could do without the petty politics of his wife's kinship and her dubious loyalties raising its ugly head at every opportunity amongst his allies, for it got in the way of the fight for Wales.

And he loved her. Angrily, Llywelyn pushed the thought aside. Love was dangerous and impractical in times of war, but since the incident with Gelert he knew that she and Dafydd meant the world to him. Simply, he would be lost without them.

Sitting back, he pondered the problem a while longer. Apart from meeting Richard at Chester, she had, to his knowledge, had no further contact with him or her father since Nottingham. And as far as he was concerned it was better it remained that way, then Maelgwn could have no reason whatsoever to challenge him about his wife's loyalties again. *Or she to flee to England …*

Making a decision Llywelyn stood, then calling for a servant to bring him a platter of food, he crossed to the hearth where several young hounds lay stretched out in front of the fire, and picking up the largest he carried it back to his seat.

'So you have chosen?' a voice said softly behind him as Joanna entered the hall. 'Tis a good choice for he is one of Gelert's - from his last litter by a neighbouring bitch.'

'He can never replace Gelert,' Llywelyn said, reaching for a leg of chicken from a platter that has just arrived with his free hand, and dangling it in front of the dog.

'You have defeated Owain and Gruffudd?' Joanna asked, changing the subject.

'Yes, and thwarted your father's naval invasion,' Llywelyn replied, watching her reaction keenly.

'Well, Father is too busy dealing with the barons and concentrating on his plans for France to be much concerned with Wales these days, so mayhap there will be no more impromptu raids.' Joanna said carefully. 'If you plan right you will soon have your heart's desire; your childhood wish fulfilled - to be the prince of the whole of Wales once again.'

'Yes, you're right,' Llywelyn said. Then putting down the dog he stood and kissed her hard on the lips. 'I think it's best if you sever any communications with your family in England for the time being, my love. Whilst your father deprives me of Gruffydd, I think it is only fair that I deprive him of any contact with his daughter. Especially after Nottingham.'

'But what about Richard?' Joanna cried, pulling away from Llywelyn. 'Can I not even communicate with him?'

'No,' Llywelyn said shortly. 'All the time you stay with me as my wife, then there can be no more contact with anyone in England - it's for your own good,' he said gruffly.'

Distressed, Joanna turned to leave.

'There is one other thing, however,' Llywelyn's voice stopped her in her tracks. 'It's news I think you will be glad to hear. I have made my decision and I intend to acknowledge Dafydd as my legal heir, but for the moment I wish it to be kept between ourselves.'

Joanna opened her mouth to speak, but Llywelyn held up a hand to stop her. 'I would that you hear me out,' he said. 'I do not do this for your father - I am in no way complying with his demands, so do not think that things will change between us for we shall never be friends. I am doing it for the good of Wales. I am heartsick of the conflict that arises when members of the same family set upon one and other in the battle for supremacy, simply because in Wales when a man dies we have no distinction between those who can inherit and those who can't. The sons of mistresses fight the sons of legitimate wives in the battle for supremacy. Brothers, cousins, uncles, they too fight each other for power - it is all too easy for a man like your father to pit one against another as he has just done by setting Owain and Gruffudd against me. But it is more than that. I have seen first-hand the destruction that arises from the Welsh custom of giving illegitimate sons as much right to inherit as a legitimate son. When I was a boy I had to fight my uncles and cousins to establish my rights here in Gwynedd, and I don't want that for my own sons. As much as I hate the Norman custom of primogeniture, I have to applaud the fact that it does at least mark out one successor from the pack by right of legitimacy. However, as I said, I wish my decision concerning Dafydd to stay between ourselves for the moment, for it will take many years of careful planning and there are those who would not like it. Moreover, I would rather that Gruffydd heard it from me and not through hearsay whilst he is still John's prisoner.'

Joanna was smiling as she took Llywelyn's large hand in hers. 'You will not regret this, Llywelyn, I swear. Dafydd will be a great leader!'

Llywelyn looked down at her gravely. 'Gruffydd will not roll over easily. He will most likely challenge Dafydd one day. Might even kill him. Are you prepared for that?'

'Yes,' Joanna said. But Llywelyn saw from the shadow that crossed her face as she spoke, that she was privately hoping her father would keep Gruffydd incarcerated long enough for Dafydd to meet that challenge as a man.

Chapter 32

Dover Castle, England, 13th May, 1213

John stood on the battlements of Dover Castle staring out to sea, searching for any sign of the threatened invasion from France. For that was what it had come to now, despite the fact that his envoys had secured a last-minute reprieve from excommunication. He sighed, the only hiccup in his eleventh-hour decision to come to terms with the pope on the matter, was that whilst he'd been prevaricating Archbishop Langton himself had paid a visit to Rome at Christmas. When he'd left, it was armed with letters formally deposing him as the king and freeing his subjects from their oaths of allegiance, thus giving dispensation for Phillip to invade the kingdom with his blessing. In the event, Langton had passed the pope's legate, Pandulf Verraccio, on the road back to France armed with the papal bulls of deposition. It was only after weeks of terrible uncertainty and much to and froing by messengers that he was finally assured that the letters of deposition had been destroyed.

It had been a tricky few months' John conceded, and not ones he wanted to live through again. There were, of course, terms attached with pope having accepted his appeal for absolution from excommunication, for he'd been deeply suspicious of his motives and not about hoodwinked easily, having been fooled more than one occasion already. Therefore, on the pope's instructions, Pandulf had given him until 1st June to endorse the terms of acceptance laid out in the letters brought back to England by his envoys. They would entail him accepting Stephen Langton as Archbishop of Canterbury, and the return of all the exiled prelates to England. Including his old adversary Giles de Braose. They would also include him welcoming back his enemies, FitzWalter and de Vesi from their respective exiles in France and Scotland.

There was one good outcome to be derived from coming to terms with the church, however, for having done so he was now able to cloak himself in the mantle of Christendom, thus denying Phillip the opportunity of that particular gesture. Even so, John was not naïve enough to think that it would deter Phillip from attempting to place his son Louis on the throne of England. Therefore, war would not be averted, no matter who claimed the protection of the church. In recognition of this threat, his half-brother, Will Longespée, was busily assembling a fleet of ships in order to defend England should the need arise - which it undoubtedly would - and a land army was being mustered from the shires and even now was gathering at Barham Downs in Kent. John knew that war was not a popular choice. But then neither was servitude under a foreign king, and his subjects seemed at least to agree upon that. Frowning, John turned away from the window as William Marshall entered the room.

'The pope's legate, Pandulf Verraccio, has just arrived, your Grace,' he said, handing over a sheaf of letters. 'He requests that you meet him down in the hall to ratify terms as soon as possible. The Earls of Salisbury, de Warenne and de Ferrers, are also present, Sire, along with the Count of Boulogne to act as guarantors as you requested this morning,' he finished, referring to Reginald de Dammartin, the fugitive Count of Boulogne, who, having quarrelled bitterly with Phillip the previous year, had promptly fled to England seeking the protection of John's court. The man was important by dint of the fact that through his marriage he held the Norman fiefs of Aumale, Domfront and Mortain. Feifs which John had lost to Phillip in his failed conquest of 1204. Moreover, an agreement in the May of 1212 at Lambeth with Dammartin had secured for John the support of the coalition of princes from the Lower Countries, one which included the Count of Flanders and Otto of Brunswick, the son of John's sister Matilda, who were also squabbling with the French King.

'Lead on then, Marshall,' John said icily, wishing only to get today over with. The pope's suspicions regarding his motives for finally accepting the terms offered the year before were beginning to grate on him. But in two days' time, he intended to call a special council meeting at Ewell, for he had something else up his sleeve. Something so cleverly constructed that hopefully it would not only prove a salve to the pope's fears, but also provide a much-needed lift to his army's spirits before he led them to war. And so, it was with a whistle that he followed Marshall down the stairs.

House of Templers, Ewell, England, two days later, 15th May, 1213

'I have bought you here today to bear witness to a very important charter concerning my promises to the pope. Promises which I agreed to in good faith in the presence of his legate at Dover two days ago,' John said, scrutinising the sea of faces assembled around the large table in the Templers Hall, which included, among others: John de Gray, Geoffrey FitzPeter, his justiciar, the earls of Salisbury, Pembroke, Surrey, Winchester, Arundal and Derby, and Reginald de Dammartin, again.

It was de Dammartin who spoke now, just as the papal legate himself entered the room late and breathlessly took a seat at the end of the table. 'What charter, Sire? What could be more important than the guarantee of faith made at Dover?'

John grinned wolfishly at the little Frenchman, before turning to Pandulf and laying the charter before him. 'As you can see, and as this charter explains to yourself, and his Holiness in Rome, I am handing over the kingdoms of England and Ireland in feudal vassalage to him, both as a gesture of our sincerity, and to make amends for our past differences.'

There was a collective gasp around the table as the importance of John's speech sank in.

'Don't tell me you have made yourself the pope's vassal!' Marshall said, half rising out of his seat in alarm.

'I have indeed pledged my resolve to pay homage and allegiance to the pope, and to repay the church its dues - so as to bring us formally back within the blessed confines of the Holy See,' John concurred smugly. 'And to that end, I have laid out terms in the charter which I trust will be acceptable to the pope as a pledge of my honour herewith.'

Silence fell over the hall as John's greatest magnates grudgingly acknowledged that, beneath the greed and madness, John still bore the mark of his old genius.

Only Pandulf himself seemed unmoved however, his gaze remaining unfathomable as he contemplated John for several long moments. Then without warning, a smile of such beauty spread across his face that John openly broke into laughter.

'I shall be honoured to present Pope Innocent with such a treasure upon my return to Rome,' he said, standing and making a little bow. Then before John could change his mind, he turned and took his leave.

John sighed happily and settled himself back in his chair with his wine. It was getting on for Vespers and the hall was empty now save for him and a few others. 'So, what did you think, Marshall? Were you not impressed by my charter?

William grinned and raised his goblet over the table to John. 'I must say Sire that it truly *was* a stroke of genius! Why, by simply by transforming England into papal fief, you have not only rescued us from our position as an outcast hovering on the edge of Christendom, but you have restored us to a position of safety and security within the church's protection. Now we no longer have to wait for the formalities of the interdict to be lifted in June as outlined in your previous agreement with the pope. Thus,' and this is the clever bit he acknowledged, 'you have not only thwarted Phillip's plans for an immediate invasion, but you have gained yourself a steadfast political ally for the future, for the pope can surely no longer have any doubts about your sincerity due to the largess of your gesture!'

John smiled, but he was hardly listening to the Marshall now, for his mind had moved onto the problem of Peter of Wakefield, the old hermit who the previous year had prophesised that someone more worthy of the crown would replace him by Ascension Day next. And he was not unaware that Ascension Day was only just a little over a week away on the 23rd May.

'Tell me,' he asked William thoughtfully. 'What do you think we should do with the old man, Peter of Wakefield? Send orders tonight to have him hung before his ... er ... prophecy ... dare I say it, is recalled - perhaps say he died in prison?

William frowned. 'I think it best you not tempt fate and hang him yet, Sire. He paused, and John suddenly realised that, despite his gushing praise of a moment before, the Marshall was secretly wondering if his last-minute submission to the pope had more to do with Peter of Wakefield's prediction, rather than actually wanting to make amends with the church. And if he was, it then begged the question as to whether or not the Marshall himself was wavering in his loyalty; perhaps secretly hoping that God would intervene and the old hermit's nonsense would come to pass, and suddenly he was angry.

'You think then that the old fool is right?' he snapped. 'That there is someone more worthy of my crown ... perhaps you yourself even harbour hopes of Phillip of France sneaking past by my defences and putting Louis on the throne of England by the end of next week, eh?'

'Good grief, no, Sire! But I urge caution. Once the day has come and gone the old man will be seen to be what he is - a charlatan. When that is proved to be the case then you can deal with him as you see fit!'

John frowned at the Marshall over his goblet for a moment, then thinking him sincere he smiled suddenly. 'If that is the case – and it surely will be -

then we shall feast on the common the day after Ascension Day and show the people that we place no store by rag-tag beggars purporting to be the agents of God!'

But still, that night John did not sleep for fear that the old man might have spoken true ...

Dover Castle 27th May 2013

John tossed restlessly in his bed again as the ghost of Matilda de Braose once more invaded his dreams. In the distance he could see her son Will, and Arthur, and then several of the Welsh hostages he had hanged calling out to him for mercy. He woke suddenly in a cold sweat. A faint crack in the bed curtains showed that it was nearing dawn.

'What day is it?' he asked as, hearing the creak of his bed, his squire opened the curtains further and began to fuss about with the pillows.

Why, it's the 27th May, Sire,' the boy replied, blinking in surprise at the question.

Running a hand across his aching head, John threw back the covers and swung his feet out onto the cold stone floor then, pushing the protesting squire aside, he began to pull on his shirt and braes. It had been three long days since Ascension Day had passed without occurrence, and he had set his tents up on the common ready to fete his deliverance from Peter of Wakefield's prophecy. But then, out of the blue, word had come that old man's followers had rallied around him and begun to claim that today, the fourteenth anniversary of his coronation, was in fact the date that the old hermit had really meant. John scowled to himself, shortly after that, word had come from Corfe castle that the execution he had planned for the old fraud had been delayed because of rising public opinion and the threat of riots. He paused for a moment, recalling the havoc he had reeked amongst the tents when he had realised that he had several more days of torture to live through before he could finally dismiss the old man's divinations as a hoax. Now though, the new day of reckoning was upon him, and he had only to get through until tonight. Already he had sent word that a new execution was to be scheduled for the morrow, come what may.

Keeping that uplifting thought in mind, he grabbed his tunic and began to make his way down to the hall where, in an attempt to forget the prophecy, and ignore lines of expectant faces that filled his court, he began his fourteenth anniversary celebrations by drinking wine and planning his invasion of France. Later that night, when it was nearly midnight and he was quite drunk, and once again sure that the old hermit's prophecy was unfounded, he consoled himself by imagining the old man being bound and dragged in the morning by a horse's tail to Wareham, where, in a spiteful fit of vengeance, he had decreed that he was to hang alongside his son as a lesson to anyone else who might think to upset his equilibrium in the future.

Then he sat back and raised a goblet of wine in a toast to the future …

Damme, France, 30th May, 1213

John's fleet of five hundred ships loaded with arms and men, paid for mostly by the fortune he'd amassed through various forms of taxes, tyranny and extortion, sailed up the river Zwyn on 30th May towards Damme under the command of William Longespée, the Earl of Salisbury, having received word from the Count of Flanders that the time was right.

At the entrance to Damme they were greeted by an incredible sight. That of Phillip's invasion fleet, beached or bobbing in the harbour, waiting for his command to sail across the channel and settle his son Louis on the throne of England.

That was not destined to happen. Without preamble, the English streamed into port, cutting adrift ships piled high with food and supplies for the French military, before storming the beached frigates and setting fire to them. The harbour was filled with choking black smoke. The very sea set on fire by the wrath of the English soldiers who drew strength from the fact that their king was, once more, an apostle of the church. A God-fearing king. A king with the might of the Lord's sword at his shoulder, and the pope's holy blessing in the bag.

Chapter 33

Aber, North Wales, June 1213

'So Father's fleet won a victory at Damme?' Joanna asked, wishing she was able to write to Richard and find out more, for she missed the gossip and the little insights that he gave in their private communications.

'Yes!' Llywelyn said angrily, throwing the letter containing the news down in front of her. 'And with the pope's holy blessing, and God almighty behind him, apparently! Though Phillip's reinforcement troops nearly caught the fleet unawares when it foolishly decided to land. They were forced to flee with their tails between their legs, else it would have been a blood bath.'

'But still, he would have been victorious with or without the pope's blessing, wouldn't he?' Joanna asked, still confused by the recent news of her father's sudden submission to Rome.

'Goodness only knows - one thing I can say about your father is that he has the luck of the gods. Though whether or not it's the one he professes to have submitted too, I know not. The Marshall has told anyone who will listen, that apart from his obvious victory, never has so much treasure come to England since the days of King Arthur! Just think how many wars all that foreign silver could fund - I can only hope it's not another with Wales!'

Joanna sighed, and picking up the letter she looked at it thoughtfully. 'Well, it might be a victory for my father, but I think it is naught to do with the offices of God for he has sinned too sorely to be redeemed. Repaying the church's stolen money and allowing a few exiled prelates back into the country, doesn't absolve him of the cold-blooded murder of innocent children or the rape and murder of baron's wives,' she said sadly.

'Or the intention of doing the same in future if things don't go his way,' Llywelyn added, stopping his pacing and looking at Joanna closely. 'Your father's submission to the pope has really riled you, hasn't it?' he said suddenly. 'You don't really believe that he has repented of his sins, or that he truly intends to abide by the terms of that submission, do you?'

'I don't really understand it,' Joanna said, crossing to the window and looking out over the bailey. 'Why, only a few months ago, you told me that the pope wrote to Archbishop Langton; to warn him and the bishops against trusting my father. Even when Pandulf Verraccio met him at Dover, he was still circumspect about father's intentions; still not ready to lift the interdict from his shoulders without further assurances. Now, according to this letter, Father can do no wrong in Innocent's eyes. He has even promised to go on a crusade! And where does that leave you, Llywelyn? What of your treaty with the pope? It counts for nothing now that he supports my father. From now on, whatever way you turn, you will be damned, for if my father is your enemy, then so is he. And, as for your treaty with Phillip, well, by its very nature it makes you an enemy of the pope, because he no longer supports France in its ambition to put Louis on the throne. As I've said, you're damned. Whatever way you turn.'

Llywelyn sighed. 'I suppose I should have told you sooner, but I met with Pandulf a few weeks ago - just over the border near Chester - and we discussed the matter. As you rightly say, for the moment I'm stuck in a cleft stick. But a meeting is being planned with Stephen Langton in June. He proposes a truce, and if the terms are right I will accept. The charter your father signed at Ewell basically wipes out any previous agreement made by me, anyway,' Llywelyn said sourly. 'His ploy to win Innocent to his side with his sudden gifts of England and Ireland as papal fiefs worked like magic. Innocent was so moved that he immediately accepted the charter and redeemed him of all sins of the past. He's written enthusiastically of your father's remarkable conversion since, and will not be lead to believe that it's anything other than that. Moreover, in the eyes of the world, John's victory at Damme is now seen to be his reward for his return to the Holy See!'

Llywelyn joined her at the window. 'You realise that there will be no stopping him now that he has his little victory,' He said thoughtfully. 'Your father wants more, and he will take his army to France again to that end. Probably in the belief that with

God on his side he cannot lose. Which will only be to my advantage, for it leaves the way open for me to reclaim the rest of my lands here without his interference,' Llywelyn finished, looking at her closely.

'Could I write to Richard please, Llywelyn?' Joanna asked suddenly. 'He's married now … to Rohese of Dover - you remember her, do you not? And now he plans to go to France with Father, for they are reconciled.'

'How do you know that?' Llywelyn asked sharply. 'You've not been corresponding with him against my wishes, I hope!'

'No! Llywelyn. No, of course not!' Joanna said, turning away so that he could not see the tide of red flooding her face, for there was one person that she had, against Llywelyn's wishes, continued to write to. And suddenly she wished she had not …

Chapter 34

Bristol Castle, England, October 1213

Gruffydd glared at his jailor in what he hoped was a suitably frightening manner as he was shoved into the cold, bare room in the tower at Bristol Castle that was to be his latest place of confinement. He was tired of travelling the length and breadth of the land at John's behest; tired of travelling from village to village with the wagon train as it was slowly piled full of riches, plundered or stolen, from those barons still wealthy enough to help fund his next expedition to France. But John would not allow him out of his sight for long, fearing that in his absence the barons would seize from him the only thing preventing him from finally losing his weakening grip on Wales altogether. For news had come that his father had finally recovered the castles of Deganwy and Rhuddlan, along with the four *cantrefi* of Gwynedd Is Conwy lost to him at his surrender.

Sighing, he threw himself on the grubby straw pallet, and pulling out his mother's brooch, he contemplated it. He had escaped being hanged at Nottingham, that was true. And although he'd been told that it was his detestable stepmother's letter that had saved him, he couldn't help thinking that, in some way, this little brooch had something to do with it. That somehow it had worked as a talisman during the long terrible days of John's madness, for why else had only he and a handful others been saved at the very last minute? He turned it over in his hand. He could feel no vibration; no warmth radiating from it. It just felt cold. Inanimate. But he was sure he hadn't imagined it. Was sure that he had felt the rushes stir and the whisper of her warm breath on his face as she had lain down beside him that first night alone in the Black Tower. He was even sure that he had derived some comfort from her ghostly presence. But if that was true, then why wasn't she here now? And why hadn't she been with him in all the other dungeons and towers he'd been incarcerated in since Nottingham?

Putting the brooch down, he stood and crossed to the narrow window that looked out across the river Avon, before hauling himself up against the bars and peering down into the bailey. The sun had crossed the main expanse of the ward and it now shone down into the far corner; the place where supplies for the reinforcements of the castle's outer walls were stacked. Gruffydd scowled. Apart from swelling his coffers, John was here to inspect the progress of the works, for it was here that he held Eleanor, Prince Arthur's sister, who, despite being a woman, some still considered to be the rightful sovereign of England following her brother's disappearance. Lowering himself to the floor, Gruffydd crossed to the pallet and picked up the brooch again. It felt warm now, even though it hadn't been in his pocket, and suddenly he felt a strange sensation - something akin to anger - spread through his body.

'Bring her to me,' John said, waving a bejewelled hand in the air with a flourish.

Immediately Eleanor was lead towards the dais where John sat with Isabella, and bobbing a small curtsey she stood quietly waiting for him to speak.

John peered at her thoughtfully for a moment, taking in her striking face with its high cheekbones and large, blue-grey eyes modestly framed by a gauzy wimple, before letting his gaze wander down over body. She was everything that a man desired. She was taller than most of the other women in the room, with voluptuous curves and a waist that a man could span with his hands. She had dressed carefully for her audience with him in a white linen shift and gown of the finest red wool with long fitted sleeves, over which she wore a shimmering red silk bliaut of a darker shade. As a final touch she had gathered the bliaut together at the waist with a silver girdle, beneath which several folds had been tucked, allowing the rest of the skirt to fall to the ground where the toes of her tiny gold slippers peeked out. John smiled, she could not complain that her captivity had been without rewards he told himself, and although they were rewards of conscience, he was sure they were still welcome in her confinement. As were her visits from neighbouring barons, who would arrive periodically with news of England and her beloved France. On several occasions, he had allowed her to ride out along the sands in the company of their daughters, even presenting her with a saddle with gilded reigns and scarlet ornaments in order for her to do so in style.

'I can see why they call you the pearl of Brittany, for you are very lovely to look at, Eleanor,' he said at last, picking up a goblet and taking a large gulp of red wine. 'In fact, you've the look of your brother,' he murmured, before putting it down again.

At once, Eleanor's head snapped up at the mention of her brother, and Isabella put a warning hand on John's sleeve.

'No! No! Sire,' she whispered, glancing at Eleanor. 'We said it was perhaps better you did not mention Arthur!'

John merely glared at her, before turning his attention back to Eleanor. 'How would you like to go back to France?' he asked. 'To be courted, even wed? Would that please you?'

'Yes, Uncle,' Eleanor replied demurely.

'Perhaps you could even make a claim for Brittany - in lieu of the fact that the title of Duchess is rightly yours, and not your half-sister Alix's, who really only holds it by marriage to the king's cousin.'

Eleanor looked pleased now. 'Your wish is my command,' she concurred, giving a little bob.

John nodded. 'Then it shall be done.'

Eleanor turned to go, but instead, she paused and turned back. 'Sire. I have correspondence from Joanna - I thought you would you like to read it? It is only frivolous girls talk really, but you are welcome.'

Immediately John leaned forward in his chair, his eyes bright. 'Yes Eleanor, I would love to read word from Joanna. I have not heard from her since -' He stopped abruptly, unwilling to make any mention of Nottingham in case Eleanor knew nothing of it.

Eleanor nodded, and turned to go again.

'Send them to me at once!' John called after her, suddenly desperate to read them.

The servants were lighting the sconces before John had the opportunity to sit down alone and read Joanna's letters to Eleanor. They were several months old and, as she had warned, they were mostly full of girl's chat: the latest fashions from France, a stallion brought for stud that would not perform, and countless other topics so trivial that John almost threw them away. However, it was last one dated the previous June that caught his attention, and pushing the others aside, he read it again. When he'd finished, he put it down on the table beside him. Then calling for his squire, he ordered Gruffydd to be fetched from the dungeons.

Gruffydd woke to a torch being thrust in his face, and a guard shaking him by the shoulder.

'King John wants you ... now!' he barked.

'Wha -'

'Move it! I told you, the king wants to see you. Now!

Feeling not a little put out, Gruffydd staggered to his feet and rubbed the sleep from his eyes. Then with his chains chinking, he obediently he followed the guard down the dark, shadowy corridors and into the main hall. The first thing he realised as he was thrust to his knees at his feet, was that John was very drunk, appearing not to recognise him as he glared at him myopically over the rim of his goblet.

'Ah, it's Llywelyn's whelp,' he said eventually, waving away a servant who was fussing over a wine stain spreading across the front of his fine linen shirt.

Gruffydd shifted uncomfortably in the guard's iron grip, wondering why he had been summoned before the king at such an indecent hour. He was about to ask, when John suddenly stood up and dismissed the guard with a jerk of his head. Then turning to Gruffydd he studied him with distaste.

'I have news from your homeland,' he said with an edge to his voice that was now wholly familiar to Gruffydd. 'It is news that I think you should hear. And it concerns your new baby brother ...'

Gruffydd was impotent with rage when he was thrown back into his tower room. So, his father was going to go ahead and name his new son, Dafydd, as his successor instead of him, was he? He swore, and spat bitterly into the rushes. During the long lonely months of his confinement, thriving only on second hand accounts of his father's rebellion, he'd actually convinced himself that Llywelyn would not comply with the John's orders and name the legitimate offspring of Joanna's womb as his heir. In fact, it was impossible to comprehend him doing so, considering he had taken trouble to renegade [renege] on all other aspects of his treaty with the king of England. What was worse, though, was that he had only found out because his detestable stepmother had crowed about it in a letter to Eleanor. Presumably his father was only going to tell him if he was ever released from John's prison. And if he was not, then Llywelyn would have saved himself the trouble. He scowled. Perhaps it would suit his father's purposes if he was never set free, for that would save him ever having to explain his motives, he could then set about having more legitimate children without having to worry about a war for supremacy breaking out upon his death. Going to his pallet, he thrust his hand down into the straw, rooting about until he found the place where he'd hidden the brooch, and finding it, he pulled it out. It felt alarmingly hot, and he almost dropped it in fright.

A sudden movement caught his eye. *She* was standing there, as clear as day beneath the moonlit window. He fell back terrified against the rough stone wall of the cell. His legs felt like jelly, and he could feel the panic rising from his belly. 'My God, it's true,' he whispered, fearfully sketching the sign of the cross in front of him. 'Gwenny always said she could see you, but I wouldn't believe her!'

Gruffydd, my son, my son ...

Her lips hadn't parted, but her words hung heavy in the air.

Gruffydd looked down at the brooch. It was vibrating slightly in his hand, its heat burning his palm. He knew immediately that with its help he had somehow summoned her to him. Suddenly, Gruffydd's fear turned to rage.

'You knew, didn't you? You knew that Father was going to pass me over for his new whelp, Dafydd? That why you're here, isn't it!'

He was shouting now. There was a rattle of keys, and a guard popped his head through the door and peered curiously at him.

'Is that why you've come to haunt me?' Gruffydd continued, oblivious of the man. 'So that you can make sure that I fulfil your precious dream! Do you think that I am not capable of doing it myself? That I am not capable of standing against a boy not yet out of the cradle? That I would let you down! Have you so little faith in me, that you had to return from the grave to get what you want!

'Oh, my God, I can't bear it!' Gruffydd sobbed hysterically. 'It's bad enough having to dance to John's tune, but at least he's still alive!' Then going to the window, he hauled himself up against the bars, and with his free arm he threw the brooch out as far as he possibly could.

That night Gruffydd dreamed of his mother. He was a boy again. Lying on the rocks alongside the salty waters of the Menai Straits with Gwenny, the *llys* at Aber behind them nestling on the hillside on the edge of the *Eryri* mountains. They were dangling their hands in the cool water, whilst Tangwystl sat on the sands, spinning stories of the great future that lay before them.

It was late afternoon and the sun had fully arced and was sinking behind the *llys,* when he finally stood and shook the drops of water from his hands. Bored with stories of her brother's impending greatness, Gwenny had long since wandered off in search of wild flowers and pebbles with which to decorate her room,

Idly, he bent and picked a bunch of primroses, contemplating their beauty in the fading light. Feeling his mother's gaze upon him, he came and sat down beside her, laying his head on her shoulder and the posy of golden flowers in her lap.

'Tell me again, Mama,' he whispered sleepily, watching as her lips curled into the slow, familiar smile.

Stroking his hair, she pulled him closer as she told him how he was destined to become a great and masterful ruler; a beloved prince, loved and revered by the people of Wales as his father had been before him. He closed his eyes in contentment as her soft, musical voice washed over him, her words painting a bright and glorious picture of his future. His future as she saw it. One as the rightful prince of Wales. A prince of the true blood who would leave a line of Welsh princes behind.

She tilted his face to hers. 'Promise me, *bach!*'

'Promise you what, Mama?'

She laughed. 'Have you not been listening, *cariad?*'

He paused. She was fading. Becoming misty, ethereal. He sat up, aware that where her shoulder had been there was now only air. Suddenly, he felt disoriented. Lost.

Promise me Gruffydd, bach ...

'Mama?' he called, reaching out a hand. 'Mama, please don't go!' But she was fading rapidly now, drifting off into the distance as the sun finally dipped behind the *llys,* leaving only deep shadows in its wake and the echo of her voice in the wind.

Gruffydd, my son, my son ...

Then suddenly the dream changed. It was dark and he was looking down on a courtyard, he could see shadowy buildings below; people were gathering and pointing up at him. He could hear crying and screaming. Someone calling his name. In the distance, he could see people running towards him.

He woke suddenly, sweating with fear. The dungeons were still bathed in darkness, but for a shaft of early morning light which spilled down through the bars on the window. Slowly, he pulled himself up on one elbow. Something glinted dully in the rushes beneath it. Rubbing his eyes, he opened them again and leaned forward curiously. It was the brooch.

Alongside it stood a raven ...

Chapter 35

Aber, North Wales, February 1214

Llywelyn was slightly drunk, his mood unfathomable when he entered the bed chamber that night, having spent the day in conference with Maelgwn and Rhys Gryg.

'Your father has left for France, taking Isabella and young Richard with him,' he said, referring to Isabella's Richard. 'He's also taking Arthur's sister Eleanor - probably with the intention of parading her in front of the Bretons to gain support against Alix, perhaps even marry her to some agreeable count and set her up as his puppet duchess.' He belched loudly, making Joanna frown. 'There is also talk of a marriage contract between Hugh's heir and your half-sister Joan - I suppose he needs to mend bridges with the Lusignans and the people of Angoulême, considering he practically kidnapped Isabella from them and married her whilst she was still betrothed to Hugh.' He picked up a fig from the window sill and inspected it closely before putting it down again and wiping his hand absently on his sleeve.

'You know he could have easily have afforded another expedition on the riches he brought back from Damme were it not for the amount he has had to pay for his reconciliation with the church,' he continued. 'Instead, as usual, he looks to the barons to pay for it. Do you know that he took ten thousand marks from William FitzAlan, just so the poor man could inherit his own family title; he charged John de Lacy seven thousand marks for similar, and widows are now charged up to a thousand pounds just to keep their dowers and secure exemption from marriage. Along with that, he holds their son's hostage. Yet still the barons remain violently opposed to the campaign; are refusing to serve him abroad again - he's had to employ mercenaries, household guards and those knights who cannot refuse him because of their debts to make up his army. No wonder he is the most unpopular king in Christendom!'

Joanna frowned, and putting her hairbrush down, she turned in her chair to look at him. 'You are remarkably well informed, husband,' she said coolly. 'And also, not a little drunk!'

'Oh, it's Maelgwn and Rhys Gryg that are remarkably well informed - they have spies everywhere these days, even in your father's court,' Llywelyn rejoined, ignoring her little jibe.

'I know all that,' Joanna said wearily, 'I am tired of the hearing of it -'

'And you have been writing to Eleanor,' Llywelyn said abruptly.

Joanna froze. 'How do you know? You cannot object to that, surely? She is my cousin after all. I thought you only expected me to cease communication with those nearest to my father … my … my brothers, Richard and John. Look, Llywelyn, I felt sorry for her!' Joanna rushed on as, crossing to her side, Llywelyn picked up her goblet and swallowed the contents in one gulp. 'I still cannot reconcile myself with Arthur's death at my father's hands, and her now being used as a pawn in his game to win back his French lands -'

'I do object, actually,' Llywelyn interrupted, swaying a little as the remains of the hot, spiced wine hit his stomach. 'I object to the fact that once more you have concealed something from me which I only found out through Maelgwn. Moreover,' he added, 'she showed those letters to your father, who showed them to Gruffydd whilst they were at Bristol.'

'But there was nothing -'

'Oh, but there was,' Llywelyn said softly. 'You told her that I have chosen Dafydd over Gruffydd as my heir, and now Gruffydd thinks I have betrayed him whilst he rots in an English prison. How your father must gloat! What's more, Maelgwn now sees this as further cause for mistrust. You know he hates you. You also know how long it took me to reconcile him to my cause last time you meddled. Well, it took all the diplomacy I had today to convince him yet again of your innocence. It also took all my powers of persuasion to convince him that I had not yet chosen my successor, for he is a patriot who firmly believes that Gruffydd, a true Welsh prince, should be the rightful inheritor of Wales and not the half-Norman son of a treacherous bitch!'

'But I didn't mean for her to show my father -' Joanna stammered.

'Where's Rhoda?' Llywelyn asked suddenly, ignoring her protestations.

'I gave her the night off - '

'So, we are alone?'

Joanna's jaw clenched and her eyes turned wary as she watched him deliberately turn and push the door closed behind him.

'Llywelyn?'

'Shush,' he said, pulling her to her feet and twisting her around so that he could pick up a handful of hair and drape it over one shoulder. Despite her obvious reluctance, he felt her knees go weak in response to the sudden warmth of his breath on her neck.

'And tell me, wife.' He said, pulling her closer so that he could slide a hand down the front of her kirtle and cup a breast. 'Are you loyal to your husband, or to your father these days?'

Joanna was leaning back against him now, relaxing as he began rolling her nipple between his rough fingers, and without knowing why he felt a sudden and overwhelming desire to punish her for her sins.

'Well, who exactly is it you are loyal to, wife?'

'You, Llywelyn,' she breathed. 'Always you -'

Emitting a noise that was a mixture somewhere between desire and rage, Llywelyn released her breast and, pulling her across the room, he threw her face down on the bed, pinning her there easily with one knee.

'Llywelyn, what -' Joanna cried, struggling to free herself.

Ignoring her protests, Llywelyn roughly grasped the hem of her shift and pushed it up around her naked backside. 'Then I suggest that you never forget where your loyalties lie again, woman!' he hissed,

Beneath him, Joanna tore at the bedcovers desperately, clawing them so hard that they bunched up around her face and she could scarcely breathe.

'Please, Llywelyn!' she whispered, her voice muffled. But Llywelyn did not heed her as he struggled to untie the lacings on his braies.

Then time stopped. Time in which Llywelyn forgot that she was his wife, and instead he took her like an animal. There was no gentleness. No forgiveness. Just simple retribution for her betrayal and treachery. Only once did he call out her name. And when he did, it was a with a roar of anguish as he tore into her body from behind, battering flesh against flesh, as if by doing so he could reach her very soul. At last, when he had finished, he let out a terrible shudder, and releasing her he flung himself from the room without a word. Leaving Joanna face down on the mattress, still clinging numbly to the sheets.

When Joanna roused herself some hours later, it was to a little giggle, and when she turned her head,

she thought she saw a pair of eyes. Eyes the colour
of honeyed mead, staring out from the shadows ...

Chapter 36

La Rochelle, France, June 1214

John's army landed in France for the second time in May, and at the beginning of June they departed their base at La Rochelle and marched north. Their mission was to distract Phillip's army sufficiently enough so that Emperor Otto and his Flemish allies could storm Paris, before heading south to trap Phillip Augustus's armies who were rallying there. However, after initial success at Ancennis on the border of Brittany and Anjou, and then at Nantes, where he took several important prisoners including King Phillip's cousin, Peter of Dreux, John was completely halted at Angers, the ancient capital of his house.

His mistake was in besieging William des Roches fortress at Roche-de-Moine, a few miles from Angers. Thinking it an important stronghold, Phillip had appointed William des Roches as its seneschal, and when it began to fall to John, Louis took it upon himself to march to its relief. Unfortunately for John, once they had learned of Louis' approach, and finding themselves faced with the might of his army, his Poitevin nobles promptly lost all heart and turned and fled for home.

In full Angevin temper John returned to La Rochelle to sit and wait it out. The news when it came was not good. On the morning of 27th July, a coalition of John's allies, including his half-brother, William Longespée, Emperor Otto, the Counts of Boulogne and Flanders, and the Duke of Brabant met Phillip Augustus at Bouvines, a tiny village next to a bridge along the River Marcq. The coalition troops rode in below a flag bearing Otto's emblem of a dragon and an eagle; the French beneath their sacred banner of the Oriflamme, the rightful symbol of France. The battle was a rout, with Otto and several other noblemen fleeing the field, leaving the Counts of Boulogne and Flanders, and the Earl of Salisbury to be captured along with thirty other high ranking knights and noblemen. Bouvines was lost. Phillip was triumphant.

'Amen!' said Llywelyn, hearing of the news. 'Amen!'

'Amen, to what?' Joanna asked, entering the room.

'You've not heard then?' Llywelyn said, handing a letter over to her. 'Your father has been defeated at Bouvines.'

'What?' Joanna cried, sitting down abruptly. 'No. No, I had not heard. Is he dead?'

'No, he was forced back to La Rochelle. Your uncle Will, and the Counts of Boulogne and Flanders were captured. However, Otto fled the field along with many others.'

Llywelyn looked at Joanna's ashen face, and taking pity on her he poured her a goblet of wine. 'Here, drink this,' he said gruffly, taking the letter from her shaking hand and thrusting it at her. 'You can read the details later if you want, but no doubt Richard will write.'

'My uncle Will,' Joanna said. 'What will happen to him? 'Mayhap they will ransom him, mayhap they will kill him, mayhap they will let him rot in prison - I care not!' Llywelyn said abruptly. Then, more gently. 'I have letters to write myself, Joanna. Your father has finally lost his war and he will have to return to England and face the repercussions of that here. I am sided with the barons who will see to it that the charter they have drawn up to curtail his excess as king is sealed by him, and that it contains the clauses I ask concerning the release of my son and the other hostages.' He paused. 'Phillip will invade eventually, Joanna. Nothing will change that. The question is, will the barons support a foreign king or not.' And with that, he gave her a slight bow and turned and strode from the room.

Gruffydd, his son, was coming home ...

Chapter 37

Aberconwy Abbey, North Wales, July 1215

Llywelyn stood at the window of the chapterhouse, looking out over the western cloisters and down towards the stone pillars flanking the abbey gatehouse. It was Sunday morning. A day of worship. It was also the day chosen for him to be reunited with his son who was to be escorted into Wales by a group of the king's men and delivered to him here at the abbey - the place he had chosen so that Gruffydd might avoid the curious gaze of the villagers back home.

The morning passed slowly as he watched the monks emerge from their cells and make their way towards the chapel for morning worship, and from there to the sparsely furnished refectory to break their fast. And the sun had fully risen over the courtyard, leaving the cloisters in shadow, before he eventually heard the door open and close behind him with a click, signalling the arrival of the abbot.

'You must be filled with happiness now that Gruffydd is coming home at last,' the old man said quietly, appearing alongside him and placing a cup of mead and a loaf of bread on the stone sill.

Frowning, Llywelyn turned, and was about to speak when he caught himself. How could he make the old man understand that following the initial joy of Gruffydd's release, he felt nothing but dread; that he was plagued with terrible doubts about the wisdom of bringing his eldest son back to Aber so soon. So much had changed in Wales during the four years in which he had been held hostage. Most importantly his place in the succession, a decision he knew the boy would never come to accept.

And then there was Joanna. Though of a similar age, his wife and son had never been friends. Llywelyn was already dreading the inevitable arguments that would arise between them when Gruffydd started to blame her for her son's elevated status on account of her Norman blood and her relationship with the King of England. He also knew that Gruffydd would never accept that he'd made his choice of successor independently of those facts. Had done it for the good of Wales, and not because he had been forced to by her father.

As if sensing that the prince was preoccupied with his own thoughts and not ready to talk, the abbot wisely pulled up a seat and sat down patiently to wait. Forgetting the abbot, Llywelyn ran a hand through his hair which was beginning to grey at the temples now that he was in his forty-third year, as he desperately sought a way to make things easier.

The idea of bypassing Aber altogether, and taking his son across the Menai Strait to Llanfaes, where he could leave him to become accustomed to his freedom and adapt to his new status appealed. But immediately he dismissed the idea. Never one to try to avoid confrontations, he was not about to start now. And so reluctantly he cast his mind about for another solution.

An hour later, frustrated and angry, Llywelyn gave up. Gruffydd was no longer a child; could no longer be placated with a new toy, or sweetmeats from the kitchen. He would just have to accept his lot. Accept that things were different now, for Wales could no longer afford to be an independent country struggling for survival on its own. It had to become part of a bigger kingdom if it were to continue to exist.

But what if he never accepts it? Perhaps you should reinstate Gruffydd in the succession? Niggling doubt prevailed.

No, that never was, and never would be, an option, his rational mind replied. There was too much water under the bridge; too much at stake. He wanted peace for Wales. The last thing he wanted to release upon his death was a war amongst his kin. He wanted … no … needed, the stability of a designated heir.

But it is the Norman way …

'But I'm married to a Norman woman!' he said out loud, jerking the abbot out of a slumber.

Seeing that he had woken the old man, Llywelyn sat down. There was only one answer. Gruffydd was no longer the boy that he had delivered up to John four years ago. He was a youth on the verge of manhood, and it was time that he acted like it; came home and accepted his place in the order of things as they were. They would have to face the consequences later. Together.

Satisfied with his decision, Llywelyn picked up the cup of mead and downing it thirstily he pushed all thoughts of Gruffydd's return aside. Then, pulling his seat up alongside the abbot's, he began to speak of the new grant of land he intended to bestow upon the Abbey, and his plans for his internment within its walls when the time came.

Stepping out into the sun later, Llywelyn nodded at one of the monks before walking down through the cloisters and on towards the heavy wooden gates - the only place outside the abbey where there was a clear view over the vineyards, and towards the mountain pass from which he expected Gruffydd to come. As he waited he turned his mind to the events leading up to his son's release. Events in which, upon returning defeated from Bouvines, his father-in-law had found himself embroiled in yet another war. A war in which he found himself finally having to capitulate to the wishes of his dissident barons at home. Having to concede that their grievances against him had not gone away. That they were still very real, and sorely needed to be redressed.

The first reprisals when they came had been swift, calculated to prevent John from re-grouping his army upon his return from France. In May, led by the Earl of Essex, the barons had stormed and taken London, outmanoeuvring John's supporters, the Earls of Chester, Derby, Salisbury and Pembroke. At the same time Llywelyn himself had marched on Shrewsbury, taking both town and castle without a fight, crucially infiltrating the Norman ring of power along the border, and weakening the ever-present threat it posed to Wales. With this victory under his belt, he'd committed himself to the task of bringing control and order to the rest of Wales, leaving the civil war to rage on in England without further need of his aid. Within weeks John had been forced to the negotiating table, and from there onto Runnymede, where he sealed the Magna Carta on the 15th June, and accepted the barons' renewed oaths of fealty on the 19th. In triumph, the barons had arranged for a meeting of the council to be held at Oxford at the end of July at which John would meet with them and personally ratify the terms of the Charter.

Llywelyn frowned. His one regret was that he had not been present at Runnymede. Had not witnessed, first-hand, the subjection of the man who'd murdered Welsh children in cold blood. He had, however, been invited to join the barons at Oxford. To discuss the concessions that would finally secure the return of the lands and liberties which he and his Welsh allies had been deprived of in the terrible summer of 1211, and, of course, the release of his son and the other hostages the king had taken during his hedonistic years of unchecked rule. And with that he had to be content.

During this time, John had only once tried to win back Welsh favour by sending William, the Bishop of Lichfield, to the border to meet with him and his allies armed with peace proposals, however, these had fallen on deaf ears as none of them were prepared to lay faith any longer in the promises of a king they could no longer trust.

But it was the arrival of Reginald de Braose, sent by his brother Giles on a mission to aid Llywelyn and his allies in the recovery of the de Braose lordships, that finally secured for Llywelyn the alliance he had been seeking, to maintain a strong presence in the Marches. Both Giles and Reginald had been absent during the negotiations that concluded the barons' war. Refusing to have any part in the Runnymede settlement, or any intention of making peace with a king who'd murdered their mother and brother in cold blood. Immediately Llywelyn had seen the opportunity to cement an alliance between himself and a powerful leading Marcher family whose resentment of the English king matched his own, and after much negotiation Reginald had agreed to marry Gwladys. Joanna's pleasure at the match had been unfeigned, for she harboured a vision of them forging further marriages with the de Braoses: not just in order to secure Anglo-Norman allies, but because she firmly believed the family were destined to play a vital part in their future lives.

Llywelyn yawned and stretched his arms above his head. He already had another marriage in mind between Marared and Reginald's nephew, John de Braose, the rightful heir to the Bramber estates in England. Then there was Will de Braose, a lad of about Joanna's age. He was already contracted to marry Eva Marshall, but you never knew, they might have a daughter who would make a good wife to the future heir of Wales.

Be warned -

The words rang loudly in his ears. As if someone standing alongside him had spoken. He turned his head cautiously. There was no one. The only tangible thing was the unnatural silence pressing down on him. Heavy and suffocating. He frowned, every sense becoming alert as a prickle of unease run down his spine.

'Who's there?' he called, straining to see. The vineyards ahead were deserted. But there was definitely something. 'Who's there?' he called again. Anxiously this time. Suddenly he heard a creaking noise in the distance, and an unexpected wave of nausea washed over him. He closed his eyes. When he opened them again, in place of the vines, there was a corpse swinging from a tree. Its face was unrecognisable. Just ribbons and empty sockets where carrion had recently feasted; its teeth bared in a deathly grin. Llywelyn reeled backwards, sickened as the vision changed. There was a room with guards at the door. A woman was sprawled across a bed, crying. Her back was to him, her long dark hair swathed about her shoulders like a mantle. He could see them heaving with each sob. Could feel her pain like daggers in his heart.

It was Joanna.

Pressing a hand to his mouth, Llywelyn grasped the gate for support as, without warning, his promises to Tangwystl surfaced like a bloated corpse bobbing to the surface of a lake. No, she couldn't be here! Not so far away from her usual haunting ground, and so near to a place of worship. And if she was, why? Gruffydd was safe ... or was he?

Be warned -

'Go, Tangwystl,' he whispered. 'Please, go! It is over, you need do no more harm for Gruffydd is coming home. Now. Today. I have kept my part of the bargain!' But he knew that he had not. He knew that he had betrayed her, and that she had followed him here for it was not yet ended. He was half expecting a ghostly reply, when the sound of bird song and the creak of a handcart being dragged along the path shattered the silence, and the vision disappeared.

Leaving Llywelyn to wonder whether he'd simply suffered from a bad turn brought on by the anxiety of his son's return. Or if, in her desperation, Tangwystl really had penetrated the abbey walls to warn him of the future, should he decide to go ahead with his plans to make Dafydd his successor now that Gruffydd was free.

Gruffydd paused and glanced behind him. A distant rumble of thunder rolled down the narrow mountain pass that he and his escort of English soldiers had just traversed, filling him with a deep sense of foreboding. When it had subsided, he flicked the reigns of his new mount, Dante, a gift from his step-uncle Richard, urging him down what was left of the flinty track and onto the final leg of his journey to the Cistercian Abbey - the place elected for his reunion with his father after four years of being hostage by the English king. After a while the track came to an abrupt end, and, holding up his hand, the leader of the escort called a halt and glanced nervously about - as if expecting to be taken by surprise by a stray band of native warriors who might not yet be aware that the English king had been defeated, and had come to terms with the prince of Gwynedd for the release and repatriation of his son into Wales under the protection of the English crown.

Ignoring him, Gruffydd leaned forward over his saddle and gazed eagerly out at the familiar landscape that lay before them. The sun had finally broken through the clouds and was now shining down on a steep valley, at the bottom of which a small stream meandered its way through a small copse on the one side, and a larger forest on the other. He smiled, recognising the valley and copse as one of his childhood haunting grounds: the place where he had learnt to hunt and wield a bow. For a moment he hesitated. His father had sent strict instructions that he skirt Aber, and proceed straight to the abbey where they could be reunited in peace without the prying eyes of the villagers upon him. But today of all days he did not feel duty bound to obey his father – he had been absent for four years, and another hour or so would make much of a difference. And so, with a sudden surge of optimism, he kicked Dante into a trot, and bypassing the head of his escort deftly, he led the way down a concealed track which he knew led into the neck of the valley.

As they neared the bottom, what was left of the mountain mist suddenly parted revealing an old shack, smoke billowing from a ragged hole in the roof. It was Mab's old hut. He frowned, wondering who lived there now, for he'd heard that the old woman was dead - had died in suspicious circumstances on the night of his new brother's birth. Suddenly curious, Gruffydd dismounted, and throwing his reigns to an English soldier he strode to the door, pulled aside the sacking, and entered. It was dark and smoky inside the room, but his eyes could just make out a figure squatting on a stool poking at the embers of a dying fire. He frowned. Her back was turned to him, but there was something familiar in the set of her head and shoulders as she sat hunched protectively over the hearth. Without thinking, his hand went to his script which hung from his belt and contained the few personal possessions he had left. He could feel the brooch vibrating through the soft leather kid; its heat was burning his fingers, and almost at once a familiar ripple of fear began to crawl its way down his spine.

Book Two

Degannwy Castle, North Wales, 1216

The light was strangely cold and bright as Bronwyn walked in solemn procession behind Gruffydd and Gwenllian to her grave, a private place within the grounds of the chapel at Degannwy. With them, they took an ancient priest; a believer of the old ways, a man who could placate the gods and settle restless spirits. They also took her enamelled brooch, wrapped in a piece of leather and bound with silver cord, the only thing left that might bind her spirit to this world other than her son.

The grave had been difficult to find at first, hidden as it was by grass and tangled with weeds; all that marked it now was its headstone, and even that was weather beaten and crumbling under the unforgiving Welsh skies. A brief inscription proclaimed it the resting place of Tangwystl, mother of Gruffydd and Gwenllian, beloved of Llywelyn ap Ioworth, prince of Gwynedd.

Gruffydd had been reticent from the first, fearful even, but Gwenny had not. She had stood calmly apart, the wind sweeping through her long red brown hair as the priest prayed over her mother's tomb, his balding tonsure bowed low, his robes billowing in the sudden wind that swept across the bleak landscape as he muttered words in an ancient language. When his job was done he had stepped back, frowning as a sudden mist rolled in from the sea, concealing the chapel and threatening to cut off their passage home. Muttering an oath Gruffydd knelt, pausing only to cross himself before he began to dig with his hands at the foot of her grave.

Only Bronwyn saw her standing behind him; she watched as slowly she reached out a hand and let it linger there, at his shoulder, then, with a look of sadness on her face she turned and slowly melted into the swirling mist ...

When Gwenny and Gruffydd had gone, Bronwyn stood for a long time, contemplating the newly turned patch of soil at the foot of her grave where the brooch was now buried, then, making up her mind, she turned and left. Knowing that they, none of them, had seen the last of it yet ...

Aber, North Wales, October 1216

The spirit of reconciliation brought about by the Magna Carta between the barons and King John, had not outlasted the summer following Gruffydd's release. By the autumn of 1215, at the demand of the king, the Magna Carta was annulled by the pope who declared it not only "shameful and base," but also "illegal and unjust." Within days of the pope's proclamation, England was once again in the grip of civil war, with John himself saying that the terms of the Magna Carta had been extracted from him under duress. In truth, John had never meant to abide by a document forced upon him by his barons.

No longer trusting the king, a more defiant group of John's barons, including his old enemy, Eustance de Vesi, turned to France again, inviting Prince Louis to press ahead with his plans to take the throne in the hope that the French king would come to their aid. The Northern barons went a step further, petitioning the King of Scots to take control of Northumberland, Westmoreland and Cumberland. John, beside himself with rage, marched North towards Scotland allowing his mercenaries to burn villages, rape, plunder, murder and steal along the way in a ruthless campaign designed to strike fear in his subjects and remind them that he was still their king. Within the first few days of 1216, his troops had taken the besieged border town of Berwick, burning it to the ground in a show of bloody vengeance that was soon to become his stamp upon a rebellion that threatened to overturn the land.

Having dealt with the North, John turned his attention to the south-east of England, ploughing down through Lincoln where Robert Fitz Walter, Saer de Quincy and a French force were besieging the castle. After a fierce battle, which left the commander dead and Fitz Walter, de Quincy and three hundred French knights prisoners, John's army proceeded on towards Fotheringay, before heading into East Anglia, down to Essex, and finally on to Oxford where they came to rest.

Along the way, resistance towards the royalist army dropped as castles were surrendered without a fight, and by March 1216, faced with inevitable defeat, even the staunchest of John's enemies were at last contemplating making peace. Wales, meanwhile, had found itself once more under interdict, any previous treaty with Rome having been inadvertently broken by John's sudden defection to Christianity. That, and the continuous allegiance of the Welsh to the French king and their support of the baron's cause, immediately made the country an enemy of the pope. Not at all disadvantaged by this, Llywelyn and his allies took the opportunity presented by the chaos in England to parade through the Welsh countryside and capture many of the castles still held by the royal demesne, including Carmarthen, which had been the centre of royal power in south-west for nearly a hundred years.

Then suddenly, in April, rumours from France filtered into England claiming that Prince Louis was about to set sail from Calais. In a state of panic, John immediately fortified the Kentish coast and sent a fleet across the channel to try to blockade Louis in port. But despite his efforts, the twenty-seven-year-old prince landed in England at the end of May, marched through Kent, and arrived triumphant in London on 2nd June, promising to restore England's laws and rule the realm justly.

During the summer that followed, Louis' army succeeded in pushing John out of the south-east of England, whilst in the North, the Scots proceeded to push back across the border. Castles held for John prepared to endure lengthy sieges as the country was split between the two rival kings. Amidst this turmoil, John was suddenly plagued with a number of damaging defections, including that of his own half-brother William Longespée, the Earl of Salisbury, and his cousin, William de Warenne, Earl of Surrey, both of whom had fled to Winchester to disavowed their allegiance to him and acknowledge Louis as their King. The loss of Salisbury and de Warenne was a huge blow to John, who, although used to the bitter taste of betrayal amongst friends, had, until that day, not experienced it amongst family. By the Autumn only a handful of loyal supporters remained faithful to him, including the Marshall and Chester.

Then, in October, things took another unexpected turn for the worst. While staying at Lynn in Norfolk, John fell ill with dysentery. On the 12th, despite advice to the contrary, he pushed on with his campaign, marching his troops across the River

Wellstream, at the point when it ran into the Wash. It was here that he suffered his final, devastating blow, when against the advice of his captain of the guard, he instructed his baggage train to take a short cut across the Walsh itself. The tide was not out far enough and the baggage train, containing his coronation regalia, ran into the dangerous quicksand that lurked beneath the surface of the sea bed. Unable to turn or move the sprawling wagons, the king could only watch helplessly as within moments it, along with several men and horses, were swallowed up by a huge wave to be lost forever beneath the waves.

Embittered, angry, and by now extremely sick, John carried on, spending a night at Swineshead Abbey in Lincolnshire, then on again to Newark. By then he was in terrible pain and was forced to be carried the last few miles on a stretcher. He died there at Newark on the evening of 18th October, in agony, having been finally persuaded by the abbot to forgive his enemies.

'He died in agony,' Joanna whispered to Llywelyn when they heard the news via a courier armed with details from among others, her brother Richard, and the Abbot of Swineshead Abbey himself.

'He died as a wicked man should!' Llywelyn re-joined harshly.

'He was my father,' Joanna said brokenly, 'and God help me, I loved him.'

'I know,' Llywelyn said, more gently this time. 'And you can take heart that at the end he repented some of his sins - according to the abbot he made a charter leaving Margred de Lacy three carucates of land in the forest of Aconbury - to build a religious house for the souls of her father, William de Braose, Matilda her mother, and William her brother, all of whom were named individually. He obviously had a conscience, albeit buried somewhere deep, Joanna, but it bobbed to the surface at the last, when it was needed.'

Joanna turned away from Llywelyn, and put the letter she still held down on the table carefully.

'Joanna, you know your half-brother Henry is now officially named as his heir?'

He's still in his minority,' Joanna murmured, thinking of the frail, fair-haired boy she had last seen at her father's court before he'd hanged the hostages. 'He's only nine.'

'Yes, and that is why Pembroke and Chester have charge of him. Now that your father is dead, as his half-sister, your job will be to help me in my negotiations with him – mayhap Wales will fare better in his hands,' Llywelyn said practically. 'But for now we are still at war.'

Joanna turned away, not listening. 'I should make arrangements to attend Father's funeral and Henry's coronation.'

'Of course,' Llywelyn said, going to her side and putting an arm round her stiff shoulders. 'Your father wills that his body be buried in the church of St. Mary and St. Wulfstan, at Worcester.'

'Why there, I wonder?' Joanna said, shrugging off his embrace and brushing away a tear. 'I always thought it would be Windsor, or Corfe even.'

Llywelyn contemplated her for a moment. 'It would not be safe to transport his body elsewhere in times of war, Joanna, you should know that. His enemies would not stop short of desecrating his body if it fell into their hands, even I would not want that for your father. As for Henry, he will remain in Corfe Castle with Isabella until the necessary arrangements have been made for his coronation I should imagine.' He paused. 'Don't think for a minute, Joanna, that I will roll over and submit to a new English King just because John is dead.' Then, more gently. 'Look, I know it is hard, the death of your father and your stepbrother now proclaimed his heir, but we will get through this you and I. I have great plans for Wales still, and now, with Gruffydd's release, I mean to grant him lands of his own to rule so that he will have purpose. I also mean to call a council soon and settle the other princes of Wales into their own lands in order to make peace between us once and for all. But all this will take time, and I still need your support to bring my plans for Wales to fruition - your skills as negotiator are now needed to be applied to those who hold council over your brother whilst he is still in his minority.'

'I wonder why Isabella is not acting as Regent?' Joanna said. 'At least we would know what we are dealing with - both the Marshall and Chester, although loyal to my father at the end, have a history of changing allegiances where it suits their pockets or their moral high ground - we are more likely to find ourselves at war with one of them, than on any whim of Isabella's.'

'That could never be allowed, you know that, my love. Anyway, you said yourself that one day she might want to return to France. She never has had a head for politics or rule, only flirtation and self-gain.'

Joanna turned to him sadly. 'Ah, Llywelyn, my love,' she said, 'tiz a sad day for me I'll not deny, but, as always, I am here to support you - more so now that we face new challenges. I ask only one thing of you, however, and that is that you let me grieve for my father in peace, that you do not ask anything of me until I am ready.' And with that she turned sadly away, and headed for the chapel to pray.

Chapter 39

Aber, North Wales, 1217

'That is so not true, you little pip-squeak. Why, I would thrash you for it, were you not such a coward that you would run and squeal to your mother!'

'But it *is* true! Your mother was a concubine, and that means you're a bastard and can't inherit!' a shrill voice rejoined, the familiar accusation carrying clearly to Gwladys who was idling the time away spinning wool with her ladies in the tower.

'Shut up! Oh, do shut up!' Another voice, Elen's, interrupted her piercing entreaty, finally dispelling any notion of a peaceful afternoon whiling away the time awaiting Reginald's return from Worcester, where he'd ridden with her father to meet Joanna and finalise a peace treaty with King Henry, who, following a spate victories against Prince Louis, was now prepared to recognise him in his conquests in Wales.

Throwing a look of resignation to the other women, Gwladys put down her distaff, and went to the window from where she could look down onto the large courtyard below. Elen stood between the brothers, her small face screwed up in an attempt not to cry as she bravely tried to intervene and prevent any further argument between the pair, both of whom she loved with an equal passion - despite the fact that only one, Dafydd, was of her true blood, and the other as he had so succinctly pointed out in his childish way, was merely the offspring of a mistress and therefore illegitimate.

Sighing, Gwladys picked up her skirts, and made her way down the turret stairs and into the *ty hir*, the familiar stone built house that she'd called home until her marriage to Reginald de Braose, Lord of Brecknock, Abergavenny and Builith had taken her beyond the fringes of Wales, and catapulted her into the Anglo-Norman and Welsh society that now existed along the Marches.

'Gruffydd -' she said, stepping purposefully out into the courtyard.

'Where's father? I wish to speak with him ...' Gruffydd growled, rounding on Gwladys immediately.

'Why, surely you know? He is in Worcester, concluding a treaty with King Henry. He is to come to terms at last.'

Gruffydd looked at Gwladys through narrowed eyes. 'And when did he mean to tell me?' he asked accusingly.

'You were not here when he made the decision. He held a council with the princes, and he consulted with us, but because you are so disagreeable these days he decided that it was best that you were left out.'

Gruffydd laughed shortly. 'Well, you would know all about being in disfavour. I must say that I'm surprised to see you here at all after Reginald's defection to Henry last summer - he actually had the cheek to pay homage to the king, didn't he? In return for his Bramber Estates in Sussex, I understand!'

'It was a politically astute decision!' Gwladys retorted, feeling her cheeks grow red with anger at the unveiled sarcasm in Gruffydd's tone. 'He only meant to aid Father in his efforts to unite the Welsh and English by regaining his Sussex lands. He was, and ever is, Father's vassal!'

'His nephews, Rhys and Owain, didn't see it that way though, did they? They saw it as betrayal, that's why they attacked Builth,' Gruffydd continued, ignoring both Dafydd and Elen now that more pleasure could be derived from his half-sister's discomfort, than from the pair of them put together. 'And what's more,' he said, warming to his theme, 'Father was so angry that he besieged Brecon, forcing your precious husband to yield the castle of Swansea as penance for rejecting his true overlord in favour of the enemy!' He looked at her narrowly. 'How did you feel being caught in the middle of it all, sister dear - did you stand by the Angevin cause, or the Welsh? After all, you have mixed blood in your veins - just like Dafydd here.' He said, shooting a look at the boy who had stood mutely by during this puzzling exchange, too young to understand grown up politics any deeper than that certain conditions of birth stood in the way of his stepbrother getting what he wanted, and that he could use them to rile him whenever his siblings' glowering presence threatened his small world.

Gwladys suppressed her anger. 'I would be careful what you say, if I were you!' she said archly. 'My mixed blood, the Angevin blood that flows in my mother's veins and that I inherited, has nothing to do with anything. I love Reginald, and I want what is best for him. I love Father, too, and now they have come to terms. It's best you remember that, Gruffydd, for you would do very well to back down and come to terms with your own plight, for I don't see a very bright future ahead of you if you cannot!'

'You still have the claws of a cat, don't you!' Gruffydd said stiffly, then looking down at Elen he smiled. 'You will make a good soldier one day, little sister. Only reserve your battle fight for those who deserve it, sweetheart, for neither your brother nor I do.' Then ruffling her hair affectionately, he turned and glared at Daffydd, who, though still mystified by the grown-up's argument, was bright red with fury at the continuous mention of his mother's Angevin origins, which on the one hand made him proud, and on the other perplexed, for they seemed to crop up in the most casual of conversations, only to cause a lot bother along the way.

'As for you,' he said regarding the boy like he would a turd stuck to the sole of his shoe. 'You will keep. There are many ways to flog a horse, and I have lots of supporters who would prefer to see a prince of the true blood succeed to Wales, rather than a mere half-Angevin, half-Welsh baby like you who has much growing up to do!'

'Will he go away again?' Elen asked miserably, moments later, staring after Gruffydd's retreating form.

Gwladys sighed. 'I expect so. Senena is with child, and they are staying on the Isle of Môn with her father until it is born. I only wish that he could accept that he is no longer father's successor, and concentrate on his wife and family, and ruling his own lands, instead of rebelling at every turn,' she added, referring firstly to the stiff, unapproachable girl that Gruffydd had married two summers ago and, secondly, to the lands in Meirionnydd and

Ardudwy that Llywelyn had bestowed upon him thinking that his eldest son would find some sort of recompense for the loss of his inheritance in their ownership.

'Papa says that he rules his lands unjustly,' Dafydd said fiercely. 'He said that if he continues that way, then he will have to take them away from him. I hope that he does, and that he locks Gruffydd up for good and throws away the key!'

Gwladys sighed. 'It does you no good taunting Gruffydd every time you see him, Dafydd, in fact it only makes things worse, and you are far too small to stand up to him if he really loses his temper.'

'I'm not afraid of him!' Dafydd said haughtily. 'And anyway, Papa will lock him up eventually because he causes so much trouble.'

'I shouldn't bank on that,' Gwladys said, suddenly losing patience with the subject of Gruffydd. 'He might well be a threat to you, Dafydd, but to Father he is also an invaluable warrior - has proved himself so, and until you are old enough to take on that role yourself, then he will stay at liberty in order to defend the realm where and when he is needed. If I were you I would take a subtler approach and let Mother fight your battles for you. Even now, whilst she is intervening in the quarrel between King Henry and Father, she extends her efforts on your behalf. You must remember that she is the king's sister, and as such she has sway!' she finished crossly. Then picking up her skirts, she made once more for the peace and tranquillity of the spinning room to await her husband's return.

Aber, North Wales, October, 1220

Celebrations had already commenced in the great hall by the time Gruffydd and his wife Senena arrived at the *llys* on the evening of Elen's betrothal to John of Scotland, the young man who was not only nephew to the King of Scotland, but also the recently titled Earl of Huntingdon. The couple were drenched to the skin, having encountered the first of the heavy rains that always beset the Welsh mountains during the early Autumn months, before the onset of the heavy snows that characterised the Welsh winters, which would have made John and Elen's journey back to his lands in the north impossible until the following year.

Shrugging off his sodden mantle irritably, Gruffydd waved for a page, before looking around at the familiar surroundings of his childhood. The first thing he noticed was that the great hall had been refurbished. It was now lavishly decorated with ornately carved panelling, and brightly coloured tapestries on every wall, all artfully lit by the warm glow of several hundred well placed sconces. Up on the dais, a vast table lined with ornately carved chairs was laid with goblets of chased silver and cutlery of the same ilk. In the middle of it all sat his father, flanked on the one side by his wife Joanna, and on the other Elen, and several members of John's family.

Gruffydd frowned, the hall rang with music and laughter as troubadours and minstrels vied with one and other for the bride-to-be's attention, and he was shocked to see an animal trainer with several monkey-like creatures on his shoulder. He turned away in disgust. Aber was fast becoming like the English courts in that it had dissolved into a veritable mummering theatre rather than the pleasantly ordered hall that he remembered. Even his father was dressed more like an elegant courtier than a Welsh chieftain, with his tunic of peacock coloured silk worn beneath an exceptionally fine fur trimmed mantle. Without warning a sudden wave of anger overwhelmed him, as memories of the sumptuously dressed courtiers and glittering surroundings of his imprisonment under King John came flooding back, reminding him of the licentiousness of the English courts he'd witnessed before being reduced to the derogation of a prison following the massacre of the Welsh hostages.

Tearing his eyes away from the disagreeable scene, Gruffydd took Senena's arm, and together they made their own way towards the dais to join Dafydd and the other guests of honour who were being seated there. It was a year or so since he had last seen the boy, and even at eight years of age Dafydd still looked like a baby, with his plump cheeks and stubby fingers, their nails bitten to the quick. Seeing Gruffydd regarding them, Dafydd quickly thrust his hands under the table and turned to whisper something to a pretty, fair-haired young girl seated between him and Elen, whom he recognised as Elen's latest companion, Isabella de Braose.

As he made his way along the row of seats, he nodded to Gwladys and Reginald. In an effort to restore equilibrium in the family, Reginald had recently passed his controversially won estates in Bramber, Sussex, onto his nephew John de Braose at his coming of age. His father, never one to miss an opportunity to strengthen ties between his family and influential Norman lords, had immediately arranged a match between Marared and the young man, a strategy that had brought about a sort of semi-quasi peace between Llywelyn, and the son-in-law whom he still regarded as a traitor.

Pausing for a moment, Gruffydd looked around. Although the chief reason they had been invited to the feast was to bid farewell to Elen, he was fast getting the impression that something else was on the agenda, not least because of the ill-disguised whispers that had followed him down the aisles as he went. Quickly dismissing the thought, he slipped his hand into Senena's and, feeling her reassuring squeeze, he smiled gratefully at her. It had come as something of a surprise to find that he actually liked the tall, timid girl that his father had elected he marry upon his return to Aber. Of good stock, she had given him a girl and a boy in a short space of time and was now expecting another, and it had soon become clear that her ambitions matched his own, for she announced that if they were blessed with second boy, then they would call him Llywelyn after his father in an effort to restore some peace between them both. Taking a seat, Gruffydd threw a reassuring smile down the table at the bride-to-be.

She had changed from the skinny waif that had championed him two summers ago. Now a tall, slender girl approaching thirteen summers, her expressive blue eyes, fringed with long, dark lashes seemed haunted. She was currently fiddling self-consciously with her hair which fell loose round her shoulders in a dark mantle, whilst at the same time throwing anxious looks at her betrothed who sat alongside her. Gruffydd felt a sudden pang of regret that, because of their differences, he had not got to see her grow up, for she was probably the only one of his half-sisters that he really liked. John was a lucky man he thought, taking measure of the pale young man who was gazing openly at the vision beside him, clearly stunned by his good fortune.

Nodding to several other people he recognised, Gruffydd once more turned his attention to Dafydd, who was now contemplating him with the usual customary scowl on his face that he reserved especially for when they were present in the same room. Gruffydd returned the look steadily, aware that others were watching them with interest - it was no secret that the brothers hated one another intensely and were usually kept apart, with him confined to the endlessly cold corridors of Degannwy overlooking the river Conway where he could not make trouble. Surprisingly, Gruffydd found himself looking away first, and he clenched his fists angrily at his side as he fought hard to swallow his bile ... *if only things had been different - if only he had been, not only the first-born son, but legitimate as well.*

Seeing his discomfort, Dafydd smiled slyly and, turning to Isabella, he whispered something that clearly shocked the girl whose eyebrows momentarily disappeared beneath her hairline. Deciding to ignore him, Gruffydd glanced briefly at his father. Llywelyn was leaning back in his chair, drumming his fingers on the table and pretending to be unaware of the tension radiating from his sons.

Gruffydd bristled. His father had made no attempt to greet him, nor did he show any intention of doing so now, making him wonder again why he had been given licence to attend this particular feast. He sighed, his father, he knew, would have a reason, and doubtless it would not be long before he was told. Moreover, he was reasonably sure that it would have something to do with the succession.

A sudden commotion at the end of the hall announced the arrival of Gwen and her husband, William de Lacey. Spotting Gruffydd seated on the dais, they immediately made their way over to him. It was a long time since he and Gwen had been together, with Gwen now residing mostly in Ireland with William. Throwing herself at her brother, Gwen hugged him with such enthusiasm that Gruffydd had to pry her arms from around his neck.

'Oh, Gwen, it's good to see you!' he said, laughing. 'How long has it been?' he asked, patting one of the empty chairs he had reserved for her alongside him.

'Too long, brother,' she said, glancing around. 'Tis quite the gathering, isn't it? And little Elen, well, isn't she turning into a beauty!'

'Why, yes ... I couldn't help noticing that myself,' Gruffydd replied, watching as Elen sipped delicately from a cup of chased silver with the one hand, whilst periodically clenching and unclenching a piece of table linen nervously with the other as she tried to ignore the young man who sat beside her battling to control his youthful blushes.

'And Father?' Gwen said, glancing thoughtfully down the table. 'He looks well enough with our stepmother, does he not?'

Following her gaze, Gruffydd's lips tightened as he saw Joanna turn and say something to Llewelyn. Her hand rested on the sleeve of his tunic, the fine silk undoubtedly stitched by her own fair hand. She was flirting with him, he thought in disgust, and Llywelyn was smiling back at her with affection. My God, he really does love her! he thought, and he wondered why he should be so surprised after all these years. After all that was just one of the reasons that he hated his stepmother. That, and the fact that she finally given birth to Dafydd. 'Yes,' he said tersely, suddenly annoyed that once again she monopolised his father's attention.

'And have you heard the news that Isabella has returned to Angoulême and married her former betrothed's son, another Hugh?' Gwen continued, oblivious to the look of hate on Gruffydd's face as he continued to stare at Joanna.

'Yes,' Gruffydd said again, his voice dull with contempt.

Gwen's diatribe about Isabella continued for some time. Then seeing that Gruffydd wasn't interested in the gossip surrounding the abandonment of her children, or her flight to France in pursuit of Hugh Lusignion the younger, Gwen huffed and turned to Senena, leaving William with the job of trying to try to distract him.

Gruffydd barely noticed as he continued to seethe.

It was an age before Llywelyn finally left his seat and came over to formally greet his son. 'I see that you are keeping well,' he said carefully, nodding briefly to Senena and Gwen, who discreetly changed places to speak with Marared and her husband who had now joined Gwladys and Reginald at the end of the table.

'Well enough,' Gruffydd replied grudgingly. 'But why do you insist on keeping me confined to Degannwy, Father?' he blurted out suddenly. 'Surely I can be of more assistance to you here?'

Llywelyn sighed. 'Because, lad, you insist on warring with your brother, you know that. If I thought that I could keep you at my side without trouble brewing, then I would, but you make it impossible for me to do so.' He paused before changing the subject. 'I have been hearing alarming tales of your rule in Meirionnydd and Ardudwy. Ednyved,' he said, speaking of the new seneschal who had replaced an ailing Gwyn after Gruffydd's return from England, 'has informed me of your treatment of your villeins, which is considered unjust.' He sighed. 'You have a wife now, Gruffydd, and a young family to think of. Is it not time that you settled for that; to raise your family and be content with the lands that I have bestowed upon you without causing further trouble?'

Once again, Gruffydd's thoughts returned unerringly to his claim as his father's successor. He could hear his mother's voice in his head, edging him on: *the people of Wales will support you in your claim, bach, they will support you over that of a half-Angevin usurper.* He ground his teeth angrily. For a moment, he'd harboured the hope that that his father had invited him here to tell him that he fully supported his eldest sons claim above Dafydd's; that he would uphold Welsh law. That now that John was dead, the Norman law of primogeniture could, once again, be ignored.

He was about to broach the subject, when trumpeters signalled the beginning of the feast.

Llywelyn rose. 'We shall speak later, Gruffydd,' he said firmly. 'For now, try not to spoil Elen's evening.'

Seeing him depart, Senena and Gwen joined him again.

'Do you think he has reconsidered?' Senena whispered, her eyes bright with anticipation. 'Do you think we can come back to Aber, to the *llys*? That maybe you will succeed after all? I do so hate it at Degannwy, it's no place for the children,' she added, looking fondly over to where, Margred, the eldest of their offspring sat wiggling on her nurse's lap, excited to be attending the feast whilst her new baby brother, Owain, remained at home in the nursery.

'I don't know,' Gruffydd said shortly. 'All I know is that the old fox has got something up his sleeve, and

I'm not sure I'm going to like it!' Then crossly he turned his attention to the feast, helping himself to a generous portion of the roast boar being offered by a page, followed by some leek pottage which had far too much garlic in it for his liking.

'Glutton!' Gwen teased an hour later, when he finally pushed his trencher away, and leaned back to wipe a trickle of sauce from his mouth with his hand.

'You can speak!' he said, grinning at her voluptuous bosom and waist line. Then more seriously. 'And there is still no happy news to impart, then?'

'No, I fear that time enough has passed to realise that I am barren.'

Gruffydd pursed his lips. 'You don't know that for sure, you might be wrong, it could be William's fault.'

Gwen sighed. 'To be sure!' she said, mimicking the Irish lilt. 'But no matter, I am content.' She hesitated.

'What is it?' Gruffydd ventured, looking at her narrowly.

'Have your visions gone now, since we buried the brooch?'

'Yes. Why?' he asked uneasily.

Gwen glanced across at her husband, then as if making a decision she said. 'Tis only that sometimes she comes to me in Ireland. In my dreams, or in the fire. But there are too many other distractions there ... too many other ghosts.' She shivered visibly. 'Tis a wicked place, Ireland. If William were to die I would leave -'

As if sensing scandal, Senena tapped Gruffydd on the sleeve with a spoon. 'What are you two whispering about?' she asked

'Ghosts,' Gwen, said airily. 'We were talking ghosts, weren't we, Gruffydd? Mother's, in particular!'

'Nonsense!' Senena said briskly, and Gruffydd saw her face darken at the mention of Tangwystl, the woman that she knew very little about other than what she had gleaned from Bronwyn's ramblings, and the various rumours that were attached to their mother's name. Suddenly he was irked, annoyed that the subject of Tangwystyl had once again raised its ugly head. Senena, however, was staring at them both intently, waiting for more, and he sighed.

'Gwenny used to see our mother all the time when we were children, didn't you, Gwen? Reckons that she only haunts us because she believes that I am destined to succeed to the throne on Father's death instead of Dafydd,'

'But that was when we still had the brooch,' Gwen clarified. 'It's gone now. Buried with her in her grave.'

There was a long silence, then Senena smiled at them both brightly. 'Well, we've seen no ghosts, have we, Gruffydd. Anyway, you are perfectly capable of succeeding your own, aren't you, my love, as I'm sure your father will tell you today. As lovely as Elen's send-off is, the summons sent implied more than that, didn't it darling?' she said, standing and kissing him affectionately on the head.

With that, she turned and began to make her way down the hall, leaving Gwen and Gruffydd staring after her with a joint sense of impending doom.

It was several hours later before Gruffydd was finally summoned to his father's well-appointed chancery behind the hall, and he'd imbued more than his fair share of wine, leaving him feeling tired and irritable.

Llywelyn was sitting behind a table, his hands linked together behind his head. Opposite him, Dafydd sat moodily in a hard-backed chair, another empty one stood alongside him. Throwing his half-brother a quick look, Gruffydd sat down in the vacant chair, and propping one booted leg across the other, he tried to look relaxed.

Llywelyn was nothing if not blunt. 'I have asked you here today to tell you that I have chosen Dafydd as my successor, and your uncle, King Henry, recognises my choice and approves it. I have also petitioned the pope to have Dafydd recognised as my heir, and to have Joanna declared legitimate in the eyes of the church. You might as well accept it lad, it was never going to be, no matter what I might have promised your mother.'

Gruffydd sat as still as a statue carved from stone, only a persistent twitch in his jaw betrayed his emotions. Then suddenly he was out of the chair and facing his father like a demented demon.

'How dare you!' he shouted. 'How dare you replace me with this half Angevin whoreson! What about your promise to my mother? What about the people - they are behind me! Even you must see that they will never support Dafydd over me, a prince who has the true blood of Wales running through his veins!'

Dafydd stood nervously. 'Don't shout at Papa like that!'

Immediately, Gruffydd rounded on his brother. 'Shut up! Shut up, you little pip-squeak! Why I -'

Caught up in a turmoil of pain and anger, Gruffydd didn't notice as Llewellyn stood and crossed over to the hearth. Nor did he notice when Llywelyn froze as he felt a familiar cold breath against his ear.

You will regret this Llewellyn Fawr, a voice breathed. *You will regret this, you'll see ...*

Degannwy Castle, North Wales, 1227

Owain was whittling. It was a pastime that he enjoyed as it gave him the chance to take his younger brother, Llywelyn, out from under his mother, father, and his sister Margred's feet in the castle. He scowled. He hated the tense, almost stifling atmosphere that seemed to always hang over the castle, one which, he had begun to understand over the years, stemmed from the night of his Aunt Elen's betrothal. Of course, he had only been a baby then, and Llywelyn had not even been born, but it was no secret that it was on that occasion his father had learned that his half-brother - his uncle Dafydd - had been formally declared as their father's successor. He frowned, he didn't really know what was meant by the word "successor," only that it caused an awful lot of rows, and that because of it his father had been mostly confined to Degannwy as grandfather Llywelyn's "guest," only being allowed out in order that he might carry out some mission or other on his behalf.

'Owain! Owain! Come look at what I've found!' a shrill voice cried from the back of the graveyard.

Owain paused, and ceasing his whittling, he began to look around, suddenly aware that despite his instructions to the contrary, Llywelyn was nowhere in sight.

He found Llywelyn stooped over a grave. It had long been left unattended, its occupants name now lost beneath the clinging lichen and fingers of creeping weed that covered it.

'Christ's bones!' Owain exclaimed angrily, forgetting where he was. 'What do you think you are doing? That's someone's grave you are disturbing!'

'But look what I've found!' Llywelyn exclaimed, emerging from his digging like a rabbit from a hole.

'Stop it! Put it back!' Owain cried. Frightened, as a sudden gust of wind disturbed the otherwise quiet graveyard, sending leaves and debris spinning around them.

'I won't! I won't! Finders keepers!' Llywelyn shrieked.

'Please, Llywelyn. Put it back!' Owain tried once again, looking around and wondering why, like him,

Llywelyn couldn't feel the power building, as above them thunderous clouds began to roll across the sky.

'Never!' Llywelyn laughed in delight. And then he was gone. Running with the wind behind him towards the castle with his treasure, where he would hide it like a magpie hides its prize - high in its nest, until it falls and is found by another.

Aber, North Wales, July 1227

Joanna looked at the letter in her hand. It was from Gwladys and it was short and to the point. Reginald was dead, and his son, Will, now Sir William, 6th Lord of Abergavenny, had inherited his father's estates in their entirety, save for the few she had brought to him by marriage which were still in her name.

Joanna put the letter down and crossed to the window to stare out across the now familiar landscape. The sun was at its highest in an impossibly blue sky, its golden rays shining down upon the purple -topped mountains of the *Eryri*; beyond the village she could see the river *Afon Aber* as it meandered lazily through the valley, and, beyond that, tiny dots of white where sheep grazed in the fields beneath the well-tended orchards cultivated at the foot of the mountains. For a moment, she wondered how Gwladys felt about the situation. Did she miss Wales and her past home life enough to return? Or would she prefer to live out her life in England as a rich widow under the protection of her late husband's family? Sir William, it seemed, was more than happy for her to stay on and become companion to his wife Ava and his children, residing in one or other of the estates that he now owned. Joanna smiled ruefully not sure which one she would prefer if she had the choice, for even after all these years she still felt the occasional pang of homesickness for her old life in France despite having becoming accustomed to the Welsh one she now lived.

Llywelyn was not in favour. 'She must come home,' he said that evening as they dined in private for once. 'Sir William is the king's man through and through,' he said, taking another bite of the fine white bread on the plate before him. 'He has pledged his services and support to your brother and, furthermore, he supports Hubert de Burgh's advancement into Wales which I will not tolerate. No, you will write to Gwladys and inform her that she will be safer here under our protection whilst we seek a new marriage alliance for her.'

Joanna frowned. 'Mayhap she doesn't want to marry again?'

'Nonsense. She will marry again and beget children of her own this time.'

'Still, she has become very fond of Reginald's son, even though he is older than her ... he's more like an uncle really, and she gets on with his mother's kin - Gracia had an extensive family; mayhap we could foster future alliances within the family there?' Joanna ventured

Llywelyn looked at her sternly. 'No. You will write. Now. Today.' He paused. 'I would not normally insist, but I cannot see any good coming out of this unless she returns home immediately. Please see to it at once, Joanna ...'

Aber, Wales, Autumn, 1228

Dawn had only just broken when the carts trundled into the courtyard, followed by Llywelyn and his *teulu*. The noise was deafening after the silence of the past few weeks, and Joanna hastened towards the door alarmed. She had barely made it out of the *ti hir* when she came to an abrupt halt. Llywelyn and several of his *teulu* were wounded. Amidst the affray, she could see him being helped down from his horse by two of his men. As his feet met the ground he stumbled and had to be half carried to a bench, where he was given a wineskin and a husk of bread by his squire before managing to bark out orders to his men.

Throwing down the armful of rushes that she had been carrying, Joanna ran to him.

'Llywelyn! Llywelyn! Holy mother of God, you are injured!'

'Tis only a shoulder wound,' Llywelyn ground out through gritted teeth. 'Tis nothing that will not heal.'

'What happened?'

'There was a battle - at Ceri -' he broke off, his face screwing up with pain before continuing. 'Against Hubert de Burgh.' He grinned, flashing his good white teeth. 'We won!'

Joanna didn't need to be told any more. De Burgh's ascendency into Wales had accelerated rapidly, having been granted the strategic castle and lordship of Montgomery by the king earlier in the year. As a result, Llywelyn's relationship with her stepbrother had steadily deteriorated, with her own attempts to intercede on his behalf resulting in the confiscation of two English manors, Rothley and Condover, granted to herself. Angry that Henry had taken lands gifted to his wife, Llywelyn had immediately engaged in conflict with de Burgh, determined to stop any further intrusion into Wales under the banner of the Crown.

'We took the castles of Neath and Kidwelly,' Llywelyn continued. 'And we've prevented de Burgh from constructing a further castle at Pen y Castell. I think we've finally managed to break the English stronghold along the Welsh borders. But we have a prisoner.' He coughed, before barking out further orders to his men, and Joanna watched as a man was pushed forward by two soldiers. He was bound at the wrists by a length of rope, and stripped of his weapons he wore only a hauberk and chausses and his dirty blond hair fell unkempt over a bruised and bloody face. Joanna might not have recognised him were it not for his impossibly blue eyes.

'Sir William!' she blurted.

They stared at each other for several long moments, before Joanna tore her gaze away, afraid that Llywelyn would glimpse the treacherous memories that passed between them.

'I mean to ransom him to the Crown - for two thousand pounds.' Llywelyn said lazily.

Joanna gasped.

'I am worth it, madam!' Will spoke for the first time.

'The sum has been agreed,' Llywelyn continued, ignoring the young nobleman. 'As have other terms. And, so,' he grinned suddenly, 'I think it's time to talk, don't you, Will?' Then struggling to his feet, he ordered the young man be released from his bonds.

'From now on you are here as our guest under house arrest. My squire will show you to your rooms whilst my wife attends to my wounds. Then we will speak,' he finished tiredly.

Indeed, that night as the household sat down to dinner, Joanna learned that in principle the sum of two thousand pounds had been agreed for the release of the young nobleman. For the time being - or for however long it took for the ransom to be paid - Will was to remain their guest under house arrest. But more importantly to Llywelyn, Joanna learned, he had extracted a promise from de Braose that he would give his daughter Isabella in marriage to Dafydd. Joanna was not unaware that this was this a major coup, for not only would it bind the de Braoses, one of the most influential Marcher families to his future heir, but it would also bring as part of Isabella's dowry the lordship of Builth, thus expanding his stronghold in Wales. Llywelyn had obviously forgotten his more unsuccessful attempts at marrying his daughters into the de Braose family, she reflected wryly as she reached for another of the sweetmeats that she so loved. Reginald de Braose, Will's father, had been an unreliable ally. As had John, Marared's husband who, despite having bought the lands of Gower along with claims on Reginald's lands, would not be pressed into politics for any cause save his own.

Looking at Llywelyn's face, now flushed with wine, and at Will's cool one, Joanna could only hope that a match between the two young people might finally fulfil Llywelyn's expectations and provide the stable foothold in the March that he desired. Along with the right connections to the crown and, ultimately, the king's ear.

She also hoped that Will's ransom would be paid soon, for she was experiencing such a strange plethora of emotions each time she met his eyes that she did not think she could survive in such close proximity to him for any longer than was necessary.

Chapter 40

Degannwy Castle, North Wales, 1228

Gruffydd paced angrily up and down the hall, viciously kicking an unfortunate hound out of the way as he went, and watching moodily as it went to take refuge under a table still laden with dishes from lunch. The servants were slack here he thought angrily, as he recalled the peace and comforts of Aber from which he had once more been banned after fighting with Dafydd again.

He scowled. In spite of his efforts, in the years following Llewelyn's announcement that Dafydd was to be his successor, there had been no improvement in his relationship with his brother, particularly as in 1222 Dafydd had gained formal recognition as Llywelyn's heir from the pope. To make matters worse, in 1226 Joanna had obtained a papal decree declaring her legitimate, placing yet another obstacle in the way of his ambitions to follow in his father's footsteps. Llywelyn's attempts at placating him with the lordships of Meirionydd and Ardudwy had also ended in disaster the year after Elen's marriage to John of Scotland, for he had deemed him a harsh and cruel overlord, and barely a year after that he had deprived him of those very same lands.

Despite all this, Gruffydd grumbled to himself, he had still led his father's war band against the English in Ystrad Tywi when problems had arisen between English and Welsh troops along the Marches. And then when Llywelyn had seized the fortresses of Kinnerley and Whittington on the Shropshire border, it had been him that his father had sent to intercept the English in South Wales where they were intent on seizing the castles of Carmarthen and Cardigan. He had even accompanied Llywelyn into Montgomery when it had fallen to Henry's troops, where they'd been surrendered the castles of Whittington and Kinnerley to the Crown rather than prolong the warfare.

But it had taken just the one, ill-advised attack on his brother to cancel all that out, when his resentment against him had had erupted into violence one afternoon and he had raised a sword to his throat. Pandemonium had broken out in the great hall at Aber and, after a brief but bitter fight, Llywelyn had had him seized and imprisoned in Degannwy Castle, only this time not as a guest but as his prisoner.

Gruffydd scowled. 'Dafydd is weak!' he said out loud for all the hall to hear. 'For all his years he clings to his mother's skirt like a limpet still. He's not strong enough to rule Wales after Father's gone!' He paused, then picking up his goblet he turned to Senena. 'I heard tell that Joanna has formed an attachment to Reginald's boy, Will de Braose, the English nobleman Father captured at *Ceri*.'

'And where did you hear that?' Senena asked, coming closer and tilting her head quizzically, before glancing to where Bronwyn sat winding her distaff on the window embrasure overlooking the bailey. 'Well?' she asked again when Bronwyn didn't look up.

'From Hubert de Burgh. I met him when we surrendered the castles of Whittington and Kinnerley to the crown at Montgomery.'

Senena raised an eyebrow. 'And why would he would he get word to you?' she asked. 'He's still deeply involved in a war with your father, or had you forgotten? In fact, *Ceri* is under siege at this very moment!'

'He and I had a lot in common,' Gruffydd said, putting his wine goblet down on the table. 'Father deplores his ambitions,' he continued carefully. 'Perhaps I do not.'

'And you think that he might be of some help in the matter of your succession?' Senena asked with some surprise.

Gruffydd shrugged. 'Mayhap he just thought the news might be of some use to me,' he replied begrudgingly, suddenly wishing that he hadn't mentioned it at all, for Senena was now regarding him with a look on her face that he had come to learn meant trouble.

Just then young Llywelyn ran and flung himself at Senena's skirts, sobbing alarmingly, followed closely by his brother Owain with a frown on his face.

'What is it, *cariad?*' she asked, smoothing his hair back from his flushed wet face, her attention diverted momentarily from Gruffydd's revelations.

'Its Margred!' he said. 'She keeps saying that there's the ghost of a lady here, she says she see her up in the tower and she wants me to see her, too, but I don't want to!' he finished on a wail.

'Don't be silly, your sister is just teasing you, Llywelyn. There's no ghosts here or anywhere else for that matter!' Senena said, and Gruffydd saw her throw an uneasy glance at Bronwyn who had finished winding her distaff, and was now standing quietly waiting to speak to them.

Suddenly cross, Gruffydd threw the eating knife he had been holding on to the trestle table. 'Have you been filling that girls head with nonsense,' he asked, turning to glare at her himself. Then without waiting for a reply he took Llywelyn's hand, and with Owain on his heels, he made his way out of the hall to seek Margred out for an explanation.

Left alone with Bronwyn, Senena's hand went to the brooch that she had found amongst Llywelyn's belongings recently. It was a pretty trinket, and she had pinned it to the inside of her girdle thinking to question Llywelyn about how he had come upon it when she had a chance. Now, though, it throbbed with a life of its own beneath her touch, and without knowing why she suddenly knew that it had something to do with the mysterious ghostly lady that Llywelyn had said Margred had seen. Immediately, her mind returned to the conversation between Gruffydd and Gwen at Elen's betrothal feast. Gwen had mentioned a brooch then, hadn't she? Said that they had buried it in their mother's grave. It was not beyond the bounds of possibility that Llywelyn had found it there and brought it home with him, he was always scrabbling amongst the stones. She shivered and looked around. Was it possible then that the ghost that Margred claimed to have seen was in fact the ghost of the mother that Gwen and Gruffydd said had haunted them in the past?

She was still contemplating this when she realised that Bronwyn was watching her closely. For a moment their eyes locked. The only sound in the hall was the moan of the wind in the rafters and the hiss of the flames in the fire.

'No good will come of it,' Bronwyn said, her eyes going to where Senena's hand still rested on her girdle.

Senena frowned. She had very little time for Bronwyn. In fact, she could never understand why Gruffydd had retained her, given the rumours of witchcraft which surrounded her and the fact that all the servants feared her. But maybe she could serve some purpose yet. 'Perhaps not,' she said. 'But pray tell me a little more about its original owner …'

Aber, North Wales, 1229

'No! No! No!' Llywelyn shouted again, his voice resounding round the *llys* like a death knoll. Moments later a door slammed in the tower, followed by sobbing and a slapping of slippers on the stone steps as Senena hurtled down them, having once again failed to secure her husband's release from his imprisonment at Degannwy. Seeing Joanna standing at the bottom she came to an abrupt halt, and then pushed straight past her, down the hall and out into the courtyard beyond.

'Trouble in paradise?' Will de Braose asked.

'Its Senena. Llywelyn refuses to release Gruffydd, and now he has ordered her and the children to stay here at Aber in punishment for his refusal to accede to the terms he recently offered him, which might have made his imprisonment easier - one of which was to apologise to Dafydd for his past behaviour and recognise him as the chosen heir to Gwynedd - which of course is something he would never do.'

'Never mind,' Will said, placing a friendly hand on her shoulder.

'Don't, Will, there are servants about!' Joanna said in warning. She could feel the warmth of his fingers through the silk of her sleeve; feel her heart flutter with the conflicting emotions that over the past few months she had fought to suppress. And it was getting harder.

'We have done nothing wrong.' Will whispered in her ear, making the nape of her neck tingle. She took a deep breath. His closeness was turning her knees to jelly, and she began to panic again as she so often did in his presence, afraid that she would reveal her true feelings, let down her guard and betray her husband.

'And neither shall we!' Joanna whispered, glancing around to check that no servants were near them. 'You must stop coming here, Will. Your ransom has been paid, and as soon as the marriage contract is drawn up, Isabella and Dafydd's wedding can go ahead - you have no reason to come anymore!'

'Joanna. Ah, Joanna, my love.' Will put a hand on her other shoulder and turned her gently to face him, before drawing her into the shadows. 'You must know how I feel about you? I have loved you since the first day I met you - when you were a girl on your wedding day, remember? And then that night in the chapel, when we made a pact not to tell on one another. We share secrets, you and I, Joanna. Would it be so wrong to share more?' He pushed a stray tendril of hair from her forehead and tilted her chin towards his face so that she could feel his breath on her cheek.

'Llywelyn is in the turret,' Joanna warned. 'Ah, Will, you play a dangerous game - you will be the death of me. I would that you were back in England for your own safety!' Immediately she regretted voicing the words; the hall was unnaturally silent, and there was a sudden chill in the air that she swore hadn't been there earlier. She shook herself. She was just being fanciful, that was all. There was nothing but stillness. That, and an absence of servants.

Will didn't seem to notice. 'Perhaps later in the stables, then?' he whispered, releasing her chin reluctantly.'

'No, Will. Never! I shall not betray my husband ... that's my last word!' And with a swish, Joanna tossed her fur trimmed mantle over her shoulder and headed towards the door, leaving Will standing alone in the hall.

Neither had seen Senena re-enter the hall where she stood watching them thoughtfully in the shadows, before slipping out to the courtyard again when they parted.

After Joanna left, Will stayed. He picked up an ivory figurine on the table and contemplated it. It was smooth and cold to his touch, and for a moment he let his fingers linger on its contours, his thoughts still on Joanna. It had become increasingly hard to stay away from her during the past year, despite the fact that he had no reason to be in Wales now, other than to discuss arrangements for when his daughter was married to the future heir of Gwynedd. In fact, it was a miracle that Llywelyn hadn't suspected that his erstwhile guest had any other reason to visit them, as he was not unaware that a certain amount of gossip was being generated amongst the servants, or that knowing looks were being thrown in his direction each time he visited. But despite that, Will found it increasingly hard to stay away. He knew he was putting them both in danger. He often contrived to meet her in a corridor, or out in the courtyard. On one occasion, he'd not been able to resist reaching out and touching one of the long braids that she'd worn that day in the manner of a young maid. She'd not objected as he'd drawn her closer in the shadows of the walls. Their bodies had almost touched, and her upturned lips had held such promise, such delight. But then she had drawn away, afraid as a servant had bustled by with a large cut of mutton thrown over his shoulder for the evening feast. Moments later she was gone like a scared doe running from the sight of a hunter, leaving him alone and full of desire. Will groaned. He had a perfectly good wife, Ava, at home in England - why lust after another's? It was total madness!

Senena leaned her head against the wall in the courtyard and contemplated what she had seen. It was not cold enough to cool her temper, but the sight of Joanna and Will de Braose together had diverted her attention from the fact that she had argued with Llywelyn again. She scowled. He had no right to remove her and the children from Degannwy, no right at all - if she wanted to share her husband's captivity, then why should she not? And as for her bitch of a mother-in-law, well, she always took Llywelyn's side because she was protecting Daffydd's interests. Kicking the wall angrily in another fit of pique, Senena retired to a low bench partly hidden by ivy, her mind working fast. Surely she could make use of what she had seen? It had been no accidental meeting ... the close proximity of their bodies, the furtive glances, and the way Joanna had fled hall, all spoke of a lover's tiff.

'May I sit down?'

'It's your bench,' Senena said shortly, unsurprised that Joanna had suddenly materialised by her side.

'Are you not happy here, Senena?' Joanna asked, sinking down beside her in a rustle of silk.

'Would you be happy if you had been forcibly parted from your husband?' Senena retorted waspishly, moving slightly so that she was not touching her mother-in-law's skirts.

Joanna frowned. 'Well, no, of course I wouldn't,' she said after a while.

'Well then, there's your answer - though of course you might find other diversions, what with Llywelyn away so often.' Senena could have bitten off her tongue as soon as the words were out. 'I'm sorry Joanna, it's my cat's tongue. I can't seem to contain it at the moment.' She threw a sideways look at her mother-in-law. Joanna's expression hadn't changed. If she knew that she had seen her with Will de Braose earlier, then she said nothing.

'I'm sorry,' Senena ventured again. 'And yes, I'm unhappy. The children are unhappy. She signed, thinking of the children who were somewhere inside the *llys* playing with their nurses.' She sighed. 'Does

Llywelyn mean to keep Gruffydd prisoner for the rest of his life?'

'Until he can behave in a civilised manner around his brother, or until Dafydd is able to protect himself against him, yes,' Joanna replied curtly. And with that, she stood up and left.

In her pocket, Senena's hand curled around the little brooch as she glared after Joanna. Angevin whoring bitch, she thought. Then she smiled as she remembered the letter she planned to write that night to Hubert de Burgh. You'll get your comeuppance, yet, you Angevin whoring bitch, you see if you don't!

Chester, England, 1229

'You're on your way to London, then?' Richard asked, passing Joanna a goblet of wine. They had just enjoyed a good meal in a tavern together, having met quite by chance at a gathering held by the Chesters to celebrate the marriage of a niece.

'Yes,' Joanna replied, 'I am travelling to meet with Dafydd and Gwladys who are already there. Dafydd is to pay homage to Henry for his father's lands - upon his death of course. It helps with his cause and guarantees the land upon his succession should Gruffydd ever contest them with the Crown - which of course he will.'

'It is unlike you not to be by his side, or carrying out the mission on his behalf; after-all you've both worked so hard to secure his position as Llywelyn's heir.'

'Dafydd must fight his own fights and carry out his own diplomatic missions from now on,' Joanna replied, taking a sip of the good red wine. 'Llywelyn and I will not always be here to protect him. After all, he's a grown man now.'

'And Llywelyn has arranged a match for him with Sir William's daughter, Isabella, I hear,' Richard said. He frowned. 'Now that de Braose's ransom has been paid, he is no longer Llywelyn's hostage I understand, yet he freely accepts your hospitality and is a regular visitor at your court still. How so? I would have thought that under the circumstances he would have returned to England - to be his wife, Ava?

Joanna felt herself blush, and she quickly took a sip of wine in the hope of recovering her discomposure at the suddenness of the question. 'The ransom has been paid, yes, but there are still matters to be sorted out with regarding an alliance between ourselves and Sir William's family. Which means, of course, that no date for Dafydd and Isabella's wedding has been arranged yet. Will stays with us often as a welcome guest - he and Ava will soon be family so it's only proper. But the subject of the marriage arrangements is one that Dafydd is hoping to broach with Henry when they meet, for the marriage will be of political importance for England as well as Wales.'

Joanna realised that she must be babbling, because Richard was gazing quizzically at her over the rim of his goblet. She paused and took a deep breath before carrying on. 'Gwladys has accompanied him because, being both the widow of an Anglo-Norman baron as well as the king's niece, she cannot re-marry without Henry's approval ... if, of course, she wishes to re-marry at all.' Joanna finished lamely.

Richard looked at her. 'You will be careful, won't you, Sis?'

'I don't understand? What do you mean?' Joanna said, putting down her goblet carefully.

'I mean that Sir William, well, he's young ... your age, I suppose. I wouldn't want you to get hurt - or worse, Sis. Do you understand what I'm saying?'

Joanna smiled her brightest smile. 'Now why would you think that, Richard? I will be fine. Now tell me about Rohese, I hear she is talking about founding a nunnery ...'

Aber, North Wales, 1229

Joanna leaned against the stable partition. Why had she come? Why now, especially when she had resisted so many times before? It must have been madness. Why could she just not have heeded Richard's subtle warnings? The questions went on in her head, hammering away like a demented woodpecker, and for a moment she was tempted to run. But then it was too late as the door opened and Will began to cross towards the stalls, soft footed in the straw.

'Joanna?'

'I'm here.' Joanna stepped forward into the flickering light of the lamp that he held in front of him.

Slipping the lamp into a niche in the wall, Will took her hand. Neither said anything as he drew her in his arms. 'You have been away a while,' he said softly.

Joanna sighed. 'I thought a long trip abroad would bring me to my senses,' she whispered.

'And did it?'

'No ... yes ... Oh, Will!' She breathed, as eagerly he slipped his hand down the front of her kirtle and cupped a breast in his hand.

Immediately, Joanna lifted her head. Waiting for his kiss. Wanting it with such urgency that she was weak at the knees. He was kneading her breast now, rolling her nipple between his fingers. She could feel his erection in his chausses, strong and hard. Could feel the wetness building between her legs.

She was on the verge of yielding herself completely, when there was a sudden rustling noise further down the stalls, followed by the sound of a door creaking as it closed. Spooked, a horse whinnied and began to stamp and kick at its stall door, sending a bucket flying, and suddenly Joanna came to her senses.

'No! Will. No, I cannot!' she cried, giving him a violent shove that sent him flying back against the stable wall.

'What? What is it, Joanna?'

'Did you not hear it? Someone was here!'

'No … no, you must have misheard. There's no one here. It's your imagination, that's all,' Will said, rubbing his arm where he had caught it on the rough stone.

'There *was* someone here, I swear!' Joanna said urgently.

Will tried to draw her back into his arms, but it was no use. Frightened now, Joanna picked up her skirts and turned to leave.

'I must never meet you like this again, Will. Never! Do you understand?'

And then she was gone, as frightened and skittish as the horses that she left behind her.

Chapter 41

Aber, North Wales, Easter, 1230

The Easter festivities were a welcome end to the long weeks of fasting during Lent, a time in which the households diet had been reduced to bread, stews made of vegetables, and endless platters of fish disguised any which way to give them appeal. Tonight, however, they had dined on roast boar dripping with delicious fat and juices, a haunch of venison cut from a deer killed in the hunt that day, along with goose, capons, and platters of tiny quails. And Joanna was tired from the eating of it all.

The revelry grew louder as the evening progressed. Around the hall, the sconces flickered as they burned down, throwing shadows into dark corners where lovers giggled as they took their guilty pleasure. Alongside her, Llewelyn's chair and several others were empty, for earlier that morning he had ridden to the border with Dafydd and a band of men, where once again the threat of invasion had reared its ugly head. She did not expect them back any time soon.

She jolted suddenly. Gruffydd had just entered the hall and was staring at her with a look of undisguised loathing on his face. He'd been released from Degannwy temporarily to attend the feast; an unexpected piece of indulgence on the part of his father who'd reasoned that a night amongst kin might divert his attention from his thwarted ambitions and his deep hostility towards Dafydd.

Dragging her eyes from his, Joanna saw that Gwladys and her husband, Ralph de Mortimor, whom she'd wed following the death of Reginald, were now seated at one of the lower tables. Quickly she sent a page down to invite them to join her, but they declined with a wave, not wishing to miss the dancing. Anxiously, she looked around, her eyes alighting on Marared and her husband, John de Braose, further down the hall. But they, too, could not be persuaded to forsake the benches for the comfort of the dais. And so, Joanna was quite alone.

At the far end of the gallery, the travelling minstrels brought from Provence for the occasion began a lively roundel as the servants joined in the dancing, swirling this way and that in their best homespun, the dowdy colours lost in the sea of bright silks worn by the ladies and gentlemen of the court.

Still desperate to fill the seats with someone to divert her attention from Gruffydd's hostility, Joanna's eyes alighted on Sir William, wondering who had invited him because she most definitely had not. Much to her chagrin she found that he was regarding her frankly, one eyebrow cocked in amusement at her predicament. Immediately she felt herself blush, recalling the way his hard chest and muscular thighs had pressed up against hers in the stables on his last visited the *llys*. Trying to hold back her panic at his unexpected appearance, she cast around looking for someone else, then suddenly angry at herself for letting him get under her skin, she threw all caution to the wind and sent a page to fetch him.

Sitting down beside her, Sir William waved the boy away and topped up her goblet from the pitcher in front of her. Quickly Joanna stole a glance at Gruffydd, and was relieved to see that for the moment his attention had been diverted by some old friends who'd found their way into the feast, and he was no longer looking in her direction.

'To the fairest woman in the room!' Will said, putting down the empty wine pitcher and raising his goblet to her in salute.

'Why are you here, Will?' Joanna blurted suddenly.

Will looked puzzled. 'Because you invited me?'

'I most certainly did not!' Joanna hissed.

'Well, if you didn't, then who did?' Will asked, putting down his goblet and raising an eyebrow.

As soon as the words were out, the hairs on the back of Joanna's neck began to prickle. Slowly, she turned her head. Senena was watching her slyly as she and her ladies formed a line on the dance floor. For a moment their eyes met and, without needing to be told, she knew that Senena had sent the invitation. Suddenly everything fell into place. It had been Senena who had interrupted them in the stables that night, and it was Senena who was spreading gossip amongst the servants. And now, with Gruffydd at her side for support, it was Senena who was hatching a plan to trap her with Sir William. In full view of everyone at the feast.

And Llywelyn had left her alone with them ...

Will was watching her intently. 'What is it, Joanna ... what's the matter?' Much to her distress her eyes began to fill with tears, clinging to her lashes like jewels, and her lips began to tremble.

Hastily Will groped for a piece of table linen, and finding one, he thrust it at her.

'Senena sent the invitation to you,' Joanna whispered. 'She knows, Will. She knows about you and me, and she has told Gruffydd, and now between them they mean to make trouble.'

'Look, Joanna,' Will was speaking reasonably. 'They know nothing, because nothing has happened. Anyway, as disagreeable as they are, the pair of them pose no threat you. Why would they? Their grudge is with Llywelyn and your son, not with you, me, or anyone else!' Still unconvinced, Joanna dabbed at her eyes, but Will ploughed on, ignoring her distress even though she was sure that it must have been obvious to him. 'I have also written to Ava and asked her to make arrangements for Isabella and Dafydd's marriage.' He put down his goblet carefully. 'Joanna, when that is over, I -'

'Don't, Will,' Joanna said, wiping her eyes. 'Whatever you are going to say, don't. Senena is looking at us and I swear she can lip read.'

'Let her look, then,' Will said, and Joanna saw a glint of recklessness creep into his eyes as he took another sup of wine. 'Joanna, I am going to divorce Ava. I shall think of a reason - or perhaps she will divorce me - she has cause enough, I'll grant. When it is done, I shall go to Chester. Or Shrewsbury.' He paused. 'I've been thinking. And I've been meaning to ask you.' He took a deep breath. 'Will you leave Llywelyn and join me? Dafydd is a grown man - his succession is secure, and your job here is done. Come with me, my love. The baron's war ended long ago. England is stable, and your brother Henry would welcome you at court. Both of them knew it was only the wine talking, but Will pressed on. 'From there we can go to France ... to Isabella ...

mayhap she and her new family would welcome us -
'

'No! No!' Joanna stood abruptly. 'No, Will, don't ask me such things – you've had too much to drink!' All at once a wave of dizziness washed over her.

Someone was going to die ...

Unsteadily she grasped the back of the chair. Her whole being was tingling now with a preternatural sensitivity. Desperately she looked at Will. His face had blurred. The features melting like candle wax and dripping onto the table before him. Suddenly, she was very frightened. The air had turned icy cold in the otherwise stuffy hall, and outside a storm was beginning to rage, she could hear it rattling at the shutters and trying to break in.

Sitting down again, Joanna grabbed Will's arm. 'Please, Will, don't talk like that! Don't ask me again! Llywelyn would hang you if he knew you speak of this - he would hang me, too!' Then releasing his arm, she stood, and knocking over her half empty goblet of wine she fled towards the safety of the wooden gallery overlooking the hall.

It was getting late, and from her position at the centre of the hall Senena watched the pair with narrowed eyes. Joanna, she thought, appeared to be distressed – she had grabbed Will's arm and was leaning close to him, speaking urgently. Then without warning she stood and began to run blindly for the stairs leading to the gallery. Senena frowned. How Prince Llywelyn had failed to see that they were a couple on the verge of becoming lovers was a mystery to her, especially when the whole of his court knew. For a moment, her thoughts lingered on the correspondence with Hubert de Burgh that lay in her room. She had been hoping that tonight she would have a chance to prove his suspicions: bolster Gruffydd's cause in the Marcher lord's eyes, and thus in England with the king, but it seemed that the pair had had a tiff, resulting in Joanna removing herself from the young nobleman's presence. Without thinking, her hand curled around the little enamel brooch that lay in her pocket. It was vibrating. Felt warm to the touch. She shivered, willing it to make her wish come true and enchant the pair into danger. Tonight. Whilst Llywelyn was absent from the *lys*.

As if in response, a violent gust of wind blew one of the shutters open with a crash, and up in the gallery a flash of lightening lit the air around Joanna's head where she now sat. She was not alone. Behind her there was another figure. Shadowy. Indistinct. No one else seemed to have noticed. Only Gruffydd, who, having made his way alongside her, promptly dropped his goblet of wine as his eyes fastened on the gallery in horror.

'Oh my God! Please, not again!' he whispered, as instinctively his hand went to the empty scabbard at his side, where, had he not been under the watchful gaze of his guards, normally his sword would have hung.

'Who ... who is she?' Senena breathed.

'My mother ...'

'You mean to say *that's* the ghost of your mother!' Senena whispered in awe, her hand curling once more round the little brooch, suddenly assailed by a mixture of elation and terror at the power it had unleashed before her eyes. And of her husband's sudden sickly pallor as he stood gazing up at the fading apparition.

'Are you alright, Princess!' It was one of Joanna's ladies shouting. 'Speak, Princess! Are you alright – were you were touched by the lightning!'

But Joanna didn't hear her. Neither did she hear the distant thunder beyond the *Ilys*, or her ladies' cries as they gathered around her, for she had drifted into a world beyond the one that they inhabited.

Tonight you will lie with Will de Braose …

The voice had come from behind her and Joanna shot to her feet, startled. There was nobody but her ladies clucking around her like a gaggle of deranged geese.

Tonight …

Frantically Joanna looked around. Had she had too much to drink. No. No, she had not, she had spilled what was left in her goblet when she had taken her leave of Will de Braose, and she had thought to send for more. *Will de Braose* ... His name rang in her head like a bell, the mere thought of him filled her with longing. It was as if somebody was standing behind her - bewitching her; filling her head with erotic pictures of the young Englishman which she could no longer control. Quickly, she pushed the images away, dismissing them as fanciful - the product of an overwrought imagination brought on by the strains of Llywelyn's absence, and too much rich food and wine. Then gathering her skirts, she dismissed her ladies and made her way down to the hall where she headed for the stairs leading to her chambers in the tower.

Behind her the *llys* was in chaos as servants fought to close shutters and re-light sconces. In the gallery, the minstrels had disbanded and were now helping to restore order and to salvage their instruments from the rain. Nobody would miss her she reasoned. The minstrels would set up their instruments in another part of the hall and they would resume their revelling, assuming that she had retired and taken to her bed after her fright.

It was only when she was alone in her chamber and had dismissed Rhoda, sending her down to the kitchen to get herself some food, that she began to relax.

Down in the hall Senena had seen her go and was now filling Will de Braose's goblet with the last of the spiced wine that she had grabbed from a nearby table, and telling him how that her father-in-law had sent word that he was not expecting to return home that night. Moreover, that she had just seen Princess Joanna heading for her rooms, and Rhoda heading for the kitchen.

Nobody noticed, only Senena who glanced triumphantly in her husband's direction when, a little while later, and somewhat worse for wear, Will de Broase rose from the table, and armed with his goblet of wine, began to make his way purposefully across the hall.

It was past Compline when Llewelyn strode unexpectedly into the *llys* amidst a flurry of startled servants. He was stripping himself of his boots and wet mantle when Senena spotted him, and grabbing Gruffydd by the arm she dragged him away from his friends. 'Your fathers just returned, and Joanna is in her chambers with Sir William!' she whispered urgently. Involuntarily, her hand closed round the brooch. It was vibrating fiercely. Its heat burning her palm. She could feel her excitement mounting. 'Tell him, Gruffydd, tell him ...'

Gruffydd looked at her strangely, before turning to see that his father had indeed returned and was stripping himself of his wet clothes by the door. Then he quickly scanned the hall looking for Joanna and Sir William, but they were nowhere to be seen.

'De Braose may have gone to his own chambers,' he said uncertainly.

'He has not. I saw him follow her up. And you know as well as I do that his chambers are across the other side of the *llys,* and not near hers,' she hissed. 'This is our opportunity,' she added, as, with a gleam of excitement in her eyes, she spun on her heels and plunged through the crowded hall, headed for

Prince Llywelyn who was now deep in conversation with Thomas Corbet.

'What is it you want, Senena?' Llywelyn asked irritably, when moments later she appeared unannounced at his elbow. His eyes hid none of the animosity that he had harboured for her over the years, and she was not surprised when he spared no courtesy, only saying bluntly. 'Can you not see that this is men's business, and I am tired after riding to the border and back for nothing and missing the festivities?'

'Yes, my lord,' Senena said sweetly, smiling to herself secretly in the knowledge that the man who stood before her would soon be reduced to nothing more than a snivelling cuckold in front of the whole court. That prince or no prince, he would be seen to be no better or worse than any other man in the room. 'But there is a matter that begs your urgent attention, Sire. One that I think you might welcome …'

'And what might that be?' Llywelyn asked. Again, without much interest, only that undercurrent of dislike.

Taking a deep breath, Senena took a step closer and leaned in towards his ear. 'Joanna charged me with a message for you,' she whispered conspiratorially. 'She heard of your unexpected, but pleasant return, and she wishes to see you, my lord.'

As she had hoped Llewelyn's demeanor towards her changed dramatically at that bit of news, and suddenly she had his undivided attention. 'Well?' he asked, cocking his eyebrows questioningly, a small smile of indulgence suddenly playing on his lips. Senena kept her expression neutral, barely able to supress the leap of excitement that assailed her when she saw the eagerness in Llywelyn's eyes as he anticipated his wife's games, and once again her hand curled around the little brooch, feeling it egging her on.

'She asked me to tell you to meet her in her chambers in the tower,' Senena confided sweetly. 'Immediately.'

Gruffydd had caught up with her now, and grabbing her arm he shook her. 'Let Father alone, Senena. Can you not see he is tired and in need of a bath and refreshment?' Then with an apologetic grin to Llywelyn, he dragged her off into a corner.

'What are you up too?' he growled.

Senena snatched her arm away. 'Oh, leave me alone you big ninny. Can you not see I have done you a favour? Do you not hate Joanna? Well, here's your chance to see her humiliated, revealed for the Angevin slut she is. It might do your cause good, Gruffydd. Gather you more friends amongst those who support Wales if they see that your stepmother is whoring with one of her own. It might also make people question who is really the father of Dafydd ap Llywelyn, for once a whore, always a whore!' And with that she turned on her heel and disappeared into throng without so much as a backward glance at her husband.

Joanna heard the footsteps on the stairs long before she heard the rap on the door. For a moment she stood quite still then, trance like, she crossed the room. In the corner a sconce flickered and went out and she hesitated, her hand hovering over the wooden bar. She could hear the distant sound of music starting again in the hall, and the shouts of the revellers as they resumed their play. In her head there was a loud buzzing noise, like a hive of bees gone mad. What was the matter with her tonight she wondered. Everything seemed to be happening as if it were to another person and she was on the outside looking in.

Another rap on the door brought her back to the present, and without needing to be told she knew that Will de Braose stood outside - she could feel his pull through the thick oak, feel his presence as if he was already in the room with her; touching her face, kissing her mouth, undoing the laces on her green silk bliaut ...

Closing her eyes, she laid her head against the against the rough-hewn wood and tried to blot out the images, but they persisted, tormenting her like demons. Somewhere in the darkness an owl hooted, and, as if obeying an unspoken command, she raised her hands once more to the bar. It was made of the same heavy oak as the door, and it rested on two iron hooks, one on either side of the frame. Without thinking her hands curled around it and she lifted it free, then, finding it too slippery to hold, she let it fall into the rushes with a thud. Immediately the door swung inwards, as if propelled by some invisible force.

Will de Braose stood at the top of the curved staircase, holding a cup of spiced wine in his hand. Behind him a single rush lamp flickered in the darkness, throwing him into sharp relief. For several long moments she stood quite still, her eyes fixed on his face. Everything about him was exaggerated: she could see every tiny line on his cheeks; every nick and scar beneath his neatly trimmed beard in extraordinary detail, as if she were seeing them for the very last time.

'Come, my love,' she whispered. The words were lost in the moan of the wind that tore through the roof timbers, and crashed into the curved walls of the tower as, dream-like, Joanna took Will's hand and slowly led him into the room.

Behind them the door closed on its own, slipping noiselessly into its frame. Neither thought to slip the bar back into place. And neither of them noticed the silent figure in the corner of the chamber, watching them from the shadows. The figure which, as they fell together on the bed, turned away and slowly faded into nothing ...

Left alone, Llewelyn frowned. Gruffydd rarely rowed with his wife, he reflected, as he watched what seemed to be a fiery exchange between the pair. Then putting them out of his mind, he grinned as Thomas brought him back to the present with a shove.

'Well, go on then you great oaf, I couldn't help but hear. Go and break your fast in the bedroom department. I've a mind to do that myself with that pretty little wench over there later!'

Llywelyn laughed, and signalled to his squire. 'Follow me with that pitcher of wine over yonder!' he ordered. Then grabbing a torch, he turned and threaded his way through the guests towards the turret stairs, running up them with the agility of a much younger man, only to come to an abrupt halt at the top. The air around him had grown cold. Apart from the torch, the only other light came from a single rush lamp flickering in the corner of the landing. He frowned and tilted his head to one side, listening. A low moan emanated from inside the chamber, followed by a muffled cry. Immediately he was consumed by a wave of panic - what if Senena had been wrong? What if Joanna had been taken ill, and had meant her to summon him immediately upon his return so that he might send for a physician without worrying their guests?

He was about to reach for the door when another moan, distinctively male this time, immediately disabused him of that notion. He fell back, suddenly angry as he found himself considering another possibility – that Senena, knowing that one of Joanna's ladies had stolen into her chamber with a man whilst she was engaged elsewhere, had sought to cause trouble by having him catch them in the act. If that was the case, he'd then be obliged to reprimand Joanna for allowing such wanton behaviour amongst her women, for unlike the serving wenches employed to cook and clean, some of them – the younger ones - were the daughters of noblemen and princes employed in the capacity as gentile companions. It would be unacceptable if word got out that they were engaging in illicit trysts whilst in his care, for it not only would ruin their reputations on the marriage market, but it would cause outrage amongst the men who had entrusted him with their daughters - men who were not likely to forget what happened to their sons, having done the same in the past.

Struggling to keep his temper, Llywelyn signalled to his squire to stay back, then holding the torch high, he pushed open the chamber door and stepped into the room. The flame flickered and went out in the draught as he entered, and he looked around. In the gloom he could just make out two figures moving slowly together on the bed, their conjoined bodies throwing an eerie shadow on the wall above them. It took a moment for Llywelyn to realise that one of them was his wife, and another to realise that she was naked, her legs spread beneath Will de Braose, whose broad shoulders gleamed with sweat in the shimmering glow of the firelight. Unable to move, he watched as Joanna's nails gouged a path down Will's back, before coming to rest on his tight white buttocks where her slender fingers began to urge him on towards his climax.

They did not finish. Joanna froze as Llywelyn let out a terrible roar, and pushing de Braose away from her, she turned towards the noise in confusion. Even to Llywelyn's eyes it was as if he had thrown a draught of ice cold water over the lovers, freeing them from a spell. He watched as Joanna pushed Will away and struggled to sit up, pulling the tumbled sheets around her naked body in her haste.

'Llywelyn! Forgive me!' she cried, her face crumbling as she looked down at herself and then at Will, as if she was only just aware of their nakedness. 'Please! I don't know what came over me. Truly, I don't!' she whispered, pushing her tangled hair from her dazed face, and scrabbling to her knees amongst a pile of pillows and furs.

Enraged, Llywelyn thrust the torch at his squire and threw himself at Joanna. 'Get dressed, and make yourself decent!' he bellowed, dragging her down from her nest, still twisted in the sheets like a rag doll. Then drawing his sword in a screech of metal, he lunged for de Braose, barely missing him as he rolled across the mattress and made a grab for his arm, trying to wrest the hilt of the sharp, double-edged weapon out of his grasp before it was turned on him again.

How long they remained locked in battle, Llywelyn didn't know, before he heard the distant sound of shouting, followed by the crash of metal on stone as men ran up the stairs and into the chamber.

'Llywelyn, stop!'

Llywelyn froze, his sword to de Braose's throat as the familiar voice brought him back to the present. Slowly, his sword arm fell and he pushed de Braose away, the rage inside him turning ice-cold as he saw Thomas's horrified face hovering on the edge of his vision. Behind him he could see Joanna, still on her knees, but surrounded now by half a dozen guards with drawn swords in their hands, and the squire holding the torch, re-lit, streaming above her for light. Her lips were trembling, and the tears were running unchecked down her cheeks, and for a moment he wondered if this was how he would always remember her: half-naked, crying tears of remorse - or was it regret - for having been caught in the embrace of her lover.

'It would be naught but cold-blooded murder like this,' Thomas' voice broke through his pain and he looked around the room desperately for support. 'Let him answer tomorrow on the gallows, in front of the people - he is already doomed, let him die as he should, by the rope on Gallows Marsh!' Thomas finished, reaching out and taking his sword.

Time seemed to pass in a blur as de Braose was dragged protesting from the room. As if in a dream, his treacherous words floated back up to them as he was escorted across the courtyard below the tower: William de Braose, their friend, and now Joanna's lover, was shouting accusations of witchcraft and black magic; words which could land Joanna on a pile of faggots with flames licking her ankles by morning if they filtered through to the village.

Left alone Llywelyn stood staring down at his wife as if she was something out of a bad dream. Her large eyes still swam with tears, and she was moaning with fear as she pulled the sheets tighter around her. None of it touched him.

'Harlot! Whore! Jezebel!' he spat. 'On the morrow, you and your Norman lover will die for this!'

Joanna let out a loud wail, and threw herself back on the bed. Behind him Llywelyn heard a sound, and he turned to find Senena hovering in the doorway. Although partly concealed by the shadows, her face was flushed with triumph, and even before he saw it in her eyes he knew the truth – that it had been Senena who had masterminded the plan to not only bring about Joanna's downfall, but Dafydd's and his own as well, if ever the question of Dafydd's paternity was raised in the future.

But even as he locked the door on his wife, and handed the key over to a guard, he knew Senena could not have done it alone …

Dawn came at last, cold and grey, as Joanna lay on the tumbled bed shuddering and sobbing. It was at this hour that the soldiers came to get her. The hall was empty apart from Ednyved. He gestured to a chair, and, with rather more force than necessary, one of the guards shoved her in it.

'Where's my husband?' she asked in a tight little voice.

Ednyved contemplated her for a long moment before replying. 'He has left, madam. Gone.' He paused. 'You are to be ferried across the strait to Llanfaes with immediate effect today. You are to be held there in confinement until Prince Llywelyn decides what to do with you.'

'And William de Braose?' she asked defiantly, afraid to show her fear in front of his sternness.

'He will be tried in due course, and hanged,' Ednyved without preamble.

'How can you be so sure he will hang?' Joanna blurted out.

'He will hang, Madame,' Ednyved said impassively. 'Just be glad that you are the king's sister and the same fate does not await you.' Then, turning on his heal, Ednyved strode from the hall. Leaving Joanna staring wordlessly at his departing back.

Joanna was not sure how long she sat in the hall before she became aware that all her possessions were being transported down from her chambers in the bower and piled up by the doors to the bailey.

Gradually the hall came alive as morning turned to early afternoon. Servants who had once treated her with deference stared openly at her now, and one even spat on the rushes at her feet. None served her with anything to break her fast, and, despite herself, she felt hunger knaw at her belly.

Finally, there was a commotion at the end of the hall and Dafydd strode towards her. He stopped a few paces away and stared at her, the pain and bewilderment on his face plain to see.

'Why, Mother?' he asked. 'Why betray Father so? And why here, in your own marital bed, with so many guests present?'

Joanna made to rise, to go to him, but the guard pushed her back down in the seat. Dafydd sighed. 'You are to go to Llanfaes, now, today, he said, trying to hide his hurt. He indicated to where her possessions were now being carried out to a waiting horse and cart, then he signalled to a girl that Joanna only knew by sight. Shyly she approached, carrying a plain bliaut that Joanna seldom wore, and a woollen cloak that she did not recognise.

'This is Nerys,' Dafydd said. 'She is to accompany you to Llanfaes.'

'What about Rhoda?' Joanna whispered.

'Rhoda has been dismissed,' Dafydd said carefully. 'She failed in her duty to protect you last night.'

'But where will she go?' Joanna asked. 'She is old ... frail.'

Dafydd sighed. 'I will see she gets some money, Mama ... she will not suffer, and she has kin.'

Nerys proved competent, pulling the bluit over her unresisting head and lacing it swiftly then throwing the non-descript cloak round her shoulders. 'So you won't be recognised,' she said, pulling the hood over Joanna's dark hair that she had not had the time to braid or tidy.

Out in the bailey Joanna saw only a blur of hostile faces, then, as Dafydd pushed her through the throng, Gwenllian stepped forward.

'You disgust me!' she hissed. 'You're nothing but an Angevin whore!' With that she spat in Joanna's face.

Dafydd pushed her back. 'You will show some respect to my lady mother,' he said angrily.' Gwen rounded on Dafydd. 'And you,' she said. 'Son of an Angevin whore. You are not fit to rule Wales in Father's stead!'

Dafydd looked at her long and hard. 'And what of your brother Gruffydd?' he asked steadily, keeping a firm grip on Joanna's arm. 'Has he fled back into exile to cower by the hearth after the damage he and Senena caused last night? Father knows of Senena's communication with de Burgh,' he added scornfully. 'Letters were found in her room. Gruffydd shall not get another reprieve!'

'Gruffydd has returned to Degannwy, yes,' Gwen conceded. 'As the terms of Gruffydd's parole dictated, and Senena and the children have gone with him,' she added defiantly. 'And not because your mother was exposed for the whore she is!'

'No! Gwen. No! They fled like cowards, with their tails between their legs. Do you think that's a fitting mantle to wear to rule Wales?' Daffydd re-joined angrily

Gwen spat on the ground at his feet, her tawny eyes black with anger.

Dafydd looked at her in disgust. 'You should go back to Ireland,' he said bitterly. 'Where you can do little harm!' And with that he practically carried Joanna the last few paces to the cart, and lifting her up unceremoniously, he deposited her alongside a frightened Nerys. Minutes later the wagon driver was making use of his crop to clear the way as they hurtled over the bridge and out onto the open road, heading towards Joanna's exile.

None of them saw the shadowy figure that lingered at the window of the tower, before turning and fading silently back into the shadows ...

Cricceith Castle, North Wales

Llywelyn had spent the night at a neighbouring manor, leaving Dafydd to deal with his wife, for he could no more deal with her than he could accept the events that had led him there. He cursed the fact that he had allowed Senena to persuade him to let Gruffydd out of exile for the Easter feast. But he could not wholly blame Gruffydd. Gruffydd had, after all, seemed not to know what Senena had planned. Had in fact tried to prevent it, in his own indomitable way.

Llywelyn rubbed his eyes and sighed. The letters they'd found discarded in the chamber she had occupied - communication between his daughter-in-law and Hubert de Burgh, alleging an affair between his wife and Will de Braose - had cut him deeply. Hubert de Burgh had probably just been meddling. Hoping to divert the attention away from the real issue of his encroachment into Wales. But Senena had understood that it was the truth. Had waited and seized the moment when it came. Llywelyn would never forget the look on her face as she had told him so sweetly that Joanna awaited him in their chamber.

Then Llywelyn remembered the day that he had told Gruffydd that he'd made provision for Dafydd to be his legal heir. And he remembered *her* voice. *Tangwystl's*. Whispering in his ear as clearly as if it was yesterday - *you will regret this, Llywelyn Fawr ... you will regret this ....*

De Broase had sworn blind all the way to the dungeon's that he had been bewitched ...

Aber, North Wales, May 1230

William de Braose was hanged on the 3rd of May 1230 at Crokein Manor. He went to the scaffold still claiming that he was innocent; that somehow, he had been bewitched into betraying Prince Llywelyn's trust and sleeping with his wife. The township turned out in full; the spectacle of a much-hated Norman lord, now 'Black William,' swinging from the rope was lure indeed. As was the imprisonment of the Angevin whore who had betrayed their trust. Whether they believed the story that the young man, half out of his mind, had babbled through his trial was never discussed as the township closed ranks around their prince. Joanna did not attend the hanging, but she was not spared the details. A polite letter from Dafydd told her that he had died with honour. Another from Gruffydd, did not. And as Joanna burnt it in the hearth she resolved that if she was ever released, she would never allow Senena or Gruffydd near her or her family again.

'You are writing to the king? Ava de Braose?' Dafydd asked, suddenly tired of the endless streams of clerks and scribes toing and froing from the chamber.

Llywelyn frowned. Then nodding to the last of the clerks hovering around him, trying to catch his eye, he bid them go. 'The hanging of de Braose could have had far reaching repercussions in England. We can only be thankful that the king has suffered his own troubles and the trial went relatively unnoticed. However, in answer to your question, I am writing to both Ava de Braose, and the king - to express my sincere regret that my wife's actions with de Braose put in jeopardy all that we had jointly achieved in the past year in order to establish trust and unity between our two countries.' He sighed. 'Ava de Braose has not expressed any wish to cancel the marriage contract, and neither has the king, and so I have no reason to suspect that it will not go ahead as planned. The only thing tarnishing this happy outcome is that Hubert de Burgh is using de Braose's fate as a method of whipping up support for his campaign in order to infiltrate himself further into

Wales. Which is, of course, no more or less than I expected him to do given the circumstances.'

Dafydd scowled. 'If Senena and Gruffydd had not been able to communicate with de Burgh's spies, then none of this would have happened. You should banish him for good - to the other end of the earth if you must, Father. I should certainly do so if I were in your shoes!'

Llywelyn threw him a sharp glance, and Dafydd wondered if he had gone too far. Over the past week he had slept little, fearful that Joanna's actions might impact upon his succession; that his father might think twice about making his youngest son, the offspring of his adulterous wife, his heir.

'I blame Senena more than Gruffydd,' Llywelyn said finally. 'He at least had the sense to try to stop her.'

'Well, I hope that all this doesn't mean that you are going to be kind to him!' Dafydd rejoined angrily, his mind still plagued by doubts.

For several long moments father and son looked at each other.

'I fear that when the dust has settled on the de Braose affair we shall have to embark on another campaign to quell de Burgh's ambitions, for he's once again fast encroaching on Wales,' Llywelyn said calmly after a while. 'Gruffydd would have been good to have on our side, but for the moment - ' he left the sentence hanging, for they both knew that it would take time to salvage any sort of relationship with Gruffydd, if indeed there was one to salvage.

'And Senena?' Dafydd asked.

Llywelyn signed. 'Senena has been fetched back to stay at Aber where she will be kept under guard and can do little more harm. So, I would ask that for the sake of peace you stay out of her way where you can. In the meantime she will be prevented from even visiting Gruffydd in exile - she has brought that upon herself because of her actions, if she had not meddled, in time I would have allowed her and the children greater access to Degannwy.

Llywelyn turned away then as if he had tired of the conversation. Moments later he was striding through the door, leaving Dafydd with no more certainty than before as to how he actually felt.

Chapter 42

Aberconwy Lodging House, North Wales, 1231

'I will not! I will not! I will not!'

'You will do as I say!' Ava de Braose said, slapping her daughter across cheek. 'Tomorrow you will marry Dafydd, if it is the last thing you do! Now,' she said, turning to the seam mistress. 'Finish the gown if you will, and if she squirms, stick a pin in her!'

Isabella let out another wail. 'But they murdered Papa! I shall never forgive Prince Dafydd for that!'

'It was hardly the boy's fault,' Ava said reasonably. 'If your father hadn't let down his chausses like a common serf rutting in the hay, he would be here to celebrate your coming nuptials with us!' Carefully she turned Isabella around so that she faced the mirror. 'How do you want your hair?' she asked, lifting a handful of the girls long flaxen tresses. 'Loose, I think. With a circlet of flowers - in white, of course. Or braided at the sides, perhaps, and held back with an ivory comb?' Abruptly, she dropped the heavy sheath of hair, and dragged her eyes away from the angry blue ones in the mirror.

For some illogical reason, she had transferred her hate of Will onto Isabella, simply because the girl resembled him so much. She sighed. Like it or not, tomorrow was the day that Dafydd was to marry Isabella. And, like it or not, tomorrow was the day that Joanna was to be released, for Llywelyn had forgiven her after only a year under house arrest. Letting her out in time to see her beloved son wed to her lover's daughter. Now there was plenty of irony in that, she thought. Had Llywelyn done it without thinking? Or had he seen how like her father Isabella had become in the last year, and found it a suitable way of reminding his wayward wife of her sins?

Throwing down the comb she was holding, she marched to the door. Either way, did he not realise that she would have to face her husband's lover in the church. Men were insufferable in their logic, she thought angrily, and marching to the door she threw it open with a crash and went to find herself another drink. Leaving Isabella staring mutinously after her.

Bangor Cathedral, Wales, 1231

Prince Dafydd ap Llywelyn, heir to the title of Prince of all North Wales, and Lord of Aberffraw, knelt beside his young bride on an embroidered faldstool at the high alter of Bangor Cathedral. It had become quite clear in the last week that she despised him and had no wish, whatsoever, to be wedded to the son of the woman that she blamed for her father's death. No amount of gifts or entreaties had softened the stony-faced countenance that she had presented on her arrival at Carmarthen Castle, where, under the chaperone of her mother, they had spent several weeks before the wedding trying to put the past year behind them. She had neither laughed or cried, nor shown any indication of being capable of emotion at all, except for the day that Gwladys, now married to Ralph de Mortimer, had arrived. She alone had reached out where no-one else could and broken through the barriers that her dead husband's granddaughter had erected around her, for she had loved his son as she might have loved a son of her own.

What Gwladys had said to Isabella in the comfort of the ladies' bower, Dafydd would never know. But whatever it was, it had been enough to place the girl at the altar on her wedding day, and for that he was glad, because regardless of the circumstances he still desired to marry her.

Isabella refused to look at her handsome husband as he knelt beside her at the altar. Instead she kept her head bowed meekly, and her hands clasped together in prayer. What she prayed for was not obvious to anyone but the girl alone. In her despair, she prayed that Princess Joanna would die slowly and in agony and as far away as possible from her home and family. And then she prayed that she would never have to suffer having to spawn a child from the man who knelt beside her, for if she did, she vowed she would kill it.

The marriage completed, she stood and smoothed down the fine lines of her richly embroidered gown trimmed with fur and, touching briefly the garland of flowers that adorned her flaxen hair, she turned to Dafydd and smiled. It was not a pleasant smile, but even in her misery she could see that to the young prince it was like the snows receding from the mountains and the sun shining down into the valleys after a long dark winter as, with a bow, he took her arm and together they turned towards the high arches and solid stone pillars that lined the nave.

For a moment Isabella felt giddy. What she'd just prayed for was a sin. And she had committed that sin in God's house. And before his own alter. Around her the strong smell of incense hung in the air making her feel sick, and the ringing of the cathedral bells was now contributing greatly to the ache that was beginning in her head. Quickly, she stole a look at her husband. He was smiling down at her; his hair a glossy blue-black in the stray beams of sunlight that spilled down from the stained-glass window above the alter before which they'd just made their vows. Although undeniably handsome, his chiselled features and dark, unfathomable eyes were so very different to the blue-eyed, golden creature that had been her father, that immediately she forgot her sickness as her hate bubbled to the surface again.

As they walked back down the aisle towards the cathedral's huge wooden doors, Isabella's eyes lingered on her mother, her beautiful face concealed by a black silk veil. Was she, Isabella wondered, the only person there who knew that Ava de Braose had despised her husband, both for his straying affections and his unbridled love of life? Then she looked at Joanna who sat beside Prince Llywelyn. Her lovely face was as cold and remote as any of the statues of the saints that lined the cathedral. If she saw resemblance to her dead lover in her son's new wife, then she hid it well.

Without faltering, Isabella glided miserably past the rest of the packed pews, her little chin thrust forward in an act of defiance that was to be the only defence mechanism available in her new life. A life with a man she hated. And a family she loathed.

The wedding feast was interminable as course after course was brought out from the kitchens. Trenchers and platters were piled high with wild boar, venison, swan, tiny quails, trout, and pike, accompanied by vegetables, salads and bread made from the finest flour available. Then came the custards, honeyed cakes, sweetmeats and marchpane figures of the bride and groom. Betwix the courses, wine and mead flowed freely, and as the roar of noise in the great hall grew louder, the jests became bawdier, with Dafydd's friends gathering around him teasing him mercilessly on the subject of his wife's hugely appealing assets which he would sample later that night.

Alone now on the high table, Isabella pushed away the half-eaten plate of food in front of her. Her mother had long disappeared with a flagon of wine, having offered her no advice except to say that she should expect no joy from her union that night and not to be surprised if there was blood, for it was to be expected. Isabella had watched her go, wretchedly aware that from now on she was truly alone, for it was unlikely that her mother would appear in the morning to bid her farewell on her journey to her new home. Miserably she stared round the room, wondering if she could choose to disappear without drawing attention to herself. She was still nowhere nearer a decision, when she suddenly found Princess Joanna staring down at her with something akin to pity on her face.

'You look worn out,' she said, helping her to her feet. For a moment she looked like she wanted to say something more, something personal, but instead she said. 'You should go to your room and prepare yourself.' With that, Isabella found herself being thrust into the arms of a group of giggling ladies and being dragged away amidst a great deal of whistling and jeering from the lower tables.

Dafydd was quite drunk when he finally appeared in the bridal chamber, and stumbling to the huge bed strewn with garlands and flowers where Isabella lay, he pitched across it in a heap. Isabella gasped, mortified as his friends hauled him upright and stripped him none too gently of his clothes, before casting them aside in a heap on the floor in their eagerness to see him bedded.

Behind them her attendant's let out little shrieks as, completely naked, the future heir to Wales was thrust into bed alongside his bride. If Isabella had thought that she could not be more embarrassed, then she was wrong. For finding himself pressed up against her body, newly sponged with rose-water and anointed with fragrant salves and oils by her ladies, Dafydd immediately became aroused, his erection clearly visible beneath the sheer silk that covered them. She was only saved from further humiliation by the appearance of the bishop, who had materialised in the doorway unannounced to bless them, lying stiffly as the holy water touched first her face, and then her breasts, before trickling down to leave a damp patch on the sheet as he turned to Dafydd to repeat the process. With the holy blessing complete, their boisterous guests withdrew from the bridal chamber, pausing only to throw last minute advice over their shoulders as they made their way down the stairs to re-join the revelry below.

Left on their own, Isabella held back her tears as Dafydd fumbled for a moment, and finding her breasts, began to knead them eagerly. If he wondered why she lay still and unresponsive when he parted her legs and crouched between them, he did not ask. Neither did he ask when he took her brutally and painfully for the third time that night, why she cried.

Chapter 43

Aber, North Wales, 1234

Llywelyn rolled over and kissed Joanna smartly on the lips.

'What was that for?' Joanna asked, stretching like a cat.

'For still being a perfect lover, a perfect wife, and a perfect mother.'

Propping herself up on her elbow, Joanna peered at him. 'What has brought this about, then?' She asked, running a finger down his chest, and tugging briefly at a crop of dark hair peppered with silver that sprouted above his navel.

Llywelyn lay back against the pillows with a sigh. 'We need to talk, Joanna.'

His voice was so serious that Joanna sat up and waved the serving girl away.

'Talk then, Llywelyn, my heart. What is worrying you?'

'You are not going to like it, *cariad*.'

'Just talk then,' Joanna said grimly, knowing that any term of endearment from her husband meant bad news these days.

'I mean to go to Degannwy. It has come to my attention that Gruffydd and Senena are expecting another child.' Llywelyn hesitated. It had been a difficult decision, but over the past year or so he had gradually allowed Senena and the children more access to Gruffydd in his confinement in the hope that re-introducing a bit of family stability might discourage Gruffydd from his vendetta against Daffydd. The result had been that Senena was, after so many years, pregnant again.

Getting no response from Joanna, Llywelyn continued tentatively. 'If Gruffydd assures me that he will cause no more harm; try not to interfere in my plans for Dafydd's future, then I mean to release him. I will give him lands to rule to keep him occupied. Llŷn to start with and, if he proves true, I shall give him Powys as an appendage. I mean for him to succeed Gwenwynwyn as leader in Central Wales so that he might have a purpose other than warring with his brother after I am gone.' He paused. I can only hope that the prospect of new family and his six years of imprisonment will have taught him a lesson - to be a better brother, a better son, and a better ruler than before. That, and the fact that land that is easily won from me is as easily lost.'

When he turned his head, Joanna had risen from the bed and was leaving the room.

An hour later she had left the *llys.*

Aber, North Wales, 1236

Bronwyn lit the fire in Mab's old hut and stared into the flames. She had not followed Senena and Gruffydd to Llŷn after his release. Instead, she had packed her own bag and slipped away without a word. Leaving them to wonder where she had gone, but not enough to have her sought out, for her presence had only ever been tolerated and never wanted. She smiled, watching as the flames caught the bundle of herbs she had found in an old cauldron by the door: marjoram, betony, fennel. It crackled, sending fragrant smoke billowing up through the hole in the roof. They would not recognise her these days, Bronwyn, with her long brown hair chopped short and her homespun clothes. She was something of a seer now. A wise woman. A witch. She was respected, feared, even worshiped in a way judging by the gifts left outside her door. People came to her as they once had Mab. They came to buy spells to win back lovers, fail crops, even cause plagues. Or they came to have her throw the runes, or read the tarot and tell their destiny. She chuckled. Mab had not seen her own destiny; had thought herself too clever by far. But there was some sort of justice to her being here in Mab's old hut, she thought. The fire was burning fully now, and giving it a poke, Bronwyn peered into the bright flames and began to concentrate on the problem in hand.

Princess Isabella was pregnant. And she was desperate. And knowing of Bronwyn's powers she had sought her out as Bronwyn had known she would. She would visit tonight, it had been arranged. Leaning closer, Bronwyn watched as the girl made her preparations. She could see the hate flowing from her; the disgust as she looked at her swelling belly in the polished metal mirror. It would be a simple enough thing to do, to rid her of the baby - all Isabella had to do was to come as they had arranged. She had already sent a message to tell her that she was waiting with the right herbs; the right salves and potions to bring about a miscarriage and rid her of the evil thing that lived inside her. There was only one thing now that gave the girl a purpose in life, and that was to never give her husband an heir. Bronwyn desired that, too. That's why she had stayed so near the princess: to ensure from afar that if her beloved Gruffydd did not succeed his father, then his son, Owain, would have first place in the succession after Dafydd was gone. To do that, however, she first had to see that Dafydd would never have an heir of his own. And there was justice in that.

She watched as Isabella carefully smoothed down the fabric of her fine silk gown edged with squirrel fur. Smiling as the girl left the *llys* under the cover of darkness, and began to make her way towards the forest.

Two days later, amidst a general furore at the *llys,* Princess Isabella miscarried.

Aber, North Wales, February, 1237

'Mama! Mama!' It was a visiting Marared who found Joanna slumped unconscious on the floor of the ladies' bower, the priceless jade figurine she had been holding smashed into several large pieces beside her. She had lost a great deal of weight and been complaining of pain in her belly for some weeks and, despite the cessation of her courses, her ladies had found bloody rags on the fire. But the physicians summoned by Ednyved and Llywelyn had all left, having failed to diagnose the cause, and advising only that Joanna be bled regularly, take the medicines they left and get plenty of rest. Joanna had disobeyed on every count.

It was Llywelyn himself who arrived next, summoned from his letter writing by Nerys and, scooping Joanna up in his arms, he carried her through to her chamber and laid her gently on the bed. He did not need to be told she was dying. He had seen for himself the dark shadows that had fallen over the house of Aber, and he had watched the sparkle in her eyes fade as her face grew thinner and her appetite waned.

In the corner of the room the shadows stirred softly. *I shall be waiting for you in hell, princess of Snowdon ... husband thief ... whore -*

Only Llywelyn heard her breathless little giggle as she faded away ...

'The princess has a condition of the womb, I believe. It is not uncommon in women past childbearing age.' The plump, red faced little physician said, propping Joanna up against the pillows following his examination. 'I have tested her humours ... her urine. There is nothing more I can do, I am afraid. Apart from continuing to leech her in order to draw forth the bad blood that devils her.'

'Nothing?' Llywelyn echoed angrily, facing the latest in the long line of incompetent doctors that had crossed their threshold lately.

'Nothing, I am afraid,' The physician said, feeling the sweat begin to poor down his face and his legs begin to shake, as it dawned on him that if the princess died in his care, then he might, too. For he was a foreigner. An Englishman sent reluctantly from

Bramber in Sussex by Marared, with assurances that he could make the princess well again. And he was not much in favour with Llywelyn.

'Then I shall call in more doctors … surgeons, leeches, even wise women if I have to! I shall send to all corners of the land!' Llywelyn shouted, rounding on the hapless young man angrily. 'Oh, get out of my sight! Get out of my sight, you worthless, shit-eating little weasel, and never come back!'

'As you wish, my prince,' the physician croaked, scurrying away as a sudden rush of urine ran down the inside of his best hose. He only looked back once at his precious instruments still lying on the bed beside the princess. He reckoned he could buy more someday.

Llywelyn kept his promise, bringing in every physician, barber-surgeon, wise man and seer within riding distance of the *Ilys*. Each in his turn came and fled. The only one he did not ask was the woman who now lived in Mab's old hut, for he knew that it was Bronwyn. And he knew that Bronwyn would never help.

Despite all his efforts, Joanna lay in her bed for weeks, growing more and more weak. Each time one of her children visited they expected the worse. Expected her to have passed away in their absence.

And then the shadows of her past began to visit. They were all there, gathered around her: her father, Arthur, Matilda de Braose ... and Will. Her Will, with his laughing blue eyes and sandy hair was standing at the end of her bed, smiling and holding out his hand to her.

'Not just yet, Will,' she whispered, as by her side, Llywelyn dropped her hand and turned his head away sharply to hide his tears.

Elen was there, holding her hand one night when she turned her face weakly to the dark shadows in the corner. 'She is waiting for me,' she whispered. 'She has waited so long ...'

'Who is waiting?' Elen breathed, feeling the tiny hairs on the back of her rise.

Joanna gave a weak smile. 'The woman in the meadow. Light a candle for her in the chapel, daughter, and say a prayer for her unhappy soul ...'

Joanna died at the beginning of February. Outside, the snow had fallen; a thick carpet of it blanketed the fields and topped the peaks of the *Eryri* mountains, where yet more clouds gathered. Wales was silent. Llywelyn, the tears rolling down his face, was holding her hand as she quietly slipped away. All her children were there with her. One by one they kissed her cold cheek and knelt down beside her to pray and wish her God speed and safe journey into the next world. The room was heavy with sorrow and mourning, and the soft weeping of her ladies. A priest in attendance said prayers with the family, and a vigil was kept at her bedside for the rest of the long night, with Dafydd, Marared, Elen and Gwladys keeping their father company by her side. Only Isabella stayed away. Afraid that someone would guess that once, years ago, she had ill wished her mother-in-law in the house of God.

The day of Joanna's funeral was a deeply moving affair. All the family, gathered at the *llys,* with her children, their husbands, wives and grandchildren waiting quietly as Joanna was prepared for burial, Then in solemn procession, they followed Llywelyn as Joanna's body was carried in state across the

Lafan sands and placed on a ferry before being borne across the straights to Llanfaes itself. Once there, she would be laid to rest in a carefully prepared burial ground on the spot where Llywelyn was already planning a Franciscan friary: along the seashore, overlooking the *llys* in her honour. Joanna and he had planned the requiem mass and the following internment in detail.

Neither had expected it to come so soon.

Southern Powys, Wales, 1237

Gruffydd looked down at the letter in his hand. The one that the breathless courier had just thrust at him, having ridden day and night so that he might receive the news before it spread throughout the land. It was penned by Prince Llywelyn's steward, and it merely told him the bare facts:

Joanna, The Princess of Snowdon, beloved wife of Llywelyn Fawr passed away at Aber Cen Garth on 2nd February last, and has been laid to rest in Llanfaes as per the wishes of her husband, Llywelyn, prince of Gwynedd, on the very spot where a friary will be built in her memory. God rest her soul.

So, she was dead. Dead, gone, and buried. And good riddance! Putting down the letter he strode over to one of the tall mullioned windows that overlooked the castle grounds, and stared out at the distance beyond. Would he have liked her a little better, he wondered, his father's wife, had she not given birth to Dafydd. No, he thought. No, I would not. And perhaps that was simply because she had so readily taken the place of his mother in his father's affections after she had died.

Tangwystl ...

He shuddered as her name popped into his head. As clearly as if someone had spoken it.

My son ...

'No! No!' he shouted, alarming a passing servant who popped his head through the door. '*No,*' he whispered. 'Not here. Not now -'

'Are you alright?' Senena asked, rising from the bed where she'd just settled little Rhodri, the child that had surprised everyone by being born despite the months of enforced separation they'd had to endure, both in the years before and after Joanna's disgrace.

'Joanna's dead.'

'Joanna's dead?'

'Yes,' Gruffydd said, taking a deep breath. 'Dead!'

Senena's eyes widened. 'Let me see!' she cried, and grabbing the letter from the table she read it quickly, before throwing it down. 'Are you not glad!' she asked exultantly. 'Because I certainly am - I couldn't stand her, what with all her plans and schemes to keep you out of the way so that she could secure the succession for her own precious son. Mayhap, now she's dead, Dafydd's weaknesses will be revealed and you can take your true place as your father's heir!'

'Hmm,' Gruffydd said thoughtfully. 'Well, for the time being I shall continue to foster the support that is growing for me here. Then I will face Dafydd squarely, with an army behind me. I shall bide my time - I do not wish to upset father and have him strip me of my lands again. Particularly while I can rally so much support from those who do not wish to see the son of a dead whore as the next prince of Wales. Now, shall we go to Mass and pray for her soul?'

Senena laughed happily. 'If you wish, my Lord!'

Chapter 44

Aber, North Wales, 1237

Dafydd threw down the letter he was holding, and turned to Isabella who was perched on a window seat beside his desk looking preoccupied and irritable. He knew that look. She was pregnant again. Not only had she got plumper lately, but her skin had taken on the sickly pallor and general pastiness that had accompanied the first pregnancy: the babe she had lost so suddenly the previous year.

'Isabella? Isabella?' he repeated. 'Are you feeling sick?'

'What?' Isabella said, startled out of her reverie. 'What? What did you say?'

'I said, are you feeling sick?

'No. No, my Lord, why I am in the greatest of health.'

'You are with child, then?'

'I am not certain.' Isabella turned her face away.

Dafydd frowned ... she was lying he was sure. He opened his mouth to speak, then seeing the set of her shoulders he changed his mind, and picking up the letter he began to read it again. It was news of Gruffydd and Senena. Gruffydd was, for the time being, abiding by their father's wishes and remaining in Powys where Llywelyn had plans for him to succeed Gwenwynwyn as leader of Central Wales. He scowled. It was not in Gruffydd's nature to obey their father, nor to ignore the deep-rooted hate that he harboured for him as his chosen heir. Gruffydd was planning something he was sure, and its roots were in the very place in which he was now firmly ensconced - a place where resistance to the rule of Gwynedd was not only rife, but well suited to his plans. Gruffydd was growing too strong to tolerate for much longer, and he was fast becoming a thorn in his side. He smiled grimly. Soon, very soon, he would lure his brother into a trap and put him back in prison – the only place he could be sure he would no longer be a threat.

With that decided, Dafydd turned his attention once more to Isabella. He could not afford for her to lose another child. Not if he was to beget an heir.

Two nights later Isabella pulled on her mantle and left the *llys* by the postern gate. It had not been easy. Daffydd was becoming suspicious, and of late he had watched her every move. It had taken all her powers of persuasion to get him to sample the new wine she had ordered from France as a gift. Wine which contained the sleeping draught Bronwyn had supplied her with. He had only become relaxed enough to accepted first one, then another cup, after she had come to the conclusion that in order for her to gain his trust she would have to mollify him in some way. And the only way she could think to do that was to hint at happy news - play the loving wife, the suffering, expectant mother whose every whim and fancy must be obeyed. She scowled. What she had not expected to do was to having to endure hours of listening to his petty grievances and increasingly vindictive plans for Gruffydd ...

Much later she arrived at her destination, and pushing aside the sacking that covered the door, she entered. The hut was hot and smoky; pungent with herbs, the mud floor scattered with clean rushes. Bronwyn nodded briefly, then bidding her to take off her mantle, she sat her down on a straw pallet in front of the fire to wait whilst she mixed the herbs and prepared the potion. It was both bitter and sweet at the same time, and in some odd way, sensual. She didn't know how long the ritual took, but by the time she left armed with a pouch full of medicines, Isabella felt both light headed and strangely euphoric.

Two days later she had her second miscarriage ...

Aber, North Wales, 1237

Llywelyn was looking at the flames in the fire when it happened. There was no warning, no indication that he was going to suffer a seizure. Only a blurring of his vision and a sudden numbness in his arms and legs before, with a strange look of puzzlement on his face, he keeled forward into the rushes towards the flickering inferno. The last thing he recalled before he lost consciousness, was Ednyved's stricken face and Dafydd's concerned one looming over him as he was pulled from the hearth.

'Your father has suffered a seizure,' the physician confirmed, looking mournfully towards the bed where Llywelyn lay, his slack features grey in the dim light of the chamber.

'But he can't have!' Dafydd exclaimed violently. 'Not so soon after Mama's death, surely?'

Bowing his head, the physician began to gather his instruments together. 'It might well be a delayed reaction to the shock of your mother's death,' he said, voicing Dafydd's own thoughts. 'It probably would have happened sooner or later. He carried on working instead of taking the time to grieve as he should have done after so great a loss.'

Dafydd frowned. 'But you can treat him, can't you?'

'Yes, yes. With the right medicines, it's possible that your father could recover his speech and even the full use of his arms.'

Sighing, Dafydd crossed over to the window to stare out at the grey mass of cloud that hung over the *Eryri* mountains, waiting as Llywelyn's steward and several servants entered the room, their arms full of clean bed linen and pewters of scented water with which to bathe their lord. Thinking that Dafydd needed a moment to contemplate the seriousness of his father's affliction, the physician put down his instruments and busied himself preparing the medicines and the poultices that he'd recommended.

But Dafydd was not thinking of his father's health at that moment. He knew that with Llywelyn lying gravely ill in his bed, the Welsh people needed a leader. But more importantly, he could see a God given opportunity to deal with the ever-present threat posed by his brother, without having to worry about the shadow of Llywelyn's censure hanging over him. He laughed suddenly, shocking the girl who was bathing Llywelyn's face. Then recovering himself quickly, he nodded to the physician and left the prince's chamber for his own, where he began to scheme.

As they sat down to dinner that night he eyed his wife. She was the only prohibitive factor in his plans for the future. She had been with child several times, but never yet carried one full term. Picking up his goblet he considered her with narrowed eyes. Each time she was with child, it had been reported that she had slipped out alone at night by the postern gate and had not returned to the early hours of the morning. The next time she was with child he vowed he would be ready.

That night he took Isabella brutally, sparing her no pain, spurred on by the thought of the power which was now in his hands and his need for an heir.

Southern Powys, Wales, 1237

Gruffydd tucked the letter he had just been reading into his tunic. It was from Elen. Her husband, John of Scotland, the Earl of Chester, was dead. He sighed. Elen, it seemed, had truly loved her husband, but his prolonged illness had robbed of them both of the chance of having children, and because he had died leaving no male heir, the Earldom of Chester had passed into the Crown's hands. Gruffydd wondered what would happen to her now. As an eligible widow, she would be put back on the marriage market by Henry until he found her a suitable husband he supposed. Poor Elen he thought, picking up a sweetmeat and taking a bite, it was not often that within a marriage arranged for political reasons love grew, and the chances of it happening again were extremely rare.

'It's the ideal time to attack!' Senena said reasonably, handing Gruffydd a goblet of hot, spiced wine. 'With your father seriously ill Gwynedd is in turmoil, and now with John of Scotland dead the eastern border is controlled by the Crown again, making Gwynedd weak on that front, too. Strike whilst the iron's hot, Gruffydd - it's your chance to remove the threat of Dafydd once and for all,' Senena urged, thinking of her own ambitions and the fact that with Isabella failing to produce heirs, and her having been restored to her own fertility with the arrival of Rhodri, she was planning another little victory herself ...

The remote footholds of the *Eryri* mountains were Gruffydd's place of choice for his rebellion against his father and Dafydd. Their familiarity; the lie of the land, and his childhood knowledge of the mountain paths and enclaves that surrounded Gwynedd, where he would get support, all convinced him that he could advance from there, burning townships and villages as he went.

In the event, his rebellion was finished before it had begun. He and his small army of Powys' men barely made it from Criccieth to the foothills of Yr Eifl, before being ambushed by Dafydd who had been forewarned of his attack. The battle was swift. Lasting less than an hour before, separated from his *teulu,* and left with only a small band of soldiers,

Gruffydd was forced to retreat back into Powys with his tail between his legs, and once again admit defeat in the face of his father's chosen heir.

Chapter 45

Strata Florida, North Wales, 19th October 1238

Prince Llywelyn had made a slow but steady recovery: he was now able to talk, use his arms, and walk without the aid of a stick, as well as being able to eat and drink and attend to his own needs. But he knew that his days were numbered, and he wanted to go Aberconwy Abbey and die there in peace, having assumed the habit of a monk. Because of this, and because of his eldest son's most recent act of rebellion, it was once more of vital importance to him that the lords and princes of Wales renew their oaths of loyalty to Dafydd, in order to secure their support for his succession when he was gone.

He sat back now in his chair in the guest house at Strata Florida Abbey, the place he had chosen for this to happen. Beyond the abbey dark clouds were gathering, presaging a storm. Even now he could hear the wind building and the sound of distant thunder, and he wondered if they would come.

'Do you think they will come?' Dafydd asked, echoing his father's thoughts. 'They might think better of it after the stream of letters Uncle Henry's dispatched, reminding them that the only homage that may be demanded is to him as their King.'

'They will come,' Llywelyn said tiredly, watching his son's attendants milling round him, adjusting his attire. 'We just have to be mindful of Henry's objections to the swearing of homage. They will come, and they will swear oaths of fealty and loyalty to you in its stead. It is more than enough for now, Dafydd, for with those oaths you will have gained friends. And once those friends have sworn allegiance to you, Gruffydd will have lost all support, along with his battle to usurp your place in the succession when I am gone.'

'But that is no more than they have done in the past,' Dafydd said bitterly, waving the servants impatiently away. 'I thought Uncle Henry had cleaved to your desire to have Wales made independent; for them to pay homage to *me* as their liege lord. After all, what is the point of all this if they are still the King of England's men and not mine?'

'The point is,' Llywelyn said irritably, 'that you will have friends who are sworn to you. I can then retire happily to Aberconwy, wear the habit of a monk, and live out my days there in prayer.'

Dafydd frowned. 'Is that really what you want, Father? To life out your life in an abbey? I still need your support, you know!'

'My days are numbered, Dafydd,' Llywelyn said, standing. 'I am tired of it all. Tired of the fight for Wales, and tired of the endless war between you and your brother. I want to be where I belong ... and that is with my wife. Besides, you have to pick up the reins sometime, and now is as good a time as any.'

He smiled suddenly, and crossing the room he put his hands on Dafydd's shoulders. 'I know that you will make a good leader, and that you will make Wales great - for both yourself, and your future sons.' He hesitated. 'Isabella is young. Despite her failures, I am certain she will bear you children yet.'

She must bear him children, Llywelyn thought grimly, as he turned away. Else, Gruffydd would have won. And Gruffydd had children aplenty, a girl and four boys now he reflected grimly, thinking of Dafydd, their latest boy born to Senena in July, and almost certainly named after his uncle Dafydd to remind him that he did not yet have a son of his own to carry on his name, Llywelyn concluded bitterly.

But despite his son's difficulties, Llywelyn had never felt prouder than when Dafydd stepped into the abbey later that day. Upon his head he wore the *talaith,* the coronet which was the symbol of his rank, and his tunic was of the finest crimson silk, over which he had thrown a fur lined cloak with a silver clasp fashioned in the shape of a stag. He watched with a lump in his throat as one by one the princes fell to their knees and pledged their allegiance to his son. And when they had finished, he knew he could retire to Aberconwy Abbey happily and live out his days in peace.

That night the festivities were the grandest they'd seen since Joanna's death. The hall was filled with the lords and princes of Wales dressed in their finest, pledging their support and good fortune for his son. Mead and wine flowed freely, as platter after platter of food was brought out for the feast: swan, wild boar, venison and fish, accompanied by dishes of salads and vegetables made their way down the tables first, followed by sweetmeats, honeyed cakes and finally, large rounds of cheeses. In the background, the soft tones of flute and harp floated down from the gallery as a group of travelling troubadours entertained them with songs and ballads from France. He only wished Joanna could have been there to see her son's finest hour.

Amidst all the festivities, Dafydd watched his wife as she sat miserably alongside him. He was suddenly convinced that she was with child again. He looked at her speculatively, some two or three months he judged by the pattern of her sickness and the way she turned away from her food. Well, this time he would not be fooled. That night he watched what he drank, and he ate little. And even then it was only food from the lower tables, as he recalled his father's earlier certainty that he would have a son to inherit what he had won.

When he went to bed, however, Isabella was already there; curled up and pretending to be fast asleep like a baby, with her ladies beside her ...

Aber, Wales, November 1238

Isabella paused only to light the torch she had concealed at her side from the glowing remains of a fire on the edge of the village. It was a full month since the princes had gathered at Strata Florida to swear fealty to her husband, and at least three before that in which she had known she was pregnant. But because of slowness of Llywelyn's recovery and the preparations for Strata Florida, she had been unable to do anything about it, and since their return to Aber she had been watched like a hawk. She glanced fearfully behind her. She had finally managed to slip past the watch, and out through the postern gate, dressed only in a simple white shift and tiny velvet slippers, over which she had thrown a fur trimmed mantle. It didn't take long to find the path she needed - the one that would take her through the silent village and on, down towards the river, where it snaked off into the forest towards where Mab's old hut stood. She had to see Bronwyn. It was imperative. She had done everything exactly as the woman had told her to: the salves, spells, potions and charms, all of which should have caused her to miscarry again, had failed. And now to her horror, she could feel the evil thing fluttering and moving inside her …

Dafydd was roused from a deep slumber by Ifan, one of the guards, who spotting the princess slipping out of the Princes Hall, had ordered a groom to saddle his master's faithful old stallion, Endeavour. Together they picked up her trail and followed her as she made her way down the dark track, holding her torch high, her hair flowing behind her like spun gold in the pale light of the moon.

Dafydd urged Endeavour on angrily. Never had his wife looked more beautiful. But that was not his concern tonight. His smile was cruel as he thought how he might punish her for the sin of leaving the *llys* without his permission, and if he was right, finding a way of ridding herself of the child that he was sure she carried.

After several miles the track ended, and they lost her trail down by the river, only to pick up her bobbing torch on the fringe of the forest near the ramshackle hut that had once belonged to the old seer, Mab.

For several minutes Dafydd sat staring down at it. He had expected Isabella's excursion to be one to gather herbs under the cover of moonlight. Herbs with which to make a potion and rid herself of the babe; perhaps accompanied by some silly pagan ritual she had learnt somewhere. He'd not expected her to come here to this ruined place.

His face darkened as she pushed aside the sacking that covered the door and slipped inside, and he found himself gripping Endeavour's reigns tighter as the anger towards his wife that had laid dormant for so long bubbled up inside him. How dare she deceive him; plot behind his back and make a laughing stock of him, as one by one she failed to hold onto the babes she had conceived, leaving others to gossip about his ability to sire a child that could go the full term.

Above them the moon was suddenly shrouded in cloud, and throwing a glance at Ifan, Dafydd saw him cross himself and mutter a curse before checking that his sword still hung by his side.

Shivering, Dafydd pulled his mantle tighter around him. Danger hung in the air. He could feel its cold fingers crawling down his back as, beneath Endeavour's hooves, something rustled in the tangled undergrowth, making him whinny nervously.

Neither spoke as they dismounted and crept the last few yards towards the dwelling on foot, coming to a halt under the cover of a thicket, close to a jagged square of light shining through a broken window in the crumbling wattle and daub wall. Inside the hut a bright fire burned in the centre of the floor, and beyond it, a cow and several sheep stood dozing behind a low partition. He could see his wife and another woman, who despite her cropped hair and advancement in age, Dafydd recognised as Gruffydd's old nurse, Bronwyn, moving around the room and arguing in low voices. The heated exchange went on for a long time before Isabella stamped a foot, and crossed to the broken window, where she stood gazing angrily out over the dark forest for a while. Then as if making a decision, she pulled the mantle from her shoulders and threw it on the floor, revealing the shape of her full breasts, and the soft curve of her belly where the baby lay through the transparent layers of her shift.

Growling in anger, Dafydd's hand flew to the jewelled dirk at his side, but Ifan grabbed his arm. 'We cannot rush in and accuse the princess of visiting - albeit in the middle of the night, and in her shift!' he said reasonably.

Dafydd hesitated, before sinking back into the shadows of the thicket with a grunt, watching as Bronwyn went and sat down on a straw pallet in front of the fire, and stared into it deeply as if searching for something in the flames. There was a long silence during which Isabella remained motionless by the window, before Bronwyn finally reached for a small metal box hidden in a pile of turves alongside the hearth and opened it, pulling out something that resembled a lump of beeswax. After a moment Isabella stirred, and with a smile of relief she went and sat alongside her, watching intently as Bronwyn's deft fingers began to knead and mould the wax, pushing and pulling it this way and that until it began to form strange shapes.

Part curious and part suspicious, Dafydd settled down to watch. An hour later he eased his position and groaned. Early dawn was creeping over the forest, and in his discomfort, he was now convinced that Isabella had come here on a whim: that she had befriended Bronwyn somewhere, and in her delicate condition her confused mind had brought her here - to seek advice and have her fortune told. Mayhap, she was even having some curiosity made out of the wax - a charm perhaps. Women did these things when confronted with the fear and pain of childbirth. He had even convinced himself that her previous miscarriages were just that, miscarriages, and he was preparing to leave and let Isabella return to the *llys* of her own accord, when suddenly Ifan stood and gripped his arm.

'Wait!'

Dafydd froze. Bronwyn had finished with the wax and it now stood upright on the straw between her and Isabella. He blinked, not quite believing what he was seeing.

It was a doll. A decidedly pregnant, naked, wax doll. Both women were staring at it with a mixture of fear and awe.

Deciding something was missing, Bronwyn pulled a small bone handled knife from her girdle, and leaning forward she cut a lock of flaxen hair from the long tresses that fell over Isabella's shoulder, before pressing it firmly onto the head of the faceless effigy. Then she did a strange thing. Leaning forward again, she loosened the ties on Isabella's shift and let it fall down over her hips, then reaching out her hands she began to run them experimentally over the smooth mound of Isabella's naked stomach where the baby lay.

Immediately, Ifan's hand went to his sword, the swish of metal in the pre-dawn silence as he withdrew it from the scabbard seemed eerily loud. The women appeared not to hear, as removing her hands from Isabella's stomach, Bronwyn picked up the doll, and using her thumbs she began to rub the little wax belly in much the same way as she had Isabella's a moment before.

Dafydd blinked. He was sure that he saw the little doll move its legs and strain as Bronwyn's thumbs began to press harder. Rubbing his eyes, he peered again. Bronwyn was holding it in one hand now, and as he watched she poked its little belly sharply with her forefinger. Almost immediately, the little doll flung its head back and began tossing its golden tresses from side to side, squirming pitifully in her grip.

'Sweet Christ, do you see what that woman doing!' Dafydd shouted, turning on Ifan. 'She is devilling that ... that ... *thing* - she must be stopped!' Before he could move, however, Isabella gave a long shudder and fell back heavily on the straw, kicking her legs and grasping her stomach as she moaned loudly.

Bronwyn watched her closely for several moments, then delving back into her girdle she brought out a pin and stabbed it hard into the doll's belly. Isabella let out an unholy shriek as the doll squirmed pitifully in Bronwyn's hand, its little arms and legs flailing in the air like a tiny trapped animal, before lolling backwards in a parody of Isabella's faint.

Ifan dropped to his knees, his eyes rolling in horror. 'I must get help, my lord!' he stammered. 'She's mad! Don't go near her … don't touch her for she's a witch! Listen! Listen! She's summoning demons to help her!' It was true. Bronwyn was casting a spell over the doll and stabbing it repeatedly with the pin, and with each prick of the pin, Isabella let out an unholy scream.

Dafydd ignored him as, frantic with fear, he sprang forward and tried to push his way through the brambles that had sprung up almost overnight around the hut.

Bronwyn was chanting louder now. Dafydd could see dark forms swirling around the room. Behind him a sudden wind had risen, howling through the trees to join with Isabella's cries.

Petrified, Ifan groped for his sword, and holding it upside down in the age-old symbol of a cross he began to pray loudly against the deafening sound.

Dafydd had finally made it to the window where, panting with fear, he began to tear at the crumbling wattle and daub wall with his bare hands.

'No!' With a roar, he scrambled through the frame and flung himself at Bronwyn. Bronwyn turned on him with a shriek, then dropping the doll she grabbed the knife and launched herself bodily at him.

Together they fell to the floor. 'No you don't, you witch!' Dafydd panted as they rolled, entwined like serpents on the cold earth.

Bronwyn's eyes were wild, her teeth barred like an animal as she fought her enemy. She was surprisingly strong and lithe for her age and she fought like a hoyden, but then Ifan finally recovered his wits, and scrambling through the wall he seized Bronwyn's arms and pulled her away from Dafydd, sending the knife flying out of her hands to come to rest harmlessly on the floor by Isabella.

Slowly all the fight went out of Bronwyn and she stood glaring, first at her captor, and then at Dafydd still crouched on the floor. Outside the wind was dying as quickly as it had risen, and dawn was now creeping over the forest, throwing a pale light into the room. It seemed impossible that the scene of a moment before had ever happened.

Suddenly, Bronwyn began to laugh. A horrible cackling sound that echoed round the room. 'Well! Well! It seems you are too late, little princeling!' she wheezed, nodding behind Dafydd. 'My particular services were not needed after all!'

Dafydd leapt to his feet and spun round in horror to see Isabella standing by the pallet. Buried in her stomach was the knife. Around it her blood oozed, sticky and red between her fingers. Beside her stood the little doll, its tiny hands curled round the pin protruding from its little belly. Isabella staggered forward a few steps. Alongside her, the little doll did the same. Then it stood upright and, turning its faceless little body towards the broken wall, it began to march - up and over the debris and out, into the eerie morning light, its golden locks streaming behind it like a banner in the last of the screaming wind.

Miraculously Isabella lived. Bronwyn, however, did not. Dafydd watched from the tower as Isabella rode her white palfrey past the blackened circle outside the walls of the *llys*, the only thing remaining of the pyre on which they had burned her, condemned by the church as a heretic and a witch.

If Isabella looked, then Dafydd did not see. She was on her way to a nunnery in Godstow where she would stay until she had learned her lesson, and it was decided if, and when, she would return.

But Dafydd knew now that even if she did return she would never have children. The pain in her womb would never go. Not as long as the little doll continued it march into the darkness, and the pin remained in its belly.

Aberconwy Abbey, North Wales, 1238

The news of Bronwyn's burning and Isabella's fate did not take long to reach Gruffydd and Senena at the castle overlooking the Lŷnn peninsula, and it did not take Gruffydd long to reach Aberconwy where, to his frustration, he had to wait two days for an audience with his father.

'You must see that he is mad, Father!' Gruffydd begged when he was finally summoned to his bare cell. 'If the rumours are right he's not fit to rule Wales! He burnt Bronwyn at the stake, for Christ's sake - accused her of witchcraft and heresy under the laws of the church. And he did so without any trial or right of appeal!'

Llywelyn sighed, and shook his head. 'Your brother rules Wales now. If you have an issue you must speak with him.'

'He rules unjustly!' Gruffydd spat.

'He rules as he sees fit!' Llywelyn rejoined angrily. 'Bronwyn was found guilty by the church of witchcraft. She helped Isabella kill the child she carried, and the others, which alone was a mortal sin. But then she was seen summoning the devil. Seen giving life to a wicked little effigy of her making, and using it for the devil's work!'

Gruffydd frowned. 'Look, I know that what Bronwyn did was wrong, but still, her punishment was carried out with unseemly haste do you not think? And what has he done with Isabella, eh? He did not burn her at the stake!'

'Isabella is safe. She has been sent to Godstow. To a nunnery, where she will do penance and learn to be a good and decent wife to Dafydd in the future. When she has learned her lesson no doubt Dafydd will have her back. Until then, she must remain where she can do no harm!' Llywelyn shuddered. The de Braose family were cursed. Bad things followed them wherever they went ...

'You should go now,' he said, his face growing pale, his words more laboured.

Gruffydd went. He rode to Aber and requested an audience with Dafydd, but he was refused. Instead he saw Elen who was visiting following a meeting with the king in Shrewsbury. On the matter of marriage. Of all his half-sisters, Elen was perhaps the closest – he recalled a time when she had stood bravely between him and Dafydd when she was just a girl no higher that his waist. They spent two days together before Elen journeyed back to her home in Huntington. But when asked if she thought he might ever rule Gwynedd, she had gazed at him sadly and said. 'I see a future for you, brother, but tiz not the same as the one that you see.'

Then, refusing to be drawn further on the matter, she had turned her horse for England and ridden away.

Chapter 46

Criccieth Castle, North Wales, 1239

'This cannot be!' Gruffydd shouted, terrifying the messenger who had delivered the news and sending the dogs fleeing, tails down, under the table. 'I will not tolerate it - Dafydd does not have the authority to evict me from my lands here in Powys!'

'Hush, now! Be calm, Father!' Owain said, nodding at the messenger to go. 'We must look at this sensibly. Clearly Uncle Dafydd is overstepping the mark, you will have to write to Grandpapa ... tell him what he is up to ... have him stopped.'

'That's easier said than done!' Gruffydd yelled, pausing only briefly to glance at the stocky, red-haired, nineteen-year-old boy that was his son, and wonder when it was that Owain, only a few years older than his brother Llywelyn, had grown up enough to become mediator between his father and his uncle, and even his grandfather Llywelyn at times. 'If your grandfather were not so busy saying his prayers at Aberconwy, then it would never have happened - would never have been allowed -!'

He stopped abruptly as the door of the hall flew open amidst a flurry of leaves and Senena entered carrying baby Dafydd in her arms, closely followed by Margred and Llywelyn with a reluctant Rhodri in tow. Gruffydd scowled, Senena had insisted the moment that Dafydd was born that they name him after his half-brother in an attempt to gull his father into thinking that he had finally accepted him as their overlord, and as a dig to remind Dafydd himself that he had yet to sire a namesake of his own. Unfortunately, it had served only to irritate him to hear the name of the person he hated most in the world now echoing twice fold around the castle walls.

'What's going on?' Senena asked, handing Dafydd over to his nurse, and rushing to Gruffydd's side. 'We've just passed a messenger on the road on our way back from morning chapel. He says that we are to be evicted from our lands here in Powys, on Dafydd's orders, and we are to go to Llŷn and stay there for the time being - surely that can't be so?'

'It is, and he has!' Gruffydd said shortly. Then turning to Owain and Llywelyn he made a decision. 'Call a council - of all the lords and nobles who will come - this must be stopped else they too will be subjected once more to the rule of Gwynedd!' Then calling for a clerk, Gruffydd ordered him to pen an urgent letter to his father, wondering bitterly if Llywelyn would even bother to part his hands from prayer this time to read it.

A reply did come, several days later, just as the household was breaking its fast. Giving a silver penny to the messenger, Gruffydd picked up a loaf of bread and headed out into the courtyard.

He was sitting on a pile of straw with his head in his hands when Senena found him later that morning in the stables.

'What is it, Gruffydd?' she asked, knowing the answer already.

Gruffydd raised his head. His white face and puffy eyes showed the signs of prolonged weeping. 'This time Papa has truly forsaken me,' he said brokenly.

'How so?' Senena whispered, sinking down beside him and trying to hide the anger that she inevitably felt whenever Gryffydd had dealings with his father.

Gruffydd sighed. 'The letter I wrote - I thought that he truly didn't know - that when he did, he would call Dafydd off. I know that he was loathe to interfere in the matter of Bronwyn, but this is different. Dafydd is taking the lands that he gave me. Surely that means something to him?'

There was a long silence. 'What *exactly* did he say?' Senena asked after a while.

'He says, as he said before,' Gruffydd said bleakly, 'that Dafydd rules Gwynedd now and that I must speak with him; that if I make my peace with him he might yet die content knowing that I still rule Powys and Llŷn when he is gone.'

Senena drew a sharp breath. 'And what say you to that, husband?'

'I say,' Gruffydd said, standing and running a hand over his face, 'that nothing will make me give up Powys without a fight; that not even father's illness or his wish to live out his days in the company of monks will make me do so. I also say that I will see Dafydd dead before I make my peace with him!'

Aber, North Wales, 1240

Dafydd ran a hand tiredly over his face as, not for the first time that morning, he mulled over the problem of his half-brother. It had been nearly three years since his father's stroke, and two since the lords and princes of Wales had renewed their fealty to him at Strata Florida, and Llywelyn had gradually begun to give him control over all his Welsh lands. He had spent those years wisely, trying to stamp his mark of authority on Wales, an exercise which he had begun by gradually depriving Gruffydd of Powys and leaving him only the lordship of Llŷn and the castle of Criccieth on the peninsula. The last thing he wanted was for Gruffydd to offer up any resistance in his bid to become Llywelyn's only heir when he was gone.

His success in restricting Gruffydd to the Llŷn peninsular had not come without a fight, however. Gruffydd, not unsurprisingly, had reacted violently to the theft of his lands by burning and laying waste to the surrounding countryside and whipping up a large contingent of supporters from amongst the disenfranchised nobility of Powys, and from amongst Senena's own kin, including her brother, Einion ap Caradog, and brothers-in-law, Walter de Clifford and Ralph de Mortimer.

Llywelyn, tired and ill, and permanently retired to Aberconwy Abbey, had made it quite clear when Dafydd had approached him with his problem that as he now ruled Gwynedd it up to him to try to sort out his differences with Gruffydd. His job was done, he said. He had fought long and hard to try to ensure that he, Dafydd, would inherit most of what he had spent a lifetime winning, but when it came down to it, Joanna's death, Henry's treachery, and his own ill health had finally taken its toll and he could no longer stand up against his eldest son's countless rebellions; nor could he interfere between the two brother's any longer. With that his father had withdrawn into the abbey, refusing to see family or friends as he began the task of spending his last days in prayer (and, more worryingly, begging the forgiveness of the ghost that he claimed haunted him in his dreams: the ghost with long, red brown hair and eyes the colour of honeyed mead that stood in the way of his Joanna and a clear conscience with which to die).

Crossing to the window, Dafydd stared moodily out at the purple-topped mountains beyond which lay the fields, the valleys, townships and land, all of which made up his inheritance. Beyond them he could see the dark clouds creeping in from the sea, gathering there before the storm. Just like the clouds that were gathering over his plans for Wales, and threatening a storm over his inheritance. Kicking a lolling hound, yet another descendent of old Gelert's, out of the way, he began to pace the floor restlessly. There was nothing for it now but to put into action the plan that had been formulating itself in his mind for many months. If Gruffydd would not be contained within the Llŷn peninsula where he could minimise the threat to his power, then he would have to take more drastic action.

It was also time to bring Isabella home, for he must be seen to have a wife by his side ... even if that wife would never give him children. Besides, he thought sadly, despite everything, he still loved her.

Llanfaes, Anglesey, February 1240

From the window in the manor where she was now under house arrest, Isabella stared out over the distant shoreline, watching the screaming gulls swoop and dive over a flotilla of tiny fishing boats moored alongside the jetty landing their shimmering catch. She was dressed now all in white, with a jewel-studded net and linen fillet, secured by a golden coronet, covering her flaxen hair - a far cry from the stiff scratchy habit and hair cloth she had been forced to wear at the nunnery.

She wasn't surprised when, a while later, she saw Senena making her way up the muddy road towards the manor riding her grey palfrey. In fact, she was expecting her, for she had not been slow in learning a few tricks from her time with Gruffydd's old nurse and she'd seen the warning in the crackling fire.

'So you're here after all. I wasn't sure what to believe!' Senena cried, her entry to the hall hampered by her heavy woollen skirts and the furs that swathed her thin shoulders. 'Well, in that case, you'll have heard what your husband has done! He has tricked Gruffydd and Owain and imprisoned them in Criccieth Castle, and he is now refusing to set them free!'

Isabella showed no surprise. She already knew of the trickery her husband had employed to trap Senena's husband and her eldest son, luring them to a meeting held under the protection of Richard, the Bishop of Bangor, at the Bishop's own manor and making them both his prisoners, for she had been party to it. If she had learned one thing during her incarceration at Godstow, it was that from now on she must support her husband if she did not want to end her days there dressed in sackcloth and ashes and praying to a God she no longer believed in.

'Well, what have you to say about it? You must surely have some objection - after all you have only just been released from a term of imprisonment yourself, so you know how it feels to be treated so unjustly!'

Taking a deep breath Isabella turned to her sister-in-law and gave her a breath-taking smile. 'Would you like some wine and cake? After all, it's a long journey home to Criccieth on an empty stomach,' she asked sweetly.

Gruffydd was still a prisoner in his own castle when Llywelyn died a few months later, on 11th April, at Aberconwy Abbey. He was not allowed out to attend his father's funeral or his internment in the abbey church. The whole of Wales was in mourning, but he was not allowed to be. He was not allowed to see his sisters or their husbands, or even his own wife and children, whilst Dafydd began the business of closing ranks against him and protecting his own interests now that their father was gone. Gruffydd paced the room restlessly; the only thing that kept him going now was that Senena was formulating a plan that might help set him free.

That, and the shadowy figure of his mother, who was coming to visit him more and more now that Llywelyn was dead and he had no friends.

Chapter 47

Gloucester, England, 15th May 1240

Dafydd stood by the window, staring moodily out at the bustling streets of Gloucester, now awash with heavy rain. His father had been dead barely a month before Wales had plunged into chaos, with rival claims being bought against him by Marcher lords and native Welsh chieftains alike, vying for Powys, Buellt, Mold and Cardigan. It had not been much longer before the king, hearing of this, had demanded that he ride to Gloucester to sign a treaty and renew his oaths of homage and fealty as soon as possible.

But even as he had ridden through the gates of the city that morning, with the sound of the cathedral bells ringing in his ears, it had been with the knowledge that his uncle, King Henry, did not intend to recognise him as his father's heir in those lands beyond Gwynedd which the old prince had ruled when he was alive. To the king he was, and would remain, the prince of Gwynedd, with no claims to a wider lordship until the dispute over his lands was settled by arbitration - if indeed it ever was - for as Dafydd was now becoming only too aware, despite his earlier assurances and pledges to Llywelyn, the King of England had no intention of allowing his nephew his father's full position as ruler of the whole of Wales.

Turning from the window, he could not help but meet Henry's sardonic eye. Then kneeling before the great assembly of lords who had gathered to see him renew his vows, he made a vow of his own: that he would not lose the lands that his father had fought so hard for and won. Not to the man before whom he now succumbed - the man who was not just his uncle, but also the most duplicitous king to ever have sat on the English throne.

Aber, North Wales, August, 1241

'Good grief!' Dafydd shouted. 'The scheming, conniving little vixen has only gone and persuaded Uncle Henry to attack us!'

'Who has?' Isabella asked, throwing frightened glances, first at her husband, and then at the exhausted messenger still on his knees before him, pressing the sodden mail bag his chest.

'Senena, of course! Who else has been threatening to petition the King of England on Gruffydd's behalf! She's ridden to Shrewsbury in secret, and begged Henry to free Gruffydd, claiming that I am confining her husband unlawfully. And now Henry is using Gruffydd's imprisonment as a pretext to invade Wales! Not only that, she was accompanied by Gwenllian who has complained that I've not awarded her the patrimony owed to her upon Father's death!'

Isabella sat down heavily on a chair. 'Who told you this?' she asked?'

'Aynnanus Wokeham, who else!'

She was not really surprised. Since the old prince's death, and Dafydd signing the Treaty of Gloucester the previous year, Wales was now simply a battle ground upon which petty arguments and wrongful claims surrounding his disputed lands were dragged out, and later fought over in the king's court amongst those who wanted to dispose of them. Aynnanus Wokeham, Dafydd's attorney, must have been present on Dafydd's behalf at one of these hearings, and overheard Senena petitioning the king on her husband's cause. And now Henry was summoning Dafydd to England again. This time to answer to him as his overlord - both for the chaos in Wales which was partly of the king's own making, and to explain the reasons why he kept his brother incarcerated without reason.

Signalling the messenger to leave, Dafydd began to pace the hall angrily. 'I knew I could not trust her,' he said. 'She's played a clever card, and I've no choice but to answer Henry's summons and ride to Shrewsbury where he orders we meet. And if he frees Gruffydd, where do I stand then in the eyes of my people? I will be a laughing stock, and Senena and Gruffydd will have won. And if Henry thinks that chaos reigns in Wales now, then he clearly has no idea what it will have to endure if Gruffydd is set free to fight me for what he regards as his rightful inheritance! What? What is it?' he asked, coming to a halt as Isabella suddenly stood and crossed to the fire.

'There is another way,' she said steadily.

'And what might that be?' Dafydd asked, peering at her with sudden interest.

'You refuse to go, and you fight Henry instead! Show him who really rules Wales! Show him you are not his lackey; his Welsh puppet that dances every time he pulls your strings. Go and claim your inheritance, Dafydd! But this time do it on the battlefield, and not on the court floor!'

Aber, North Wales, One Month Later

Dafydd entered the hall and pulling up a chair he sat down wearily by the hearth, carless of his blood-stained hauberk acquired in yet another skirmish with the king's men.

'You have to surrender,' Ednyved said.

Dafydd frowned, wondering if he should not have replaced his father's old adviser upon his death, for he was certain that Ednyved would not have said the same to Llywelyn, had he found himself in the same position.

'You cannot continue to fight them,' Ednyved continued, regarding him with grave concern. 'Not with so many of your father's old allies now pledging their support to Gruffydd, and welcoming the king's invasion. You have to face it, my lord. All your friends have deserted you, and you are now alone and at the king's mercy. If you do not accept that and lay down your arms you will surely loose Gwynedd!'

Dafydd pounded his hand with his fist in frustration. He also wished he had never listened to Isabella. His dream of defeating Henry had died in less than a month with the loss of his allies, many of whom had defected to Gruffydd's cause. Henry, emboldened, had marched into Wales with a seemingly unstoppable force. Dafydd could not fight him, and, powerless, he had fallen back in the face of his mighty army, burning his own castles behind him on the way in frustration.

Isabella, standing at Ednyved's elbow, nodded in agreement and Dafydd glared at her. 'That's not what you thought a month ago when you advised me to fight,' he growled. 'You were all for me standing firm and challenging the king then!'

Isabella sighed. 'I don't see you have any choice now,' she said, smiling to herself inwardly. 'You must go to Gwern Eigron as the king demands. Negotiate with him. Mayhap you can win him back to your side, and he will help you put down the insurrections. You just have to ask him as your overlord. Explain the situation to him, ask him to -'

'His terms will be harsh,' Ednyved interrupted. 'You will be permanently stripped of your lands, and he will force you to release Gruffydd, and –' He hesitated and glanced at Isabella before continuing. 'And he may well demand that if you die without an heir, Gwynedd will pass to the royal demesne - until he decides whether or not he recognises Gruffydd or one of his children as its rightful successor.'

'See what you have done, woman!' Dafydd shouted, rounding on Isabella. 'If we'd children as we might have had, then at least I need not have worried on that score!'

'You know why we don't have children,' Isabella spat. 'Because your father murdered mine, and I was forced to marry you - the son of a murderer!' For a moment she glared at him. 'Of course, if you'd not murdered Bronwyn, then I might have been able to go to her and ask her to lift the spell -'

'Enough!' Ednyved barked at Isabella, his tone making it clear that he would not tolerate such dangerous talk in public from a woman, before rounding on Dafydd. 'Go to the king and hear his terms! Go, before you lose everything your father won for you!'

But he was already speaking to an empty chair, for Dafydd was already half way out the *llys*.

Gwern Eigron, Wales, August 29th 1241

Dafydd stood before the king, his dream of ruling the lands his father had before him now in tatters. He had lost everything that his father had fought for in a few swift and frightening months, and now he was defeated.

As Ednyved had predicted, Henry's terms were cruel: he had lost all claims to the lands beyond Gwynedd that were under dispute, had been forced to release Gruffydd into the king's custody, and, most bitterly of all, if he died without an heir, Gwynedd would pass into the coffers of the royal demesne.

Chapter 48

Criccieth Castle, North Wales, September 1241

Senena pulled her shawl tighter around her shoulders, and stared out over the marshes beyond the castle wall forlornly. She was pregnant again, expecting yet another child sometime in the spring of next year. And she was once more alone, for the king, in the aftermath of his invasion of Wales, had immediately reneged on his promises to her. Far from releasing Gruffydd from Criccieth, and restoring him to his lands following Dafydd's surrender at Gwern Eigron in August, he had taken both him and Owain to London, where they were now prisoners in the tower as surety against any threat that Dafydd might pose in the future. Now, suddenly, Henry's position in Wales was very strong.

And it had been of her doing, for with Dafydd now completely stripped of his disputed lands, and with Gruffydd out of the way, Henry had placed allies of his own there: Marcher and Welsh lords, who'd begun strengthening his position by rebuilding castles and enforcing royal judicial power on behalf of the Crown. In addition to this, the key fortresses of Cardigan, Carmarthen and Degannwy had also fallen to the Crown and become centres of royal power, leaving what was left of Wales to be fought over by the remaining pack of disgruntled lords and chieftains, like wolves over what was left of the kill.

Turning, she kicked out bitterly at a log that had fallen from a pile by the hearth, disturbing a pup who was dozing there and waking Llywelyn who was sleeping in a chair after a long night of border patrol.

'What? What is it, Mother?' he asked, rubbing his eyes.

'We must pack,' Senena said, making her decision. 'I shall leave for London on the morrow. Henry has written to assure me that Gruffydd and Owain are kept in honourable confinement as his guests in the White Tower, where they are being treated well as befits members of his own family. He assures me that I shall have full access to them both whilst it is decided what is to be done with them.'

'Henry is using them as pawns in his game, Mother,' Llywelyn grumbled irritably. 'And moreover you are playing a part in it.'

Senena sighed. Llywelyn, now a tall, thin young man still not yet in his twenties, with wavy brown hair and a permanent frown, had surprised her by calmly taking over the role as her protector and adviser after Grufffydd and Owain had been taken into captivity, showing quiet determination and far better grasp of the politics of the matter than she might have given him credit for had he not been forced to do so. For a moment she paused, knowing that he referred to the fact that she had promised to hand either him, Rhodri or Dafydd over to Henry should either Gruffydd or Owain die in captivity, in the hope that he would eventually stand by their previous agreement. But what choice did she have? Henry was determined to use her husband and son as tools to keep Dafydd in check, for if he continued to challenge the Crown over the loss of his lands, he faced the very real prospect of having to share what was left with his half-brother, or even worse, being displaced entirely. She sat down irritably. None of it had worked out as it should. Her promise of six hundred marks for her husband and son's freedom, along with promises of livestock and regular future payments, were now of little use. Really all she had done was to have her husband and son transferred from one prison to another.

Standing, she aimed another kick, this time at Llywelyn's foot. 'Come on, help me pack my coffers, and then we can write letters to the King of England. I will not sit by and watch my husband and son rot in jail any longer!'

'And you will be of no help to Father if you travel in your condition!' Llywelyn retorted, following her out of the door.

'I know, but he has need of us,' Senena whispered silently, as between the folds of her skirt, her fingers curled around the little brooch.

Chapter 49

The Tower of London, England, 1242

Gruffydd leaned his large bulk back against the pile of pillows and furs on his bed in the White Tower, the place where he and Owain had been held as the king's 'honourable guests' for the last year whilst he considered where their loyalties lay. Outside, he could hear the roar of the leopards coming from the menagerie where Henry housed his strange and exotic animals: gifts from Emperors and princes around the world. Like them, he was locked behind bars, and he was now bored, frustrated, and very overweight from the inactivity of life with nothing to do but read, play chess and eat. Henry, it seemed, was not overly concerned with his welfare now that he was his prisoner, and he was not allowed out to ride, hunt, or partake in any activity at all, save for a few short strolls with Senena carried out under the watchful eye of the wardens and guards on duty all the time.

Sighing, he looked into the corner where the shadows stirred, growing longer in the fading evening light. Then with a smile, he poured himself another goblet of wine. He was no longer afraid of her, the shadowy figure that visited him each and every night. They both knew now that her dream for him was dead and gone. But still she came. Came and whispered to him each night of another dream; one in which his two eldest sons, Owain and Llywelyn would rule Gwynedd in his stead. He smiled sadly. He had seen his father, too; wearing his crown, with Joanna, but always with the shadow of Will de Braose and Tangwystl between them. And he had seen Bronwyn. Bronwyn had not been afraid to die; not when her job with Isabella had been done so efficiently and so well for, unlike Mab, she had seen the spectre of death coming ...

Sighing again, Gruffydd turned to the lacquered table beside his bed, and pulling the draw open he took out the little brooch, wondering, not for the first time, how it had got from being buried in Tangwystl's grave in Wales, to be hidden amongst his belongings in the Tower. Then, as he carefully put it back in the draw, he wondered again whose shadow it was that he so often saw, walking amongst the ravens in his dreams ...

London 1243

Gwenllian sat back in the chair in the sparsely furnished lodging house she had rented near to the Tower of London. That her choice of lodgings did not reflect her status as a rich widow - for she was that - owning lands in Ireland and Wales, some of which King Henry still refused to acknowledge, was deliberate, for it was prudent to remain low for the time being, out of sight of the king's watchful eye as she continued her fight for Gruffydd's freedom.

There was a knock and the door opened, admitting Elen, accompanied by Senena, who had in tow with her a messenger sent to England by her brother, Einion ap Caradoc.

'What news have you from Wales?' Gwenllian asked without preamble.

The messenger nodded in turn to each of the ladies, before accepting the goblet of wine offered by Gwenllian's maid. Then casting an eye round the room to ensure they were alone, he passed over the document with Enion's seal upon it containing the list of Welsh noblemen who, unhappy with Dafydd's rule and Henry's growing influence in Wales, had been enlisted in the plan that was slowly being devised to break Gruffydd free of the great keep in London.

'There are not so many as I'd hoped,' Senena said, her voice heavy with disappointment as she passed it on to Gwenllian and Elen.

'No, but we still have the support of many of those who made pledges for you when you petitioned the king last,' Gwenllian said encouragingly. 'Including Gwladys's husband and Marared's, and some of Father's extended family ... and of course there are those nobles and families who are contracted to marry cousins, and so forth,' she finished lamely.

'We might as well face it,' Elen broke in, 'we are rapidly losing support to Dafydd. If we are to break Gruffydd free we need money and support now. Gruffydd's not getting any younger and, if we're honest, he's not getting any fitter - which suits Henry's plans of course, for the less fit he is the less likely he is to escape.'

'Yes, but what of Robert?' Gwenllian asked, referring to Robert de Quincy, the husband forced on her by King Henry after the Earl of Chester's death. 'You have not told him you are here I hope, because I have heard say that he is Dafydd's man ... and the king's -'

Turning, Elen spat on the floor. 'He doesn't even know I'm in London,' she said viciously. 'The last time I saw him, he was lying drunk on the floor of his chambers at his manor near Fotheringhay.' She stood and pulled back the barbette and veil that concealed the lower part of her face, revealing the fading bruises of the recent beating endured during the last hours in her husband's presence.

'He did that?' Gwladys whispered.

'Yes,' Elen spat. 'So you can be sure that I shall never inform him of our plans, for with Gruffydd back in power I intend to divorce him, for by then I would have endured the seven years of required marriage first.'

Senena scowled. 'Dafydd would not agree to it I suppose, him being the king's man.'

Elen's eyes narrowed. 'He will pay for that, sister. With Gruffydd free, and with his help, I shall finally be rid of my husband and Wales will be rid of an impotent ruler. If he thought the wrath of Isabella was bad, then he has a lot to learn - he led Robert to believe that I poisoned John and that his death was my doing, and now because Robert fears me, he beats me.' She smiled. 'But they will both regret their treatment of me one day ...'

The Tower of London, March 1244

'Elen! Gwen! At last! I thought you would not come!' Gruffydd said, watching as the guards withdrew.

Elen sighed. 'We nearly could not. Robert -'

'Knows of your plans to free me,' Gruffydd finished the sentence for her.

'Yes.' Elen turned and looked out of the narrow window, down onto the cobbled courtyard three stories below. Never one for heights, Gruffydd saw her flinch at the thought of the spine chilling drop between them and the ground, and for a moment she looked as if someone had just walked over her grave.

Crossing to her, Gruffydd put an arm around her shoulder. 'He is cruel to you, little sister.' It was not a question, merely a statement.

Turning out of the circle of his arms, Elen went and sat down by Gwen. In the adjoining chamber, they could hear Owain laughing with one of the women Henry turned a blind eye to visiting and providing him with the comfort that young men of his age sought.

'How are Senena and the children?' Gwen asked, trying to cover her embarrassment.

'They're fine, only Catherine does not fare well in the London air, so they have gone back to Criccieth to be with Margred for a while.'

Gwen nodded. Catherine, their youngest, had been born whilst Gruffydd was a prisoner in the tower and, being a sickly child, she needed the country air rather than the cloying London smoke and cold rain.

'What has happened to you, Gruffydd?' Elen asked suddenly, ignoring Gwen's glare. 'You look so unwell - do they not allow you any air? Any exercise?'

Gruffydd grunted, and patted his expansive girth. 'Not since they got wind of our plans to have me freed,' he said. 'But then no-one has actually ever escaped the Tower, have they? And now it seems, thanks to Robert de Quincy, I'm not going to be the first!' He sighed. 'Why don't you leave him, *cariad*? Run away, be free. If not for yourself, then do it for me!'

Elen sighed. 'It is easier said than done, brother. He has control of my lands, my dowry is his, and Dafydd will not listen to my pleas - will not believe that Robert is a cruel and vicious man.'

Gruffydd sighed. 'How did he know of our plans?' he asked.

It was Gwen who answered. 'He beat it out of her,' she said steadily. 'He beat her within an inch of her life. She was nearly dead when she was brought to me.'

'I'm sorry,' Elen whispered, wringing her hands in anguish. 'So sorry … if I'd been stronger … if I hadn't -'

Gruffydd growled. 'I would kill him myself, if only I could escape this God-forsaken tower!' he said, crossing to a table and pouring her a goblet of wine from a pitcher there.

Gwen stood, spotting something lying on the table as Gruffydd poured. 'Where did you get this?' she whispered, picking it up fearfully and crossing to the window so as to see it better. 'I thought we had buried this long ago ... why's it here ... *how's it here?'*

Gruffydd paused. 'I found it among my belongings in my drawer,' he said defensively. 'According to Owain, Llywelyn dug it up years ago and kept it until Senena discovered it amongst his things one day. She must have left it here when last she visited, for I cannot think how else it might have got there.' He crossed to the window and took it from her, rubbing his fingers over the faded enamel. Outside he could hear the caw of the ravens as they squabbled over a piece of carrion, and he felt a sudden chill run down his spine.

'Does she come to you?' Gwen whispered, crossing herself quickly.

'Yes,' Gruffydd said, smiling wryly. 'I thought I would be afraid, but I do not fear her any longer. She keeps me company. Her, and Bronwyn.'

'Bronwyn?' Gwen shivered. 'Let me take it away, Gruffydd. Your mind will become crazed if you keep it here with you.'

For a moment Gruffydd did not answer, he was staring down into the courtyard, could see people running towards the Tower ...

'No,' he said, his fingers curling around the brooch. 'No, it came back to me for a reason ...'

Chapter 50

Tower of London, St David's Day, 1244

Gruffydd moved another piece on the chess board. 'Checkmate!' he said triumphantly, watching as Owain threw down his queen and leaned back in his chair, deep in thought.

'Are you serious about what we discussed last night?' Owain asked after a moment, throwing a glance at his father's fellow conspirator, Hal, a manservant of Gwen's, who'd chosen to share their exile in the Tower whilst she continued to petition the king.

Gruffydd nodded. Despite Robert de Quincy's intervention, his thoughts had seldom strayed from the idea that he might one day escape from prison. More so lately after Gwen and Elen's visit, for he now thought another plan possible, and with that in mind he had a pile of sheets stuffed in a coffer at the foot of his bed, though still not as many as he would have liked. Dreamily, he looked past Owain and into the fire, and just for a second he thought he saw something there: a figure, her arms outstretched, reaching for him ...

Frightened, he turned away. In the background, he had seen again the shadowy figure of the stranger. Walking amongst the ravens ...

Peter de Vallibus, the Constable of the Tower, leaned back in his chair in his apartments and regarded Gwenllian thoughtfully. She was an attractive woman: a bit on the plump side now, but still youthful, with her strange eyes the colour of honeyed mead, and her red brown hair coiled and tucked neatly beneath her crisp wimple.

'So you are leaving us soon?' he asked sorrowfully.

Gwen sighed. 'Yes,' she said, crossing to the window and looking out over to the Royal Apartments; her lodgings during a fresh round of negotiations with the king to release her brother and award her the lands her father had bequeathed her.

'Then Henry has still not come to a decision about your claims - or Gruffydd's? Not even now that Dafydd is raising an army against him once again?'

Gwen turned and accepted the cup of wine and one of the sweetmeats that Peter's servant was offering. 'It's difficult,' she said. 'On the one hand, Henry sees it as an opportunity of setting the brothers against each other once more, but on the other, he is not unaware of the fact that he has left it too long. Gruffydd no longer has the support he once had, you see. Not whilst he remains locked away here in London. I know that Senena does her best from Criccieth to keep his cause fresh in the minds of the people, but Dafydd has grown too strong, and he is now winning allies amongst those who resent Henry's growing presence in Wales. The truth is that the king's trump card has grown fat and friendless, and is now of little use to him. With that in mind, he is no longer concerned with keeping the pledges he made to Senena or myself to put him on the Welsh throne and into his inheritance where he belongs.'

Peter sighed. 'I shall miss you,' he said, coming and dropping a kiss on her shoulder. 'You have been excellent company.'

Gwen turned into the circle of his arms. 'It's getting late, past midnight - I shall have to go back to my rooms in a moment else my reputation will suffer,' she paused at the sound of the chapel bells ringing out loudly in the darkness.

Peter smiled wryly and prepared to kiss her again, but she jerked away suddenly as a loud commotion began out in the in the courtyard and people began to shout and run towards the tower ...

Gruffydd was only a little drunk when he, Owain, and Hal began knotting the sheets, but his resolve to try to escape was not shaken by Owain's pleas to the contrary.

'I can do this!' he said, panting as he pulled the rest of the linen off his bed and threw it onto the growing pile by the window.

He paused to drink the last of his of wine; it was strong, pungent and spicy and he let it linger on his tongue for a moment before swallowing the last mouthful. Then, heedless of the strange, reckless laughter that was beginning to well in his throat, he fell to his knees and began to scrabble around, pulling the loose ends together, and tugging them repeatedly in a frenzied effort to ensure that they were tight. He was so engrossed in his task that he didn't notice Hal and Owain exchange worried looks over his head. Neither did he notice the distant roar of the lions, or the growl of the bears as, caught up in the sense of foreboding that hung over the Tower, they too began to pace back and forth in their cages.

'Look,' Owain ventured at last as Gruffydd grabbed the ends of his makeshift rope and, hauling himself unsteadily to his feet, began to look wildly around. 'Look, this is madness! Can you at least not wait and see what Aunt Gwen has to say tomorrow after her audience with the king? Or indeed, what news there is from Mother who is fighting your cause back home!'

'No!' Gruffydd said, taking a deep breath and turning towards the shadows as they moved restlessly in the corner. 'No, I have to try now! Tonight! If I can make it down into the courtyard, mayhap I can conceal myself somewhere: get out via a ship off Tower Warf, or hide myself amongst the merchants leaving after selling their wares on the morrow. Either way, Gwen will help me!'

'Father, please reconsider ... this is madness!' Owain repeated, watching as Gruffydd reached for Hal and began to tie the first lot of sheets around his waist. 'Please! Don't you realise that you are putting Aunt Gwen at risk!'

But Gruffydd was not listening. He was peering down at the cobbles below, listening for any sound of the guards changing, or a clue that their plan had been discovered. Then turning he tied the loose end of the sheets firmly around the stone mullion that divided the window, and glancing around the room once more, he began to push Hal into the terrifying darkness beyond ...

Disturbed by the all the noise and the sudden pounding of feet on the walkway beyond the window, Gwen pushed Peter aside and ran to the door. Wrenching it open, her first instinct was to follow the crowd ...

Gruffydd gripped the edge of the window embrasure in relief. Hal had made it to the bottom, he could see him peering up at him through the mist, his face white and triumphant before he disappeared into the shadows beyond the tower wall. Taking a deep breath, he turned and slapped his son on the shoulder.

'You're next. Just pull the sheets back up when I reach the ground, and tie them round your waist tightly. Just remember, there is no one behind you, and the only way is down. Oh, and make sure that your woman unties the sheets after you're gone. You have paid her, haven't you?' he asked anxiously, glancing at the door behind which she waited.

Owain nodded, and Gruffydd could see the sweat running cold and damp down the front of his tunic as he, too, threw a swift look at the door.

'I will wait for you with Hal at the bottom and we shall find somewhere safe to conceal ourselves tonight,' he said, turning away sharply before Owain could see the fear beginning to gather in his eyes. Then, swinging a leg over the deep sill, he threw one last glance into the corner where she waited.

'I will be back soon, Mother. In Wales where I belong,' he whispered. *'You are right, it's no life for a prince of the blood to be locked in a tower far away from the land of his birth!'*

Gwen arrived at the foot of the tower frenzied with fear. Around her, the swirling torches made patterns in the darkness, their glowing embers sparking amber and blue as they danced on the breeze and faded like fireflies into the night.

Above her, the moon suddenly came out from behind the clouds, lighting the scene from afar like a theatre A figure was climbing down the side of the tower, his large form dangling from a makeshift rope, his feet dancing against the bricks as they tried to make purchase with the wall. Without needing to be told, Gwen knew it was Gruffydd.

Gruffydd paused, and repositioning his feet against the wall, he stared up at the stars above the battlements, just as the moon freed itself from the clouds. Cursing, he hung there, clinging tightly as above him the knots in the rope creaked and stretched ominously, making his heart miss a beat. Below him, he could hear the roar of the lions in the menagerie and the sound of the river lapping against the distant wharf. He could also hear feet pounding in the direction of the Tower, and the shouts of the guards as they realised something was afoot.

'*I can do this!*' he whispered through gritted teeth, looking down through the mist below. Then shifting his heavy bulk, he began to lower himself down again; hand over hand, easing himself carefully towards the ground and freedom ...

Freedom, when it came, was the yawning, empty space into which he fell when the sheets unravelled and parted above his head ...

Wildly Gwen looked around her. She could hear a woman keening loudly, but it was only when Peter pulled her into his arms that she realised the sound was coming from her. Pushing him aside, she picked up her skirts and began to scramble over the rose borders, careless of the thorns tearing at her arms and face.

'No!' Peter shouted, pulling her back. 'No! There is nothing you can do!'

'I must!' Gwen sobbed, freeing herself from his grip as people began to gather around them ...

Gruffydd lay where he had fallen, twisted and broken on the ground like a doll, surrounded by smoking torches and panic-stricken guards. In the distance, he could hear a woman weeping, keening loudly. Then as the darkness swirled around him and he closed his eyes, he saw the ravens crowding in ...

Gwen saw *her* first: misty and ethereal as she floated across the cobbles, her red brown hair swirling around her shoulders in the ghostly breeze that blew in from the wharf.

Mama ...

Drawing a sharp breath, her eyes went to the object that lay glinting dully in the light of the torches beside the heel of Gruffydd's broken foot. For a moment, she hesitated. Then diving forward, she began to scrabble amongst the dirt, tearing at the cobbles until her hand closed over the little brooch.

Behind her a woman screamed: the sound tore across the courtyard, and in the silence that followed she heard Peter's whispered gasp -'Holy Mother of God, who are you?' as in front of her Tangwystl hovered uncertainly, trapped on the threshold between two worlds, gazing down in anguish at the broken body of her son ...

Too late ...

Gwen scrambled back into the safety of Peter's arms, clinging to him fiercely as the ghostly wind blew wildly around them, sending showers of sparks and smoke billowing dangerously from the burning torches.

My son, my son, where are you ...

A deathly silence fell as everybody froze and stared. Then slowly a shadow, tall and indistinct, rose and hovered for a moment, before gazing down in puzzlement at the body that lay beneath him.

Gruffydd ...

Tears coursed down Gwen's face as pandemonium broke out. Then suddenly Hal launched himself from the shadows and threw himself at his prince's ghostly feet, as above them, trapped in the Tower, Owain collapsed into his lover's arms and let out an unholy wail.

Come, my son ....

Screams and the sound of panic almost drowned the words, as with one last look at his body, Gruffydd turned and began to walk. Slowly amongst the ravens. Towards his mother. Then he was gone, as together they turned into the mist and the veil between the two worlds fell once more ...

But not before Tangwystl paused, and looked in her daughter's direction. For a moment their eyes met - two pairs of eyes the colour of honeyed mead, locked between two worlds. Fiercely, Gwen's hand curled around the little brooch as Tangwystl hovered, drifting uncertainly, before finally giving her a sad little smile of farewell.

Now that she had the son that she loved so much, she could wait for her daughter ...

EPILOGUE

Gwenllian stood before the fresh mound of her brother's grave at Aberconwy where his body finally had been laid to rest alongside his father's four years after his fatal fall from the Tower of London.

In those four years much had changed in Wales, for Dafydd, too, had died at Aber barely two years after Father's death, and as Isabella had remained childless he was succeeded by two of Gruffydd's sons, Owain and Llywelyn, who had now divided Gwynedd between them. The last that Gwen heard of Isabella, was that she'd retired from court life and gone to England in order to seek permission from the king to re-marry. Rumour had it that now she was free of Dafydd, she longed to have children, and so she'd offered a reward to the person who could find the wax doll that still roamed the length and breadth of the kingdom and remove the pin from its little belly.

With a shudder, Gwen reached into her pocket and withdrew the little enamelled brooch that had been burning a hole there during the long journey from her lands in Ireland to her brother's grave. For a moment she stared at it, then turning to Senena who had materialised like a ghost alongside her, she dropped it into the hole she had dug with her bare hands earlier.

Finally, with a last look at the little object that had caused so much trouble and pain, she crossed herself. Then taking Senena's hand, together they turned and walked away.

Afterword

As the author of this novel I wish to point out that I am not a historian. I do however have a deep and abiding love of history and I have enjoyed every minute of the research I have done in order to try to bring history alive for my readers. I hope that, allowing for artistic/author interpretation, it is correct. As for the supernatural elements ... well, you have only to read books by medieval contemporary writers such as Gerald of Wales, *The Journey Through Wales and The Description of Wales,* to know that my imagination is not too far-fetched ...

Select Bibliography:

Gerald of Wales, The Journey through Wales and the description of Wales. (Penguin Classics 2004)

Bartlett, Robert, Gerald of Wales. A voice of the middle ages. (Tempus Publishing Limited)

Maund, Kari, The Welsh Kings, Warriors, Warlords and Princes. (Tempus Publishing Limited 2006)

Turvey, Roger, Llywelyn the Great. (Gomer Press 2007)

Turvey, Roger, The Welsh Princes, The Native Rulers of Wales 1063-1283, (Pearson Education)

Weir, Alison, Eleanor of Aquitaine, (Pimlico)

Warren, W L, King John, (Yale University Press, 1997)

Herbert, Norris, Medieval Costume and Fashion, (Dover Publications inc)

Labarage, Wade, Mistresses, Maids and Men; Baronial Life in the Thirteenth Century, (Eyre and Spittiswoode 2003)

Hammond, Peter, Food and Feast in Medieval England, (Sutton Publishing Limited, 2005)

Hudson, Roger, Hudsons English History, A Compendium, (Weidenfudd & Nicolson, 2005)

McLynn, Frank, Lionheart & Lackland, King Richard, King John and the Wars of Conquest, (Vubtage Books, 2007)

Hindley, Geoffrey, A Brief History of the Magna Carta, (Constable & Robinson, 2008)

Dan Jones, The Plantagenets, The Kings Who Made England, (William Collins, 2013)

Dan Jones, Magna Carta, The Making and Legacy of The Great Charter, (Head of Zeus Ltd, 2014)

Acknowledgements:

Thank you to Nicky Galliers who gave up her time and expertise to assist in the production of my book as a much valid editor and, I hope, friend.

Final Note:

I found the most wonderful thesis online some years ago, however, the only title I could see that it owned was: 'Languishing in the Footnotes: Women and Welsh Medieval Historiography?' It was the most wonderful piece of work regarding the women behind the men in Welsh Medieval history; most notably, several of Llywelyn Fawr's daughters, and his daughter-in-law Senena. One day *mayhap,* I shall meet the author and know her name...for I am assuming it is a *her!*

Printed in Great Britain
by Amazon

MASTERING PUBLIC AFFAIRS

Strategies, Pitfalls, and Case Studies

OSMAN KARAKAS

2023

About Book

Book Title: **MASTERING PUBLIC AFFAIRS:**

Strategies, Pitfalls, and Case Studies

Type: Digital E-Book
Format: PDF
Size: 6X9 inches - 15.24X22.89 cm
Total Pages: 215

© All Right Reserved - 2023 - Osman KARAKAS
Copying, in full or in part, for reuse is prohibited. It can be used partially by acknowledging the source.

E-mail: okarakas@hotmail.com

Web: www.osmankarakas.com

CONTENTS

PREFACE 4

CHAPTER 1: INTRODUCTION TO SUCCESSFUL PUBLIC AFFAIRS 7
- UNDERSTANDING THE ROLE OF PUBLIC AFFAIRS 11
- THE IMPORTANCE OF EFFECTIVE PUBLIC AFFAIRS STRATEGIES 14
- OVERVIEW OF COMMON MISTAKES AND THEIR IMPACT 17

CHAPTER 2: BUILDING A SOLID FOUNDATION 21
- ESTABLISHING CLEAR OBJECTIVES IN PUBLIC AFFAIRS 24
- STAKEHOLDER MAPPING AND ANALYSIS 28
- CRAFTING A COMPELLING PUBLIC AFFAIRS NARRATIVE 31

CHAPTER 3: AVOIDING PITFALLS: COMMON MISTAKES TO STEER CLEAR OF 35
- NEGLECTING COMPREHENSIVE RESEARCH AND ANALYSIS: 36
- IGNORING PUBLIC PERCEPTION AND SENTIMENT: 40
- LACKING TRANSPARENCY AND AUTHENTICITY: 43
- MISJUDGING CULTURAL AND SOCIETAL CONTEXT: 47
- NEGLECTING ETHICAL CONSIDERATIONS: 50
- REACTING POORLY TO CRISES: 52
- INEFFECTIVE MEDIA RELATIONS: 55
- OVERLOOKING DIGITAL AND SOCIAL MEDIA: 58
- FAILING TO UNDERSTAND PUBLIC PERCEPTION AND SENTIMENT 62
- OVERLOOKING ETHICAL CONSIDERATIONS IN PUBLIC AFFAIRS 64

CHAPTER 4: STRATEGIES FOR SUCCESSFUL PUBLIC AFFAIRS 68
- UNDERSTANDING THE POWER OF MESSAGING: 69
- DEVELOPING A TARGETED MEDIA RELATIONS PLAN 72
- LEVERAGING STAKEHOLDER ENGAGEMENT: 77
- PROACTIVE CRISIS MANAGEMENT: 80
- HARNESSING THE POWER OF DIGITAL AND SOCIAL MEDIA: 84
- ENGAGING WITH KEY DECISION-MAKERS AND INFLUENCERS 88
- NAVIGATING CULTURAL SENSITIVITY: 91
- REAL-WORLD CASE STUDIES: 97

CHAPTER 5: NAVIGATING COMPLEX PUBLIC AFFAIRS LANDSCAPES 103
- MANAGING CRISIS SITUATIONS AND REPUTATION DAMAGE 109
- LOBBYING AND ADVOCACY: BALANCING INFLUENCE AND INTEGRITY 114
- INTERNATIONAL PUBLIC AFFAIRS: CHALLENGES AND OPPORTUNITIES 118

CHAPTER 6: CASE STUDIES IN PUBLIC AFFAIRS 124

CASE STUDY 1: STARBUCKS' "RACE TOGETHER" CAMPAIGN 131
CASE STUDY 2: VOLKSWAGEN'S EMISSION SCANDAL RECOVERY 134
CASE STUDY 3: CHICK-FIL-A'S APPROACH TO CONTROVERSIAL STANCES 137

CHAPTER 7: LEARNING FROM SUCCESS AND FAILURE....................141

ANALYZING THE FACTORS BEHIND SUCCESSFUL PUBLIC AFFAIRS CAMPAIGNS..145
LESSONS TO BE LEARNED FROM HIGH-PROFILE FAILURES 149
ADAPTING STRATEGIES BASED ON REAL-LIFE SCENARIOS 152

CHAPTER 8: ETHICAL CONSIDERATIONS IN PUBLIC AFFAIRS............158

BALANCING CORPORATE GOALS WITH SOCIETAL IMPACT...........................161
TRANSPARENCY AND AUTHENTICITY IN PUBLIC COMMUNICATIONS 164
ADDRESSING PUBLIC AFFAIRS IN SENSITIVE INDUSTRIES 168

CHAPTER 9: CRAFTING YOUR PUBLIC AFFAIRS ROADMAP 171

DEVELOPING A COMPREHENSIVE PUBLIC AFFAIRS STRATEGY........................175
SETTING MEASURABLE GOALS AND MILESTONES......................................179
CONTINUOUS IMPROVEMENT: ADAPTING TO CHANGING LANDSCAPES...........183

CHAPTER 10: THE FUTURE OF PUBLIC AFFAIRS 187

EMERGING TRENDS IN PUBLIC AFFAIRS AND COMMUNICATIONS...................191
THE ROLE OF TECHNOLOGY AND DATA ANALYTICS 196
ANTICIPATING CHALLENGES AND STAYING AHEAD.......................................200

APPENDIX B: GLOSSARY OF KEY TERMS 205

DEFINITIONS OF ESSENTIAL PUBLIC AFFAIRS CONCEPTS 209

Preface

Welcome to "Mastering Public Affairs: Strategies, Pitfalls, and Case Studies." In a world where communication and perception play pivotal roles in shaping organizations and their interactions with society, the realm of public affairs has gained unparalleled significance. This book is a comprehensive guide designed to provide readers with the tools, knowledge, and insights needed to excel in the dynamic field of public affairs.

Public affairs is not merely about managing external perceptions or engaging with stakeholders; it is a strategic discipline that influences decisions, policies, and reputations. Whether you are a seasoned public affairs professional looking to refine your approach or someone new to the field seeking to grasp its nuances, this book aims to equip you with the essential strategies, best practices, and real-world examples to succeed.

Throughout the chapters of this book, you will embark on a journey that covers a spectrum of topics – from establishing clear objectives and crafting compelling narratives to understanding the intricate interplay of media, technology, and public sentiment. You will learn how to navigate the complexities of crisis management, ethical considerations, and the delicate balance between corporate goals and societal impact.

At the heart of this book are the case studies that illuminate both successful campaigns and cautionary tales. By examining the experiences of companies like Starbucks, Volkswagen, and Chick-fil-A, you will gain a deeper appreciation for the art and science of public affairs. These case studies serve as windows into the real challenges, decisions, and outcomes that define the field.

It's important to note that public affairs is a dynamic landscape, continuously evolving in response to societal shifts, technological advancements, and global events. As such, this book not only delves into current best practices but also provides insights into emerging trends and the future of public affairs.

We invite you to engage with this book as both a reference and a study guide. Each chapter offers practical takeaways, thought-provoking questions, and opportunities for reflection. The goal is not only to impart knowledge but also to encourage critical thinking and the application of concepts to real-world scenarios.

Whether you are a communication professional, a business leader, a policymaker, or a student aspiring to enter the world of public affairs, this book has something to offer you. As you embark on this learning journey, remember that mastering public affairs is not just about following a set of guidelines; it's about understanding the nuances, making informed decisions, and ultimately contributing positively to the broader societal conversation.

We hope that "Mastering Public Affairs" becomes a valuable companion on your path to becoming a more effective and insightful public affairs practitioner. Your journey starts here.

Sincerely,

Osman Karakas
Author

Chapter 1: Introduction to Successful Public Affairs

Public affairs is the art and science of managing an organization's interactions with various stakeholders, including the public, media, government bodies, interest groups, and more. In an increasingly interconnected and information-driven world, the role of public affairs has grown in importance, as organizations recognize the need to effectively communicate, advocate, and navigate the complex landscape of public perception.

This chapter serves as a foundational exploration of the key concepts and principles that underpin successful public affairs strategies. By the end of this chapter, readers will have a clear understanding of the fundamental elements that contribute to effective public affairs and the impact it has on an organization's reputation, growth, and societal relevance.

Key Concepts:

1. **Defining Public Affairs:** Public affairs encompasses a broad range of activities, including government relations, media engagement, stakeholder outreach, and advocacy. It involves shaping public opinion, influencing policies, and building relationships that advance an organization's objectives.

2. **Stakeholder Analysis:** A critical aspect of public affairs is identifying and understanding various

stakeholders, from customers and employees to regulatory bodies and community groups. Mapping stakeholders' interests, concerns, and influence helps shape targeted communication strategies.

3. **Strategic Communication:** Successful public affairs hinges on clear and coherent communication. This involves crafting messages that resonate with different audiences while aligning with an organization's values and objectives.

4. **Reputation Management:** Public affairs plays a central role in safeguarding and enhancing an organization's reputation. By actively managing how the public perceives an organization, public affairs professionals can mitigate potential crises and foster trust.

The Importance of Successful Public Affairs:

In today's fast-paced and information-rich environment, public affairs is not just an optional aspect of organizational operations; it's a necessity. Effective public affairs can lead to several key benefits:

1. **Informed Decision-Making:** By staying attuned to public sentiment and stakeholder concerns, organizations can make more informed and

strategic decisions that align with societal expectations.

2. **Legitimacy and Credibility:** Organizations that engage in transparent and ethical public affairs are more likely to be perceived as credible and trustworthy by the public and other stakeholders.

3. **Influence and Advocacy:** Public affairs allows organizations to advocate for their interests and influence policies that affect their industry or sector.

4. **Risk Mitigation:** Proactive public affairs can help organizations anticipate and mitigate potential crises by addressing concerns before they escalate.

5. **Business Growth:** Positive public perception can attract customers, investors, and partners, contributing to long-term business growth and sustainability.

Throughout the following chapters, we will delve deeper into the strategies, pitfalls, and case studies that exemplify the multifaceted nature of public affairs. By mastering the principles outlined in this chapter, you'll be better equipped to navigate the challenges and opportunities that arise in the realm of successful public affairs.

Understanding the Role of Public Affairs

At its core, public affairs serves as a bridge between organizations and the external world. It encompasses a wide array of activities and strategies designed to manage an organization's interactions, communications, and relationships with various stakeholders, both internal and external. The role of public affairs extends far beyond traditional public relations; it involves shaping perceptions, influencing policies, and navigating complex societal landscapes.

A Multifaceted Responsibility:

Public affairs professionals are tasked with navigating a complex web of stakeholders, each with their own interests, expectations, and concerns. This includes government bodies, regulatory agencies, customers, employees, investors, media outlets, interest groups, and the general public. The ability to effectively communicate and engage with these diverse stakeholders is a hallmark of successful public affairs.

Shaping Perceptions:

A significant aspect of public affairs is shaping how an organization is perceived by the public and key stakeholders. This involves crafting narratives, messages, and communication strategies that highlight an organization's positive contributions, values, and initiatives. Public affairs professionals work to ensure that an organization's image aligns with its goals and resonates with the values of its target audiences.

Influencing Policies:

Public affairs extends into the realm of policy advocacy. Organizations often have a vested interest in influencing government policies, regulations, and legislation that affect their industry or sector. Public affairs professionals engage in lobbying efforts, build relationships with policymakers, and contribute to public debates to advocate for policies that align with their organization's objectives.

Crisis Management and Reputation Building:

A critical role of public affairs is managing and mitigating crises. When issues arise that could potentially damage an organization's reputation, public affairs professionals step in to provide timely and transparent communication, address concerns, and develop strategies to restore trust. Effective crisis management is essential for preserving an organization's credibility and long-term success.

Collaboration and Coordination:

Public affairs is rarely an isolated function within an organization. Instead, it requires collaboration and coordination across different departments, including communications, legal, marketing, and government relations. Public affairs professionals often serve as liaisons between these departments, ensuring that messaging and actions are aligned and consistent.

Measuring Impact:

Measuring the impact of public affairs efforts can be challenging, as success is often subjective and long-term in nature. However, key performance indicators (KPIs) such as media coverage, stakeholder engagement, public sentiment analysis, and policy changes can provide insights into the effectiveness of public affairs strategies.

In the chapters that follow, we will delve deeper into the strategies, techniques, and case studies that illuminate the multifaceted nature of successful public affairs. By grasping the nuances of public affairs and its role in shaping organizational outcomes, you'll be better prepared to navigate the complexities of this dynamic field.

The Importance of Effective Public Affairs Strategies

In today's interconnected and information-driven world, organizations are constantly under the scrutiny of various stakeholders, ranging from consumers and investors to government agencies and advocacy groups. Effective public affairs strategies have emerged as essential tools for organizations to navigate this complex landscape and build relationships that are founded on transparency, trust, and mutual understanding.

Building Trust and Credibility:

Trust is the cornerstone of any successful organization. Effective public affairs strategies help foster trust by promoting open and honest communication. When organizations proactively address concerns, provide accurate information, and engage with stakeholders in a meaningful way, they enhance their credibility and reputation.

Influencing Decision-Making:

Public affairs strategies provide organizations with the means to influence decision-making processes that impact their industry, operations, and bottom line. By engaging with policymakers, regulators, and legislators, organizations can contribute their expertise, share insights, and advocate for policies that align with their goals.

Navigating Public Opinion:

Public opinion can have a profound impact on an organization's success. Public affairs strategies enable organizations to monitor and understand public sentiment, identify potential issues, and take proactive measures to address concerns before they escalate. By effectively managing public perception, organizations can mitigate reputational risks and maintain a positive image.

Managing Crises Effectively:

No organization is immune to crises. However, organizations with robust public affairs strategies are better equipped to manage crises when they arise. These strategies involve clear communication, swift action, and a commitment to transparency. When organizations take responsibility, offer solutions, and demonstrate a genuine commitment to rectify mistakes, they can weather crises with minimal damage to their reputation.

Engaging Stakeholders:

Stakeholder engagement is a fundamental aspect of public affairs. Organizations must identify and understand the expectations, needs, and concerns of their stakeholders. By engaging in meaningful dialogue and incorporating stakeholder feedback into their strategies, organizations can build stronger relationships and ensure their actions align with broader societal values.

Enhancing Competitive Advantage:

Effective public affairs strategies can provide organizations with a competitive edge. A positive public image, strong relationships with policymakers, and a track record of responsible practices can set an organization apart from its competitors. Such advantages can attract customers, investors, and talent, contributing to long-term success.

Contributing to Sustainability:

Sustainability goes beyond environmental initiatives; it also involves maintaining positive relationships with communities, regulators, and other stakeholders. Public affairs strategies that prioritize sustainable practices and responsible corporate behavior demonstrate an organization's commitment to its social and ethical responsibilities.

In the chapters ahead, we will delve into practical techniques, real-world case studies, and actionable insights that will empower you to develop and implement effective public affairs strategies. By understanding the significance of these strategies, you'll be better equipped to navigate the intricate landscape of public affairs and contribute positively to your organization's reputation and success.

Overview of Common Mistakes and Their Impact

In the realm of public affairs, even minor missteps can have significant repercussions on an organization's reputation, relationships, and long-term success. Understanding and learning from common mistakes is crucial for public affairs professionals to navigate the complexities of the field and proactively avoid pitfalls that could undermine their efforts.

Neglecting Comprehensive Research and Analysis:

Mistake: Failing to conduct thorough research and analysis of stakeholders, public sentiment, and the broader societal landscape before formulating public affairs strategies. Impact: Without accurate insights, organizations risk crafting messages that do not resonate, engaging with the wrong stakeholders, and misinterpreting public sentiment, leading to ineffective strategies and missed opportunities.

Ignoring Public Perception and Sentiment:

Mistake: Disregarding public perception and sentiment when making decisions or communicating with stakeholders. Impact: Ignoring public sentiment can lead to misunderstandings, backlash, and damaged relationships. Organizations may find themselves out of touch with their audience, leading to decreased trust and credibility.

Lacking Transparency and Authenticity:

Mistake: Failing to communicate transparently or presenting a message that appears disingenuous. Impact: Lack of transparency erodes trust and credibility. Inauthentic messaging can lead to accusations of manipulation, making it difficult for organizations to recover public trust.

Misjudging Cultural and Societal Context:

Mistake: Overlooking cultural nuances and societal context when crafting messages or launching campaigns. Impact: Cultural insensitivity can lead to public outrage, accusations of cultural appropriation, or perceptions of tone-deafness. Organizations may alienate key demographics and damage their reputation.

Neglecting Ethical Considerations:

Mistake: Pursuing strategies that compromise ethical principles for short-term gains. Impact: Ethical lapses can tarnish an organization's reputation and lead to public backlash. Long-term damage can outweigh any short-term benefits gained from unethical practices.

Reacting Poorly to Crises:

Mistake: Mishandling crisis situations by providing inadequate or delayed responses, downplaying the severity of the issue, or failing to take responsibility. Impact: Poor crisis management exacerbates the situation, damages an organization's reputation, and erodes trust among stakeholders. Negative public perception can persist long after the crisis is resolved.

Ineffective Media Relations:

Mistake: Mismanaging relationships with media outlets or providing inaccurate or incomplete information to journalists. Impact: Media can play a pivotal role in shaping public opinion. Failing to build positive relationships with media professionals or providing misleading information can result in negative coverage and damage an organization's reputation.

Overlooking Digital and Social Media:

Mistake: Underestimating the impact of digital and social media on public affairs strategies or failing to engage effectively in online conversations. Impact: In today's digital age, online platforms are powerful tools for communication. Ignoring these channels can result in missed opportunities to connect with audiences and address concerns.

In the chapters that follow, we will delve into real-world examples and case studies that illustrate these common mistakes and their consequences. By understanding these pitfalls, you'll be better prepared to develop strategies that avoid these missteps and set your public affairs efforts on a path to success.

Chapter 2: Building a Solid Foundation

In the dynamic realm of public affairs, success hinges on a solid foundation built upon clear objectives, thorough research, and strategic planning. This chapter delves into the essential elements that lay the groundwork for effective public affairs strategies. By establishing a robust foundation, organizations can navigate complexities with confidence and ensure that their efforts resonate with stakeholders and the broader public.

Setting Clear Objectives in Public Affairs:

Setting objectives is the compass that guides an organization's public affairs efforts. Objectives provide a clear sense of purpose and direction, helping organizations prioritize actions and measure success. Whether the goal is to influence policy changes, enhance public perception, or manage a crisis, clearly defined objectives ensure that efforts are aligned and focused.

Stakeholder Mapping and Analysis:

Understanding the landscape of stakeholders is pivotal for effective public affairs. Stakeholder mapping involves identifying key individuals, groups, and organizations that have an interest in or impact on an organization's operations. Thorough stakeholder analysis provides insights into their concerns, expectations, and influence, enabling organizations to tailor their strategies to address specific needs.

Crafting a Compelling Public Affairs Narrative:

A well-crafted narrative is the cornerstone of successful communication in public affairs. A narrative is not just a collection of messages; it's a cohesive story that encapsulates an organization's values, goals, and contributions. Crafting a narrative involves identifying key themes, framing messages, and conveying information in a way that resonates with diverse audiences.

Aligning Messaging with Organizational Values:

Effective public affairs strategies align messaging with an organization's core values and mission. When messaging is consistent with an organization's identity, it fosters authenticity and trust. Public affairs professionals must ensure that their messaging reflects the organization's commitment to ethical practices, social responsibility, and long-term sustainability.

Strategic Planning and Adaptability:

A solid foundation also involves strategic planning that considers potential challenges and opportunities. However, the ability to adapt is equally important. The public affairs landscape is dynamic, and organizations must be prepared to adjust their strategies based on changing circumstances, stakeholder feedback, and emerging trends.

Measuring Success and Refining Strategies:

A strong foundation includes mechanisms for measuring the success of public affairs efforts. Key performance indicators (KPIs) such as media coverage, stakeholder engagement, and policy changes can provide insights into the effectiveness of strategies. Regular evaluation allows organizations to refine their approaches and make informed adjustments.

By establishing a solid foundation, organizations can navigate the complexities of public affairs with clarity and purpose. In the chapters that follow, we will delve into practical techniques and real-world examples that illustrate how to apply these foundational principles to develop effective public affairs strategies. Through meticulous planning and a deep understanding of objectives, organizations can build a strong framework for success in the public affairs arena.

Establishing Clear Objectives in Public Affairs

At the heart of any successful public affairs endeavor lies a set of well-defined and achievable objectives. These objectives serve as the guiding stars that illuminate the path toward impactful communication, strategic engagement, and meaningful change. Establishing clear objectives in public affairs is not just a preliminary step; it's a fundamental cornerstone that informs every aspect of an organization's interactions with its stakeholders.

Why Clear Objectives Matter:

1. **Direction and Focus:** Clear objectives provide a sense of direction and purpose for public affairs efforts. They help organizations prioritize activities and allocate resources effectively.

2. **Measurement and Evaluation:** Objectives offer a basis for measuring success. By setting specific goals, organizations can track progress and evaluate the effectiveness of their strategies.

3. **Alignment with Organizational Goals:** Public affairs objectives should align with an organization's broader goals and mission. This alignment ensures that public affairs efforts contribute to overall success.

4. **Stakeholder Engagement:** Well-defined objectives guide how organizations engage with stakeholders. They help tailor communication to address stakeholder concerns and expectations.

Key Components of Effective Objectives:

1. **Specificity:** Objectives should be clear, precise, and focused on a particular outcome. Vague objectives make it challenging to measure success or allocate resources appropriately.

2. **Measurability:** Each objective should be measurable. This means that progress and achievement can be quantified or assessed using concrete indicators or metrics.

3. **Achievability:** Objectives should be realistic and attainable. Setting overly ambitious goals can lead to frustration and unrealistic expectations.

4. **Relevance:** Objectives should align with the broader context and goals of the organization. They should address issues that are meaningful to stakeholders and the organization itself.

5. **Time-bound:** Setting a timeframe for achieving objectives adds a sense of urgency and accountability. This helps prevent objectives from lingering without progress.

Examples of Clear Objectives:

1. **Objective:** Increase positive media coverage by 20% within the next six months.
    - Specific: Increase positive media coverage
    - Measurable: 20% increase

- Achievable: Depending on current coverage trends
- Relevant: Enhancing public perception
- Time-bound: Within six months

2. **Objective**: Engage with key legislators to influence the inclusion of favorable policy provisions in the upcoming industry legislation.
    - Specific: Engage with key legislators
    - Measurable: Influence policy provisions
    - Achievable: Based on established relationships
    - Relevant: Affecting industry legislation
    - Time-bound: Before legislation review

3. **Objective**: Enhance transparency by launching a quarterly stakeholder dialogue series to address community concerns.
    - Specific: Launch stakeholder dialogue series
    - Measurable: Address community concerns
    - Achievable: Organizational commitment to dialogue
    - Relevant: Improving transparency and community relations
    - Time-bound: Quarterly

By establishing clear objectives, organizations provide a roadmap for their public affairs efforts. These objectives serve as the foundation upon which strategies, messaging, and engagement plans are built. As we delve deeper into the chapters ahead, the significance of setting clear objectives will become increasingly evident as an essential element of successful public affairs practices.

Stakeholder Mapping and Analysis

In the intricate tapestry of public affairs, stakeholders play a pivotal role in shaping an organization's reputation, decisions, and overall success. Stakeholder mapping and analysis are powerful tools that allow organizations to identify, understand, and engage with the individuals and groups that have a vested interest in their operations. This chapter explores the significance of stakeholder mapping and analysis in effective public affairs strategies.

Understanding Stakeholders:

Stakeholders encompass a broad spectrum of individuals, organizations, and groups that can significantly impact or be impacted by an organization's actions. These stakeholders range from customers, employees, and investors to government agencies, regulatory bodies, advocacy groups, and the general public.

The Importance of Stakeholder Mapping:

1. **Identifying Key Players:** Stakeholder mapping enables organizations to identify the most

influential and relevant stakeholders within their ecosystem. This identification is essential for allocating resources and prioritizing engagement efforts.

2. **Understanding Interests and Concerns:** Mapping helps organizations understand the interests, needs, and concerns of different stakeholders. This insight allows for tailored communication and strategic decision-making.

3. **Predicting Reactions:** By understanding stakeholders' perspectives, organizations can anticipate how different groups might react to their actions or decisions. This foresight is crucial for managing expectations and potential risks.

Stakeholder Analysis Process:

1. **Identification:** Begin by identifying all potential stakeholders that may have an interest in or impact on your organization.

2. **Categorization:** Group stakeholders into categories based on their level of influence, interest, and involvement. Categories may include primary stakeholders (directly affected), secondary stakeholders (indirectly affected), and tertiary stakeholders (external influencers).

3. **Prioritization:** Prioritize stakeholders based on their level of influence and impact. High-priority

stakeholders are those with significant influence and interest.

4. **Analysis:** Conduct a thorough analysis of each stakeholder group. Understand their motivations, concerns, expectations, and potential areas of alignment or conflict.

5. **Engagement Strategy:** Develop tailored engagement strategies for each stakeholder group. Determine the most effective channels and messages to communicate with them.

Benefits of Stakeholder Mapping and Analysis:

1. **Informed Decision-Making:** A comprehensive understanding of stakeholders informs strategic decision-making that considers their needs and concerns.

2. **Effective Communication:** Tailored communication strategies resonate with stakeholders, building trust and enhancing relationships.

3. **Mitigating Risks:** Anticipating stakeholder reactions helps organizations mitigate potential conflicts or backlash.

4. **Building Alliances:** Building positive relationships with stakeholders can lead to valuable alliances and partnerships.

Real-World Application:

For instance, in a corporate sustainability initiative, stakeholder analysis might identify investors, environmental NGOs, local communities, and regulatory agencies as key stakeholders. By understanding their concerns and motivations, organizations can develop sustainable practices that align with stakeholder expectations.

Stakeholder mapping and analysis are not static processes; they require continuous monitoring and adaptation. As we progress through this book, you'll see how stakeholder engagement strategies are tailored based on the insights gained from this analysis.

Crafting a Compelling Public Affairs Narrative

In the realm of public affairs, where communication shapes perceptions and influences decisions, the power of storytelling cannot be overstated. Crafting a compelling narrative is an art that allows organizations to connect with stakeholders on an emotional and intellectual level, conveying not just information, but also values, purpose, and impact. This chapter delves into the intricacies of creating a narrative that resonates, engages, and drives meaningful change.

The Essence of a Narrative:

A narrative is more than a sequence of events; it's a cohesive and structured storytelling framework that weaves together facts, emotions, and values. A well-crafted narrative gives context to an organization's actions, helping stakeholders understand its journey, motivations, and contributions.

Elements of a Compelling Narrative:

1. **Clarity of Purpose:** A narrative should clearly articulate the organization's purpose, mission, and core values. It answers the question, "Why does this organization exist?"

2. **Central Theme:** Every narrative revolves around a central theme or message that encapsulates the essence of the story. This theme serves as the guiding thread that ties together different elements.

3. **Human Connection:** A narrative is most impactful when it resonates on a human level. It should evoke emotions, empathy, and relatability to make stakeholders feel personally connected.

4. **Conflict and Resolution:** A narrative often includes challenges, conflicts, or obstacles that the organization overcame. Highlighting these aspects adds depth and authenticity.

5. **Visual Imagery:** Paint a vivid picture through descriptive language. Use metaphors, anecdotes, and visual imagery to help stakeholders visualize the story.

The Role of Authenticity:

Authenticity is a cornerstone of a compelling narrative. Stakeholders value genuine stories that reflect an organization's true character, successes, and challenges. An authentic narrative creates a sense of trust and resonates more deeply with audiences.

Tailoring the Narrative:

Different stakeholders have different interests and perspectives. To create a narrative that resonates with diverse audiences, tailor the storytelling approach while maintaining consistency in the core message.

Narrative in Action:

Imagine an organization in the tech industry with a mission to bridge the digital divide in underserved communities. Their narrative could revolve around the journey of a young student whose life was transformed by access to technology. This narrative would highlight the challenges faced, the impact of the organization's work, and the broader societal significance.

Strategies for Effective Storytelling:

1. **Identify Core Messages:** Define the key messages that align with the narrative's theme and purpose.

2. **Choose the Right Medium:** Different narratives may be better suited for written articles, videos, social media posts, or speeches.

3. **Consistency:** Ensure that the narrative aligns with the organization's actions and values consistently.

4. **Engage Emotions:** Use emotional storytelling to make the narrative relatable and memorable.

5. **Include Diverse Perspectives:** Incorporate stories from various stakeholders to create a well-rounded narrative.

A compelling public affairs narrative is a strategic tool that can shape perceptions, build connections, and foster change. By mastering the art of storytelling, organizations can inspire action, strengthen relationships, and leave a lasting impact on their stakeholders and society as a whole.

Chapter 3: Avoiding Pitfalls: Common Mistakes to Steer Clear Of

In the intricate world of public affairs, where perception and reputation are paramount, even the most well-intentioned efforts can go awry due to common mistakes. This chapter sheds light on the pitfalls that organizations must be vigilant to avoid. By understanding these pitfalls and learning from the missteps of others, public affairs professionals can navigate the challenges of the field with greater wisdom and effectiveness.

Neglecting Comprehensive Research and Analysis:

Mistake: Failing to conduct thorough research and analysis before formulating public affairs strategies. Impact: Inadequate research can result in misguided messaging, missed opportunities, and strategies that do not resonate with stakeholders.

In the fast-paced world of public affairs, the allure of swift action and immediate communication can sometimes overshadow the importance of thorough research and analysis. Neglecting these crucial steps can lead to strategies that are based on assumptions rather than evidence, resulting in missed opportunities, misaligned messaging, and ineffective engagement with stakeholders.

Why Research and Analysis Matter:

1. **Informed Decision-Making:** Comprehensive research provides the insights necessary for making well-informed decisions. It ensures that strategies are based on accurate data and a deep understanding of the landscape.

2. **Tailored Messaging:** Research allows organizations to understand the preferences, concerns, and expectations of different stakeholder groups. This understanding enables the crafting of messages that resonate and address specific needs.

3. **Identifying Opportunities:** Research uncovers opportunities for engagement, collaboration, and advocacy that might otherwise go unnoticed. It helps organizations identify gaps in the market, emerging trends, and potential allies.

The Consequences of Neglect:

1. **Misguided Strategies:** Skipping research can result in strategies that miss the mark. Organizations may fail to address the real concerns and priorities of stakeholders.

2. **Inaccurate Assumptions:** Without data-backed insights, assumptions about stakeholder preferences and public sentiment can be

inaccurate, leading to decisions that don't align with reality.

3. **Missed Opportunities:** Neglecting research can cause organizations to overlook valuable opportunities for engagement, partnership, or industry leadership.

4. **Reputational Risks:** An absence of research can lead to messaging that is tone-deaf or misaligned with public sentiment, resulting in reputational risks and backlash.

Components of Effective Research and Analysis:

1. **Stakeholder Mapping:** Identify the individuals, groups, and organizations that are relevant to your organization's objectives.

2. **Public Sentiment Analysis:** Gauge public sentiment through surveys, social media monitoring, and media coverage analysis.

3. **Competitor Analysis:** Understand the strategies and initiatives of competitors to identify gaps or areas of differentiation.

4. **Industry Trends:** Stay updated on industry trends, regulations, and emerging issues that could impact your organization.

5. **Data Collection:** Gather data from reputable sources, conduct surveys, and analyze trends to inform your strategies.

Real-World Application:

Imagine an organization in the healthcare sector launching a campaign to promote a new medical treatment. Neglecting research could lead to messaging that doesn't address patients' concerns, misses key influencers, or fails to understand the healthcare landscape. With thorough research, the organization can tailor its messaging to resonate with patients, engage with healthcare professionals, and navigate regulatory challenges.

Balancing Speed and Research:

While swift action is important in dynamic environments, it should not come at the expense of research and analysis. Organizations must strike a balance between speed and thoroughness to ensure that their strategies are grounded in reliable insights.

By emphasizing the importance of comprehensive research and analysis, organizations can ensure that their public affairs efforts are well-informed, targeted, and more likely to achieve their intended outcomes.

Ignoring Public Perception and Sentiment:

Mistake: Disregarding public perception and sentiment when making decisions or communicating with stakeholders. Impact: Ignoring public sentiment can lead to misunderstandings, backlash, and damage to an organization's reputation.

In the intricate dance of public affairs, the court of public opinion holds immense influence over an organization's success and reputation. Ignoring the perceptions, attitudes, and sentiments of the public can lead to misalignment, misunderstandings, and reputational damage. Effective public affairs strategies are those that remain attuned to the pulse of public sentiment, leveraging it to inform decisions and communication.

Why Public Perception Matters:

1. **Reputation Impact:** Public perception directly impacts an organization's reputation. A negative public image can lead to decreased trust, customer attrition, and diminished brand value.

2. **Stakeholder Engagement:** Ignoring public sentiment can result in misaligned communication with stakeholders, leading to disconnects and strained relationships.

3. **Business Impact:** Positive public perception attracts customers, investors, and partners, fostering business growth and sustainability.

The Consequences of Ignoring Perception:

1. **Misunderstood Messaging:** Disregarding public sentiment can lead to messages that don't resonate or address real concerns, causing confusion and miscommunication.

2. **Backlash and Criticism:** Ignoring public sentiment can trigger backlash, as stakeholders feel unheard or dismissed. Negative reactions can spread rapidly through social media and news outlets.

3. **Loss of Trust:** When organizations appear disconnected from public sentiment, trust erodes, and stakeholders may question their motives and authenticity.

4. **Missed Opportunities:** Ignoring positive public sentiment can cause organizations to miss opportunities for advocacy, collaboration, and positive brand reinforcement.

Listening to and Addressing Public Sentiment:

1. **Social Media Monitoring:** Monitor social media platforms to gauge public sentiment, identify trends, and address emerging concerns.

2. **Surveys and Feedback:** Conduct surveys and gather feedback from stakeholders to understand their perceptions and preferences.

3. **Media Coverage Analysis:** Analyze media coverage to identify how the organization is portrayed in the public eye.

4. **Engagement and Dialogue:** Engage in meaningful dialogue with stakeholders to address concerns, clarify misconceptions, and demonstrate responsiveness.

Real-World Application:

Consider an organization in the food industry introducing a new product line. Ignoring public sentiment could result in the launch of a product that doesn't align with consumers' dietary preferences or concerns about sustainability. By actively listening to public sentiment, the organization can tailor its messaging, ingredients, and packaging to better resonate with the target audience.

Striking a Balance:

While organizations can't cater to every individual sentiment, they should be mindful of overarching trends and concerns that could impact their brand reputation and public perception. Striking a balance between aligning with public sentiment and staying true to organizational values is essential.

By recognizing the importance of public perception and sentiment, organizations can shape their public affairs strategies to align with the expectations and values of their stakeholders. This alignment fosters authenticity, trust, and positive relationships, contributing to long-term success in the complex landscape of public affairs.

Lacking Transparency and Authenticity:

Mistake: Presenting a message that appears disingenuous or failing to communicate transparently. Impact: Lack of transparency erodes trust and credibility. Inauthentic messaging can lead to accusations of manipulation.

In the realm of public affairs, where credibility and trust are paramount, the absence of transparency and authenticity can erode an organization's reputation and hinder its ability to foster meaningful connections with stakeholders. Transparent and authentic communication is not just a best practice; it's a fundamental requirement for building trust and maintaining positive relationships in the public eye.

Why Transparency Matters:

1. **Trust Building:** Transparency is the cornerstone of trust. When organizations are open and honest in their communication, stakeholders are more likely to trust their intentions and actions.

2. **Crisis Management:** During crises, transparent communication helps organizations manage the situation, address concerns, and maintain credibility.

3. **Accountability:** Transparent organizations take responsibility for their actions and decisions. This accountability enhances their credibility and demonstrates a commitment to ethical conduct.

The Consequences of Lacking Transparency:

1. **Distrust and Skepticism:** A lack of transparency can lead stakeholders to doubt an organization's motives and intentions, fostering skepticism and cynicism.

2. **Reputation Damage:** When organizations are perceived as withholding information or being deceptive, their reputation can suffer irreparable damage.

3. **Legal and Regulatory Issues:** Lacking transparency can lead to legal and regulatory challenges if stakeholders feel their rights or interests have been compromised.

4. **Stakeholder Alienation**: Lacking transparency can alienate stakeholders who expect openness and honesty in their interactions with the organization.

The Essence of Authenticity:

Authenticity is the foundation upon which meaningful relationships are built. Authentic communication reflects an organization's true values, intentions, and actions. It involves being genuine, honest, and consistent in all interactions.

Strategies for Transparency and Authenticity:

1. **Open Communication**: Communicate openly about organizational decisions, practices, and challenges. Address concerns promptly and accurately.

2. **Honesty About Limitations**: Acknowledge limitations and challenges. Avoid overpromising and underdelivering.

3. **Stakeholder Engagement**: Engage with stakeholders in meaningful dialogue. Seek their input and feedback on relevant matters.

4. **Crisis Communication**: During crises, provide timely and accurate information. Acknowledge mistakes and communicate steps being taken to rectify the situation.

Real-World Application:

Consider an organization in the fashion industry facing allegations of unethical labor practices. Lacking transparency could worsen the situation, damaging the organization's reputation. By transparently acknowledging the allegations, conducting internal investigations, and sharing steps taken to address the issue, the organization can demonstrate a commitment to change and regain stakeholder trust.

Balancing Confidentiality:

While transparency is crucial, not all information can be shared openly due to legal, proprietary, or sensitive reasons. Striking the right balance between transparency and the need for confidentiality is essential.

By embracing transparency and authenticity, organizations can build lasting relationships based on trust and credibility. In the evolving landscape of public affairs, these principles serve as the bedrock for effective communication, stakeholder engagement, and long-term success.

Misjudging Cultural and Societal Context:

Mistake: Overlooking cultural nuances and societal context when crafting messages or launching campaigns. Impact: Cultural insensitivity can lead to public outrage, accusations of insensitivity, and damage to an organization's reputation.

In the global arena of public affairs, cultural sensitivity and an understanding of societal context are indispensable. Organizations that fail to recognize the nuances of different cultures and societies risk alienating stakeholders, triggering backlash, and damaging their reputation. Navigating cultural and societal contexts with respect and awareness is an essential skill for effective public affairs strategies.

Why Cultural and Societal Context Matters:

1. **Respect and Inclusivity:** Acknowledging cultural diversity and societal norms demonstrates respect for different perspectives and values.

2. **Avoiding Offense:** Misjudging cultural context can lead to actions or communication that are perceived as offensive or inappropriate.

3. **Effective Communication:** Tailoring messaging to cultural context ensures that messages are relatable and meaningful to diverse audiences.

The Consequences of Misjudgment:

1. **Cultural Insensitivity:** Misjudging cultural context can lead to actions that are perceived as culturally insensitive, leading to public outrage and reputational damage.

2. **Backlash and Boycotts:** Missteps related to cultural or societal context can trigger backlash and calls for boycotts from offended stakeholders.

3. **Loss of Trust:** Organizations that fail to understand and respect cultural differences can lose the trust of diverse stakeholders.

Navigating Cultural and Societal Context:

1. **Research and Education:** Thoroughly research the cultural norms, values, and sensitivities of the regions and communities you are engaging with.

2. **Local Partnerships:** Collaborate with local experts and partners who can provide insights into cultural nuances.

3. **Language and Symbolism:** Pay attention to language nuances and symbolism that could be misinterpreted or offensive in different cultural contexts.

4. **Adaptation, Not Assimilation:** Adapt your strategies to align with cultural context while respecting the authenticity of your organization.

Real-World Application:

Imagine an organization launching a marketing campaign that uses symbols considered sacred in a particular culture. Misjudging the cultural context could lead to accusations of cultural appropriation and significant backlash. By working with cultural experts and understanding the significance of these symbols, the organization could adapt the campaign to be culturally respectful.

Continuous Learning and Adaptation:

Cultural and societal contexts are not static; they evolve over time. Organizations must commit to continuous learning and adaptation to remain culturally sensitive and relevant.

By recognizing the importance of cultural and societal context, organizations can navigate the global landscape of public affairs with cultural intelligence. Adapting strategies to align with local values and norms demonstrates a commitment to inclusivity, respect, and meaningful engagement with diverse stakeholders.

Neglecting Ethical Considerations:

Mistake: Pursuing strategies that compromise ethical principles for short-term gains. Impact: Ethical lapses can tarnish an organization's reputation and lead to public backlash.

In the intricate dance of public affairs, ethical considerations serve as a moral compass, guiding organizations toward decisions and actions that align with principles of integrity and responsibility. Neglecting these ethical considerations in the pursuit of short-term gains or objectives can lead to reputational damage, erosion of trust, and long-term consequences that far outweigh any initial benefits.

Why Ethical Considerations Matter:

1. **Maintaining Trust:** Ethical behavior fosters trust among stakeholders, including customers, investors, employees, and the general public.

2. **Long-Term Sustainability:** Ethical decisions contribute to an organization's long-term sustainability and positive reputation.

3. **Stakeholder Loyalty:** Organizations that prioritize ethical behavior are more likely to earn the loyalty of stakeholders who value principled conduct.

The Consequences of Neglect:

1. **Reputational Damage:** Ethical lapses can lead to negative media coverage, public backlash, and damage to an organization's reputation.

2. **Legal and Regulatory Issues:** Ignoring ethical considerations can result in legal and regulatory challenges, leading to fines and legal actions.

3. **Loss of Stakeholder Confidence:** When organizations disregard ethical principles, stakeholders may lose confidence in their leadership and intentions.

Prioritizing Ethical Considerations:

1. **Ethical Leadership:** Leaders must set an example of ethical behavior and create a culture that values integrity.

2. **Stakeholder Impact:** Consider the potential impact of decisions on various stakeholders, including employees, communities, and the environment.

3. **Transparency:** Communicate openly about ethical decisions and practices to maintain trust and accountability.

4. **Ethical Review:** Establish mechanisms for ethical review of strategies, decisions, and actions.

Real-World Application:

Imagine an organization facing a situation where exploiting a legal loophole could lead to significant financial gains. Neglecting ethical considerations could result in exploiting the loophole, even if it harms customers or stakeholders. Prioritizing ethics might lead the organization to close the loophole to maintain fairness and integrity.

Ethical Compass in a Complex Landscape:

Public affairs often involve navigating complex situations where ethical considerations might be challenged. Organizations must remain committed to their ethical compass even in the face of pressure or uncertainty.

By recognizing the significance of ethical considerations, organizations can align their public affairs strategies with principles of integrity, transparency, and responsibility. Ethical behavior not only safeguards an organization's reputation but also contributes to the creation of a more just and responsible society.

Reacting Poorly to Crises:

Mistake: Mishandling crisis situations by providing inadequate responses or downplaying the severity of the issue. Impact: Poor crisis management can exacerbate the situation, damage an organization's reputation, and erode trust among stakeholders.

In the realm of public affairs, crises are inevitable, and how organizations respond during challenging times can profoundly impact their reputation and stakeholder relationships. Reacting poorly to crises, whether through inadequate communication, mismanagement, or dismissive attitudes, can amplify the negative effects, erode trust, and result in lasting damage to an organization's credibility.

Why Crisis Management Matters:

1. **Reputation Preservation:** Effective crisis management helps protect an organization's reputation by addressing issues promptly and transparently.

2. **Stakeholder Trust:** Responding well during a crisis demonstrates accountability and care for stakeholders, maintaining their trust.

3. **Damage Mitigation:** Skillful crisis management can mitigate the potential damage to an organization's brand and bottom line.

The Consequences of Poor Reaction:

1. **Escalation:** Reacting poorly to a crisis can lead to its escalation, as stakeholders demand transparency and appropriate action.

2. **Reputational Damage:** A mishandled crisis can lead to negative media coverage, social media backlash, and a tarnished reputation.

3. **Loss of Stakeholder Confidence:** Poor crisis management can result in stakeholders losing confidence in an organization's leadership and ability to handle challenges.

Elements of Effective Crisis Management:

1. **Timely Communication:** Swift and accurate communication is crucial during a crisis to keep stakeholders informed and address concerns promptly.

2. **Transparency:** Openly communicate the extent of the issue, the steps being taken to address it, and any potential impact.

3. **Accountability:** Take responsibility for any mistakes, apologize if necessary, and demonstrate a commitment to rectifying the situation.

4. **Stakeholder Engagement:** Engage with stakeholders to address their questions, concerns, and feedback, showing empathy and understanding.

Real-World Application:

Imagine an organization facing a data breach that exposes sensitive customer information. Reacting poorly could involve downplaying the severity of the breach or delaying communication. A well-managed response, on the other hand, would involve immediate disclosure, proactive steps to mitigate harm, and offering support to affected customers.

Preparedness and Adaptability:

Effective crisis management requires both preparedness and adaptability. Organizations should have a crisis communication plan in place while remaining flexible enough to address unique situations.

By recognizing the significance of crisis management and avoiding poor reactions, organizations can maintain their credibility even in the face of challenges. Skillful crisis management showcases an organization's commitment to accountability, transparency, and the well-being of its stakeholders.

Ineffective Media Relations:

Mistake: Mismanaging relationships with media outlets or providing inaccurate information to journalists. Impact: Poor media relations can result in negative coverage, miscommunication, and damage to an organization's reputation.

In the intricate landscape of public affairs, the relationship between organizations and the media can significantly shape public perception and influence stakeholder attitudes. Ineffective media relations, characterized by poor communication, mismanagement, or a lack of transparency, can lead to negative coverage, misinformation, and strained relationships with journalists and the broader public.

Why Effective Media Relations Matter:

1. **Information Dissemination:** Media serves as a vital channel for sharing information, updates, and organizational narratives with the public.

2. **Reputation Shaping:** Media coverage plays a pivotal role in shaping an organization's reputation and influencing public sentiment.

3. **Crisis Management:** Effective media relations are essential during crises to manage communication, clarify facts, and address concerns.

The Consequences of Ineffectiveness:

1. **Negative Coverage:** Ineffective media relations can lead to biased or negative coverage, which can

impact an organization's credibility and reputation.

2. **Misinformation Spread:** Poor communication can result in the spread of misinformation, causing confusion and eroding trust.

3. **Media Hostility:** Mismanaged relations with media outlets can lead to strained relationships and a lack of cooperation during critical times.

Elements of Effective Media Relations:

1. **Transparency:** Be open and transparent with the media, providing accurate and timely information, especially during crises.

2. **Accessibility:** Maintain accessibility to journalists, responding promptly to inquiries and providing necessary resources.

3. **Message Consistency:** Ensure that messaging is consistent across all communication channels to avoid confusion and misinformation.

4. **Relationship Building:** Foster positive relationships with media professionals based on mutual respect and understanding.

Real-World Application:

Imagine an organization launching a new product. Ineffective media relations could involve providing incomplete or misleading information to journalists, resulting in inaccurate coverage. Effective media relations, on the other hand, would involve providing journalists with comprehensive information, addressing their questions, and maintaining open lines of communication.

Navigating Challenging Situations:

Effective media relations involve not only positive coverage but also navigating challenging situations with transparency and professionalism.

By recognizing the importance of effective media relations, organizations can establish a strong and positive presence in the media landscape. Building relationships with journalists, providing accurate information, and fostering open communication contribute to a positive media image and enhance an organization's credibility and reputation.

Overlooking Digital and Social Media:

Mistake: Underestimating the impact of digital and social media on public affairs strategies. Impact: Neglecting these channels can result in missed opportunities to connect with audiences and address concerns.

In the dynamic realm of public affairs, digital and social media have emerged as powerful tools that can amplify an organization's message, engage stakeholders, and influence public perception. Overlooking the potential of these channels can result in missed opportunities to connect with diverse audiences, address concerns, and stay relevant in an increasingly digital world.

Why Digital and Social Media Matter:

1. **Widespread Reach:** Digital and social media platforms provide access to a global audience, allowing organizations to reach stakeholders beyond traditional boundaries.

2. **Real-Time Engagement:** These platforms facilitate real-time communication, enabling organizations to address issues, respond to feedback, and engage in conversations instantly.

3. **Targeted Messaging:** Digital and social media allow for precise targeting, ensuring that messages reach specific demographics or interest groups.

The Consequences of Overlooking:

1. **Missed Engagement:** Neglecting digital and social media means missing out on opportunities to engage with stakeholders where they are most active.

2. **Limited Reach:** Organizations that don't utilize these platforms might struggle to reach younger or digitally savvy audiences.

3. **Lack of Responsiveness:** In a world where news spreads rapidly through social media, overlooking these platforms can result in being left out of important conversations.

Strategies for Effective Digital and Social Media Engagement:

1. **Platform Selection:** Choose the digital and social media platforms that align with your target audience and objectives.

2. **Engagement Plan:** Develop a comprehensive plan for content creation, scheduling, and responding to comments or messages.

3. **Consistent Branding:** Maintain consistent branding and messaging across all digital and social media channels.

4. **Interactive Content:** Utilize interactive content like polls, quizzes, and live sessions to engage and involve stakeholders.

Real-World Application:

Imagine an organization in the travel industry aiming to promote sustainable tourism. Overlooking digital and social media could mean missing opportunities to share informative videos, engage with travelers, and collaborate with eco-conscious influencers. Embracing these platforms could enable the organization to spread awareness about responsible travel practices and build a community of like-minded individuals.

Staying Adaptable and Relevant:

Digital and social media landscapes evolve rapidly. Organizations must remain adaptable to new trends, technologies, and communication strategies.

By recognizing the significance of digital and social media, organizations can harness the power of these platforms to connect with stakeholders, share their narratives, and stay engaged in meaningful conversations. A robust digital presence ensures that organizations remain relevant and responsive in an increasingly digital-centric world.

By delving into real-world examples of these pitfalls and their consequences, organizations can gain insights into the potential risks and challenges that lie ahead. Armed with this knowledge, public affairs professionals can take proactive measures to avoid these pitfalls and chart a course toward more successful and impactful strategies.

Failing to Understand Public Perception and Sentiment

In the intricate landscape of public affairs, the pulse of public perception and sentiment serves as a critical compass that guides organizations in shaping their strategies and messages. Failing to grasp the nuances of how the public views and feels about an organization can lead to misaligned communication, missed opportunities, and a disconnect between an organization and its stakeholders.

Why Understanding Perception Matters:

1. **Informed Decision-Making:** A deep understanding of how the public perceives an organization informs strategic decisions and helps tailor messages effectively.

2. **Reputation Management:** Accurate perception management is crucial for maintaining a positive reputation, as public sentiment can influence an organization's brand image.

3. **Crisis Preparedness:** Understanding how the public perceives the organization prepares it for better crisis management and effective communication during challenging times.

The Consequences of Failing to Understand:

1. **Misguided Strategies:** Failing to comprehend public perception can lead to strategies that don't resonate with stakeholders, causing confusion and misalignment.

2. **Communication Gaps:** Organizations might miss addressing concerns or expectations that stakeholders have if they are unaware of public sentiment.

3. **Reputational Risk:** A disconnect between an organization's self-perception and public perception can lead to reputational risks and backlash.

Strategies for Understanding Public Perception:

1. **Media Monitoring:** Monitor media coverage and social media conversations to gauge how the public views the organization.

2. **Surveys and Feedback:** Gather feedback from stakeholders through surveys, focus groups, and online feedback forms to understand their perceptions.

3. **Third-Party Research:** Utilize independent research and reports to gain an unbiased view of public sentiment.

Real-World Application:

Consider an organization in the energy sector that is perceived by the public as environmentally insensitive. Failing to understand this perception could lead the organization to overlook the importance of sustainable initiatives, thereby missing opportunities to shift public sentiment and improve their reputation.

Continual Assessment and Adaptation:

Public perception is not static; it evolves based on various factors, including industry trends, news cycles, and social changes. Organizations must continually assess public sentiment and adapt their strategies accordingly.

By recognizing the importance of understanding public perception and sentiment, organizations can bridge the gap between their goals and stakeholder expectations. A comprehensive grasp of how the public perceives an organization empowers it to communicate effectively, engage authentically, and navigate the intricate landscape of public affairs successfully.

Overlooking Ethical Considerations in Public Affairs

In the complex realm of public affairs, where decisions and actions can reverberate through society, ethical considerations stand as a crucial compass that guides organizations toward responsible and principled conduct. Overlooking these ethical considerations can lead to decisions that compromise integrity, damage reputation, and undermine the trust that organizations have worked tirelessly to build.

Why Ethical Considerations Matter:

1. **Trust and Credibility:** Ethical behavior is the bedrock of trust. Organizations that prioritize ethics demonstrate integrity, fostering credibility with stakeholders.

2. **Reputation Preservation:** Ethical conduct safeguards an organization's reputation, preventing the erosion of trust due to unethical decisions.

3. **Long-Term Sustainability:** Ethical behavior contributes to long-term sustainability, as it aligns organizations with societal expectations and values.

The Consequences of Overlooking Ethics:

1. **Reputational Damage:** Overlooking ethical considerations can lead to negative media coverage, public backlash, and damage to an organization's reputation.

2. **Loss of Trust:** Stakeholders may lose trust in an organization that places short-term gains above ethical principles, leading to diminished loyalty.

3. **Legal and Regulatory Consequences:** Unethical behavior can lead to legal and regulatory challenges, resulting in fines, legal actions, and reputational harm.

Incorporating Ethical Considerations:

1. **Ethical Framework:** Establish an ethical framework that guides decision-making, ensuring alignment with core values.

2. **Stakeholder Impact:** Consider the potential impact of decisions on various stakeholders, including employees, customers, communities, and the environment.

3. **Transparency:** Communicate openly about ethical decisions and actions to maintain trust and accountability.

Real-World Application:

Imagine an organization facing a choice between cost-cutting measures that could harm employee well-being and more ethical alternatives. Overlooking ethical considerations might lead to pursuing the cost-cutting measures, risking a backlash from employees, customers, and the public. Prioritizing ethics would involve exploring alternatives that align with the organization's values.

Balancing Complexities:

Ethical considerations are often complex and multifaceted. Organizations must carefully weigh different factors and perspectives when making ethical decisions.

By recognizing the significance of ethical considerations in public affairs, organizations can uphold their values, foster stakeholder trust, and contribute positively to society. Ethical behavior not only benefits organizations in the long run but also promotes a culture of responsibility and integrity in the wider business landscape.

Chapter 4: Strategies for Successful Public Affairs

In the dynamic landscape of public affairs, where perception and communication intersect, the formulation and execution of effective strategies are paramount to an organization's success. This chapter delves into key strategies that organizations can employ to navigate the complexities of public affairs, enhance stakeholder relationships, and achieve their objectives while upholding ethical principles and cultural sensitivity.

Understanding the Power of Messaging:

Effective public affairs strategies start with messaging that resonates with stakeholders. Crafting compelling narratives that align with organizational values and address stakeholder concerns is the cornerstone of successful communication.

In the intricate dance of public affairs, messaging stands as a fundamental pillar that shapes perceptions, drives engagement, and conveys an organization's values and objectives. Understanding the art and science of crafting powerful messaging is essential for effective communication and the successful realization of public affairs goals.

The Essence of Effective Messaging:

1. **Clarity and Consistency:** Effective messaging is clear, concise, and consistent across all communication channels. It conveys information in a manner that resonates with stakeholders.

2. **Alignment with Objectives:** Messaging should align with an organization's overarching goals, reflecting its vision, mission, and strategic priorities.

3. **Stakeholder-Centric:** Successful messaging focuses on addressing stakeholder needs, concerns, and aspirations. It answers the question, "What's in it for them?"

Crafting Compelling Narratives:

A compelling narrative captures attention, evokes emotion, and tells a story that stakeholders can connect with. Whether conveying an organizational journey, a social impact initiative, or a product launch, narratives have the power to create a lasting impression.

Building Trust Through Transparency:

Transparency is the bedrock of trustworthy messaging. Openly sharing relevant information, even when it's challenging, builds credibility and fosters trust among stakeholders.

Navigating Complex Issues:

Effective messaging is particularly important when communicating about complex or controversial issues. Simplifying intricate topics without oversimplification requires a strategic balance that informs and engages stakeholders.

Real-World Application:

Imagine an organization operating in the renewable energy sector. Crafting effective messaging involves not only explaining the technical aspects of renewable technologies but also highlighting the positive environmental impact and the organization's commitment to a sustainable future.

The Role of Multichannel Communication:

Messaging extends across various communication channels, including traditional media, social media, websites, and public events. Consistency in messaging across these platforms reinforces the organization's key messages.

Continuous Feedback Loop:

Effective messaging is a result of an ongoing feedback loop that involves listening to stakeholder responses, gauging reactions, and refining messaging based on the insights gained.

Strategic Alignment:

Messaging should be strategically aligned with an organization's overall communication and business objectives. It should support and reinforce the organization's values and long-term goals.

By grasping the power of messaging, organizations can articulate their stories, connect with stakeholders, and shape perceptions in ways that resonate and inspire action. Thoughtful messaging isn't just about words; it's about conveying the heart and soul of an organization to build lasting relationships and drive positive impact in the world of public affairs.

Developing a Targeted Media Relations Plan

In the dynamic realm of public affairs, an effective media relations plan stands as a strategic blueprint for cultivating positive relationships with journalists, managing communication during crises, and influencing public perception. Developing a targeted media relations plan empowers organizations to navigate the media landscape with precision, ensuring that their messages reach the right audiences through credible and impactful channels.

Defining Media Relations Objectives:

1. **Messaging Alignment:** Ensure that media messages align with the organization's overarching goals and values.

2. **Positive Perception:** Foster positive media coverage that enhances the organization's reputation and credibility.

3. **Crisis Preparedness:** Develop strategies for addressing media during crises, ensuring swift and accurate communication.

Identifying Key Stakeholders:

1. **Media Outlets:** Identify the media outlets that resonate with the organization's target audiences and industry focus.

2. **Journalists and Influencers:** Build relationships with journalists, reporters, and industry influencers who cover relevant topics.

3. **Audiences:** Consider the audiences that the organization aims to reach through media coverage, such as customers, investors, or policymakers.

Crafting Tailored Messages:

1. **Message Customization:** Tailor messages to the preferences and interests of different media outlets and their audiences.

2. **Value Proposition:** Highlight the unique value that the organization brings to the industry, community, or society.

3. **Transparency and Accuracy:** Ensure that all messages are accurate, transparent, and consistent across media channels.

Creating Engaging Content:

1. **Press Releases:** Develop well-crafted press releases that communicate newsworthy developments and initiatives.

2. **Story Pitches:** Craft compelling story pitches that capture journalists' attention and offer unique angles.

3. **Op-Eds and Thought Leadership:** Contribute opinion pieces and thought leadership articles to establish the organization as an industry authority.

Building Relationships:

1. **Media Briefings:** Organize media briefings, press conferences, and interviews to share important updates and foster direct communication.

2. **Response Speed:** Respond promptly to media inquiries and requests, demonstrating accessibility and cooperation.

3. **Networking:** Attend industry events and conferences to build relationships with journalists and stay updated on industry trends.

Monitoring and Measurement:

1. **Media Monitoring:** Regularly monitor media coverage to gauge how the organization is portrayed and identify opportunities for improvement.

2. **Impact Assessment:** Evaluate the impact of media coverage on organizational objectives and adjust strategies accordingly.

Crisis Communication Preparedness:

1. **Crisis Scenarios:** Anticipate potential crisis scenarios and develop communication strategies to address them.

2. **Spokesperson Training:** Ensure that designated spokespersons are trained to handle media inquiries during crises.

Real-World Application:

Imagine an organization in the technology sector launching a groundbreaking innovation. A targeted media relations plan would involve identifying technology-focused media outlets, crafting messages that emphasize the innovation's impact, and arranging interviews with the organization's experts.

Adaptability and Evolution:

Media landscapes evolve, and organizations must adapt their media relations strategies to embrace new platforms, trends, and communication preferences.

By developing a targeted media relations plan, organizations can harness the power of media to shape perceptions, communicate their value, and engage with stakeholders in meaningful ways. Strategic media engagement enhances an organization's credibility, reputation, and impact in the intricate world of public affairs.

Leveraging Stakeholder Engagement:

Engaging with stakeholders in meaningful ways fosters collaboration, understanding, and a sense of ownership. Strategies that prioritize stakeholder engagement create a feedback loop that informs decision-making and enhances organizational credibility.

In the dynamic landscape of public affairs, where relationships are the cornerstone of success, leveraging stakeholder engagement stands as a strategic imperative. The art of engaging stakeholders effectively empowers organizations to foster trust, co-create solutions, and build a community of advocates who share in the organization's journey and contribute to its growth.

Defining Stakeholder Engagement:

1. **Collaborative Approach:** Stakeholder engagement involves fostering collaboration and dialogue with individuals or groups who have a vested interest in or are affected by the organization's activities.

2. **Listening and Responding:** Engaging stakeholders means actively listening to their concerns, ideas, and feedback and responding in ways that reflect their interests.

3. **Shared Value Creation:** Through engagement, organizations work together with stakeholders to identify areas of shared value and collaboratively shape strategies that benefit both parties.

The Power of Engagement:

1. **Trust Building:** Engaging with stakeholders authentically builds trust, demonstrating that the organization values their input and is committed to open communication.

2. **Informed Decision-Making:** Stakeholder insights provide valuable perspectives that inform strategic decisions, ensuring alignment with real-world needs.

3. **Issue Resolution:** Engagement allows organizations to address concerns proactively, preventing issues from escalating and damaging relationships.

Strategies for Effective Stakeholder Engagement:

1. **Identifying Stakeholders:** Identify key stakeholders who are directly or indirectly impacted by the organization's activities, including customers, employees, investors, communities, and advocacy groups.

2. **Tailored Communication:** Customize communication approaches for different stakeholder groups, addressing their unique interests and concerns.

3. **Inclusive Dialogue:** Create platforms for open dialogue, such as town hall meetings, focus groups, surveys, and online forums, to encourage participation.

4. **Transparency:** Be transparent about the organization's goals, challenges, and decision-making processes, fostering a culture of openness.

Measuring Engagement Effectiveness:

1. **Engagement Metrics:** Track engagement metrics, such as participation rates, feedback volume, and sentiment analysis, to gauge the effectiveness of engagement initiatives.

2. **Impact Assessment:** Evaluate how stakeholder engagement efforts have influenced decision-making, improved relationships, and contributed to organizational success.

Real-World Application:

Imagine an organization in the healthcare sector working on a new healthcare solution. Engaging with healthcare professionals, patients, and regulatory authorities through focus groups, online surveys, and expert consultations ensures that the solution addresses real-world needs.

Sustainability Through Engagement:

Effective stakeholder engagement is an ongoing process that requires dedication and adaptability. Organizations that prioritize engagement build a foundation for long-term sustainability and impact.

By leveraging stakeholder engagement, organizations can harness the collective wisdom of diverse perspectives to drive innovation, navigate challenges, and make decisions that resonate with their stakeholders' values and aspirations. Genuine engagement builds bridges, empowers stakeholders, and enriches the fabric of public affairs.

Proactive Crisis Management:

Preparing for and effectively managing crises is a critical aspect of public affairs. Organizations should have well-defined crisis communication plans in place, enabling them to respond swiftly, transparently, and empathetically to unforeseen challenges.

In the intricate landscape of public affairs, where unforeseen challenges can emerge at any moment, proactive crisis management stands as a cornerstone of organizational resilience and reputation preservation. This strategic approach empowers organizations to anticipate, prepare for, and effectively navigate crises while maintaining transparency, credibility, and stakeholder trust.

Anticipating and Preparing for Crises:

1. **Scenario Planning:** Identify potential crisis scenarios that could impact the organization's reputation, operations, or stakeholders.

2. **Risk Assessment:** Evaluate the likelihood and potential impact of each scenario, prioritizing those with the highest risk.

3. **Crisis Teams:** Establish cross-functional crisis management teams with defined roles and responsibilities for swift response.

Developing Crisis Communication Plans:

1. **Communication Protocols:** Outline communication protocols that detail how information will be disseminated, who the designated spokespeople are, and how stakeholders will be informed.

2. **Message Framework:** Create a message framework that guides the tone, content, and

timing of communications during different stages of a crisis.

3. **Media Response:** Develop strategies for addressing media inquiries, sharing accurate information, and maintaining consistent messaging.

Transparency and Open Communication:

1. **Swift Response:** Respond to crises promptly, even if complete information is not available. Acknowledge the situation and commit to providing updates as more information becomes available.

2. **Transparency:** Be open and honest about the situation, acknowledging any mistakes, and communicating the steps being taken to address the crisis.

3. **Stakeholder Engagement:** Engage with stakeholders through various communication channels, addressing their concerns and providing reassurance.

Employee Preparedness and Support:

1. **Training:** Train employees on crisis response procedures, ensuring they know their roles and responsibilities.

2. **Internal Communication:** Keep employees informed about the crisis, the organization's response, and any measures they should take.

3. **Supportive Environment:** Create a supportive environment for employees affected by the crisis, offering resources and assistance as needed.

Learning and Continuous Improvement:

1. **Post-Crisis Analysis:** Conduct thorough post-crisis analysis to assess the effectiveness of the response and identify areas for improvement.

2. **Adaptation:** Incorporate lessons learned from each crisis into updated crisis management plans for ongoing improvement.

Real-World Application:

Imagine an organization facing a product recall due to safety concerns. Proactive crisis management involves swiftly communicating the recall, providing clear instructions to consumers, and collaborating with regulatory authorities to address the issue.

A Culture of Resilience:

Proactive crisis management is not just about reacting; it's about building a culture of preparedness, transparency, and adaptability that extends throughout the organization.

By embracing proactive crisis management, organizations can navigate challenges with confidence, demonstrate leadership, and uphold their reputation even in the face of adversity. Effective crisis management not only safeguards an organization's credibility but also showcases its commitment to ethical conduct and stakeholder well-being.

Harnessing the Power of Digital and Social Media:

Digital and social media platforms are powerful tools for amplifying messages and engaging with diverse audiences. Organizations must harness the potential of these platforms to connect with stakeholders, disseminate information, and stay relevant in a digital-centric world.

In the ever-evolving landscape of public affairs, the emergence of digital and social media has transformed the way organizations communicate, engage with stakeholders, and shape public perception. Harnessing the power of these platforms is essential for building an impactful and responsive presence in the digital age, where information travels at the speed of a click and engagement transcends geographic boundaries.

Reaching Diverse Audiences:

1. **Global Reach:** Digital and social media enable organizations to communicate with a global audience, breaking down geographical barriers.

2. **Diverse Demographics:** These platforms provide access to diverse demographics, allowing organizations to tailor messages to specific target groups.

3. **Real-Time Engagement:** Digital and social media facilitate real-time interactions, allowing organizations to respond promptly to comments, questions, and feedback.

Strategies for Effective Digital Engagement:

1. **Platform Selection:** Identify the digital and social media platforms that align with the organization's target audience and objectives.

2. **Content Strategy:** Develop a content strategy that includes a mix of informative, engaging, and visually appealing content tailored to each platform.

3. **Interactive Elements:** Utilize interactive elements like polls, quizzes, live videos, and stories to enhance engagement and encourage participation.

4. **Engagement Monitoring:** Regularly monitor engagement metrics, such as likes, shares,

comments, and click-through rates, to measure the impact of content.

Crisis Communication in the Digital Era:

1. **Swift Response:** Digital and social media demand immediate response during crises to manage rumors, misinformation, and stakeholder concerns.

2. **Transparency:** Communicate openly about the crisis, its impact, and the steps being taken to address it, maintaining trust through transparency.

3. **Timely Updates:** Provide timely updates as the situation evolves, keeping stakeholders informed and minimizing uncertainty.

Building a Digital Brand:

1. **Consistent Branding:** Maintain consistent branding, including visual elements and messaging, across all digital and social media platforms.

2. **Thought Leadership:** Share thought-provoking content that positions the organization as an industry leader and engages stakeholders on relevant topics.

3. **Storytelling**: Utilize the power of storytelling to connect emotionally with audiences, making messages memorable and relatable.

Real-World Application:

Imagine an organization launching an environmental sustainability initiative. Digital and social media platforms can be used to share engaging videos about the initiative's impact, host live Q&A sessions with experts, and encourage user-generated content showcasing sustainable practices.

Adapting to Evolving Trends:

Digital and social media trends evolve rapidly. Organizations must stay adaptable and embrace new features and technologies to maintain relevance.

By harnessing the power of digital and social media, organizations can amplify their messages, engage stakeholders authentically, and stay at the forefront of conversations in the ever-connected world of public affairs. An effective digital presence enhances an organization's reach, impact, and credibility in a digital-centric society.

Engaging with Key Decision-Makers and Influencers

In the intricate tapestry of public affairs, the art of engaging with key decision-makers and influencers plays a pivotal role in shaping policies, perceptions, and the broader discourse. Establishing meaningful connections with individuals who wield influence and hold decision-making power empowers organizations to navigate regulatory landscapes, drive change, and foster alliances that resonate far beyond their immediate circles.

Identifying Decision-Makers and Influencers:

1. **Policy Makers:** Identify policymakers, legislators, and government officials who play a role in shaping regulations and policies relevant to the organization's industry.

2. **Industry Leaders:** Recognize thought leaders, experts, and influential figures within the organization's industry or sector.

3. **Community Leaders:** Engage with community leaders, activists, and organizations whose interests align with the organization's values.

Building Relationships:

1. **Personalized Outreach:** Tailor communication to each individual, demonstrating a genuine interest in their work and perspectives.

2. **Networking Opportunities:** Attend industry events, conferences, and workshops where key decision-makers and influencers gather.

3. **Thoughtful Engagement:** Engage in thoughtful discussions, contributing valuable insights and showcasing the organization's expertise.

Collaboration and Partnerships:

1. **Shared Objectives:** Identify common goals and objectives that align the organization with decision-makers and influencers.

2. **Collaborative Initiatives:** Explore opportunities for joint initiatives, projects, or campaigns that drive mutual benefits.

3. **Mutual Advocacy:** Build a relationship where the organization and influencer advocate for each other's interests and amplify each other's messages.

Contributing to Public Discourse:

1. **Thought Leadership Content:** Share informative and thought-provoking content that contributes

to industry discussions and showcases the organization's expertise.

2. **Op-Eds and Panels:** Participate in public discussions, contribute opinion pieces, and engage in panel discussions to share insights and perspectives.

3. **Social Media Engagement:** Engage with decision-makers and influencers on social media platforms by sharing their content, offering insights, and participating in conversations.

Real-World Application:

Imagine an organization operating in the education sector. Engaging with key decision-makers could involve collaborating with educational policymakers to shape policies that enhance learning experiences for students.

Influence Beyond Borders:

Effective engagement with decision-makers and influencers has the potential to extend an organization's influence beyond its immediate sphere, shaping conversations and impacting policies on a larger scale.

By proactively engaging with key decision-makers and influencers, organizations can foster relationships that drive positive change, advocate for their values, and position themselves as valuable contributors to discussions that shape the trajectory of industries, societies, and public affairs at large.

Integrating Ethics and Responsibility:

Ethical considerations are at the heart of responsible public affairs. Strategies that prioritize ethics not only safeguard an organization's reputation but also contribute to a culture of integrity, accountability, and societal well-being.

Navigating Cultural Sensitivity:

In a globalized world, cultural sensitivity is imperative. Strategies that consider and respect cultural nuances enhance an organization's ability to connect with diverse audiences and foster positive relationships.

In the intricate mosaic of public affairs, cultural sensitivity stands as a fundamental compass guiding organizations toward respectful engagement with diverse communities and societies. Navigating this terrain with empathy and understanding is essential for forging meaningful connections, avoiding misunderstandings, and fostering relationships built on mutual respect and shared values.

Respecting Cultural Nuances:

1. **Cultural Awareness:** Develop a deep understanding of cultural norms, customs, values, and sensitivities that influence the target audience.

2. **Language Considerations:** Pay careful attention to language nuances and potential translations that could impact how messages are perceived.

3. **Symbolism and Traditions:** Recognize symbols, gestures, and traditions that might hold significant meaning in a particular culture.

Tailoring Communication:

1. **Contextual Messaging:** Craft messages that consider the cultural context, ensuring that they resonate positively and avoid unintended offense.

2. **Visual Representation:** Use visuals that are inclusive and respectful of diverse cultures, avoiding stereotypes and misrepresentations.

3. **Adapting Tone:** Adjust the tone of communication to align with cultural sensitivities, recognizing that humor or directness may be perceived differently.

Engaging Authentically:

1. **Engaging Local Experts:** Collaborate with local experts or advisors who possess cultural insights and can provide guidance on engagement strategies.

2. **Building Relationships:** Foster relationships with individuals from diverse backgrounds, demonstrating genuine interest and respect for their perspectives.

3. **Addressing Concerns:** Be open to addressing concerns raised by stakeholders regarding cultural insensitivity and taking corrective actions.

Cultural Competence in Global Contexts:

1. **Global Diversity:** Recognize that cultural sensitivity is crucial not only in local contexts but also in global interactions and partnerships.

2. **Research and Learning:** Continuously learn about new cultures, societal changes, and evolving sensitivities to remain culturally competent.

Real-World Application:

Consider an organization launching a campaign promoting health and well-being. Navigating cultural sensitivity could involve ensuring that visuals, messaging, and concepts resonate positively across diverse communities while respecting cultural variations in health practices.

Fostering Harmony and Understanding:

Cultural sensitivity fosters a climate of understanding, inclusivity, and respect that transcends boundaries and strengthens relationships within and beyond an organization's immediate sphere.

By navigating cultural sensitivity in public affairs, organizations can build bridges of understanding, contribute positively to social harmony, and cultivate a reputation as entities that honor and embrace diversity in all its forms. A commitment to cultural sensitivity enriches organizational narratives and embodies a dedication to the harmonious coexistence of global societies.

Striking a Balance: Speed vs. Accuracy:

While agility is essential in public affairs, it must not come at the cost of accuracy. Organizations must strike a balance between responding swiftly to changing situations and ensuring that their communication is accurate and well-considered.

In the fast-paced realm of public affairs, the delicate equilibrium between speed and accuracy is a critical tightrope that organizations must navigate. While the urgency of rapid communication is undeniable, maintaining a commitment to accuracy ensures that messages are reliable, credible, and aligned with the organization's values and objectives. Finding the harmonious balance between these two imperatives is essential for effective communication and stakeholder trust.

The Temptation of Speed:

1. **Real-Time News Cycle:** The digital age demands rapid responses to breaking news and emerging developments to remain relevant in the ongoing news cycle.

2. **Social Media Pressure:** Social media platforms amplify the pressure to respond swiftly, as stakeholders expect instant engagement.

3. **Crisis Management:** During crises, the urge to provide immediate information can lead to quick responses that lack thorough verification.

The Imperative of Accuracy:

1. **Credibility:** Accuracy is the foundation of credibility. Inaccurate information erodes trust and can lead to misinformation spreading rapidly.

2. **Reputation Preservation:** Missteps due to inaccurate information can damage an

organization's reputation and impact long-term relationships.

3. **Legal and Ethical Considerations:** Providing accurate information aligns with legal and ethical obligations, preventing potential legal liabilities.

Strategies for Balancing Speed and Accuracy:

1. **Preparedness:** Develop crisis communication plans in advance, enabling swift but accurate responses during emergencies.

2. **Verification Protocols:** Establish rigorous verification protocols to ensure information accuracy before dissemination.

3. **Designated Spokespeople:** Designate trained spokespeople who can respond swiftly while maintaining accuracy.

4. **Transparency:** If immediate information is not available, communicate that the organization is working to provide accurate updates.

Real-World Application:

Imagine an organization facing a sudden crisis. Balancing speed and accuracy could involve acknowledging the situation promptly while emphasizing that accurate information will be provided as soon as it's verified.

Strategic Decision-Making:

Balancing speed and accuracy requires strategic decision-making that takes into account the potential consequences of rapid response without thorough verification.

By finding the equilibrium between speed and accuracy, organizations can demonstrate responsiveness without compromising their commitment to truthfulness. This delicate balance allows organizations to maintain stakeholder trust, uphold ethical standards, and navigate the intricate terrain of public affairs with resilience and credibility.

Real-World Case Studies:

Throughout this chapter, real-world case studies provide insights into how organizations have applied these strategies to achieve their public affairs objectives. These examples demonstrate the impact of effective messaging, stakeholder engagement, crisis management, and ethical decision-making.

Throughout the intricate landscape of public affairs, real-world case studies offer invaluable insights into how organizations have navigated challenges, seized opportunities, and leveraged strategic approaches to achieve their objectives.

These case studies illustrate the application of various strategies, the impact of decisions, and the lessons learned, providing a tapestry of experiences that inform and inspire effective public affairs practices.

Case Study 1: Crisis Communication Mastery

Scenario: A global technology company faces a data breach that exposes sensitive customer information.

Approach:

- Swift Response: The organization acknowledges the breach publicly within hours, demonstrating a commitment to transparency.

- Accurate Information: Despite the urgency, the company ensures all statements are accurate and verified.

- Timely Updates: Regular updates are provided as the investigation progresses, keeping stakeholders informed.

Impact:

- Trust Preservation: Stakeholders appreciate the swift and transparent response, preserving trust.

- **Positive** Reputation: Media and public recognize the organization's responsible approach, enhancing its reputation.

Lessons Learned:

- Swift response with accurate information builds trust even in challenging situations.

- Transparent communication fosters goodwill and demonstrates commitment to stakeholders.

Case Study 2: Stakeholder-Centric Engagement

Scenario: An energy company faces opposition from local communities regarding a new project.

Approach:

- Local Consultations: The company conducts town hall meetings to understand community concerns.

- Collaboration: Based on feedback, the project is adjusted to address local interests.

- Ongoing Dialogue: Regular engagement is maintained to provide updates and gather feedback.

Impact:

- Community Support: The project gains community support due to the inclusive approach.

- Enhanced Reputation: The organization is recognized for valuing community voices and collaboration.

Lessons Learned:

- Engaging stakeholders collaboratively builds positive relationships and garners support.

- Ongoing dialogue demonstrates commitment to addressing concerns and maintaining transparency.

Case Study 3: Cultural Sensitivity in Global Markets

Scenario: A consumer goods company expands to a new cultural market.

Approach:

- Cultural Research: Extensive research is conducted to understand local customs, values, and sensitivities.

- Customized Messaging: Marketing and communication materials are tailored to resonate with the local culture.

- Respectful Engagement: The organization engages with local influencers to introduce the brand authentically.

Impact:

- Market Acceptance: The brand gains acceptance and popularity due to culturally appropriate messaging.

- Positive Reception: The organization is praised for its respect for cultural nuances.

Lessons Learned:

- Cultural sensitivity demonstrates respect and authenticity, fostering positive brand reception.

- Tailored messaging connects with audiences on a deeper level, transcending cultural barriers.

These real-world case studies illustrate the multifaceted nature of public affairs and the diverse strategies organizations employ to navigate challenges, enhance relationships, and achieve their goals. By examining these examples, organizations can draw inspiration and insights to shape their own strategic

approaches and cultivate success in the complex realm of public affairs.

Continuous Learning and Adaptation:

Public affairs is a dynamic field, and strategies must continually evolve to meet changing circumstances and stakeholder expectations. Organizations should prioritize a culture of learning, adaptation, and improvement.

By delving into these strategies, organizations can arm themselves with the tools and insights needed to navigate the complex landscape of public affairs successfully. Each strategy contributes to building a holistic approach that aligns communication, stakeholder engagement, ethics, and cultural sensitivity for a more impactful and sustainable public affairs journey.

Chapter 5: Navigating Complex Public Affairs Landscapes

In the intricate realm of public affairs, the ever-evolving landscapes demand an astute understanding of the multifaceted dynamics that shape perceptions, policies, and stakeholder relationships. This chapter delves into the complexities that organizations encounter as they navigate the intricate web of public affairs, providing insights, strategies, and perspectives to thrive in a world where change is constant and challenges are diverse.

Understanding Regulatory Frameworks:

1. **Navigating Regulations:** Explore the complexities of regulatory environments and the impact of policies on industries and organizations.

2. **Advocacy and Compliance:** Understand the balance between advocating for favorable policies and ensuring compliance with regulatory requirements.

Global and Local Dynamics:

1. **Globalization Challenges:** Examine the challenges and opportunities of operating in a globalized world, where local and international interests converge.

2. **Cultural Nuances:** Navigate cultural sensitivities to resonate with diverse audiences and avoid misinterpretations.

Industry-Specific Considerations:

1. **Sectoral Analysis:** Analyze how public affairs strategies differ across industries, from healthcare and technology to energy and finance.

2. **Emerging Trends:** Stay ahead of industry trends and disruptions to adapt public affairs strategies accordingly.

Digital Transformation and Ethics:

1. **Digital Engagement:** Explore the digital transformation's impact on public affairs, from social media activism to online advocacy.

2. **Ethical Digital Practices:** Discuss ethical considerations in the digital age, including data privacy, misinformation, and digital inclusion.

Inclusive Stakeholder Engagement:

1. **Diverse Stakeholders:** Navigate engaging with a diverse range of stakeholders, from communities and NGOs to shareholders and policymakers.

2. **Collaboration for Impact:** Explore how collaboration with stakeholders can drive positive societal impact beyond organizational goals.

Future-Proofing Strategies:

1. **Adaptive Strategies:** Discuss the importance of adaptability in public affairs, where strategies must evolve with changing circumstances.

2. **Scenario Planning:** Embrace scenario planning to anticipate potential challenges and opportunities, enhancing strategic decision-making.

Real-World Complexity:

Case Study: Navigating a Complex Merger in the Telecommunications Sector

Scenario: A leading telecommunications company embarks on a merger with a global competitor to enhance market share and technological capabilities.

Challenges Addressed:

- Regulatory Hurdles: The merger involves multiple jurisdictions with differing regulatory requirements, requiring careful navigation to gain approvals.

- Stakeholder Concerns: Employees, customers, and shareholders express concerns about the impact of the merger on job security, service quality, and investments.

- Industry Implications: The merger's effect on market competition and innovation raises industry-wide implications that demand strategic foresight.

Approach and Strategies:

- Regulatory Expertise: The organization assembles a team of legal experts to navigate the complex regulatory landscape and secure necessary approvals.

- Stakeholder Communication: A comprehensive communication plan addresses employee, customer, and shareholder concerns with transparent and consistent messaging.

- Innovation Commitment: The merged entity pledges continued investment in research and development to drive industry innovation.

Outcomes and Lessons Learned:

- Successful Approval: Through strategic advocacy and compliance efforts, regulatory approvals are obtained across multiple jurisdictions.

- Stakeholder Buy-In: Open and transparent communication fosters stakeholder confidence, mitigating concerns and ensuring a smooth transition.

- Industry Leadership: The merged company leverages its enhanced capabilities to position itself as an industry leader in telecommunications innovation.

Expert Insights:

Telecommunications Industry Expert: Gain insights from an industry expert who shares their perspectives on navigating complex mergers in the telecommunications sector.

Strategic Foresight:

1. **Learning from Complexity:** Discuss how organizations can learn from complex case studies to enhance their strategic foresight and decision-making.

2. **Adapting Lessons:** Encourage readers to adapt lessons from the case study to their own industries and scenarios.

By exploring a case study of a complex merger, this chapter provides a tangible example of the challenges and strategies organizations face in the intricate world of public affairs. By understanding how an organization successfully navigated regulatory, stakeholder, and industry considerations, readers can gain valuable insights into the complexities of real-world scenarios and apply them to their own public affairs endeavors.

Managing Crisis Situations and Reputation Damage

In the intricate tapestry of public affairs, the specter of crisis looms as an ever-present reality that organizations must be prepared to face. This chapter delves into the art of crisis management, offering insights, strategies, and best practices for navigating turbulent waters while safeguarding an organization's reputation, stakeholder trust, and long-term viability.

Understanding Crisis Management:

1. **Defining Crisis:** Explore the diverse range of crises organizations may face, from product recalls and data breaches to leadership controversies.

2. **Crisis Lifecycle:** Examine the stages of a crisis, from initial detection to resolution, and the communication strategies required at each phase.

Proactive Crisis Preparedness:

1. **Crisis Communication Plans:** Delve into the development of comprehensive crisis communication plans that outline roles, protocols, and communication strategies.

2. **Scenario Planning:** Discuss the importance of scenario planning to anticipate potential crises and formulate effective responses.

Effective Crisis Communication:

1. **Timely and Transparent Communication:** Explore the significance of swift and honest communication during crises, minimizing speculation and misinformation.

2. **Coordination:** Understand the importance of coordination among different organizational departments to ensure consistent messaging.

Managing Reputation Damage:

1. **Reputation Impact:** Analyze the impact of crises on an organization's reputation and the strategies for reputation repair.

2. **Rebuilding Trust:** Explore the steps needed to rebuild trust with stakeholders after a crisis, including actions and communication.

Media Relations in Crisis:

1. **Engaging Media:** Discuss how to engage with media during a crisis, including effective spokesperson training and managing media inquiries.

2. **Monitoring and Responding:** Examine strategies for monitoring media coverage and responding to inaccuracies or misinterpretations.

Post-Crisis Analysis and Learning:

1. **Post-Mortem Analysis:** Learn the importance of conducting post-crisis analysis to assess what worked, what didn't, and how to improve.

2. **Lessons Learned:** Explore how organizations can glean valuable lessons from crises to enhance preparedness and response in the future.

Real-World Case Studies:

Real-World Case Study: Navigating a Data Breach Crisis

Scenario: A multinational financial institution experiences a significant data breach compromising customer information.

Challenges Addressed:

- Privacy Concerns: Protecting customer privacy while addressing the breach's impact on clients and the organization.

- Regulatory Compliance: Navigating legal requirements for reporting data breaches and informing affected parties.

- Rebuilding Trust: Reassuring clients, investors, and the public while restoring the organization's tarnished reputation.

Approach and Strategies:

- Rapid Response: Activating the crisis communication plan immediately, providing accurate information to stakeholders.

- Transparency: Sharing the scope and extent of the breach while outlining steps taken to address the issue.

- Collaborative Efforts: Coordinating with regulatory authorities, law enforcement, and cybersecurity experts to contain the breach.

Outcomes and Lessons Learned:

- Stakeholder Confidence: Transparent communication restores confidence among customers, shareholders, and the public.

- Regulatory Compliance: By complying with reporting requirements, the organization avoids legal repercussions.

- Enhanced Preparedness: The crisis prompts the organization to enhance its data security measures and response protocols.

Expert Insights:

Cybersecurity Expert: Gain insights from a cybersecurity expert who shares strategies for managing data breach crises.

Strategic Learning:

1. **Applying Lessons:** Discuss how the lessons learned from the case study can be applied to other crisis scenarios.

2. **Building Resilience:** Explore how crisis management enhances an organization's overall resilience and preparedness.

By examining a real-world case study involving a data breach crisis, this chapter provides a concrete example of how crisis management strategies can be applied in complex situations. Through the organization's response, readers can gain insights into the challenges, approaches, and outcomes of crisis management efforts, enabling them to better navigate their own crisis situations and protect their reputation and stakeholder relationships.

Lobbying and Advocacy: Balancing Influence and Integrity

In the intricate landscape of public affairs, the realms of lobbying and advocacy hold the potential to shape policies, legislation, and public discourse. This chapter delves into the complexities of lobbying and advocacy, offering insights into the ethical considerations, strategies for effective engagement, and the delicate balance between wielding influence and upholding organizational integrity.

Understanding Lobbying and Advocacy:

1. **Defining Terms:** Explore the distinctions between lobbying and advocacy, highlighting their roles in influencing decision-making.

2. **Influence Dynamics:** Examine the power dynamics at play when organizations engage in lobbying and advocacy efforts.

Ethics and Transparency:

1. **Ethical Considerations:** Discuss the ethical dilemmas associated with lobbying, including conflicts of interest and transparency.

2. **Transparency and Disclosure:** Explore the importance of transparent reporting of lobbying activities and financial support for campaigns.

Effective Advocacy Strategies:

1. **Message Crafting:** Delve into the art of crafting compelling messages that resonate with policymakers and stakeholders.

2. **Building Alliances:** Understand the value of forming alliances with like-minded organizations to amplify advocacy efforts.

Navigating Regulatory Frameworks:

1. **Legal Compliance:** Examine the legal and regulatory landscape surrounding lobbying activities and the importance of compliance.

2. **Staying Informed:** Discuss the need for organizations to stay updated on evolving lobbying regulations and requirements.

Balancing Influence and Integrity:

1. **Strategic Engagement:** Explore the balance between effective advocacy and maintaining an ethical approach to influence.

2. **Long-Term Impact:** Discuss how short-term wins should be balanced with the long-term impact of advocacy efforts.

Public Perception and Reputation:

1. **Reputation Implications:** Analyze how lobbying and advocacy efforts can impact an organization's reputation and stakeholder perceptions.

2. **Ethics and Image:** Discuss the importance of aligning advocacy efforts with an organization's values to avoid reputation damage.

Real-World Case Study: Advocacy for Environmental Conservation

Scenario: An environmental organization advocates for stricter regulations on industrial waste disposal to protect local ecosystems.

Challenges Addressed:

- Industry Opposition: Powerful industries resist regulatory changes due to potential economic impacts.

- Public Engagement: Engaging the public to rally support for environmental regulations in a complex issue.

Approach and Strategies:

- Compelling Messaging: Crafting messages that emphasize the importance of protecting local environments and long-term sustainability.

- **Coalition Building:** Forming partnerships with other environmental groups, scientists, and community activists.

- **Expert Testimony:** Presenting scientific evidence and expert testimonies to influence policymakers' decisions.

Outcomes and Lessons Learned:

- **Policy Change:** Successful advocacy leads to the introduction of stricter waste disposal regulations.

- **Public Support:** Public engagement efforts result in widespread support for the regulations, putting pressure on policymakers.

- **Industry Adaptation:** Industries eventually adapt to the new regulations, fostering a more environmentally conscious approach.

Expert Insights:

Environmental Advocate: Gain insights from an environmental advocate who shares strategies for effective advocacy in complex issues.

Strategic Integrity:

1. **Ethical Decision-Making:** Discuss how organizations can make ethical decisions while leveraging influence for advocacy.

2. **Balancing Priorities:** Explore how organizations can balance their advocacy goals with their broader ethical responsibilities.

By examining a real-world case study of environmental advocacy, this chapter offers a tangible example of the challenges, strategies, and outcomes of lobbying and advocacy efforts. Through the organization's approach to advocating for environmental protection, readers can gain insights into the ethical considerations and strategic decisions necessary for effective influence while maintaining integrity.

International Public Affairs: Challenges and Opportunities

In the intricate global arena of public affairs, the complexities of international engagement present both challenges and opportunities for organizations seeking to navigate diverse cultures, regulations, and stakeholder landscapes. This chapter delves into the multifaceted world of international public affairs, offering insights into the unique challenges organizations face when operating across borders, as well as strategies to leverage the opportunities presented by a connected global landscape.

Navigating Cultural Diversity:

1. **Cultural Nuances:** Explore the importance of understanding cultural differences and adapting communication strategies for diverse audiences.

2. **Cultural Sensitivity:** Discuss the risks of cultural insensitivity and the need to engage with stakeholders in ways that respect their customs and values.

Regulatory Variations:

1. **Global Regulatory Landscape:** Examine the challenges of operating within varying regulatory frameworks across different countries and regions.

2. **Compliance and Adaptation:** Explore strategies to ensure compliance with international regulations while adapting to local requirements.

Stakeholder Engagement Across Borders:

1. **Global Stakeholder Mapping:** Discuss the complexities of identifying and engaging with stakeholders in different countries and cultural contexts.

2. **Building Global Networks:** Explore the value of building global networks and alliances to enhance international public affairs efforts.

Global Crisis Management:

1. **Crisis Across Borders:** Examine the challenges of managing crises that span multiple countries and the importance of consistent communication.

2. **Crisis Preparedness:** Discuss the need for robust crisis preparedness plans that account for international considerations.

Cultural Intelligence and Communication:

1. **Cultural Intelligence:** Understand the concept of cultural intelligence and its role in effective cross-border communication.

2. **Language and Messaging:** Explore the challenges of language barriers and the strategies for crafting messages that transcend linguistic differences.

Building Global Reputation:

1. **Reputation Transcendence:** Analyze how an organization's reputation extends beyond borders and the strategies for building a consistent global image.

2. **Global Thought Leadership:** Discuss the opportunities for organizations to establish themselves as global thought leaders in their respective industries.

Real-World Case Study: Expanding Market Presence in Asia-Pacific

Scenario: An international technology company seeks to expand its market presence in the Asia-Pacific region.

Challenges Addressed:

- Cultural Adaptation: Navigating cultural differences and preferences in marketing, messaging, and customer engagement.

- Regulatory Compliance: Ensuring compliance with varied data protection and business regulations across multiple countries.

- Local Stakeholder Engagement: Building relationships with local partners, customers, and governments to establish credibility.

Approach and Strategies:

- Localized Marketing: Developing region-specific marketing campaigns that resonate with cultural preferences and values.

- Legal Expertise: Assembling legal experts to ensure compliance with diverse regulations and minimize legal risks.

- Government Relations: Engaging with local government officials and regulatory bodies to understand and meet regulatory requirements.

Outcomes and Lessons Learned:

- Market Growth: The company's tailored approach leads to increased market share and customer engagement in the region.

- Compliance Success: Diligent regulatory compliance prevents legal issues and reinforces the company's commitment to ethical practices.

- Positive Image: Local engagement efforts lead to a positive reputation among stakeholders and governments in the region.

Expert Insights:

Asia-Pacific Market Expert: Gain insights from an expert in Asia-Pacific markets who shares strategies for successful market expansion.

Global Success Strategy:

1. **Learning from Experience:** Discuss how organizations can learn from the case study to develop effective strategies for global expansion.

2. **Sustainable Engagement:** Explore the long-term benefits of building strong relationships with stakeholders in international markets.

By exploring a real-world case study of expanding market presence in the Asia-Pacific region, this chapter provides readers with a concrete example of the challenges and strategies organizations face in international public affairs. Through the company's approach, readers can gain insights into the cultural intelligence, regulatory compliance, and stakeholder engagement required for successful global expansion efforts.

Chapter 6: Case Studies in Public Affairs

In the realm of public affairs, the power of case studies lies in their ability to illuminate real-world challenges, strategies, and outcomes that organizations have encountered on their journeys. This chapter serves as a collection of insightful case studies that delve into various aspects of public affairs, offering readers the opportunity to learn from the experiences of diverse organizations, industries, and contexts. Through these illuminating narratives, readers can gain practical insights, strategic wisdom, and a deeper understanding of the complexities that shape effective public affairs practices.

Case Study 1: Navigating Regulatory Change in the Energy Sector

Scenario: An energy company faces shifting regulatory policies that impact its operations, requiring a strategic pivot to comply while minimizing disruptions.

Challenges Addressed:

- Regulatory Uncertainty: Navigating a changing regulatory landscape with potential implications for business viability.

- Stakeholder Engagement: Addressing concerns of employees, communities, and shareholders while adapting to new regulations.

Approach and Strategies:

- Regulatory Analysis: Conducting in-depth analysis of regulatory changes and their potential impact on the company's operations.

- Stakeholder Communication: Engaging transparently with stakeholders to share the company's plans for compliance and address concerns.

- Innovation Integration: Incorporating innovative solutions to align with new regulatory requirements and enhance business sustainability.

Outcomes and Lessons Learned:

- Successful Compliance: The company's strategic efforts result in seamless adaptation to new regulations while maintaining operations.

- Stakeholder Confidence: Transparent communication fosters stakeholder confidence, demonstrating the company's commitment to responsible operations.

- Industry Leadership: The company's innovative solutions position it as a leader in sustainable energy practices.

Case Study 2: Crisis Management in the Retail Sector

Scenario: A retail chain faces a crisis of consumer trust due to product quality issues, requiring rapid crisis management to salvage its reputation.

Challenges Addressed:

- Reputation Damage: Managing negative media coverage and public perception while addressing the root cause of the crisis.

- Consumer Confidence: Rebuilding trust among consumers who are concerned about product safety and quality.

- Legal Implications: Mitigating potential legal challenges while addressing consumer concerns.

Approach and Strategies:

- Swift Response: Initiating a rapid response team to investigate the issue, determine the scope of the problem, and develop a resolution plan.

- Transparent Communication: Sharing timely and honest updates with the public, acknowledging the issue, and outlining corrective actions.

- Consumer Engagement: Providing channels for consumers to voice concerns, offer feedback, and receive information on product improvements.

Outcomes and Lessons Learned:

- Reputation Recovery: Transparent communication and effective resolution efforts restore consumer trust and confidence.

- Enhanced Quality Control: The crisis prompts the company to implement rigorous quality control measures, preventing similar issues in the future.

- Stakeholder Appreciation: The public recognizes the company's efforts to address the crisis responsibly, bolstering its reputation for ethical practices.

Case Study 3: International Stakeholder Engagement in the Nonprofit Sector

Scenario: A nonprofit organization seeks to expand its global reach by engaging with stakeholders in diverse countries to advance its humanitarian mission.

Challenges Addressed:

- Cultural Sensitivity: Navigating cultural differences and customs to build meaningful connections with stakeholders from various backgrounds.

- **Donor Engagement:** Establishing trust and credibility with potential donors in different regions to secure funding for projects.

- **Regulatory Variations:** Ensuring compliance with local regulations and legal requirements while maintaining the organization's mission.

Approach and Strategies:

- **Cultural Adaptation:** Tailoring communication approaches to resonate with the cultural values and norms of different regions.

- **Partnerships and Collaborations:** Collaborating with local organizations and community leaders to amplify the impact of projects.

- **Ethical Fundraising:** Ensuring that fundraising efforts align with local customs and ethics while remaining transparent and accountable.

Outcomes and Lessons Learned:

- **Global Impact:** The organization's culturally sensitive engagement efforts lead to successful projects that positively impact diverse communities.

- Donor Trust: Building strong relationships with donors based on mutual respect and shared values enhances fundraising efforts.ww

- Local Empowerment: Collaborations with local partners empower communities to actively participate in and benefit from the organization's initiatives.

Expert Insights:

Public Affairs Thought Leader: Gain insights from a prominent public affairs expert who reflects on the key takeaways from the case studies.

Strategic Learning and Application:

1. **Practical Wisdom:** Discuss the practical insights and lessons that readers can draw from the case studies.

2. **Applied Knowledge:** Encourage readers to apply the strategies and approaches showcased in the case studies to their own public affairs endeavors.

This chapter presents a collection of diverse case studies that shed light on the complexities and triumphs of public affairs practices. Through these narratives, readers can gain valuable insights, learn from real-world challenges, and apply strategic approaches to their own public affairs efforts. Each case study serves as a testament to the dynamic nature of public affairs and the importance of adaptive strategies and ethical engagement in achieving impactful outcomes.

Case Study 1: Starbucks' "Race Together" Campaign

In 2015, Starbucks, the global coffeehouse chain, launched the "Race Together" campaign as an ambitious initiative to address issues of racial inequality and promote conversations about race in the United States. The campaign aimed to encourage dialogue among customers and employees on topics related to race and social justice. However, the campaign faced a mixture of support, criticism, and challenges that ultimately led to its premature discontinuation.

Challenges Addressed:

- **Sensitivity and Complexity:** Addressing racial issues requires careful handling due to their sensitivity and the complex historical context.

- **Consumer Perception:** Balancing genuine social responsibility with concerns that the campaign might be perceived as a marketing stunt.

- **Employee Engagement:** Encouraging employees to initiate conversations about race while ensuring their readiness and comfort.

Approach and Strategies:

- **Barista Training:** Starbucks trained its baristas to engage in respectful conversations about race with customers who expressed interest.

- **Cultural Sensitivity:** The campaign aimed to foster cultural sensitivity by creating a platform for open dialogue.

- **Support for Employees:** Starbucks provided resources and support for employees to facilitate meaningful conversations while addressing any discomfort.

Outcomes and Lessons Learned:

- **Mixed Reactions:** The campaign faced both praise for addressing important issues and criticism for being inappropriate for a coffee shop setting.

- **Communication Missteps:** Some customers felt that the campaign was not effectively communicated and appeared as if the company was forcing conversations.

- **Premature End:** Due to the challenges and mixed reactions, Starbucks ended the campaign sooner than originally planned.

Lessons for Public Affairs:

- **Balancing Act:** The case highlights the challenge of addressing sensitive social issues while balancing public perception and authenticity.
- **Stakeholder Readiness:** It underscores the importance of gauging stakeholder readiness and receptiveness for such initiatives.
- **Communication Clarity:** Effective communication is crucial to convey the intentions and goals of the campaign accurately.

Expert Insights:

Public Relations Expert: Gain insights from a public relations expert who reflects on the campaign's challenges and implications for public affairs.

Strategic Learning:

1. **Engagement Complexity:** Discuss the complexities of engaging with sensitive social issues in public affairs campaigns.
2. **Ethical Considerations:** Explore the ethical considerations organizations should take into account when addressing societal topics.

The Starbucks "Race Together" campaign serves as a significant case study that underscores the intricacies of addressing social issues through public affairs initiatives. While the campaign aimed to encourage meaningful conversations, its challenges and eventual discontinuation provide valuable insights for organizations considering similar efforts to engage with social justice and equality topics.

Case Study 2: Volkswagen's Emission Scandal Recovery

In 2015, German automobile manufacturer Volkswagen (VW) faced a major crisis when it was revealed that the company had manipulated emissions tests for its diesel vehicles, leading to significantly higher emissions levels than reported. The scandal, often referred to as "Dieselgate," resulted in substantial fines, legal actions, and a severe blow to VW's reputation. The company's response and recovery efforts provide a compelling case study in crisis management and reputation rebuilding.

Challenges Addressed:

- **Reputation Damage:** The scandal tarnished VW's reputation for environmental responsibility and integrity.

- **Legal and Regulatory Consequences:** VW faced fines, lawsuits, and investigations from regulatory authorities around the world.

- **Consumer Trust:** Restoring trust among consumers who felt betrayed by the company's actions.

Approach and Strategies:

- **Immediate Accountability:** VW admitted wrongdoing and issued public apologies, taking responsibility for the deception.

- **Regulatory Compliance:** The company worked to meet emissions standards and regain regulatory compliance.

- **Product Innovation:** VW committed to transitioning to electric and hybrid vehicles, focusing on sustainability and transparency.

Outcomes and Lessons Learned:

- **Financial Impact:** VW incurred significant financial losses due to fines, legal settlements, and reputational damage.

- **Reputation Recovery:** The company launched campaigns to rebuild trust and demonstrate commitment to ethical practices.

- **Shift to Electric:** VW's efforts to innovate toward more sustainable vehicles aligned with changing consumer expectations.

Lessons for Public Affairs:

- **Transparency:** The case underscores the importance of transparency and immediate accountability in crisis management.

- **Ethical Redemption:** VW's commitment to addressing the issue and transitioning to cleaner technologies showcases ethical redemption.

- **Long-Term Strategy:** The recovery emphasizes the need for sustained efforts and strategic shifts to regain stakeholder trust.

Expert Insights:

Crisis Management Expert: Gain insights from a crisis management expert who reflects on the challenges and strategies VW employed in its recovery.

Strategic Learning:

1. **Crisis Communication:** Discuss the significance of transparent communication and swift action in crisis situations.

2. **Reputation Regaining:** Explore strategies for organizations to regain trust and rebuild their reputation after a major scandal.

Volkswagen's Emission Scandal Recovery case study serves as a poignant example of the challenges organizations face in times of crisis and the strategies required for successful recovery. The case underscores the importance of ethical conduct, accountability, and sustained efforts to rebuild trust and reposition the organization as a responsible industry leader.

Case Study 3: Chick-fil-A's Approach to Controversial Stances

Chick-fil-A, a popular fast-food restaurant chain, has garnered attention not only for its chicken sandwiches but also for its stances on social and political issues. The company's positions on topics such as LGBTQ+ rights and traditional marriage have led to both support and backlash from various stakeholders. This case study explores Chick-fil-A's approach to managing controversies and the implications for its public affairs strategies.

Challenges Addressed:

- **Polarizing Positions:** Chick-fil-A's stance on certain social issues has drawn strong opinions from customers, employees, and advocacy groups.

- **Public Perception:** Balancing the company's values with the potential impact on its reputation and customer base.

- **Employee Morale:** Navigating potential impacts on employee satisfaction and inclusion due to the company's positions.

Approach and Strategies:

- **Clarity of Values:** Chick-fil-A openly communicates its Christian values and positions on social issues, aligning with its identity.

- **Community Engagement:** The company focuses on community involvement, philanthropy, and supporting local initiatives.

- **Employee Support:** Chick-fil-A emphasizes an inclusive workplace environment while acknowledging differing viewpoints.

Outcomes and Lessons Learned:

- **Loyal Customer Base:** The company's transparency and consistency in values have garnered support from customers who share similar beliefs.

- **Controversy Management:** The approach has sometimes led to public backlash and calls for boycotts from those who disagree with the company's positions.

- **Balancing Act:** Chick-fil-A's success underscores the challenge of maintaining a loyal customer base while addressing issues that divide public opinion.

Lessons for Public Affairs:

- **Value Alignment:** The case highlights the importance of aligning organizational values with public positions.

- **Stakeholder Engagement:** Chick-fil-A's emphasis on community engagement showcases the role of local involvement in managing controversy.

- **Ethical Considerations:** Organizations must consider how their stances align with their values and the potential impact on stakeholders.

Expert Insights:

Ethics and Diversity Expert: Gain insights from an expert in ethics and diversity who reflects on Chick-fil-A's approach and its implications.

Strategic Learning:

1. **Values-Driven Engagement:** Discuss the strategy of openly communicating values even if they are controversial.

2. **Reputation Management:** Explore the complexities of managing reputation when organizational values intersect with divisive issues.

Chick-fil-A's Approach to Controversial Stances case study highlights the intricate dance organizations must perform when addressing sensitive topics that resonate with their values. By examining Chick-fil-A's strategy, organizations can gain insights into navigating controversies, upholding values, and fostering inclusive environments even when confronted with differing perspectives.

Chapter 7: Learning from Success and Failure

In the dynamic landscape of public affairs, success and failure often serve as the most illuminating teachers. This chapter serves as a reflective platform that delves into the stories of organizations that have experienced both triumphs and setbacks in their public affairs endeavors. By examining real-world examples, readers can glean valuable insights, strategies, and cautionary tales that provide a deeper understanding of the strategies that lead to success and the pitfalls to avoid.

Embracing Success:

1. **Strategies that Worked:** Explore the effective approaches organizations have taken to achieve their public affairs goals.

2. **Adaptive Innovation:** Discuss how successful organizations adapt to changing landscapes and innovative strategies to stay ahead.

Learning from Failure:

1. **Identifying Pitfalls:** Examine the missteps and decisions that led to the failure of public affairs initiatives.

2. **Failures as Catalysts:** Discuss how failures can serve as catalysts for improvement and strategic reevaluation.

Success Case Study: "Ice Bucket Challenge" for ALS Awareness

Scenario: The "Ice Bucket Challenge" became a viral sensation, raising awareness and funds for amyotrophic lateral sclerosis (ALS) research.

Strategies that Worked:

- **Viral Nature:** The challenge's viral spread harnessed the power of social media, engaging participants globally.

- **Simplicity:** The simplicity of the challenge made it accessible and easy for participants to join.

Outcomes and Lessons Learned:

- **Global Awareness:** The challenge significantly increased public awareness of ALS and its impact.

- **Fundraising Success:** The campaign raised substantial funds for ALS research, leading to breakthroughs in treatment.

Failure Case Study: Pepsi's "Live for Now Moments" Ad

Scenario: Pepsi faced backlash for an ad that was criticized for trivializing social justice issues.

Identifying Pitfalls:

- **Insensitive Messaging:** The ad's portrayal of a protest scene was seen as inappropriate and offensive.

- **Tone-Deafness:** The ad failed to grasp the sensitivity of social justice matters, leading to public outrage.

Learning from Failure:

- **Contextual Awareness:** The case highlights the importance of understanding social and cultural contexts when crafting messaging.

- **Ethical Considerations:** Organizations must carefully consider the implications of their messaging on societal issues.

Expert Insights:

Communication Strategist: Gain insights from a communication strategist who reflects on the lessons organizations can draw from both success and failure.

Strategic Reflection:

1. **Applied Wisdom:** Discuss how the lessons learned from success and failure can be applied to readers' own public affairs efforts.

2. **Continuous Improvement:** Explore the concept of continuous improvement through the iterative process of learning from both triumphs and mistakes.

"Learning from Success and Failure" provides a platform for organizations to gain valuable insights from the experiences of others in the realm of public affairs. By examining the strategies that led to success and the missteps that resulted in failure, readers can sharpen their strategic thinking, refine their approaches, and cultivate a mindset of continuous learning and improvement in their public affairs endeavors.

Analyzing the Factors Behind Successful Public Affairs Campaigns

Behind every successful public affairs campaign lies a combination of strategic planning, effective execution, and a deep understanding of the factors that contribute to positive outcomes. This chapter delves into the intricate mechanisms that drive successful public affairs campaigns, dissecting the essential elements that organizations must consider to craft impactful strategies, engage stakeholders, and achieve their objectives. By examining these factors, readers can gain a comprehensive understanding of what sets successful campaigns apart and how to apply these insights to their own endeavors.

Strategic Planning and Goal Setting:

1. **Clear Objectives:** Explore the importance of defining clear and measurable goals for a public affairs campaign.

2. **Aligned Strategies:** Discuss the need to align strategies with overall organizational objectives to ensure coherence and effectiveness.

Stakeholder Identification and Engagement:

1. **Stakeholder Mapping:** Examine the process of identifying key stakeholders and understanding their needs, concerns, and expectations.

2. **Engagement Strategies:** Explore approaches for engaging stakeholders through tailored communication, collaboration, and relationship-building.

Effective Messaging and Communication:

1. **Message Consistency:** Discuss the significance of maintaining consistent messaging across various communication channels.

2. **Audience Relevance:** Explore the art of crafting messages that resonate with the target audience's values, interests, and aspirations.

Adaptive Strategies and Flexibility:

1. **Dynamic Landscape:** Analyze the importance of adapting strategies to changing circumstances and unforeseen challenges.

2. **Iterative Approach:** Discuss the value of ongoing assessment and adjustment based on real-time feedback and results.

Innovative Tactics and Creative Approaches:

1. **Out-of-the-Box Thinking:** Explore the impact of innovative tactics that capture attention and stand out in a crowded media landscape.

2. **Harnessing Technology:** Discuss the role of technology and digital platforms in amplifying campaign reach and engagement.

Ethical Considerations and Reputation Management:

1. **Ethical Integrity:** Examine the significance of ethical decision-making and transparent practices in maintaining credibility.

2. **Reputation Impact:** Discuss how ethical behavior and responsible practices contribute to positive reputation outcomes.

Measuring Success and Evaluation:

1. **Key Performance Indicators (KPIs):** Explore the importance of defining KPIs to measure the success and impact of a campaign.

2. **Lessons Learned:** Discuss the value of post-campaign analysis to identify successes, challenges, and areas for improvement.

Expert Insights:

Public Affairs Strategist: Gain insights from a seasoned public affairs strategist who reflects on the critical factors that drive successful campaigns.

Strategic Reflection and Application:

1. **Strategic Application:** Discuss how readers can apply the insights gained from analyzing successful campaigns to their own public affairs initiatives.

2. **Ongoing Learning:** Explore the concept of continuous learning and improvement as a foundation for achieving success in public affairs.

By dissecting successful campaigns and understanding the interplay of planning, engagement, messaging, and ethics, readers can develop a comprehensive toolkit for designing and executing impactful public affairs strategies that resonate with stakeholders and achieve meaningful outcomes.

Lessons to Be Learned from High-Profile Failures

In the realm of public affairs, failures can serve as powerful teaching moments, offering valuable insights into the pitfalls, missteps, and challenges that organizations can encounter. This chapter delves into the lessons that can be gleaned from high-profile public affairs failures, analyzing the factors that contributed to these setbacks and distilling key takeaways for organizations to avoid similar pitfalls. By examining these failures, readers can cultivate a deeper understanding of the complexities of public affairs and develop strategies to mitigate risks and enhance their own success.

Transparency and Authenticity:

1. **Honest Communication:** Discuss the importance of transparent and authentic communication, especially in times of crisis or controversy.

2. **Deceptive Practices:** Examine cases where organizations' lack of transparency led to mistrust and reputational damage.

Cultural Sensitivity and Awareness:

1. **Cultural Nuances:** Explore the significance of understanding cultural contexts to avoid inadvertently offending or alienating stakeholders.

2. **Cultural Insensitivity:** Analyze cases where organizations' actions or messaging clashed with cultural norms, resulting in backlash.

Ethical Considerations and Decision-Making:

1. **Ethical Missteps:** Discuss instances where organizations compromised ethical values, leading to reputational damage and loss of trust.

2. **Consequences of Unethical Behavior:** Examine the repercussions of unethical decisions, both legally and in terms of public perception.

Lack of Preparedness and Crisis Management:

1. **Inadequate Planning:** Explore the impact of failing to have robust crisis management plans in place, resulting in chaotic responses.

2. **Crisis Response Evaluation:** Analyze how organizations' crisis response strategies either mitigated or exacerbated the impact of failures.

Miscalculated Messaging and Audience Perception:

1. **Messaging Misalignment:** Examine cases where organizations' messaging did not align with their target audience's values or expectations.

2. **Public Backlash:** Discuss the consequences of messaging that was perceived as insensitive, tone-deaf, or out of touch.

Poor Stakeholder Engagement and Communication:

1. **Neglected Stakeholders:** Explore instances where organizations failed to engage with or listen to key stakeholders, leading to resentment.

2. **Lost Opportunities:** Analyze the missed opportunities resulting from organizations' failure to effectively communicate with stakeholders.

Learning from Consequences:

1. **Analyzing the Impact:** Discuss how organizations can analyze the consequences of high-profile failures to identify areas for improvement.

2. **Preventing Recurrence:** Explore the strategies organizations can employ to prevent similar failures and enhance their public affairs practices.

Expert Insights:

Crisis Management Expert: Gain insights from a crisis management expert who reflects on the lessons organizations can learn from high-profile failures.

Strategic Application:

1. **Mitigating Risks:** Discuss how readers can apply the lessons learned from high-profile failures to anticipate and mitigate risks.

2. **Ethical Alignment:** Explore the importance of aligning organizational actions and decisions with ethical values to avoid failures.

Adapting Strategies Based on Real-Life Scenarios

The dynamic landscape of public affairs demands a nimble and adaptable approach to strategy development and execution. This chapter delves into real-life scenarios where organizations faced unexpected challenges, shifts in public sentiment, or changing circumstances, and how they adapted their strategies to navigate these complexities. By examining these scenarios, readers can uncover the strategies organizations employed to stay agile, maintain stakeholder engagement, and achieve their objectives, even in the face of unforeseen hurdles.

Scenario 1: Natural Disaster Response and Relief

Context: An organization faces the challenge of responding to a natural disaster that affects its operations, employees, and the communities it serves.

Adaptive Strategies:

- **Immediate Response:** The organization shifts its focus from regular operations to providing immediate support and resources to affected employees and communities.

- **Engagement through Action:** The organization engages stakeholders by actively participating in relief efforts and demonstrating a commitment to social responsibility.

Scenario 2: Shifting Public Perception

Context: A company experiences a shift in public sentiment due to changing societal attitudes or emerging controversies.

Adaptive Strategies:

- **Listening and Understanding:** The organization conducts thorough research to understand the reasons behind the shift in public sentiment and identifies areas for improvement.

- **Transparent Communication:** The organization openly addresses concerns, communicates its commitment to change, and demonstrates accountability for past actions.

Scenario 3: Regulatory Changes and Compliance

Context: An industry faces new regulations that impact business operations, requiring organizations to adapt quickly to remain compliant.

Adaptive Strategies:

- **Regulatory Analysis:** Organizations thoroughly analyze the new regulations to understand their implications and requirements.

- **Operational Adjustments:** Organizations implement necessary changes to their processes, products, or services to ensure compliance while minimizing disruptions.

Scenario 4: Social Media Crisis

Context: A negative incident involving an organization goes viral on social media, leading to a reputational crisis.

Adaptive Strategies:

- **Swift Response:** The organization addresses the crisis promptly by acknowledging the issue and providing accurate information to counter misinformation.

- **Open Dialogue:** The organization engages in a transparent dialogue with stakeholders through social media platforms, addressing concerns and providing updates.

Scenario 5: Technological Advancements

Context: An industry experiences rapid technological advancements that reshape customer preferences and market dynamics.

Adaptive Strategies:

- **Innovation Integration:** Organizations embrace new technologies and incorporate them into their products or services to meet changing customer demands.

- **Educational Engagement:** Organizations engage stakeholders in conversations about the benefits and implications of technological advancements.

Scenario 6: Political and Policy Changes

Context: Organizations must navigate shifts in political leadership and policy priorities that impact their industry.

Adaptive Strategies:

- **Policy Analysis:** Organizations analyze the potential impact of policy changes on their operations and stakeholders.

- **Government Relations:** Organizations engage with policymakers, advocating for policies that align with their interests and values.

Expert Insights:

Adaptation Strategist: Gain insights from an expert in adaptation strategies who reflects on the significance of flexibility and responsiveness in public affairs.

Strategic Application:

1. **Proactive Preparedness:** Discuss the importance of proactive planning and scenario analysis to anticipate challenges and adapt strategies.

2. **Agility Mindset:** Explore how organizations can foster an agility mindset that enables them to respond effectively to unforeseen circumstances.

   By examining how organizations navigated challenges, seized opportunities, and maintained stakeholder engagement in ever-changing environments, readers can learn to develop flexible and effective strategies that lead to successful outcomes.

Chapter 8: Ethical Considerations in Public Affairs

Ethics lie at the heart of effective public affairs practices, shaping how organizations engage with stakeholders, make decisions, and contribute to society. This chapter delves into the intricate web of ethical considerations that influence public affairs strategies and decisions. By examining the ethical dimensions of communication, engagement, transparency, and accountability, readers can gain a deeper understanding of the principles that guide responsible and impactful public affairs endeavors.

Ethics and Stakeholder Engagement:

- **Inclusivity:** Explore the ethical imperative of engaging diverse stakeholders and ensuring their voices are heard in decision-making.

- **Genuine Engagement:** Discuss the importance of sincere and respectful interactions that reflect a commitment to stakeholders' well-being.

Transparency and Authenticity:

- **Truthful Communication:** Examine the ethical obligation to provide accurate and transparent information to stakeholders.

- **Avoiding Deception:** Discuss the consequences of deceptive practices that erode trust and credibility.

Balancing Conflicting Interests:

- **Ethical Dilemmas:** Explore scenarios where organizations face conflicting stakeholder interests and must make ethical decisions.

- **Fair and Just Solutions:** Discuss approaches for resolving ethical dilemmas in a manner that upholds fairness and equity.

Responsible Lobbying and Advocacy:

- **Influence and Integrity:** Analyze the ethical boundaries of lobbying and advocacy efforts to ensure they align with organizational values.

- **Accountability in Influence:** Discuss the importance of accountability when using influence to shape policies and decisions.

Cultural Sensitivity and Respect:

- **Cultural Nuances:** Explore the ethical necessity of understanding and respecting cultural differences in communication and engagement.

- **Avoiding Cultural Insensitivity:** Discuss the repercussions of failing to consider cultural contexts in public affairs initiatives.

Long-Term Societal Impact:

- **Social Responsibility:** Examine the ethical imperative of considering the broader societal impact of public affairs strategies.

- **Sustainable Practices:** Discuss how organizations can align their public affairs efforts with sustainable and responsible practices.

Expert Insights: Ethics Expert: Gain insights from an expert in ethics who reflects on the complexities of ethical decision-making in public affairs.

Ethical Reflection and Application:

1. **Guiding Principles:** Discuss how organizations can develop a set of guiding ethical principles to navigate complex public affairs scenarios.

2. **Stakeholder Trust:** Explore the role of ethical behavior in building and maintaining trust among stakeholders.

Balancing Corporate Goals with Societal Impact

The intricate dance between corporate goals and societal impact lies at the heart of responsible and effective public affairs strategies. This theme is a constant reminder that organizations must consider not only their bottom line but also the broader implications of their actions on society, communities, and the environment. This section delves into the complexities of finding equilibrium between corporate interests and the well-being of stakeholders and the world at large.

Strategic Alignment:

- **Organizational Objectives:** Discuss the importance of aligning public affairs strategies with overarching business goals.

- **Social Responsibility:** Explore how organizations can integrate societal impact into their strategic planning.

Ethical Stewardship:

- **Economic Success and Ethical Behavior:** Examine the ethical responsibilities organizations have to achieve economic success while upholding ethical standards.

- **Long-Term Viability:** Discuss the correlation between ethical behavior, reputation, and sustained success.

Inclusive Decision-Making:

- **Stakeholder Engagement:** Explore the role of involving diverse stakeholders in decision-making processes to ensure holistic considerations.

- **Equitable Outcomes:** Discuss how inclusive decision-making can lead to more equitable and just outcomes for all stakeholders.

Sustainability Integration:

- **Environmental Responsibility:** Examine strategies for incorporating environmental sustainability into corporate practices and public affairs efforts.

- **Mitigating Negative Impact:** Discuss how organizations can mitigate negative environmental impact through responsible actions.

Social Impact Initiatives:

- **Community Investment:** Explore the role of community engagement and investment in building positive relationships and enhancing societal well-being.

- **Creating Shared Value:** Discuss the concept of creating shared value through initiatives that benefit both the organization and society.

Evolving Consumer Expectations:

- **Conscious Consumerism:** Examine how changing consumer preferences and values influence organizations' approaches to societal impact.

- **Brand Loyalty:** Discuss how organizations that prioritize societal impact can build stronger brand loyalty among conscious consumers.

Strategic Learning:

1. **Ethical Decision Framework:** Discuss the development of ethical decision-making frameworks that guide organizations in balancing their goals with societal impact.

2. **Stakeholder Mapping:** Explore techniques for identifying and prioritizing stakeholders based on their potential impact on societal goals.

Transparency and Authenticity in Public Communications

Effective public communications hinge on the pillars of transparency and authenticity, which build trust, credibility, and lasting relationships with stakeholders. This section delves into the profound impact of transparent and authentic communication on public affairs efforts, highlighting their role in fostering understanding, promoting ethical behavior, and ultimately achieving organizational goals. By examining the principles and practices of transparent and authentic communication, readers can develop strategies that resonate with audiences and stand the test of public scrutiny.

The Power of Transparency:

- **Open Information Sharing:** Discuss the importance of providing accurate and comprehensive information to stakeholders.

- **Building Trust:** Explore how transparency builds trust by demonstrating honesty and a commitment to stakeholders' interests.

Authenticity as a Foundation:

- **Sincere Engagement:** Examine the significance of authentic interactions that reflect an organization's true values and intentions.

- **Emotional Connection:** Discuss how authenticity creates emotional connections with stakeholders, fostering loyalty and support.

Crisis Communication:

- **Open Acknowledgment:** Explore how transparent communication is pivotal in addressing crises and challenges head-on.

- **Rebuilding Trust:** Discuss how authenticity in crisis communication can facilitate the process of rebuilding trust.

Addressing Controversies:

- **Honest Discussion:** Examine the role of transparent and authentic communication in addressing controversies or conflicting viewpoints.

- **Constructive Dialogue:** Discuss how authenticity promotes respectful dialogue and understanding among diverse stakeholders.

Ethics and Accountability:

- **Truthful Representation:** Explore how transparent communication aligns with ethical values and responsible behavior.

- **Accountability Mechanisms:** Discuss how transparency supports organizations' accountability to stakeholders.

Strategies for Authenticity:

- **Stakeholder Inclusion:** Examine how involving stakeholders in decision-making enhances authentic communication.

- **Storytelling:** Discuss the power of storytelling to convey authentic narratives that resonate with audiences.

Strategic Learning:

1. **Communication Audits:** Explore the value of conducting regular communication audits to ensure transparency and authenticity.

2. **Crisis Simulation:** Discuss the benefits of crisis communication simulations to prepare for transparent and authentic responses.

By understanding the impact of transparency and authenticity on stakeholder relationships, organizations can foster credibility, loyalty, and support. Ultimately, transparent and authentic communication not only shapes public perception but also shapes organizational values and behavior, contributing to a more ethical and responsible public affairs landscape.

Addressing Public Affairs in Sensitive Industries

Certain industries, due to their nature or impact, navigate unique challenges in the realm of public affairs. This section delves into the intricacies of managing public affairs in sensitive industries, where factors such as environmental concerns, social impact, and ethical considerations play a significant role. By exploring the strategies and practices employed in these industries, readers can gain insights into how organizations can effectively navigate complexities and build positive relationships with stakeholders.

Navigating Environmental Concerns:

- **Sustainable Practices:** Discuss the role of transparent communication in addressing environmental impact and promoting sustainable practices.

- **Engagement with Advocacy Groups:** Explore strategies for engaging with environmental advocacy groups to foster collaboration and understanding.

Healthcare and Ethics:

- **Patient-Centric Communication:** Examine the importance of transparent communication in the healthcare industry to build patient trust.

- **Ethical Considerations:** Discuss the need to navigate ethical dilemmas related to patient care, privacy, and research.

Financial Services and Trust:

- **Transparency and Regulation:** Explore how transparent communication fosters trust in the financial services industry, especially in relation to regulations.

- **Crisis Preparedness:** Discuss strategies for handling financial crises with honesty and accountability.

Technology and Privacy:

- **Data Protection:** Examine the role of transparent communication in addressing privacy concerns related to technology and data usage.

- **Regaining Trust:** Discuss strategies for rebuilding public trust after data breaches or misuse.

Energy and Social Impact:

- **Community Engagement:** Explore how organizations in the energy sector engage with communities to address concerns and build relationships.

- **Balancing Economic Growth and Sustainability:** Discuss strategies for aligning economic interests with environmental responsibility.

Food and Agriculture Responsibility:

- **Supply Chain Transparency:** Examine how transparent communication addresses concerns about food safety, sourcing, and ethical practices.

- **Engagement with Consumer Advocates:** Discuss strategies for engaging with consumer advocates to address concerns and improve practices.

Strategic Learning:

1. **Stakeholder Collaborations:** Explore the benefits of collaborating with stakeholders to address challenges unique to sensitive industries.

2. **Ethics Workshops:** Discuss the value of ethics workshops to help professionals in sensitive industries navigate ethical considerations.

By examining the strategies employed in environmental, healthcare, financial, technology, energy, and food sectors, organizations can develop a nuanced understanding of how transparent and ethical communication can shape stakeholder perceptions and foster sustainable relationships.

Chapter 9: Crafting Your Public Affairs Roadmap

Crafting an effective public affairs strategy requires a carefully planned roadmap that guides organizations through the complex landscape of stakeholder engagement, communication, and impact. This chapter serves as a practical guide for readers, offering step-by-step insights into how to develop a comprehensive public affairs roadmap that aligns with organizational objectives, navigates challenges, and drives positive outcomes. By following this roadmap, organizations can build a solid foundation for their public affairs initiatives and navigate the intricacies of the field with confidence.

Setting Clear Objectives:

- **Defining Goals:** Discuss the importance of setting clear and measurable objectives that align with organizational mission and values.

- **SMART Approach:** Explore the SMART (Specific, Measurable, Achievable, Relevant, Time-bound) framework for goal-setting.

Stakeholder Mapping and Analysis:

- **Identifying Stakeholders:** Examine the process of identifying key stakeholders, both internal and external.

- **Understanding Needs:** Discuss strategies for understanding stakeholders' needs, concerns, and expectations.

Crafting a Compelling Narrative:

- **Defining Key Messages:** Explore how to distill complex information into concise and impactful key messages.

- **Storytelling Techniques:** Discuss the power of storytelling to convey messages that resonate with stakeholders.

Selecting Communication Channels:

- **Multi-Channel Approach:** Examine the importance of selecting a mix of communication channels to reach diverse audiences.

- **Digital Engagement:** Discuss strategies for leveraging digital and social media platforms effectively.

Engagement and Relationship Building:

- **Two-Way Communication:** Explore the value of fostering open and two-way communication with stakeholders.

- **Building Trust:** Discuss how consistent engagement builds trust and strengthens stakeholder relationships.

Monitoring and Measurement:

- **Key Performance Indicators (KPIs):** Examine the role of KPIs in measuring the effectiveness and impact of public affairs efforts.

- **Continuous Improvement:** Discuss the iterative process of monitoring, analyzing, and improving strategies based on results.

Crisis Preparedness:

- **Crisis Management Plan:** Explore the importance of having a robust crisis management plan in place to address unforeseen challenges.

- **Scenario Planning:** Discuss the benefits of scenario planning to prepare for potential crises.

Ethical Considerations:

- **Ethical Framework:** Examine how to integrate ethical considerations into every step of the public affairs roadmap.

- **Balancing Interests:** Discuss strategies for making ethical decisions that align with organizational values.

Strategic Reflection:

1. **Roadmap Customization:** Discuss how organizations can tailor the public affairs roadmap to their specific goals, challenges, and industry.

2. **Adaptive Agility:** Explore the concept of being agile and adaptable in implementing the roadmap based on changing circumstances.

"Crafting Your Public Affairs Roadmap" serves as a comprehensive guide for organizations seeking to navigate the complexities of public affairs. By following the steps outlined in this chapter, readers can develop a strategic roadmap that not only achieves organizational objectives but also fosters meaningful stakeholder relationships, ethical behavior, and positive societal impact.

Developing a Comprehensive Public Affairs Strategy

A robust public affairs strategy is essential for organizations to navigate the intricate landscape of stakeholder engagement, communication, and reputation management. This section offers a comprehensive approach to developing an effective public affairs strategy that aligns with organizational goals, values, and the evolving needs of stakeholders. By following this strategic framework, organizations can proactively shape their public image, influence policy discussions, and build lasting relationships with key audiences.

Strategic Alignment:

- **Organizational Goals:** Explore the process of aligning public affairs strategies with overarching organizational objectives.

- **Mission Integration:** Discuss how public affairs strategies can reflect an organization's mission and values.

Stakeholder Identification and Analysis:

- **Stakeholder Mapping:** Examine the identification of primary and secondary stakeholders and their influence on organizational success.

- **Stakeholder Needs:** Discuss strategies for understanding stakeholders' needs, concerns, and motivations.

Setting Clear Objectives:

- **Defining Measurable Goals:** Explore the significance of setting specific, measurable, achievable, relevant, and time-bound (SMART) objectives.

- **Outcome-Oriented Goals:** Discuss how outcome-focused goals guide public affairs efforts toward meaningful results.

Message Development:

- **Crafting Key Messages:** Examine the process of developing clear and compelling key messages that resonate with target audiences.

- **Consistent Messaging:** Discuss the importance of maintaining consistent messaging across various communication channels.

Engagement Strategies:

- **Multi-Channel Approach:** Explore the role of leveraging diverse communication channels to reach a wider range of stakeholders.

- **Personalized Engagement:** Discuss strategies for tailoring communication approaches to different stakeholder groups.

Advocacy and Lobbying:

- **Policy Influence:** Examine how organizations can strategically engage in advocacy and lobbying efforts to shape policies.

- **Ethical Advocacy:** Discuss the ethical considerations of advocating for policy changes that align with organizational values.

Crisis Preparedness:

- **Crisis Management Plan:** Explore the development of a comprehensive crisis management plan to respond effectively to unforeseen challenges.

- **Scenario Planning:** Discuss the benefits of scenario planning to anticipate and mitigate potential crises.

Ethical Considerations:

- **Ethical Decision Framework:** Examine how ethical considerations are integrated into the development and execution of public affairs strategies.

- **Transparency and Accountability:** Discuss strategies for transparently addressing ethical challenges and dilemmas.

Measurement and Evaluation:

- **Key Performance Indicators (KPIs):** Explore the role of KPIs in measuring the effectiveness and impact of public affairs strategies.

- **Adaptive Learning:** Discuss how ongoing evaluation informs strategy refinement and adaptation.

Strategic Reflection:

1. **Customization:** Discuss how organizations can customize the comprehensive public affairs strategy to their industry, culture, and goals.

2. **Long-Term Vision:** Explore the importance of aligning the strategy with long-term organizational vision and sustainability goals.

"Developing a Comprehensive Public Affairs Strategy" serves as a foundational guide for organizations aiming to build effective public affairs initiatives. By following this strategic framework, organizations can navigate challenges, seize opportunities, and foster meaningful stakeholder relationships that contribute to their success and positive societal impact.

Setting Measurable Goals and Milestones

The success of any public affairs initiative hinges on the clarity and measurability of its goals and milestones. This section delves into the strategic process of setting specific and quantifiable objectives, as well as defining key milestones that guide the progression of public affairs efforts. By understanding the significance of setting measurable goals and milestones, organizations can track progress, assess impact, and make informed strategic decisions to achieve their desired outcomes.

Strategic Goal Setting:

- **Clarity and Specificity:** Explore the importance of setting clear and specific goals that leave no room for ambiguity.

- **Alignment with Vision:** Discuss how goals should align with the broader organizational vision and mission.

Measurable Objectives:

- **Quantifiable Metrics:** Examine the process of defining metrics that allow for the measurement of progress and success.

- **SMART Framework:** Discuss the SMART (Specific, Measurable, Achievable, Relevant, Time-bound) framework for goal-setting.

Defining Milestones:

- **Key Progress Points:** Explore the role of milestones as markers of progress and achievement along the journey.

- **Strategic Pivot Points:** Discuss how milestones can inform strategic adjustments based on evolving circumstances.

Outcome-Oriented Approach:

- **Focusing on Impact:** Examine the importance of framing goals and milestones around desired outcomes and impact.

- **Measuring Tangible Results:** Discuss how an outcome-oriented approach enhances accountability and demonstrates value.

Stakeholder Engagement Benchmarks:

- **Measuring Engagement:** Explore strategies for quantifying and evaluating stakeholder engagement and interactions.

- **Quality and Quantity:** Discuss the balance between quality and quantity of engagement for effective relationship building.

Tracking Public Perception:

- **Sentiment Analysis:** Examine tools and techniques for tracking public sentiment and perception over time.

- **Adapting Strategies:** Discuss how insights from sentiment analysis can inform strategy refinement.

Crisis Response Benchmarks:

- **Response Time:** Explore the importance of setting benchmarks for swift and effective crisis response.

- **Communication Effectiveness:** Discuss how benchmarks can guide the assessment of crisis communication strategies.

Ethical and Social Impact Indicators:

- **Ethical Behavior:** Examine indicators for assessing the ethical alignment of public affairs efforts with organizational values.

- **Social Contribution:** Discuss strategies for measuring the societal impact of public affairs initiatives.

Strategic Reflection:

1. **Customization:** Discuss the adaptability of goals and milestones based on the unique characteristics of each public affairs initiative.

2. **Learning from Data:** Explore the role of data analysis in refining strategies, making informed decisions, and continuous improvement.

"Setting Measurable Goals and Milestones" provides a roadmap for strategically defining objectives, metrics, and markers of progress in public affairs initiatives. By embracing a data-driven and outcome-oriented approach, organizations can quantifiably measure their impact, make evidence-based decisions, and ensure that their efforts are aligned with their broader goals and mission.

Continuous Improvement: Adapting to Changing Landscapes

In the dynamic world of public affairs, the only constant is change. This section delves into the concept of continuous improvement as a foundational principle for staying relevant and effective in the face of evolving landscapes. By understanding the importance of adaptability, learning, and refinement, organizations can proactively navigate challenges, seize opportunities, and ensure their public affairs strategies remain agile, responsive, and impactful.

Embracing an Adaptive Mindset:

- **Flexibility as a Priority:** Explore why an adaptive mindset is crucial for public affairs professionals to thrive in changing environments.

- **Anticipating Change:** Discuss strategies for staying ahead of trends and anticipating shifts in public sentiment.

Learning from Data and Feedback:

- **Data-Driven Decision-Making:** Examine how data analytics and insights inform strategy refinement and optimization.

- **Stakeholder Feedback:** Discuss the value of soliciting feedback from stakeholders to identify areas for improvement.

Scenario Planning:

- **Future Readiness:** Explore the benefits of scenario planning as a tool for preparing for potential challenges and disruptions.

- **Strategic Alternatives:** Discuss how scenario planning enables organizations to develop multiple response strategies.

Iterative Strategy Refinement:

- **Regular Assessments:** Examine the significance of regularly assessing the effectiveness of public affairs strategies.

- **Adapting Tactics:** Discuss how ongoing assessments inform tactical adjustments to align with goals.

Agile Execution:

- **Quick Response:** Explore the role of agility in swiftly adapting strategies in response to unexpected events.

- **Testing and Learning:** Discuss the value of testing new approaches and learning from the outcomes.

Monitoring Trends and Emerging Issues:

- **Environmental Scanning:** Examine techniques for monitoring trends, emerging issues, and public sentiment shifts.

- **Proactive Engagement:** Discuss how staying informed helps organizations proactively engage with relevant topics.

Learning from Setbacks:

- **Failures as Learning Opportunities:** Explore how setbacks and challenges can serve as valuable learning experiences.

- **Course Correction:** Discuss strategies for adjusting strategies based on lessons learned from setbacks.

Strategic Reflection:

1. **Cultivating Learning Culture:** Discuss how organizations can foster a culture that values continuous improvement and embraces change.

2. **Adaptive Leadership:** Explore the role of leadership in championing adaptive strategies and promoting a culture of continuous improvement.

"Continuous Improvement: Adapting to Changing Landscapes" emphasizes the importance of embracing change and refining strategies in the ever-evolving field of public affairs. By fostering an adaptive mindset, learning from data and feedback, and proactively staying informed, organizations can navigate uncertainties, seize emerging opportunities, and ensure that their public affairs efforts remain effective, relevant, and responsive to the shifting tides of the environment.

Chapter 10: The Future of Public Affairs

As the world continues to evolve at an unprecedented pace, the field of public affairs stands at the forefront of change and innovation. This chapter takes a forward-looking approach, examining the emerging trends, challenges, and opportunities that will shape the future of public affairs. By exploring the potential impact of technology, globalization, societal shifts, and ethical considerations, readers can gain insights into how organizations can stay ahead in this dynamic landscape and continue to drive positive outcomes.

Technological Advancements:

- **Digital Transformation:** Explore the role of emerging technologies, such as artificial intelligence and automation, in reshaping public affairs strategies.

- **Data Analytics:** Discuss how data-driven insights will play a pivotal role in shaping communication, engagement, and decision-making.

Globalization and Cross-Cultural Dynamics:

- **Borderless Communication:** Examine how globalization will influence the need for culturally sensitive and internationally relevant communication.

- **Navigating Diversity**: Discuss strategies for engaging with diverse audiences across cultural and geographical boundaries.

Sustainability and Social Responsibility:

- **Environmental Considerations**: Explore how the growing emphasis on sustainability will influence public affairs efforts, especially in environmentally sensitive industries.

- **Ethical Practices**: Discuss the increasing importance of ethical behavior and social responsibility in shaping public perception.

Advocacy and Grassroots Movements:

- **Empowered Citizens**: Examine the role of grassroots movements and advocacy groups in driving public discourse and policy change.

- **Engagement Strategies**: Discuss how organizations can effectively engage with empowered citizens and grassroots initiatives.

Media and Disinformation:

- **Combatting Disinformation**: Explore strategies for addressing the challenges posed by the spread of misinformation and fake news.

- **Media Literacy:** Discuss the importance of promoting media literacy to empower audiences to discern credible information.

Data Privacy and Security:

- **Protection of Information:** Examine the evolving landscape of data privacy and security and its implications for public affairs efforts.

- **Trust Building:** Discuss how organizations can build trust by safeguarding stakeholders' sensitive information.

Ethical AI and Decision-Making:

- **Ethical Considerations:** Explore how the integration of AI into public affairs strategies requires ethical decision-making frameworks.

- **Accountability in AI:** Discuss the importance of transparency and accountability in AI-driven communication.

Strategic Reflection:

1. **Foresight and Innovation:** Discuss the value of embracing innovation and anticipating trends to remain competitive in the future.

2. **Continuous Learning:** Explore the importance of staying informed about emerging trends and adapting strategies accordingly.

"Chapter 10: The Future of Public Affairs" provides with a glimpse into the exciting and challenging landscape that lies ahead. By understanding the potential impact of technology, globalization, ethics, and societal changes, organizations can proactively position themselves to navigate these shifts, seize opportunities, and continue to make meaningful contributions to their stakeholders and the world at large.

Emerging Trends in Public Affairs and Communications

The field of public affairs and communications is in a constant state of evolution, driven by technological advancements, societal shifts, and changing stakeholder expectations. This section explores the emerging trends that are reshaping the way organizations engage with their audiences, manage their reputation, and navigate complex landscapes. By staying informed about these trends, professionals can proactively adapt their strategies to remain effective and relevant in a rapidly changing environment.

1. Digital Transformation:

- **Virtual Engagement:** Explore the increasing reliance on virtual platforms for stakeholder engagement, events, and communication.

- **Digital Advocacy:** Discuss the role of social media and online platforms in amplifying advocacy efforts and mobilizing support.

2. Personalized Communication:

- **Segmented Messaging:** Examine the trend of tailoring communication to specific audience segments for more personalized engagement.

- **Microtargeting:** Discuss the use of data-driven insights to microtarget messages and campaigns to individual preferences.

3. Purpose-Driven Communication:

- **Social Impact Alignment:** Explore how organizations are focusing on social causes and aligning their communication with purpose.

- **Values-Based Engagement:** Discuss the importance of communicating values to resonate with socially conscious audiences.

4. Visual and Video Communication:

- **Visual Storytelling:** Examine the rise of visual content and its effectiveness in conveying complex messages.

- **Video Live Streaming:** Discuss the trend of using live video to engage audiences in real-time interactions.

5. Ethical AI and Automation:

- **AI-Driven Insights:** Explore how AI is used to analyze data and provide actionable insights for strategic decision-making.

- **Ethical Considerations:** Discuss the importance of transparency and ethical AI use in communication and engagement.

6. Stakeholder Activism:

- **Empowered Audiences:** Examine the trend of stakeholders actively advocating for change and holding organizations accountable.

- **Collaborative Solutions:** Discuss strategies for engaging with activist stakeholders in productive dialogues.

7. Sustainability Communication:

- **Environmental Responsibility:** Explore the emphasis on transparent communication about sustainable practices and environmental impact.

- **Climate Advocacy:** Discuss how organizations are engaging in conversations about climate change and advocating for sustainable policies.

8. Data Privacy and Trust:

- **Transparency in Data Use:** Examine the growing importance of transparent data collection and usage practices.

- **Trust Building:** Discuss strategies for building and maintaining trust by safeguarding stakeholders' data.

9. Inclusive and Diverse Communication:

- **Representation Matters:** Explore the trend of inclusive communication that reflects diversity in both content and representation.

- **Cultural Sensitivity:** Discuss the importance of understanding diverse cultural contexts in communication efforts.

10. Virtual Reality and Augmented Reality:

- **Immersive Experiences:** Examine the potential of virtual and augmented reality for creating immersive stakeholder experiences.

- **Visualizing Complex Concepts:** Discuss how these technologies can simplify the communication of intricate information.

Strategic Reflection:

1. **Agility and Adaptation:** Discuss the need for professionals to be agile and adaptable in integrating emerging trends into their strategies.

2. **Continuous Learning:** Explore the value of staying updated on emerging trends and evolving best practices in public affairs and communications.

"Emerging Trends in Public Affairs and Communications" sheds light on the transformative shifts that are shaping the landscape of stakeholder engagement and communication. By embracing these trends, professionals can stay ahead of the curve, foster meaningful relationships, and position their organizations for success in an ever-evolving digital and societal environment.

The Role of Technology and Data Analytics

In the modern landscape of public affairs and communications, technology and data analytics have emerged as powerful allies, reshaping the way organizations engage with stakeholders and make informed decisions. This section delves into the transformative role of technology and data analytics, highlighting their potential to drive strategic insights, enhance engagement, and optimize communication efforts. By harnessing the capabilities of technology and data analytics, organizations can unlock new levels of efficiency, effectiveness, and impact in their public affairs initiatives.

1. Data-Driven Insights:

- **Strategic Decision-Making:** Explore how data analytics provide actionable insights that inform strategic choices and direction.

- **Identifying Trends:** Discuss the ability of data analytics to uncover trends and patterns within stakeholder behavior and sentiment.

2. Audience Segmentation:

- **Tailored Engagement:** Examine the power of data to segment audiences based on preferences, demographics, and behavior.

- **Personalized Messaging:** Discuss the effectiveness of tailored messages that resonate with specific audience segments.

3. Real-Time Monitoring:

- **Instant Feedback:** Explore how real-time data monitoring enables organizations to capture immediate stakeholder feedback.

- **Crisis Response:** Discuss how real-time monitoring helps organizations respond swiftly to emerging issues and crises.

4. Engagement Tracking:

- **Measuring Impact:** Examine how data analytics measure the impact of engagement efforts, from social media interactions to event participation.

- **ROI Assessment:** Discuss how engagement tracking informs the evaluation of the return on investment in public affairs initiatives.

5. Predictive Analytics:

- **Anticipating Trends:** Explore how predictive analytics forecast future stakeholder behaviors and preferences.

- **Strategic Planning:** Discuss how predictive insights guide long-term planning and resource allocation.

6. Social Media Insights:

- **Sentiment Analysis:** Examine how social media data can be analyzed to gauge public sentiment and perceptions.

- **Engagement Metrics:** Discuss the significance of engagement metrics in understanding the effectiveness of social media strategies.

7. Crisis Preparedness:

- **Early Detection:** Explore how data analytics can aid in early detection of potential crises through monitoring online conversations.

- **Response Optimization:** Discuss the role of data-driven insights in optimizing crisis communication strategies.

8. Transparency and Accountability:

- **Data Transparency:** Examine how data transparency builds trust with stakeholders concerned about data privacy.

- **Demonstrating Impact:** Discuss how organizations can use data to transparently showcase the impact of their initiatives.

9. Continuous Improvement:

- **Iterative Refinement:** Explore how data analytics inform iterative refinement of strategies based on real-time feedback.

- **Adaptive Learning:** Discuss how organizations can continuously learn and improve through data analysis.

Strategic Reflection:

1. **Balancing Human Insights:** Discuss the importance of complementing data insights with human judgment and qualitative analysis.

2. **Ethical Use of Data:** Explore the ethical considerations surrounding data collection, storage, and usage in public affairs.

"The Role of Technology and Data Analytics" underscores the transformative potential of technology and data-driven insights in the realm of public affairs and communications. By embracing these tools and leveraging their capabilities, organizations can foster deeper connections with stakeholders, make informed decisions, and drive positive outcomes that resonate in an increasingly data-driven world.

Anticipating Challenges and Staying Ahead

In the intricate landscape of public affairs and communications, staying ahead requires a proactive approach that involves not only addressing current challenges but also anticipating future obstacles. This section delves into the importance of anticipating challenges, preparing for uncertainties, and implementing strategies that position organizations for success in the face of evolving dynamics. By embracing a forward-looking mindset, professionals can navigate complexities, mitigate risks, and secure their place as leaders in the ever-changing field of public affairs.

1. Environmental Scanning:

- **Trend Analysis:** Explore the value of scanning the external environment to identify emerging trends and shifts.

- **Early Warning:** Discuss how early detection of trends allows organizations to adapt before challenges escalate.

2. Scenario Planning:

- **Future Exploration:** Examine the process of creating scenarios that simulate potential challenges and opportunities.

- **Strategic Preparedness:** Discuss how scenario planning enhances organizational readiness for various scenarios.

3. Risk Assessment:

- **Identification of Vulnerabilities:** Explore how risk assessments help organizations identify potential vulnerabilities and threats.

- **Impact Evaluation:** Discuss how assessing potential risks aids in understanding their potential impact.

4. Stakeholder Engagement:

- **Proactive Dialogue:** Examine the role of stakeholder engagement in understanding concerns and challenges before they escalate.

- **Collaborative Solutions:** Discuss how engaging with stakeholders leads to collaborative problem-solving.

5. Contingency Planning:

- **Response Strategies:** Explore how contingency plans outline actionable steps to address potential challenges.

- **Flexibility in Execution:** Discuss the importance of having adaptable plans that accommodate changing circumstances.

6. Ethical Dilemmas:

- **Anticipating Ethical Challenges:** Examine how organizations can foresee ethical dilemmas and navigate them transparently.

- **Ethical Decision-Making:** Discuss strategies for making ethical choices that align with organizational values.

7. Rapid Response Mechanisms:

- **Agile Strategies:** Explore the implementation of agile response mechanisms to address unexpected challenges.

- **Crisis Communication:** Discuss how rapid response plans are crucial for effective crisis communication.

8. Learning from Failures:

- **Failure Analysis:** Examine the practice of analyzing failures to understand their causes and prevent recurrence.

- **Continuous Improvement:** Discuss how learning from failures contributes to strategic refinement.

9. Adaptive Leadership:

- **Leadership Agility:** Explore how adaptive leaders foster a culture of agility and forward thinking.

- **Inspiring Innovation:** Discuss the role of leaders in encouraging innovative approaches to challenges.

Strategic Reflection:

1. **Cultivating Forward-Thinking Culture:** Discuss strategies for fostering a culture that values proactive anticipation and preparation.

2. **Long-Term Vision:** Explore how maintaining a long-term perspective enhances an organization's ability to anticipate challenges.

"Anticipating Challenges and Staying Ahead" underscores the importance of proactive preparedness in the world of public affairs and communications. By staying vigilant, engaging stakeholders, and developing flexible response strategies, organizations can navigate challenges with confidence, maintain their reputation, and seize opportunities even in the face of uncertainty.

Appendix B: Glossary of Key Terms

This glossary provides definitions for key terms and concepts frequently encountered in the realm of public affairs. Understanding these terms is essential for effective communication, strategy development, and successful engagement in the field of public affairs and communications.

1. Advocacy: The act of supporting or promoting a cause, idea, or policy through strategic communication, lobbying, and engagement efforts.

2. Stakeholder: An individual, group, or organization with a vested interest in the activities, decisions, or outcomes of an organization. Stakeholders can include employees, customers, shareholders, communities, and more.

3. Lobbying: The practice of influencing government policies, regulations, and decisions through direct communication with policymakers and legislators.

4. Crisis Communication: The strategic communication efforts undertaken during and after a crisis to manage reputation, inform stakeholders, and address challenges effectively.

5. Key Messages: Concise and impactful statements that convey the core ideas, values, and information an organization wishes to communicate to its stakeholders.

6. Public Perception: The collective opinions, beliefs, and attitudes that individuals hold about an organization, issue, or topic based on their experiences and exposure to information.

7. Ethical Considerations: The reflection and decision-making processes that take into account moral principles, values, and societal norms in public affairs strategies and actions.

8. Media Relations: The management of an organization's interactions with media outlets and journalists to ensure accurate and positive coverage.

9. Policy Advocacy: Engaging in efforts to influence policies, laws, regulations, and decisions made by government bodies, often to align with an organization's goals.

10. Transparency: The practice of openly sharing information about an organization's activities, decisions, and operations to build trust and credibility.

11. Stakeholder Engagement: The strategic process of involving stakeholders in an organization's decision-making processes, fostering open communication and collaboration.

12. Social Impact: The effect an organization's actions and decisions have on society, communities, and the broader environment.

13. Data Analytics: The process of collecting, analyzing, and interpreting data to uncover insights, trends, and patterns that inform decision-making.

14. Scenario Planning: The strategic exercise of creating hypothetical scenarios to anticipate potential challenges, opportunities, and outcomes.

15. Grassroots Movement: A collective effort of individuals and organizations to advocate for change or address issues from the ground up, often with local and community-level initiatives.

16. Inclusive Communication: Communication that embraces diversity and ensures that all stakeholders, regardless of background, are included and represented.

17. Crisis Preparedness: The proactive planning and readiness efforts undertaken by organizations to effectively respond to and manage crises.

18. Media Monitoring: The systematic tracking and analysis of media coverage to gain insights into public sentiment, trends, and coverage of specific topics.

19. Predictive Analytics: The use of historical data and statistical algorithms to forecast future trends, behaviors, and outcomes.

20. Sustainable Practices: Actions and strategies aimed at minimizing negative environmental, social, and economic impacts while promoting long-term viability.

Strategic Reflection:

1. **Vocabulary Mastery:** Discuss the importance of mastering these key terms to communicate effectively in the field of public affairs.

2. **Integration into Practice:** Explore how these terms can be integrated into strategies and conversations to enhance understanding and clarity.

"Appendix B: Glossary of Key Terms" offers a comprehensive reference to the terminology commonly used in public affairs and communications. By familiarizing themselves with these terms, professionals can engage in meaningful discussions, make informed decisions, and navigate the complexities of the field with precision and confidence.

Definitions of Essential Public Affairs Concepts

This section provides clear and concise definitions of fundamental concepts in the field of public affairs. These definitions serve as a foundation for understanding the intricacies and nuances of public affairs strategies, engagement, and communication.

1. Public Affairs: The strategic management of an organization's relationship with its stakeholders, including government entities, the public, interest groups, and the media. Public affairs involves shaping public perception, advocating for policies, and building positive relationships.

2. Stakeholder Engagement: The intentional and strategic process of involving individuals, groups, or organizations that have an interest in or are affected by an organization's actions, decisions, or outcomes. Engagement aims to foster communication, collaboration, and mutually beneficial relationships.

3. Lobbying: A form of advocacy involving the active effort to influence government policies, regulations, and decisions by communicating with legislators and policymakers. Lobbying aims to shape public policy in alignment with an organization's goals.

4. Crisis Communication: The strategic communication efforts undertaken during and after a crisis to manage reputation, address challenges, and inform stakeholders. Crisis communication aims to minimize damage, restore trust, and provide accurate information.

5. Ethics in Public Affairs: The consideration and application of moral principles, values, and ethical frameworks in decision-making and actions related to public affairs. Ethical behavior ensures transparency, accountability, and responsible engagement.

6. Key Messages: Concise and targeted statements that encapsulate an organization's core values, ideas, and information. Key messages are crafted to effectively communicate with specific audiences and convey a consistent narrative.

7. Media Relations: The strategic management of an organization's interactions with media outlets, journalists, and reporters. Media relations aims to secure positive coverage, respond to inquiries, and maintain a positive public image.

8. Stakeholder Mapping: The process of identifying and categorizing stakeholders based on their level of interest, influence, and impact on an organization. Stakeholder mapping helps prioritize engagement efforts.

9. Transparency and Accountability: The practice of openly sharing information about an organization's activities, decisions, and performance. Transparency builds trust with stakeholders and ensures responsible behavior.

10. Social Impact: The measurable effect an organization's actions and decisions have on society, communities, and the environment. Social impact reflects an organization's contribution to positive change.

11. Data Analytics: The systematic analysis of data to uncover insights, trends, and patterns that inform decision-making. Data analytics supports evidence-based strategies and enhances understanding.

12. Grassroots Movement: A collective and often decentralized effort by individuals and organizations to advocate for change at the local or community level. Grassroots movements mobilize public support through direct engagement.

13. Crisis Preparedness: The proactive planning, training, and readiness efforts undertaken by organizations to effectively respond to and manage crises. Preparedness minimizes potential damage and facilitates swift responses.

14. Policy Advocacy: Engaging in efforts to influence policies, laws, regulations, and decisions made by government bodies. Policy advocacy aligns an organization's interests with legislative changes.

15. Inclusive Communication: Communication that embraces diversity and ensures all stakeholders, regardless of background, are included and represented in messages and engagement efforts.

Strategic Reflection:

1. **Foundational Knowledge:** Discuss the importance of understanding these concepts as building blocks for effective public affairs strategies.

2. **Contextual Application:** Explore how these definitions can be applied in various scenarios and contexts within public affairs.

These definitions of essential public affairs concepts provide readers with a solid grounding in the terminology and principles that shape the field. By grasping these concepts, professionals can navigate challenges, make informed decisions, and engage stakeholders effectively in the dynamic realm of public affairs.

Recommended Books

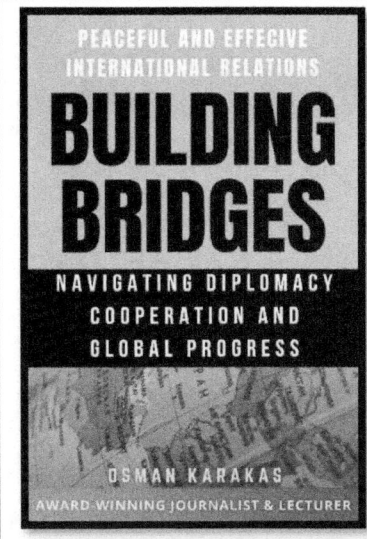

The collection of books is accessible for purchase on Amazon.com platform.

Printed in Great Britain
by Amazon